Lucas decided to act. He knelt down and tried to pull the young man's hands away from his eyes. But upon touching Melville's wrists, Lucas found them as hot as a pair of branding irons. Reaching down to Melville's waist, Lucas tried to help him up. But it was hopeless. Melville was going into seizures, ripping at his face, his neck, his clothing. All the poor guy could manage was a trembling, garbled cry . . . "Ruh-rrrruuuh—RRRRRRUUHHHH-HHHHHNNNNNNNNNNNNNN!!"

Then the fire came.

It erupted from Melville's eyes, bursting forth like two orange jets of cooking gas. The blast of heat startled Lucas and sent him falling backward. It felt almost like the discharge of the Mariah's vertical exhaust stack. An instant puff of supercharged flame, hot enough to singe the eyebrows off your face and knock the wind out of your lungs.

The sick furnace rose all around . . .

"Reading THE BLACK MARIAH was like watching a mobilized version of Hitchcock's classic *Rear Window*. A cast of rich characterization and unrelenting suspense! This is a wild ride through darkest voodoo and your very own soul, on board a fine, fast rig. 10-4, good buddy, this may be the scariest death race of them all!"   —Ron Dee, author of *Succumb*

"It's not fair that a first novelist should be this good. Mr. Bonansinga gives us a tight, taut novel filled with people you care about and scenes that are genuinely scary. This is one of the most enjoyable novels I've read in a long, long time."

          —Ed Gorman, author of *The Autumn Dead*

JAY R. BONANSINGA

THE BLACK MARIAH

WARNER BOOKS

A Time Warner Company

Enjoy lively book discussions online with CompuServe. To become a member of CompuServe call 1-800-848-8199 and ask for the Time Warner Trade Publishing forum. (Current members GO:TWEP.)

WARNER BOOKS EDITION

Cover design by Elaine Groh

Warner Books, Inc.
1271 Avenue of the Americas
New York, NY 10020

 A Time Warner Company

Printed in the United States of America

First Printing: May, 1994

10 9 8 7 6 5 4 3 2 1

Dedicated with love
to Bratch

AUTHOR'S ACKNOWLEDGEMENT

Several people were indispensible in the creation of this book. A special thanks to Sully and Diane Bonansinga, Dr. Harry Jaffe, Joyce Norman, Febronio Zatarain, Graham Watkins, Tom Leavens, Peter Hawley, Normann Pokorny, Tod Bonansinga, Jeb Bonansinga, David À. Johnson, M.S.W. and Rick Horgan. An extra special thanks to my editor Mauro DiPreta, my creative guru Jennifer Robinson, the good folks at Warner Books and PMA Literary and Film Management, and Jeanne M. Bonansinga. A major heavy-duty thanks to my irrepressible manager, Peter Miller.

PART I

Superslab

"The moving finger writes; and, having writ/Moves on: nor all your Piety nor Wit/Shall lure it back to cancel half a line/Nor all your Tears wash out a Word of it."

—Omar Khayyam
Rubaiyat

Superlab

1

Ratchet Jaw

"Somebody, please help me . . . ."

At the stroke of ten the voice ripped through the noisy darkness of the cab like shears through black muslin. Lucas reached up, adjusted the volume on his CB, and grabbed the handset. The mike felt cool in his hand.

"Ten-nine on that, Channel Eleven. Say again."

"I'm sorry, y'all . . . it's just—it's an emergency type situation."

Lucas thumbed the mike switch and replied as quietly as possible, careful not to awaken his partner in the rear sleeper. "Copy that, Channel Eleven. Recommend switching over to channel nine. Get you a Band-Aid wagon or County Mountie, pronto."

There were a few seconds of static as Lucas waited for a reply. A thick-boned black man with a grizzle of a goatee and gentle brown eyes, Lucas cut an imposing figure in the Kenworth cab. In fact, as he approached his fortieth birthday Lucas had grown into what his mama used to call a "big old house of a body." Of course, his preference in clothes didn't help any. With his steel-toed cowboy boots, oily black jeans,

Chambray shirt, sweaty black leather vest, and trademark Charley One-Horse hat, he looked somewhat larger than life.

The voice suddenly crackled back through the speaker, "I don't need no ambulance and I don't need no policeman. . . ."

Then there was a pregnant pause, followed by a simple explanation that was delivered with such gravity that Lucas imagined hearing those melodramatic organ strains used by old soap operas before they cut for commercials.

"I need fuel."

The mystery voice belonged to a young black man. Lucas was sure of it. The deep southern drawl suggested Shreveport or Jackson. Maybe even New Orleans. A more pertinent question, however, was just why this ratchet jaw was tying up channel eleven. The national calling channel was universally respected among truckers as a temporary hailing frequency for air checks. But this dude had no intention of following CB protocol.

"Listen, bro," Lucas said, "you got the big Black Mariah here. What's your moniker?"

After a burst of static, the voice said, "—Black what?"

Lucas grinned. "Mariah, with an *H*. Used to be my mama's middle name—rest her soul. What's your handle, bro?"

Another moment of noisy silence. "Don't have no cute CB tag. Name's just Melville. Melville Benoit. I'm driving a '72 Camaro eastbound on Eighty outside of Macon."

"Melville, do me a favor," Lucas said. "Switch that ole 'radidio' on over to channel twenty-one. Be able to chat with ya without tying up air checks. *Comprendo?*"

"Okay . . . alright . . . I'm switchin'!"

Lucas dialed over to channel twenty-one and waited for the kid to come back. Listening to the Kenworth rumbling beneath him, Lucas felt that warm feeling of power. The K-Whopper's engine was roaring happily; no suspicious pings, knocks, or rattles.

A moment later, the voice returned in a flurry of popping static. "Y'all still there? Black Mariah? Y'all there?"

"Ten-Roger, kiddio," said Lucas. "Comin' back at ya."

"Great—y'all think you can help me out?"

"Sure can," Lucas said with a grin. " 'Bout ten miles outta Macon near the seventy-third mile marker there's a coffee pot called Burdettes. Six full islands of diesel. Three for gas. Gift shop. Restaurant. Folks say the chicken-fried steak is almost edible."

Static. Indistinguishable rustling noises. "Y'all don't understand . . . it ain't . . . it ain't that easy."

Lucas rolled his eyes. After sixteen years as an independent trucker, Lucas had seen just about every kind of highway hot dog imaginable. Rednecks out looking for bobtail races. Frustrated salesmen gear-heading their company cars. Pissed-off wives taking it out on the family wagon. And even rogue stock-car drivers high on Benzedrine. But Melville was a member of the worst tribe imaginable—*the chatterboxes*—those frustrated four-wheelers who got their radio for $29.95 at Crazy Larry's and just had to yack with every hauler within a hundred-mile radius.

Lucas usually couldn't stomach chatterboxes.

Tonight, however, Lucas was just bored enough to play along for a while. He was returning home to Los Angeles after a cross-country trip hauling apples from Seattle to Jacksonville, a journey that seemed doomed from the start. While Lucas was *en route*, the L.A. broker had gone belly up and the apple deal had nearly died on the vine. By the time he got to Jacksonville, the warehouse people had decided to cut the original transport fee in half and Lucas had been forced to take it up the butt. Then, on the first leg of the return trip, his driving partner, Sophie Cohen, had weathered a blow-out on some Godforsaken backwater road. Lucas had been dozing when it happened and had nearly gone through the wall of the coffin box. The repairs burned up over two hundred bucks.

Now Lucas was tooling along Interstate 75 toward Atlanta, chain-smoking miniature cigars, trying to figure out the rest of his life, and talking to some chowderhead on the squawk box for kicks. At least it was better than sitting in some Motel Six coffee shop, mourning his rapidly approaching bankruptcy.

Shaking his head, he thumbed the send switch. "You want to explain that last break, Melville?"

Another pause. "It's . . . complicated."

"I got my ears on. Tell me all about it."

Through the tiny grille on the radio came the feverish reply. "I can't stop."

Lucas laughed. It was a big, hearty guffaw that made him shake against his contour seat. Stifling his laughter, he brought the mike back up to his face and said, "Old Buddy, I know just how you feel. I surely do."

Melville's frantic voice returned. "Whattya mean? Whattya mean y'all know how I feel?!"

"I hate stopping. I really do. I hate the downtime."

"No, man . . . no, no, no," Melville's voice came back through the static. "Y'all don't understand . . . I want to stop . . . believe me—y'all don't know how much I want to stop . . . but I can't—I can't stop—not in a million years."

"You can't or you *won't*?"

A long, noisy pause. "I can't."

"How come?"

"I just can't."

"Why not?"

"Trust me on this, brother—I can't."

Lucas was losing his patience. "You gonna tell me about it or am I gonna cut the coax?"

After another long pause filled with static and crackling interference, the voice said, "I know it sounds crazy but it's a goddamn hex."

Lucas stared through the windshield at the strobing white lines for a moment. "Negative copy on that, bro. Come back again."

"I said I got a motherfuckin' curse visited on me."

"Curse?"

Static. Then a feverish litany followed, which threatened to deteriorate into tears. "That's right—I been cursed . . . cursed to never stop moving . . . never stop no matter—"

There was a sudden surge of interference, momentarily drowning Melville's words and fizzing through the tiny speaker on Lucas's CB. Lucas shook his head and chuckled.

This dude was definitely some small-town yahoo trying to pull a trucker's leg on a Saturday night. He probably lived in one of the little wide-spots in the Mississippi asphalt like Yazoo City or Kokomoville. Lucas had to hand it to him, though; the kid knew how to tell a story.

"Okay, bro," Lucas finally transmitted. "I get the joke. Now why don't you back on out and give some other jammers a chance?"

Silence.

"Break two-one for ol' Melville . . . come back."

More silence.

"Yo, Melville . . . do you copy?"

No answer.

"Yo, Melville . . ."

The sudden rush of ghostly A.M. voices and bleed from other channels were the only reply. Lucas shrugged and said into his mike, "This is the big ole Black Mariah, backin' out and backin' down, copyin' the mail northbound on Seventy-Five . . .

"Ten-Roger and out."

An hour later, Lucas woke Sophie for her shift. Over the years, the two drivers had developed a system for waking each other which went something like this: The driver started the process off by rolling down his or her window. The rush of fresh oxygen and highway noise would fill the cab and gradually drift back into the sleeper compartment. Then the driver would put on a worn-out cassette of his or her favorite song (Lucas was partial to Public Enemy's "Welcome to the Terrordome," while Sophie preferred anything by Bonnie Raitt). The next phase, which was optional, depended on who was doing the waking. Sophie usually opted to fire the air horn off a few times and sing along with her music. But Lucas preferred the more direct approach of hollering back toward the sleeper. Tonight was no exception.

"Yo! Cohen!" Lucas barked over the shotgun rhythms of the rap music. "Time for school!"

A few moments later, Sophie Cohen emerged from the coffin box, dressed in Levi's and a sleeveless work shirt, rubbing her eyes and moaning hoarsely. "Stop with the noise already."

Lucas grinned and rolled up the window. "What are you sayin'? You don't like rap music?"

"Is that what they call that stuff? Music?" Sophie climbed into the shotgun seat and stretched her weary limbs. A compact little woman with short auburn hair and a row of gold earrings in her earlobe, Sophie looked more like a rock-and-roll roadie than a lady trucker. And tonight, in the green glow of the interior, broken only by the occasional strobe of the highway, she looked more like an extra from *The Rocky Horror Picture Show*.

"Where the hell are we?" she finally asked.

" 'Bout twenty miles outside Atlanta on Seventy-five."

"What country is this?"

"America—last time I checked."

Sophie reached up to the glove box, clicked it open, and rooted out a crumpled pack of Marlboros. Lighting one up, she took a long drag and sighed. "I'm getting too old for this."

She was referring to a sadistic system of time management popular among many independent truckers. In order to make the best time, each co-driver sleeps in five-hour alternating shifts. They stop only for fuel, food, weigh stations, or a shit-and-shower at a truck stop. Utilizing this method, a team can go coast to coast in two and a half days. The only trouble was, tonight The Black Mariah team had no job on the other end. No broker, no bookings, no need to hurry.

And that bothered Lucas.

Downshifting into a curve, Lucas said, "Whattya mean, you're getting too old? I've got shoes older than you. You're still a rookie."

"Don't start with me tonight, Lucas."

Grinning, Lucas shot a quick glance over at Sophie. She was lying back against the headrest, rubbing her temples, trying to wake up. It was hard to believe that she was turning out to be a fairly decent partner.

Lucas remembered the first time he had laid eyes on her. It was nearly three years ago. She had answered his ad in *Truck and Driver* and had impressed Lucas enough over the phone to win an interview. But the next morning she had shown up on Lucas's Santa Monica doorstep in her torn jeans and surly attitude. With that butchy aura about her, she had been pretty overpowering; but somehow Lucas couldn't help but be intrigued. Single-minded, stubborn, and tough, Sophie Cohen had all the right trucking credentials. Three years with Beeline Express in their tractor-purchase program. A year driving refrigerated trucks, known as *reefers,* up and down the western seaboard. Plus she had damn good skills.

After Lucas had driven a few jaunts with her, he had learned just what was behind all the denim and tough talk. Born and raised in San Francisco, the only daughter to wealthy parents, Sophie Cohen had grown up not only with a silver spoon in her mouth but the entire goddamn table setting. She'd been showered with the best of everything—the finest grammar schools, the best private tutors, the most expensive music lessons, the whole shot. By the time she'd made it to college in the early seventies—first as a poly-sci major at Berkeley and later as a history major at USC—she was a full-blown debutante. In fact, before you could say "doctor's wife," her mother had her slated to marry a nice, rich Jewish boy and live happily ever after in some Encino suburb.

But Sophie had two problems: She was too rebellious and too smart. She turned her schooling into a sword of Damocles over the heads of her parents. Drifting aimlessly through academia, absorbing esoteric subjects with a ravenous yet indiscriminate appetite, Sophie became an intellectual hobo. She never intended to graduate, never intended to marry, and certainly never intended to live in a suburb.

When her father finally lowered the boom and threatened to cut off her flow of tuition money, Sophie had already decided what she wanted to do. She'd been inspired by a book called *White Lines.* This popular tome dramatized the mystique of trucking in colorful, salty lore that really sunk a hook into Sophie. It seemed like such a poetic way out of her bourgeois fate—an earthy, egalitarian, spontaneous way to live. The day after her father's ultimatum, she went out and enrolled in trucking school and started studying for her Class-A license. The rest, as they say, is history.

"You still bent outta shape about the broker?" Lucas finally asked her over the rumbling song of the engine.

"You're the one who should be bent out of shape."

Lucas shrugged. "Who'd listen?"

Sophie snubbed her Marlboro out in the side tray and crossed her arms defensively. "We need another load for the flip-flop, Lucas—you know that as well as I do. We're driving out of our own pockets now and I dunno about you, but mine aren't real deep."

Lucas wiped his mouth with the back of his hand. "We'll land something."

"Where? When?"

He turned to her and frowned. "What am I? The Amazing-motherfuckin'-Karnack? I dunno where or when . . . but I got some calls out there already. When we stop, I'm gonna buzz Jake Sunnheimer."

Sophie rolled her eyes. "That's great. Jake the Snake. He'll have us hauling contraband weapons down to the Florida Keys for some mafia kingpin." Sophie lowered her voice into a sinister gangster's drone. "Tank you very much, Mr. Hyde. Been a pleasure doing business wit ya. Now if you don't mind, we'd like to get yer shoe size for dese lovely cement Florsheims."

Lucas began to say something, then paused and glanced over at his partner. She sat in the dimness, her head bobbing ridiculously, her face contorted into a Don Corleone impression. Suddenly all Lucas could do was laugh. "You need psychiatric help, girl. I swear to God, you need help."

"You may be right," said Sophie, a malicious grin replacing the mobster face. "Considering the fact that after three years I'm still sitting here beside you."

Lucas growled. "Keep it up, shithead, and you'll get kicked outta this rig faster than you can say 'racial tension.'"

"You wouldn't dare touch me, Hyde. You couldn't afford any more lawsuits."

"You got me there." Lucas shook his head and gazed out through the windshield at the white lines clocking by. Sophie was referring to his past experiences with small-claims courts. Over the last decade, Lucas had been sued three times. Once in Sacramento for chipping a chunk out of the Eagle Foods loading dock. Once in Kansas City for failing to cross a teamster picket line at Amalgamated Stockyards. And once in Florida for crossing a private road and knocking out countless reflectors, guardrails, and mailboxes along the way. In each case, Lucas had lost and was forced to pay the judgments out of his own pocket.

Personal responsibility was the bane of the independent trucker's existence.

Not that Lucas had any complaints. He had dreamed of being a gypsy trucker for years. In fact, growing up on the tough side of Torrance, California, the young Lucas Hyde had always been a restless boy. When he was eleven, his father, a grocery store manager, had been shot and killed by a petty thief. His mother and sisters had pulled the family together through the rough times that followed. But little Lucas had always seemed troubled . . . running away from home, getting mixed up with local street gangs, and even getting caught for stealing from his late father's store. Finally, a few stints in the Pico Rivera Reformatory got his attention and toughened him into a streetwise homeboy.

But Lucas wanted out. Out of the gangs, out of the neighborhood, and out of the racial barriers that limited a young black man's options. When he was nineteen, after three years of high school, he got a job driving a delivery van for a local electrical contractor. The job seemed to motivate him in ways he never thought possible. Driving days, he went to night school and got his high school diploma. He took on more responsibility. He enlarged his delivery routes. Eventually, he got his Class-A license and started driving the company's rusty old Freightliner.

From that moment on, he was hooked.

He began dreaming of owning his own rig. On weekends he'd drive up to Bakersfield and visit Wenona's, an infamous trucker hangout complete with a full-service repair center, a four-star restaurant, a 600-bed motel, and a triple-X adult theater. But the real attraction to Wenona's was the unofficial game room out behind the restaurant. In this smoke-filled den of iniquity, the truckers would gather to play poker, throw die, bet on sports events, pitch pennies, and make fools out of themselves gambling on banal affairs such as what time the sun would come up that day or how many miles a new set of retreads would last. The young Lucas quickly fell under their spell. He hung out with the weathered old drivers, heard all their tall tales, and absorbed their culture like a sponge. Before long, Lucas was a full-fledged owner/operator himself—with his own truck, a string of bookings, and an incurable case of white-line fever.

Unfortunately, the years spent hanging out at Wenona's also infected Lucas with a severe gambling addiction. Not only did he become a compulsive bettor on basketball games and football games, he also found a plethora of side wagers to make along the way. One driver in Des Moines would bet Lucas on the number of stops he would have to make going cross-country. Another guy in a Tucson diner would put money on how many patrons sitting along the counter that day had received speeding tickets. Lucas would find each and every bet irresistible. In fact, the trucker's lifestyle itself made gambling almost obligatory. There was so much time to think, to speculate, to muse.

Looking back over his formative years, however, Lucas had always known deep down in his heart what drew him to trucking. It wasn't the freedom of the open road or the romance of travel or the allure of being your own boss or any of those clichéd reasons he'd heard the weekend warriors tossing around. It was more likely because of one singularly strange and liberating aspect: *You were anonymous.* As long as you were moving along that superslab in your box of iron, making time, minding your own business, you were invisible. You weren't good or bad. You weren't a minority small-business owner. You weren't judged. You were simply another voice on the CB radio.

You were The Black Mariah.

"Tell you what," Sophie said, breaking the noisy stillness of the cab. "Buy me some strong coffee when we stop and I'll forgive you for ruining my life."

"Sounds fair enough."

A mileage sign loomed in the headlights. It said: JONES-BORO STOCKBRIDGE—HIGHWAY 54—2 MILES. Lucas made a mental note of it and calculated the remaining fuel. "Guess we should stop at the junction," he said. "Then you can be captain and I can finally get some relief from all these back-woods chatterboxes."

Sophie stretched her arms, rubbed the sleep from her eyes. "Lotsa schlemiels on the radio tonight?"

"You wouldn't believe it."

"For instance . . . ?"

"For instance, 'bout sixty miles back, this young brother comes over channel nine yappin' for help. Figured he was legit, so I tried to help him."

"Yeah? So?"

Lucas began to chuckle, shaking his head and downshift-ing the truck into the oncoming exit. "Kid was a mother-fuckin' CB clown. Trying to tell me he couldn't stop because he was cursed." Then Lucas lowered his voice and spoke in a pseudo-spooky, sinister, warning voice. "He be *cursed*, this poor soul . . . *cursed* to never stop moving . . . *cursed*, I tell ya . . ."

Sophie exhaled a ring of smoke and said, "You're right, Lucas. You need a break."

Lucas laughed, then pulled the truck off the highway and up the exit ramp.

"How about Montford's?"

"What about 'em?"

"Anything out of St. Louis? Omaha?"

There was a rustling sound on the other end, papers being shuffled. "Nope—nothing right now."

Lucas took a deep breath. He was standing in the corner of Lovejoy's Truck Stop, talking on the phone with some Nazi surf punk from some unfamiliar trucking bureau in Bakers-field. Frustration was making Lucas's stomach churn. He held a vise grip on the receiver. "How about cancellations?"

"Nope—negatory, dude."

"You telling me there's nothing from here to the fucking Continental Divide?!"

There was a pause, then the voice returned. "Tell you what, gimme a call, like, tomorrow morning—'round ten Pacific—we'll try to locate something on your way through Missouri or Kansas."

"That's it?"

"Sorry, dude."

Lucas hung up and mumbled, "Thanks for nothing . . . *dude*." He opened his logbook and began to record his last stretch of mileage when a voice croaked up behind him.

"Ya'll said large?"

Lucas glanced up from his book. " 'Scuse me?"

"The coffee . . ." The old diesel jockey was standing behind a cluttered counter across the office. "Ya'll ordered one large coffee—right?"

"You got it," Lucas said and walked over to the counter.

"Comin' right up." The old man smiled, teeth the color of coffee beans. He shoved a large Styrofoam cup across the counter, then snapped his imprinter across Lucas's Amex card. Handing the carbon over, he told Lucas, "Hundred fifty gallons of diesel, half gallon of solvent, and one large cuppa mud. Damage comes to two hundred and fifty-two dollars and ninety-three cents."

Lucas felt his stomach roil as he signed the carbon form, tore off his copy, and handed it back. His expenses were edging him closer and closer to the poorhouse. At less than five miles to the gallon, Lucas's rig typically burned over a thousand gallons per trip. At that rate, he needed a broker working around the clock to find two-way jobs. But now all he had was Mr. Surf Dude from Bakersfield.

"Ya'll should stick around for breakfast," the old man added, checking his Timex. " 'Round dawn Mary Jane comes in and makes the best damn flapjacks this side of the Smokies."

"Gonna have to take a rain check," Lucas said as he closed the logbook and zipped it shut. "By morning light we're gonna be three hundred miles down the road."

The old man looked genuinely sorry. "Maybe someday y'all can come back and visit."

"Sure hope so," Lucas said.

"Me too," the old man said, winking and showing his rotten teeth. "Y'all take care of yourself now."

"You too."

Lucas took the coffee, turned, and walked out of the office into the humid Georgian night. Crossing the parking lot toward his truck, he silently marvelled at the old man's warmth. Contrary to popular belief, it was Lucas's experience that most southern hospitality was extended to all races, including African Americans. Of course the contrasts down here were more dramatic. The southern racist was much more up front with his poison than his northern counterpart. But in some ways, Lucas almost preferred the blatant hatred of the Dixie klansman over the subtle discrimination of middle-class northerners. At least the KKK were honest about their ignorance and hate. The northern white was a slick motherfucker who would treat you like a friend as long as you stayed in your place and kept out of his neighborhood. As long as you were a good nigger.

But none of that really mattered to Lucas Hyde anymore. As long as his beloved rig was tanked and lubed and ready to go, he was nobody's boy.

The Kenworth tractor was idling like a dormant black bear between two diesel islands. Its ebony finish was gleaming in the silver vapor light. Pockets of moths swarmed angrily above it. A plume of heat rose up from its vertical exhaust pipe and shimmered majestically. Behind it, almost like an afterthought, was its dusty, battered trailer. Rented from a Sacramento leasing company, the trailer was a fifty-foot box of rusty iron. Even the nifty TIGER LEASING emblem on its side, which depicted a Bengal tiger in flight, didn't help much. To Lucas, the trailer was like an insult to the beautiful sleeper cab in front.

A full-blown 1987 K-Whopper COE, the power unit had been lovingly customized by Lucas over the years. Starting with its standard aluminized frame, he had added a high-performance European DAF engine boosted to 750 horsepower and intercooled with experimental injectors. Around this power plant he installed a thirteen-ton rear axle, a Phoenix beltless power-steering system, and a sophisticated diagnostic computer that stores information for later retrieval by mechanics. But the sexiest part of the tractor was its body. Custom painted and pin-lined by Roth Design in Palm Beach, Florida, the black cab was the color of purest obsidian, trimmed in bright scarlet pinstriping. At night, under the lights, it looked almost liquid.

Approaching the cab, he paused and watched Sophie straining to reach the corner of the windshield with her squeegee mop. It was another one of her rituals. At the beginning of each shift, she would scrub the glass like it was family china. Then she'd inspect every nook and cranny for the slightest sign of wear. Maybe it was a little anal-retentive, but Lucas didn't mind. The tractor was their baby. Any effort to keep it in shape was highly appreciated.

"While you're futzin' around with the windshield," Lucas said as he strolled up behind her, "check the washer nozzles."

Sophie stopped scrubbing. "Something wrong with 'em?"

"Don't know for sure. Left side might be a little clogged."

"Roger, Dodger."

Lucas stepped around to the passenger side, climbed up the chrome step, and paused. "Your coffee'll be waiting for you in the center rack. I'm hanging the DO NOT DISTURB sign 'til we get to Music City. Don't wake me 'til you see the whites of Conway Twitty's eyes."

Sophie nodded and continued mopping. Lucas turned and climbed into the cab.

It was a custom sleeper with all the extras. In the front, a fully loaded control console wrapped around a pair of ergonomic high-back seats. Embedded in the dashboard was a small video screen attached to closed-circuit cameras for monitoring backward maneuvers. Above the center dash was a deluxe Blaupunkt stereo, Trapshooter radar detector, and cordless CB. In the rear sleeper compartment, affectionately referred to in trucker parlance as *the coffin box,* was a fully furnished apartment. In addition to a good-sized twin bed and working sink, there was a host of extras. A 12-volt microwave, refrigerator, and laptop computer. All of it installed by Lucas, with a little help from the Santa Monica First National Bank and Trust.

Collapsing into bed, Lucas kicked off his boots and tossed his cowboy hat onto a shelf above him. In the three years since Lucas had purchased the Kenworth for a hundred and fifty grand, he had spent over fifty thousand additional bucks lovingly customizing her. Now, after surviving the aftermath of Reaganomics, S & L crises, recessions, and mini-depressions, he was in danger of going belly-up because of one little incompetent asshole of a broker. It was enough to give him terminal indigestion.

He closed his eyes. He needed sleep and he needed it bad. But somehow, his mind wasn't ready to shut down quite yet. He kept hearing a faint refrain somewhere deep in the recesses of his middle brain like a chorus from some Top-40 hit that won't go away. *I want to stop . . . believe me . . . ya'll don't know how much I want to stop. But I can't . . . I can't stop . . . not in a million years . . .*

There was something about young Melville Benoit's lunatic rant that bothered Lucas. Something about the tone of the young man's voice. Even filtered through the squelch of the airwaves and that tiny loudspeaker, it sounded . . . what was the word? . . .

. . . grave.

I been cursed . . . cursed to never stop moving . . .

Lucas rolled over on his side and tried not to think about Melville Benoit.

A few feet across the cabin, pinned up on the paneled wall, was a yellowed glossy of James Brown. In the picture, the Godfather of Soul was caught leaning backward in orgiastic rapture, howling into his floor mike, surrounded by his posse. At the bottom was a runny, blurred autograph. The photo was a gift from Lucas's older sister. For years it had been both godhead and good-luck charm for Lucas, who had come to idolize The Hardest Working Man in Show Business back in the early seventies.

Above the photo of Brown, taped in haphazard decoupage, were photos of other rebels such as Jimi Hendrix, Sun Ra, Screaming Jay Hawkins, and Chuck D. A ravenous music fan, Lucas had encyclopedic knowledge of the black underground. He could talk circles around most grad students. Completely self-educated, Lucas had overcompensated for his lack of a college sheepskin with a compulsive devotion to learning the street, the real world, and the renegades who shape it. It was an attitude that led to many spirited debates with his partner.

"You ought to be drifting off to dreamland by now," Sophie suddenly called back to him as she climbed into the driver's seat and strapped herself in. "I thought you were tired."

"I might be able to sleep if my partner would refrain from yacking at me."

"Grouch." Sophie put the truck into gear and pulled out of the parking lot.

Within moments they were back on the highway.

Lucas listened to Sophie wind her way back up through the eleven forward gears. The truck rattled slightly with each shift, then hummed deeply as the weight displacement fell into sync with the trailer's momentum. Before long they were roaring along at seventy miles per hour. And Lucas settled back and listened to his favorite sound—eighteen wheels singing in unison.

He felt himself drifting into slumber. It always happened as soon as he was in motion; the soothing vibration would wrap around him like a blanket. In fact, he had been that way since early childhood. If his mama wanted to knock him out, all she had to do was throw him in the back of the Buick and take a ride. Before they got to the corner stop sign, little Lucas would be out cold.

But tonight, even as the truck skimmed along the bone-dry superslab, sleep was hard in coming. Too many troubling thoughts were nagging at Lucas. Too many disturbing, incongruous images swimming around beneath the surface of his consciousness.

And that desperate, tortured voice, seeping into his thoughts like an unexpected chill on a summer night. *I been cursed . . . cursed to never stop moving . . . never stop no matter what . . .*

An hour later, with the voice ringing in his ears, Lucas finally drifted into what would turn out to be the evening's first nightmare.

2

The Man with the Silver Eyes

It was 1962 and Lucas was back in Torrance, crouching in the green darkness of a tomato patch, waiting for the man with the silver eyes. Beside Lucas there were two other boys, both coiled and breathing hard: Dez Washington, his best friend and lab partner from Mr. Kozlowski's biology class, and Grady Foster, Dez's cousin from Detroit. All around them rose the pithy smell of tomato vines, manure, and peat. Below them a flurry of ants poured across their sneakers. Lucas felt a pearl of sweat track down his back and into his gym shorts. But nobody budged. They knew within moments the big black hearse would be sliding past them on its journey back to its garage outside Blakemoor Mausoleum.

Behind the wheel, the tall man with the mirrored sunglasses would be sitting there grinning his crooked grin.

Lucas turned and inspected his assault team. Dez was kneeling by the compost pile, his little brown face glistening with sweat, his fists wrapped around a pair of big rotten beefsteaks. Next to him crouched Grady, the youngest boy. Grady's expression was twisted into a mask of intensity like a parachutist preparing to jump. Grady also held a couple of overripe tomatoes.

"Don't throw 'em 'til I give you the signal," Lucas whispered. His voice seemed suspended in molasses.

"Okay," said Dez.

"Okay," Grady echoed.

Turning back toward the street, Lucas gazed through a break in the foliage. He could see the corner of Monterey and Hamilton streets less than fifty yards away. Baking in midafternoon sun, the four-way stop sat on the edge of a working-class neighborhood. Spreading off to the south were rows of dirty ranch homes separated by cyclone fencing. To the north was a vast encampment of mobile homes. But most importantly, lying just beyond the trailer park, stewing in the distant rays of heat-bleached grass and Joshua trees, was Blakemoor Cemetery. Somewhere out there in the cemetery's farthest reaches was the body of Lucas's father . . . which was precisely why the hearse driver was now the object of the boys' contempt.

On the day of Charles Hyde's burial, the driver had made an offensive comment to Lucas that had started a private feud.

A feud that was about to escalate.

"Luke—!" Grady yelped, frantically pointing through a break in the foliage. "Over by the willow tree! It's him! He's coming this way!"

Lucas glanced through the break and saw a vehicle coming down Hamilton Street. It was a block and a half away, gleaming in the sun, silky black and impossibly long.

"Quick," Lucas hissed. "Get ready."

The other boys struggled toward the opening at the edge of the patch. Lucas picked up his ammunition and followed them into the breach. They lined up, side by side, poised and ready to fire.

The hearse came tooling down the blacktop like a cancer, slow yet inevitable. Panic burned in Lucas's stomach. The hearse was steadily closing the distance, now only fifty yards away. Now only forty. Now thirty. Soon Lucas could see the reflection of passing objects in the hearse's silken quarter panels. The gleam of sunlight on its windshield. And behind it, the milky, diffuse ghost of the driver's face.

Taking a deep breath and holding it, Lucas waited until the hearse passed directly across from their vegetable patch. Fifteen yards. Ten. Five. Three, two, one.

"Now!"

The boys let the tomatoes fly. The projectiles arched over the vegetable patch and struck the hearse dead center. On impact, the sound they made was incredible. A watery barrage of tiny farting explosions, with juice and meat splattering everywhere.

The hearse locked its brakes. Tires screeched. The bulbous rear end hunched up like an angry animal. Then, the sound of gears grinding and shrieking rubber signalled the hearse's explosion into reverse.

"Run!" *Lucas heard himself yell. But his voice sounded puny and disembodied.*

The other boys sprang from the foliage and dispersed into the vacant lots behind the vegetable patch. Lucas followed. Behind them, the hearse slammed on its brakes, jammed into forward, and came up over the curb toward them.

The motherfucker is coming after us, *Lucas thought frantically.* He's coming right through the tomatoes!

Lucas slipped on a wet spot and tumbled to the ground. Behind him, the black monster was approaching in a cloud of noxious dust and gas fumes, its metal grille plowing through the vines and plants and support sticks like the jaws of a dragon.

It was heading straight for Lucas.

Struggling to his feet, Lucas made a beeline for his bicycle. It rested against a tree about twenty feet away. The other boys had already grabbed their bikes and were halfway across the vacant lot toward safety. But Lucas had lost precious time. The hearse was only fifty or sixty yards away now.

He reached his bike, hopped on, and began to torque toward the far end of the lot. The bike—a modified Schwinn Stingray with a banana seat, reinforced frame, and oversized tires—was a natural for trail hopping. But today it somehow felt flimsy and loose against the bumpy, sun-dried ground of the vacant lot.

Behind him, the hearse was gaining.

Lucas pedalled as fast as he could toward the service road at the end of the lot. The bumps vibrated his teeth. His skinned and bleeding knees sang with pain. His Stingray rattled noisily as he pushed it as hard as he could.

A moment later he reached the road. His balloon tires hit the pavement with a bump and a reassuring hum.

Ahead of him, the service road descended steeply into a narrow valley. At the foot of the downgrade the road took a hairpin turn and disappeared into a wooded lot. If Lucas could just make it to the bottom he was home-free.

But something was wrong. Ahead of him, Dez and Grady had already disappeared around the bottom of the hill; but Lucas didn't seem to be making any progress. Glancing down at his speedometer, he felt his stomach tighten. It said he was standing still.

The hearse was close enough now to vibrate the pavement behind him.

Lucas struggled toward freedom but the faster he pedalled, the less progress he made. The bottom of the hill seemed to recede farther and farther into the distance like a mirage. His wheels seemed to be bogging down into a thick, syrupy, taffylike mire.

He was moving in slow motion.

Gazing back over his shoulder, Lucas saw that the hearse was only inches away. An enormous black obscenity, its steel maw gaping hungrily. Behind its windshield, the pasty face of the driver hovered. With his mirrored sunglasses. His smirk.

Lucas strained to move. But now he was on a hopeless treadmill to nowhere. His joints seemed frozen. The wheels of the Stingray seemed to be spinning impotently. He refused to look back at the monstrosity behind him. He refused to look back into the pale face behind the glass.

Soon he felt the warmth of the hearse's engine on his back. The gasoline stench. The particles of gravel and grime. Then, he felt the worst feeling of them all.

The slimy cold touch of the hearse's grille on his back.

It was like the kiss of a corpse.

* * *

Lucas came awake with a jerk.

Sitting up and shaking off the nightmare, he stretched his sore limbs. He had been dozing in the back of the gently vibrating cab for nearly three hours. He was filmed with sweat. His jaw ached from the grinding of his teeth. And his blankets were balled up at his feet from his feverish tossing and turning.

He had just witnessed the return engagement of a dream which had been plaguing him for years. Sometimes he dreamed mere snatches of it. Other times he experienced wide-screen technicolor versions that seemed to go on all night. But it was always the same scenario. A childhood incident that he vaguely remembered was re-created in all its garish, subconscious imagery. Thinking back, he could barely remember ever encountering the hearse driver in real life. But in his twilight thoughts, the driver took on an inexorably potent form.

Lucas climbed out of bed, steadied himself against the bed frame, and took a few moments to find his footing. The sleeper compartment was the only area in which one could actually stand up and stretch; and it usually took Lucas a few seconds to find his truck legs. He rubbed sleep from his eyes, found his coffee cup, and drew some hot water from the tank in the corner. Then he added a heaping teaspoon of instant coffee and slugged it down. Although he usually couldn't stand the flinty taste of instant, he needed it badly tonight. The cobwebs were extra thick.

For a moment, Lucas considered popping a pill. He had a stash of Dexedrine—commonly known as "Pedal Pushers"—in the locker over the bed. Just one capsule would make him sharp as a tack. But he decided against it. He really wasn't on a schedule tonight and he didn't need the inevitable migraine a day later. Instead, he just chugged down the cup of instant and grimaced at the aftertaste.

"Jesus Christ," he said aloud, "that's fucking awful."

Sophie's voice came through the dividing wall. "The sleeping giant awakens . . . ahead of schedule, yet."

Lucas shoved the accordion door open, climbed out into

the cab, and took a seat in the shotgun chair. "God I love instant coffee."

Sophie gently urged the truck around a curve, downshifting, keeping her gaze riveted to the darkness ahead of them. "Want me to stop for some fresh stuff?"

"Nah."

"You're ahead of schedule. I've got at least an hour left in my shift."

"Couldn't sleep."

Sophie gave him an odd look. "Lucas Hyde, the Yogi Bear of the trucker world, couldn't sleep?"

"I'm sorry to disappoint you but it even happens to *me* once in a while." Lucas reached up to the glove box, opened it, and fished out his box of Garcia Vegas. There was one slender stogie left. He took it out and fired it up. "Guess I'm just anxious about the goddamn broker situation."

Sophie cracked her side vent and let in the whistle of night air. "Maybe the Bakersfield boys will find us something by morning, something on the way home."

"Maybe," Lucas said, chewing his cigarillo. "I'll tell ya this much, it's a goddamn shame we don't have a reefer. We'd grab some business in Colorado on our way and make our money back in one trip."

Sophie groaned. "Don't gross me out, Lucas. The last thing I want to do is haul murdered animals."

"Excuse me. For a second there I forgot you were a communist pinko hippie."

"Flattery will get you nowhere."

Lucas grinned. He took great pleasure in teasing Sophie about her eating habits. She'd been a vegetarian for most of her life. It was a commitment she'd made after spending childhood summers at a relative's beefalo ranch outside of Denver, witnessing the whole slaughtering process up close. For a child, it was a formative experience. Of course, as a vegetarian trucker, Sophie was forced to improvise at greasy spoons and coffee counters along the way. Her usual strategy was to order toast with peanut butter and a chef salad, picking out the bacon bits by hand. Sometimes she'd even torment a perplexed waitress into bringing her a plate of garnishes only—parsley, lettuce, pickle, or whatever—and a bowl of hot water for making soup.

Early on in their partnership, the vegetarian routine drove Lucas up the wall. It was typical quasi-intellectual bullshit. Typical upper-class crap. Besides, out here on the open road you usually spent more time selecting the proper weight of motor oil than a high-fiber breakfast. This whole-grain bohemian stuff was best left to the eggheads in college towns and yuppies out in the valley.

But over the passing months, after thousands upon thousands of hard-earned miles, a strange thing began to happen. Lucas found himself thinking twice about where they stopped for grub. At first it was so subtle that Lucas hardly noticed it. He might merely glance at the bottom of a billboard to see if a place had a salad bar. Or he might drive an extra ten miles to find a joint that would offer a wider variety on their steam table or a better array of soups. It wasn't any big deal. He simply found himself taking meal stops more seriously nowadays. But perhaps the real reason he was paying more attention to their food breaks was because of something he had been dreading for over a year now—the fact that he might actually *like* this woman.

It was the little stuff that got to him at first—the tiny tray of herbs she was growing in the window of the sleeper cabin, the odors of mint and rosemary that seemed to hang around her like a wreath when she entered the cab . . . the way she told a story, imitating each character's voice and providing the appropriate sound effects . . . the sharp aroma of her hair as she passed by Lucas every night on her way to the sleeper. It was all this and much more that seemed to sneak up on Lucas one day while he wasn't looking and make him realize that maybe this hotshot little Jew from the suburbs wasn't so bad after all. In fact, maybe she was downright okay.

Regardless of his softening toward Sophie, however, Lucas knew the score. Smart partners never, *under any circumstances*, got attached. It was an unspoken code of the road. No personal crap on the superslab. It would make life miserable. Period.

"What the hell is our twenty anyway?" Lucas finally said,

using the ten-code for location. He was staring out at the dark passing landscape. Ahead of them, the interstate cut through a mountain of granite. In the spray of their headlights the rock looked like bleached bone.

Sophie filled him in. They were on U.S. 24, a few mile markers north of Nashville, Tennessee. Conditions were good. Traffic was light. And CB chatter was minimal. "Although," she added with an odd hitch in her voice, "I copied your little CB joker once or twice in the last hour."

Lucas had to pause and think for a moment. "You mean old Melville? Melville what's-his-name?"

"The very same."

"Jesus Christ, this dude doesn't give up easy." For a moment, Lucas wondered how Melville could still be in range. Most forty-channel rigs from the local Radio Shack had an effective reach of about five miles. Consequently, there were only three conceivable ways Melville Benoit could still be sending them mail: either he was tailing them, he was hovering out in front, or he was traveling along a parallel path. Each scenario seemed highly improbable. "You sure it was my guy?"

"Absolutely," Sophie said with that ·strange catch in her voice. "Who else is gonna be babbling about a curse?"

"Did you get back to him?"

"Negative. Too many other breakers on the line, teasing the hell out of the guy."

"Teasing him?"

"It seems a lot of folks copied your original conversation and wanted to get into the act."

Lucas drew on his stogie for a moment, amused. "Jesus—I bet that was rich. Buncha hard-core rednecks killing time with that crazy little brother. I bet Melville was thrilled to be drawing such a big audience."

"I don't think so."

Lucas studied Sophie for a moment. Staring at the white lines, her arms cradling the steering wheel, she was concentrating grimly; and Lucas could see that something was eating at her. "What do you mean, you don't think so?"

Sophie shot him a glance. "I don't think the guy was thrilled."

"What do you mean?"

Taking a breath, Sophie measured her voice. "I don't really know how to explain it . . . but I think the guy was telling the truth."

"Get outta town."

"I know what you're thinking," she said, again with that crazy hitch in her voice, "but it's not like that. I don't mean he's telling the truth about being cursed. I mean he's *sincere* about his *belief* that he's cursed. There's a big difference."

"What are you saying? The kid's nuts?"

"Exactly. I think the kid is seriously ill. Maybe a schizophrenic, maybe a renegade patient from some mental institution. It was in his voice, Lucas. His *voice*. There was real terror in that voice."

An inexplicable chill feathered up Lucas's spine. He agreed with her. In fact, he could still hear that crackling, distant yammer of Melville Benoit's voice. *I can't stop . . . not in a million years . . . not never!* Stamping out his cigarillo in the side tray, Lucas said, "What the hell do you want me to do about it?"

Sophie looked at him. "I think we ought to break for him again. Try to talk to him and settle him down. You're the only one that didn't tease him, Lucas. You ought to talk to him."

"Are you outta your head?! We got better things to do than tie up channel eleven with some head case from Podunk."

"I'm just asking you to talk him down, Lucas. The guy could really be in trouble. Might end up hurting himself . . . or maybe . . . somebody else, for that matter."

For quite a spell Lucas sat in the rumbling darkness, listening to the whine of the tires and pondering her suggestion. Assuming he could still find the kid, what the hell was Lucas going to say? "Hey, bro—don't mind these dudes in white suits, just step into this nice little straitjacket and everything will be peachy." And suppose the dude really was crazy— how the hell was Lucas supposed to deal with it? Lucas was a trucker, not a fucking social worker.

After a few more seconds of vibrating silence, Lucas finally said aloud, "Alright, what the hell—"

He snatched the CB handset off its cradle. "Break one-one for Melville Benoit. You got The Black Mariah here. Come on back, bro."

Silence. Lucas reached up and adjusted the squelch, cranked up the volume. A wave of ghostly voices filled the cab. But still no sign of the terrified young man with the southern drawl.

"Try it again," Sophie urged.

Lucas grunted. "Breaker one-one. This is The Black Mariah calling old Melville Benoit. You got yer ears on, Melville? Come on back. Over."

Again, staticky silence filled the Kenworth.

"Break one-one. Come in, Melville."

Nothing.

Then a voice came squawking through the CB speaker like a tin can being ripped apart. "Four-Roger, Blacky. You got The Stud Muffin on the side. Whattya say we give all this voodoo bullshit a rest tonight. Okay? Come back."

It was a new voice. Although Lucas didn't recognize the handle, he recognized the tone of voice. Just another gypsy trucker with a chip on his shoulder and a belly full of Methedrine. Sometimes Lucas couldn't stand honky motherfuckers behind the wheels of semis. Of course, trucking was like any other subculture; there were good and bad apples wherever you went.

He was about to answer when Sophie grabbed the mike from him. "We copied that, smart ass. I wonder which is smaller—your IQ or your penis?"

Through the static, the voice replied, "Ten-nine on that, Blacky. Sounds like a nasty beaver comin' over the wires."

Lucas grabbed the handset. "Listen, motherfucker—if you want to eyeball me at the next exit I'll be happy to take this up with you in person."

Through the speaker: "Sounds like a good idea, black boy. Wish I had the time."

Lucas replied, "That's what I figured."

"Fuck you," said the voice.

"Copy that, Stud Muffin. Same back at ya."

Lucas replaced the handset, sat back, and rubbed his eyes. He felt Sophie's angry glare like a heat ray on the side of his face. Opening his eyes, he turned and saw her biting her lip and staring at the road, her expression tight with rage. It was a habit of hers whenever she was pissed. The dry silence and the gnawing of her lip. "Fucking rednecks," she said at last. "I hate 'em."

Lucas fished around the glove box for another cigar. "Look . . . at least I tried."

"I'd call that a pretty feeble attempt."

Sighing to himself, Lucas was about to say something else when another breaker came over the air.

"Break-one-one, come in." It was a soft, elderly, southern voice. "Breaking for The Black Mariah. Over."

Lucas retrieved the hand mike. "You got The Black Mariah, here. Go ahead, channel eleven."

The elderly voice: "You got The Boomer on this end. If ya'll are lookin' for that mixed-up boy named Melville, I last heard him on channel nineteen."

"Thanks, Boomer. What's your twenty?"

Through the speaker, the old man answered lazily. "Westbound on rural route ninety-six. Right outside Almaville."

"What are you driving there, Boomer?"

There was a pause, then a hoarse giggle: "Just a li'l pick-'em-up truck. Been deliverin' papers for the *Sentinel* for over twenty years now. Just love to jaw with the big rigs."

Grinning to himself, Lucas imagined the old man's routine. Out each morning before dawn with a sheaf of newspapers. Moving from mailbox to mailbox, farm to farm, just like clockwork. Just like a little old rooster. Thumbing the send button, Lucas finally said, "Appreciate the info, Boomer. You take care of yourself, alright?"

"Ten-four," came the old man's reply. "Roger and out."

Lucas flipped over to channel nineteen and listened for Melville Benoit's anguished voice. Again, only the hiss of disconnected voices and static greeted his ears. Lucas clicked the send button and said, "Breaking for old Melville Benoit.

This is The Black Mariah calling Melville Benoit. Come back, Melville."

Again, only static. Lucas was getting frustrated. He just couldn't believe he was scooping around for this messed-up brother, preparing himself for another drawn-out, psychotic litany. But there was something about Sophie's concern that bothered Lucas. She was not one to be suckered by some small-town joker. If she thought this kid was sincere, then maybe—

Somebody was weeping on the CB.

At first, Lucas wasn't sure what he was hearing. Through the rush of static, it sounded almost like an animal panting, hyperventilating. Faintly at first, but growing, it touched a weird nerve deep down inside Lucas like the onslaught of a high-pitched dog whistle.

It was the sound of Melville Benoit crying his heart out.

Lucas glanced over at Sophie. Keeping the truck at full steam ahead, she was half concentrating on the road, half cocking her head toward the CB. Lucas could tell the sound was affecting her the same way it was affecting him.

Lucas spoke softly into the mike: "Melville Benoit? Can you hear me? This is The Black Mariah."

At first, the crying continued. Then, through a gurgle of phlegm and hoarseness, the kid's voice replied, "Heh . . . hello . . . hello, Black Mariah?"

"Melville?"

Through the speaker: "Yeah . . . it's me . . . but I ain't doing too well . . ."

"Calm down, bro."

Over the air came a choked sound vaguely resembling a laugh. "Got myself in some deep shit, Mariah. Auxiliary tank's almost gone. Maybe forty . . . maybe fifty more miles . . . and then . . . shit, man, y'all gotta believe me . . . I'm dyin' out here. . . ."

Lucas listened to the young man fight back his tears. "Listen, Melville . . . you gotta try and calm down. Just calm on down."

There was another noisy moment of silence, then the voice

returned. "What do y'all expect?! I already told y'all—I been cursed! What do y'all want from me!?!"

Lucas thought about it for a moment. It seemed this guy was walking along the ledge about a hundred stories above the ground and was about to fall. Whether it was all imaginary or not, the only way to talk him off that ledge was to humor him for a few moments.

Pressing the call switch, Lucas said very softly, "Why don't you tell us about it."

It took less than five minutes for Melville to relate his feverish tale. For most of those five minutes Lucas and Sophie simply listened. But occasionally, Lucas found himself wondering what all the other truckers who were out there copying the mail might be making of this thing.

The story was grand opera.

Melville Benoit was a cook. Not an ordinary fry cook either, but a full-blown gourmet chef. He had learned his trade in the navy. After his stint overseas he had studied at the prestigious Escoffier School in New Orleans.

A little over a year ago, Melville had fallen head over heels for a fellow cooking student, a beautiful young white girl named Samantha Mosby. The twosome set up housekeeping in the French Quarter and eventually announced their engagement. There was only one problem. Samantha's family was none too happy about having an African American joining the fold. One of the wealthiest, oldest-money, conservative families in Mobile, the Mosby clan was dead set against integration in any form. Especially unhinged was Samantha's loony old great-aunt.

Melville never really knew that much about eighty-nine-year-old Vanessa DeGeaux. Through local rumors he learned that the old woman lived on a deserted atoll off the Gulf Coast, an old antebellum enclave known as Egg Island. Some said she was a vegetable in some asylum, paraplegic and crazy as a loon. Others said she was a witch. In reality, not even Samantha knew very much about great-aunty. But as the wedding approached, Melville began to worry that the Mosby family—especially old Vanessa—might be up to something.

Three nights ago, Melville's suspicion was confirmed.

Melville was out in the alley behind his apartment, changing the oil in his Camaro, when he heard a sound. Someone tapped him on the shoulder. He turned around and immediately ate somebody's fist. The punch sent him sprawling back against the car and down to the ground. Melville tried to glimpse his attacker but quickly ran out of time.

Within moments he had passed out.

"That's when I woke up in my car . . ."

The amplified voice pierced the noisy silence of the cab. Filtering through the tiny CB speaker, Melville sounded like a man holding on to a life raft, beyond desperation, going under for the last time.

"What happened then?" Lucas asked, though he wasn't buying any of it. Next to him, commanding the Kenworth, Sophie sat listening with intense concentration. Her cigarette had burned down so low the ash looked like one of those Chinese snakes the kids play with on the Fourth of July.

"That's the real strange part," Melville suddenly replied through the speaker. "I realized I was movin' like a motherfucker. Somebody had propped me behind the wheel of the Camaro and sent me singin' down Dolphine Street—"

"Yeah, so . . . ?"

"There was some weird-ass stuff hanging in my car, stuff written all over my seats. Like somebody dipped their fingers in shit and wrote messages all over the interior of my rod, man. Then it hit me. Stars and magic words and charms and shit—somebody done put a fuckin' hex on me. Probably the old DeGeaux bitch. The old DeGeaux bitch put a fuckin' hex on me. There was something else, too—"

Lucas thumbed the call button. "Whattya mean—something else?"

There was a pause. Then the voice returned through the static. "I know y'all ain't swallowing any of this—but somehow I knew this shit in my car was from somebody's grave. Dirt and dead flowers and some weird-ass trinket copped right outta somebody's grave—"

Sophie and Lucas exchanged a glance. Snuffing out her

cigarette, Sophie grabbed the handset and pressed the switch. "How did you know it was from somebody's grave?"

"I just knew," the voice replied. "On account of the smell of the shit, the way my neck hairs was standin' at attention— man, I just knew this whole thing was the work of that crazy old racist DeBeaux bitch."

Another long pause. Sophie finally spoke up. "What did you do then?"

"Got my wheels under control, first of all. Headed for a pay phone to call Sam and the cops. But I knew something was wrong, seriously wrong. Felt it in my gut, man . . . and when I stopped and got out to make the call, I found out what was what."

Sophie waited for a moment. "Go on, Melville. We're listening."

His voice was taut with anguish. "Parked the car and got out and tried to dial . . . but . . . I don't know how to explain it . . . I felt it deep down in my belly . . . just couldn't stay put . . . couldn't stop moving. Just had to get back into this fuckin' Camaro and take off . . ."

There was another long pause before the young man finally continued. He sounded close to tears. "That was when I found the note."

Sophie looked at Lucas, then thumbed the switch. "The note?"

"This motherfuckin' note was stickin' outta the corner of my glove box. Written on yellowed stationery in India ink and dainty little squiggles. I just knew it was from the DeGeaux hag. It said that they took Samantha back to Mobile and that I should say my prayers. Said I was doomed. Rest of it was written in Latin gobbledygook."

Lucas sat back, rubbed his eyes, and chuckled under his breath. ". . . the men in white coats will be here any minute . . ."

Sophie shushed him.

"That's almost three days ago now," Melville added. "Since then I been trying to keep moving, trying to find Samantha, trying to get help . . . but the girl done disappeared off the face of the earth. . . ."

Sophie pressed the call switch. "Why haven't you run out of gas already?"

The voice returned. "Been rollin' real slow through fillin' stations, throwin' dollar bills at gas jockeys, beggin' 'em to stick a gallon in my rear while I bawl like a baby from the pain."

"The pain?" Lucas was becoming amazed at the complexity of this lunatic's rant.

"That's what I said," Melville replied in his strangled voice. "Pain from stoppin' comes in waves . . . and it gets worse every time I stop . . . and it feels like . . . like . . ."

Another break in the babble. Lucas rubbed his eyes, thumbed the switch, and said, "Yo, Mel—you still there?"

On the speaker, Melville was beginning to whimper. "Can't you understand what I've been tellin' y'all? Can't you recognize a motherfuckin' curse when you hear one?!"

Lucas had heard just about enough. "Got a news flash for ya, Captain. There's no such thing as voodoo curses. *Comprendo?* You're a victim of the power of suggestion!"

A long stretch of noisy silence.

"Melville?"

Silence.

"Breaking for Melville—come back."

Nothing. Lucas glanced over at Sophie. Her eyes were on the road, but her expression was knotted with intense deliberation. She licked her lips and grabbed the mike. "Melville, if you copy this, please respond—over?"

Again, nothing but white noise and the whine of eighteen Goodyears. Turning to Lucas, Sophie said, "Apologize to him."

"What?!"

"Guy spends twenty minutes telling you his story. Whether it's all delusion or not, he opens up to you and what do you do? You spit in his face. Please, Lucas, if not for him, do it for me—please apologize."

Lucas wrinkled his nose. "Jesus Christ . . ." Taking the handset, thumbing the switch, Lucas said, "Breaking for Melville . . . this is The Black Mariah, young brother . . . real sorry 'bout coming down on you like that."

He lifted the switch and listened. Through the static came the faint sound of Melville sobbing, trying to gather his breath. Finally, the weak voice returned. "Can't blame y'all for not believin' any of it—but it's the God's honest gospel truth. . . ."

"Melville," Lucas uttered softly across the surface of the mike, careful not to agitate or disturb. "Suppose we were to help ya—just suppose—okay? What exactly do you want us to do?"

After another long, staticky pause, Melville's answer came over the air.

"Refuel me while I'm still moving."

Again, Lucas shot a glance over at Sophie and said, "Ten-nine on that, Melville. Say again."

Melville explained. "I can slow way down—maybe twenty, twenty-five miles an hour—and you can somehow get a gas spout into a tank in back. I know you can do it. A full tank will keep me going through the night."

Rolling his eyes, Lucas said, "Melville, listen, if what you say is true—if you really can't stop . . . isn't this refueling shit just a temporary fix? I mean, isn't it gonna just prolong the inevitable?"

After a staticky pause, "I'm hoping . . . I'm praying . . . if I can just make it through one more night, Samantha will find me . . . and she'll know how to deal with—"

"Listen," Lucas interrupted, "I don't want to—"

Lucas suddenly felt Sophie punch his arm.

"Mute the mike," she said. "I want to ask you something."

"Stand by, Melville." Lucas clipped the handset on its cradle and turned to Sophie. In the emerald glow of the dash she looked almost ghostly. Her eyes were shifting across the middle distance. Her lips were pursed. Lucas knew the look all too well.

The lady's wheels were turning.

"Feel like a ramblin' gamblin' man tonight?" Sophie's voice was suddenly full of mischief.

"What are you saying?"

"Bet you a hundred bucks you can't do it."

Lucas was flabbergasted. "Get outta here."

Sophie grinned wickedly. "We got no flip trip scheduled, nothing on the books, no timetable, I'm bored to tears, and you're getting to be a fat old man. I'll bet you two hundred bucks you can't refuel this guy while he's still in motion."

Rubbing his eyes, Lucas groaned painfully. He couldn't believe what he was hearing. "Do you have any idea what smokie bear would do to us for a stunt like that? Hell, the County Mounties have probably been copying Melville's mail all night. You're talking reckless endangerment and God knows what else."

"Fuck the bears."

"Yeah, that's easy for you to say; you're not holding the fucking paper on this operation. We'd lose our license faster than you could say Buford T. Justice."

Sophie refused to stop grinning. "Two hundred bucks says you couldn't do it."

Lucas felt his stomach twist. She was tapping into his weakness for the wager. She'd done it many times before. A couple of years back, she'd goaded him into a high-stakes poker game in the basement of a warehouse in Loughlan, Nevada—an indiscretion that ultimately cost Lucas six hundred bucks and a brand-new set of chrome mud flaps. On another occasion she'd bet him three hundred bucks that he couldn't drive the Kenworth tractor up the hairpins of Trail Ridge Drive near Estes Park, Colorado. Lucas had won that bet, but not before clipping a side mirror and puncturing two tires. After that he'd grown leery of Sophie's dares.

He pursed his lips and said, "You don't have a dollar ninety-eight to put up on a bet."

"You don't believe me, go look in my purse."

"I'm not doing it."

"Chicken."

"Forget it."

"You're scared."

"Gimme a break with the female psychology." Lucas fished in his pocket for another cigarillo, found one, and lit it up. "I hung up my betting shoes."

Sophie was relentless. "Come on, Pilgrim."

"I said no."

Sophie grinned. "You gotta admit, your curiosity is piqued."

Lucas grunted irascibly, pretending to scorn the idea. But the truth was, he did have a hankering to eyeball young Melville—if for nothing else, just to simply confirm the fact that it was all a scam. Besides, there was some truth in what Sophie was saying. Lucas was becoming rather boring in his old age, always playing it safe, just marking time until he had enough in his banking account to retire.

But, of course, these were all halfhearted rationalizations. The real reason Lucas would even consider doing it was the bet itself. The joy of the wager.

"Lemme ask you something," Lucas finally said, staring at Sophie and pondering her Cheshire-cat smirk. "You trying to goad me into doing this because you want to help the kid . . . or because you just want to see me make another ass outta myself like the last little bet?"

Sophie thought about it for a moment and then told him it was a little of both.

Laughing, Lucas asked, "So, who the hell's gonna bail us outta jail afterwards?"

"You'll think of something," Sophie said, her grin widening.

"You are one sick mama."

"Stop stalling, Lucas."

"Why me?" Lucas moaned, chewing his cigar.

"Two hundred's my final offer."

Lucas grunted. It was over. The fat lady was about to sing. Sophie's team had just kicked the winning field goal. Lucas was history. "I'll be a motherfucker," he said to himself and reached up to the glove box. Nestled inside was a sheaf of maps and brochures bundled together with a rubber hand. Lucas pulled it out, thumbed through the pages, and found the proper document. Then he grabbed the mike and called back to Melville.

"All right, young brother—this is your lucky night."

A beat of silence followed, as the words slowly registered. "Shit, man—thank you, Black Mariah—thank you." But instead of relief, there was pain in the young man's voice.

"Put your ears on good, Melville," Lucas said, and with his thumbnail he traced a double line along the periphery of his map. "I want you to pull the plug, back down, and look for the junction of I-Twenty-four and Seventy-nine. You copy?"

"Yeah, Mariah."

"Big fours on that, young bro. Take us approximately fifteen minutes to get some extra go-juice and get close enough to eyeball ya. Be coming in through your back door."

A moment of static, then Melville's trembly voice, "I'll be there."

Lucas glanced over at Sophie, rolled his eyes, and said, "Ten-four, Melville. Be seeing you soon."

Then, after replacing the handset, flipping the radio off, and sighing wearily, Lucas added, "This oughtta be good."

3

Everybody and
Their Brother

In the middle of the night there were essentially only two ways for Sheriff Dick Baum to achieve any significant level of arousal with his beloved wife of twenty-three years.

First, he could talk Gloria into wearing the pink crotchless panties that his brother Maynard had brought back from the French Quarter in the spring of '79 and had given to Baum as a gag at the Pennington County Policemen's Ball. Over the subsequent decade, Gloria had worn the panties on three occasions, each time giving Baum a steadfast erection that lasted well past the couple's usual ten-minute line of demarcation. Unfortunately, Gloria was a stout woman and the novelty panties were not up to the rigorous quality standards of her preferred Lane Bryant Super-Support Trico Underwear with the special double stitching. After three daring trysts, the pink panties were beginning to resemble a mangled doggie toy.

Second, there was fantasy. Since his glory days at Bartonville High School, Baum had always been a champion dreamer, especially when it came to matters of the libido. In his late teens he favored Amazonian burlesque queens like Chesty Morgan, Mamie Van Doren, and Ann Marie. Their pneumatic bobbing breasts would inform every waking and nonwaking dream of the young Ritchie Baum. Later, after two years of junior college and the successful completion of his state trooper's exam, he began to favor the sirens of cinema. In his mind, Gloria Henkle, his faithful girlfriend, could materialize at any moment into Angie Dickinson in a wet T-shirt or Janet Leigh in handcuffs. After getting elected sheriff in '77 and celebrating his tenth wedding anniversary, Baum turned to real-life fantasy girls. Gloria would transform into the leggy checkout girl at the Piggly Wiggly or the red-haired legal aide over at the county courthouse.

At this very moment, in fact, Gloria was transforming into the olive-skinned Italian receptionist from the Peterborough Dental Clinic.

"Mi amore," the fantasy girl whispered in Baum's ear, her breathy voice feathering through the darkness of the Baum bedroom.

Baum felt his manhood stirring, He rolled over and pulled Gloria into his arms. Groggy, half asleep, she sighed and stroked his thinning hair. Baum gently removed the top of her cotton nightie, revealing her prominent breasts. In the moon-strafed shadows, he didn't notice her stretch marks, didn't notice the delicate lacing of blue veins and wrinkles along Gloria's neck and collarbone. She was his fantasy girl right now and that was okay with both of them.

"Hello, Mr. Frisky," Gloria said, and urged Baum between her legs. Baum was ready. His knees wobbled beneath him as he positioned himself for insertion. He could smell Gloria's scent, a mixture of Vicks VapoRub and cold cream wafting up at him. He imagined it was the receptionist's musky perfume.

"Take me, you wild animal," Gloria whispered.

The sudden sound of beeping filled the room.

"You gotta be kidding me," Baum groaned as he wrestled his erection back into his boxer shorts.

It was his beeper. Clipped to his belt, which was draped over a chair across the room, it signalled official police business. Probably an emergency.

"Goddamnit," Gloria said, shoving Baum away from her. "Just as I was imagining you were James Brolin."

Baum looked down at his wife and grinned. He brushed the dishwater-gray hair from her eyes, leaned down, and planted a kiss on her nose. Gloria returned the kiss, then pulled her nightie back over herself.

The beeper continued beeping.

Sheriff Dick Baum climbed out of bed, clicked off the beeper, and checked his watch. It was 3:45 A.M. He went over to the phone and dialed his office. A squat little man with very little neck to speak of, Baum had the physique of a small German automobile. Square-jawed, chiselled, sun-burned to a brick red, his face looked hewn from granite. But at the moment, his toughness was belied by a pair of bony white legs poking out of his boxers.

The night receptionist answered on the third ring. She told Baum it was Deputy Morrison who had beeped him. Baum told her to get the deputy on the phone. A moment later, Del-bert Morrison came over the line. "Hey, Sheriff, how's it goin'?"

"Delbert, you better have a sure-fire good reason to get me outta bed at four o'clock in the friggin' morning."

"Something brewing out on Highway Twenty-four, Sheriff. Heard it on the scanner about ten minutes ago."

Baum rubbed his eyes. "I'm listening."

The deputy's voice was tense, anxious. "Couple truckers planning to pull some kind of stunt out there. Gonna refuel somebody while still in motion."

"Run that by me again."

"Said they're gonna refuel some kid in a car while he's still moving. I'm thinking reckless endangerment and FCC violations up the butt and that's just for starters."

"Is that right?" Baum shot a look over at Gloria, who was propped up on her elbow, watching.

The man on the line was a continual thorn in the sheriff's side. Young and earnest and naive, Morrison was like a hy-peractive puppy dog. He wanted to bring the sheriff every old shoe or dead bird lying along the side of the road from here to Memphis. Unfortunately, Morrison was all Baum had at the moment. His other deputy, a sharp black gal from At-lanta named Arlene Williams, was out with the flu this week, which had forced Baum to split the shifts between himself and this twitchy kid.

"I'm telling ya, Sheriff," the deputy added, "we're talkin' fuel on the highway, people leaning out of vehicles. Could develop into something very dangerous."

Baum yawned and arched his sore back. "Sounds like a job for the state police."

"But these hot-dog truckers are headed for the Pinkneyville junction."

"So?"

"That's Pennington County."

"So what?"

"That's our jurisdiction, Sheriff."

Baum gazed over at his wife. She had already lost interest and had gone back to sleep. Shaking his head, Baum silently cursed his luck. His erection was a distant memory now. The sweat on the back of his neck had turned clammy. "Whattya saying, Delbert?"

"I'm saying we should nip this in the bud before anybody gets hurt."

"Delbert, if you recall, the last time you got bent outta shape over something on the CB scanner, it turned out to be two truckers picking up a couple of whores."

After an awkward silence, the voice said, "This is different, Sheriff."

"Alright, cool your jets for a second." Baum glanced at his watch again. He was due back at the office in a little over three hours. Since his romantic interlude had been so irrevocably trashed, he figured he might as well come in early. Better to lose a little sleep than have Delbert out there on some wild goose chase. "You stay put, Delbert," Baum finally said. "I'll be there by four-thirty and we'll see what develops."

"But—"

"I'll swing by the junction on my way in and make sure the sky ain't fallin'."

"But I—"

"If something develops, I'll let you have the collar."

"But I thought—"

"That's an order, Delbert. You got plenty of paperwork to do. You hear me?"

"Yes, sir."

Baum hung up the phone and started getting dressed. His arthritic knees were beginning to throb, his back was knotted with pain. Oh yes, sports fans, this was starting out to be a great day.

Angel Figueroa sensed trouble. Flipping off his Cobra scanner, he quickly grabbed his broom and started looking busy. The manager, Guillermo, was coming through the garage entrance; and the last thing Angel wanted to do was get caught listening to the scanner instead of doing his duties. But tonight, with the bizarre interchange between Melville Benoit and The Black Mariah, the temptation to listen was just too strong. Angel had been copying Melville's ranting and raving since midnight.

It was now almost 4:00 A.M.

Guillermo approached, wiped his greasy hands on his apron, and said, "Not gonna have you hanging around here all night again. You oughtta be done with the garage and halfway through the walk-in by now."

"Almo'th done," Angel replied, head down, lisping softly, grabbing for a broom. He wore a greasy denim vest over a Metallica T-shirt that hung loosely over faded blue jeans. His arms were covered with dozens of braided Indian bracelets.

Guillermo frowned. "What did you say, boy?" As owner and sole proprietor of the Dixie Boy Truck Stop for over eleven years, Guillermo wasn't about to let this young squirt take advantage of him. He wanted a straight answer.

"Almo'th done." Angel spoke a little louder this time, his cleft palate and harelip softening the consonants and creating a severe speech impediment. He was seventeen years old going on sixty. Deformed from a congenital birth defect, Angel's scarred, oblong face, obscured by a mane of obsidian-black hair, gave off a look of chronic sullenness. But underneath all the hair lurked timid brown eyes filled with intelligence and passion. Passion hard won from years of torment. "Took a little longer tonight," he added, "on account of the th'emi-truck we had in here earlier."

Guillermo wasn't buying the excuse. "Don't give me that shit, kid—you've been listening to the two-way for hours. I'm not springing for any more overtime."

"I can wa'th the fridge right away." Angel hurried over to the big iron washbasin in the corner of the garage and began filling a bucket with hot water.

Behind him, Guillermo watched, pursing his lips sourly. "Not gonna stand for any more fuck-ups—understand?"

"Yeth-thir."

"Got a business to run here."

Angel nodded. "Be done in fifteen minuth."

Guillermo grunted. "What the fuck did you say?!"

Angel paused, turned to his boss, and enunciated as best he could. "Be done in fifteen minnnnn—uhhhhth."

Sighing wearily, Guillermo turned and headed back toward the restaurant, mumbling under his breath. "Goddamnit to hell . . . what the fuck was I thinking . . . hiring a retard. . . ."

Across the garage, Angel tried to ignore the words and concentrate on filling the bucket with Mr. Clean. The restaurant door slammed shut behind him. Angel jumped slightly. He was on edge. The words hurt. They always hurt him deep down. Ever since he tried to go to high school and suffered the cruel teasing of those pack dogs known as teenagers. His mother had always said it's what's inside that counts. But after they locked her away in the sanitarium down in Chattanooga, her words of encouragement had all but faded away. For over two years now, Angel had been on his own; and it was no picnic.

He finished filling up the bucket, swished the detergent around a bit, and tossed in a sponge. Then he carried the bucket across the garage to the narrow corridor leading into the back of the restaurant.

Inside the corridor, there were two enormous, white metal doors. He opened the first door and went inside. A fog bank of cold vapor met his face. On either side were metal racks brimming with trays of hamburger patties, pats of butter, tanks of milk, cartons of cream, and cocktail sauce. The room smelled of freezer-burned meat, rancid cheese, and icy stains of unidentifiable spills.

Angel knelt down by the first shelf and began to scrub the empty bottom rack. There were patches of congealed mustard and egg welded to the grillework. He scrubbed violently, compulsively, attempting to forget his troubles.

From out in the garage came a familiar sound: the clang of a service bell and the sound of air brakes. At first, Angel paid little attention to it. But when he heard the familiar baritone of a certain trucker's voice, Angel's ears instantly perked up.

He shoved the bucket aside, hopped to his feet, and rushed out of the walk-in toward the garage.

"You want how much?"

"Twenty gallons."

"In a can?"

Lucas had no time to explain. "That's correct. Can's in the back of my rig. But I'll need a needle-neck funnel instead of the normal spout."

It took several moments for the wiry little attendant named Bob to understand the request. A fiftyish man with a receding hairline and bulbous Adam's apple, Bob was dressed in oily blue coveralls and a sheepish expression. He stared at Lucas for a moment, then shuffled toward the rear of the truck.

Lucas watched, fidgeting.

The moment Bob reached the rear of the truck, the corrugated sliding door jumped open and revealed Sophie, standing inside, illuminated by a pool of dusty light from the overhead lamp. She was holding the can. " 'Evening," she said, nodding down at Bob. "Sorry to be hurrying like this but we've got a schedule to keep—you know how it is."

Bob reached up and took the can. "That gonna be regular or premium?"

Sophie grinned nervously. "Regular would be fantastic."

"Yes ma'am."

Back at the front of the rig, Lucas quickly scanned the length of the Dixie Boy Truck Stop. It was a modest-sized oasis, bathed in yellow vapor light, consisting of two main buildings in an *L* configuration around a half-dozen fuel islands. The building on the left was a cozy little coffee pot filled with dozens of truckers having early-morning breakfast. A couple of them had come to the windows and were gazing out at the Mariah, pointing, yacking. The structure on the right was a cavernous service area. A couple of tractors were up on lifts, walls were covered with ancient parts, oil pits, diagnostics, the works.

Reaching into his pocket, Lucas rooted out his last cigarillo and lit it up. Then he checked his watch: 4:17 A.M. Jesus, what the hell was he doing in the middle of the Tennessee boonies at four-seventeen in the morning screwing around with some idiotic backwoods psycho?! Was it worth a measly two hundred bucks? Was winning some candy-ass wager that important? Could Sophie Cohen manipulate him that easily? Somehow, the questions were moot now. There was something deep inside Lucas that had been awakened, something indescribable. It was as if the gauntlet had been flung to the dirty pavement and the game had begun and now there was no stopping it.

A sudden voice snapped Lucas out of his reverie. " 'Scuse me, mister?" It was Bob. He stood there with the can of gas. "Couldn't find no needle-neck funnel."

Lucas chewed his cigar. "Got any flex pipe?"

"No, sir."

"Any tubing? Old radiator hoses?"

Bob rubbed his mouth. "We got radiator hoses comin' out our asses, but I ain't sure them'll work on your can. If y'all could just tell me what it was gonna be used for."

Lucas glanced across the parking lot, past clouds of moths dancing beneath the vapor lamps. He wasn't sure how many other haulers had been listening in out there, on the side, copying their conversation with Melville. Must have been a couple. In fact, ole Bob here probably knew what they were up to and was just playing dumb (which wasn't too far of a stretch for the wiry little man). Lucas wasn't even convinced the local County Mounties didn't already know. Of course, that was what made it so interesting. Finally, Lucas said, "Just helping out a fellow trucker."

Just then, Sophie came walking up, wiping her hands on a towelette and nodding nervously. "All the levels are groovy. Pay the tab and let's roll."

Puffing the cigarillo, Lucas tried to control his gathering anger. "Yeah, except there's a problem with the funnel. Can't find a needle-nose."

Sophie turned to Bob, smiled artificially. "Wouldn't by any chance have some flexible tubing?"

Bob sniffed up a wad, hocked, and spat. "Like I told your partner, it ain't gonna fit the can."

Lucas took a breath. "Okay, I got an idea. What about one of those plastic oil cans with the long necks? We could cut the neck off and stick it on the can."

"Sorry," Bob shrugged. "Them ain't for sale."

"You're shitting me, man?!" Lucas was losing his temper. "You mean to say we couldn't buy one of those plastic moth-erfuckin' oil cans?"

Sophie stepped in between them, raising her hands. "Okay, alright, we'll figure this out. We're all big grown-up boys and girls."

Tossing his stale cigar to the pavement, Lucas ground the ashes under his cowboy boot. "Tell you what, Bob—why don't you take a second and go in and scrounge around—"

Another voice, soft and inarticulate, drifted across the shadows of the parking lot behind them, interrupting Lucas. "Would thith work?"

Lucas and Sophie wheeled around. Angel Figueroa, his hair falling across his face, obscuring his eyes, approached through the shadows just outside the garage, an extra-large funnel in his hands. Nearly four feet long, covered with grease, the funnel appeared to be made of extra-heavy-duty plastic or fiberglass.

Sophie reached out and took the funnel. Then she handed it to Lucas. Lucas inspected it for a moment, squeezed it, tested its strength. "Yeah, this is perfect."

Gazing downward, Angel said nothing.

Lucas stepped forward and extended his hand. "Thanks a million, man."

Angel kept his gaze averted, remained silent.

"We really appreciate it," Sophie added. "You're a life-saver."

Still no reply.

"This is Angel," said Bob. "Angel's kind of a retard. Nice kid, though. Really knows his way around a bucket and a mop."

"How much do we owe you, Angel?" Lucas asked the boy.

"Nothin'," Angel muttered. A soft breeze suddenly gusted past them and tossed Angel's hair away from his face. For an instant, his malformed features were revealed in the harsh glare of vapor light. Both Lucas and Sophie saw it. And in that instant of recognition, Angel waited for the inevitable mixture of pity, repulsion, and fascination that always came from "normal" people. But amazingly, neither of these two strangers reacted negatively to the ravaged face. They simply saw it, made note of it, and kept their gaze focused on Angel's eyes—almost as if it didn't occur to them to treat Angel any differently from any other poor son of a bitch.

"Appreciate the help, Angel," Sophie finally said and patted the boy on the back.

Turning to Bob, Lucas said, "What's the damage?"

The wiry man glanced at the pump. "Twenty-four-thirty-six for the gas."

Lucas paid the tab and nodded at Sophie. The twosome quickly headed for the cab. They were climbing the access ladders and opening their respective doors when Angel came running after them, calling out, "Excu' me! Mithter? Excu' me!"

Pausing on the last step, Lucas gazed down at the boy. "Yeah?"

Angel approached cautiously and made a concerted effort to enunciate his words. "I was li'thenin' to y'all on the tincanner tonight."

Shooting a glance over at Sophie, Lucas paused and said, "You don't say."

"I wa' thinking y'all might need help."

Again, Lucas and Sophie exchanged a glance. Finally, Lucas said, "And you were thinking you might help out?"

Angel gazed down at his shoes. "Yeth-thir."

Lucas stared at the boy. "You have any idea how dangerous this stunt is gonna be?"

"Yeth-thir."

Thinking for a moment, Lucas said, "Love to take you along, kid, but I'd rather not have to come all the way back here to drop you off afterwards, know what I mean?"

"You kin drop me at the I-Thevinty-Five overpa'th," Angel replied. "My uncle liveths near there."

There was an awkward pause. Sophie began to smile. Lucas glanced over and saw the woman grinning like an idiot and just threw his hands upward, exasperated. "Why not? Jesus, we've gone this far out on a limb. Might as well pull everybody down with us."

Angel grinned. "Need to put my mop away firth. It'll juth take a thecond."

The boy turned and rushed back into the garage. Lucas started the truck, revved it for a moment, and waited for Angel to return. A strange sight suddenly caught Lucas's eye. Off to the left of the parking lot, a row of truckers had gathered outside the restaurant. Standing in the silvery light, they were watching like some bizarre gallery on the edge of some strange outdoor performance. Some of them began to clap. Others whistled and hollered like they were at a sporting event.

"Oh, my God," Sophie uttered from the passenger side.

"Unavoidable," Lucas said. "Everybody and their brother has a CB down here."

Outside, the truckers were approaching the Kenworth, clapping merrily, cheering.

One of them hollered, "Good luck!"

Another yelled, "Go get 'em, Blackie! I got fifty bucks on y'all!"

Biting his lips, slightly unnerved by the attention, Lucas watched them surround the truck. Some of them seemed to be passing money to and fro, probably laying bets on the charade. Lucas felt like a rube, like one of those rodeo clowns with the baggy pants about to get spiked by an angry bull. He imagined the cops showing up any second now, shutting the whole gag down and slapping Lucas with some kind of FCC fine.

But no such luck. Angel had returned with a bandanna around his head and his vest buttoned to the neck. The boy scurried up the ladder on Sophie's side, squeezed into the cab, and took a seat on the edge of the sleeper behind them. He smelled like a mixture of ammonia and bubble gum.

"Here goes nothing," Lucas said as he flipped on the high beams, threw it in low, and started for the exit. "Warp factor three, Scotty . . . and God help us all."

As they pulled out of the parking lot, the other truckers jogged alongside for a few moments, laughing, urging them on. Lucas could only shake his head in dismay. But Sophie couldn't resist leaning out her window and bowing theatrically.

For several moments after the big black truck pulled out of the Dixie Boy lot, Guillermo stood on the steps of the restaurant, scratching his whiskered chin. Dark eyes narrowing, toothpick clenched in his teeth, the owner of the truck stop simply couldn't believe what he was seeing.

In the vapor light of the parking lot the truckers were hurriedly finishing their business, refueling, and preparing to chase after Lucas and Company. One driver from Memphis had offered to hold the entire pot of cash that had been wagered. There were nearly twelve hundred dollars in twenties sitting in a cigar box on his dashboard. Another lady trucker from Birmingham had filled up a large Coleman cooler with ice, bottles of orange juice, six-packs of beer, plastic cups, Slim Jims, and hard-boiled eggs—like she was gong to some goddamned picnic brunch, for Christ's sake.

Then they all started pulling out of the lot, one by one, into the gray, predawn light. They were heading for the junction of I-24 and Highway 79, which was about ten miles down the road, in a gentle valley near the border of Kentucky.

Guillermo just couldn't believe it. Within five minutes, the entire Dixie Boy had become deserted. A goddamn ghost ship. Bad enough that the black son of a bitch had lured Angel away before he had finished his duties. Now the screwy Yankees had stolen his entire breakfast crowd. Hundreds—maybe thousands—of pesos down the tubes.

Grunting angrily, Guillermo turned and went back into the restaurant. There were only three human bodies left in the joint. Bob, the gas jockey, was sitting on a stool near the soda fountain, nursing a cup of mud. Phyllis, his third-shift gal, was behind the register, snapping her Juicy-Fruit. And Cody, his gangly, pimply faced short-order cook, was lurking back in the galley, peering out of the pass-through window at the sudden emptiness.

"Hey, boss," Cody shouted at him from the kitchen. "Whattya say we hop in my Jimmy and bop out to Sheridan Ridge? Place has got a great view of the junction. Phyllis can mind the store."

From the cash register, Phyllis piped in. "Oh, sure, let's let Phyllis do the shit work again."

Guillermo trudged over to the diner bar and sat on the first stool. "Goddamnit to hell, I ain't tailin' after some goddamn black Yankee with a death wish."

Cody pulled his apron off, emerged from behind the pass-through, and approached the end of the bar. "C'mon, boss—let's check it out."

"I said no, Cody."

"Ain't no customers here anyhow."

Guillermo gestured at the barren restaurant. "I'm well aware of that fact."

"Then, come on. Let's go watch."

A moment of terse silence passed, then Guillermo stood up and kicked the edge of his stool. "Oh, for Christ's sake, alright."

Cody yelped triumphantly and headed for the rear exit. Guillermo followed begrudgingly. Outside, they found the battered four-wheel parked next to a fossilized old Buick up on cinder blocks. They climbed in, Cody fired it up, and they screeched out of the lot.

* * *

On the other side of the county, Baum stopped at a deserted 7-Eleven for a large cup of coffee. He also got a newspaper and fresh tin of Copenhagen. His doctor had warned him about cutting down on the cigars and Baum had decided that smokeless tobacco would make an acceptable alternative. The only problem was the mess he created by constantly spitting the vile juice into whatever container was handy at the moment.

On his way back to the cruiser he put a gob of tobacco behind his cheek. Then he climbed back into the car, pulled out of the lot, and headed for work.

En route, Baum rolled down his window and let the cool predawn air blow the sleep from his brain. The smell of pine and manure swirled through the car. It was bracing. Baum took a sip of coffee and scanned the horizon. A moment later, Gainesboro Road appeared around a gentle bend. He took a left and sped down the two-lane blacktop toward the highway.

Gainesboro Road was a narrow access drive that wound through a maze of old factories and rotting textile mills. At one time the most lucrative industry in the area, the textile business had fallen on lean years in the recent past. Mills started closing up faster than you can say *recession.* All the little neighboring towns and trailer parks had become ghost towns.

Baum took another sip of coffee and gazed out at the passing landscape. It was a crying shame how raggedy this area had become. All along Gainesboro the empty factories rose up into the dawn, their once billowing smokestacks now cold and silent, their once gleaming windows now boarded over. They reminded Baum of haunted castles from some lost Vincent Price picture. Brooding, coated with soot, and frozen in time, they were constant reminders of that shit storm they used to call Reaganomics.

"What the—?" Baum did a double take. Something had caught his attention up in the shadows of the factories. Something near the roof of the old Hawkshaw Mill at the end of the road.

"I'll be a son of a bitch."

He pulled over to the shoulder and took a harder look. Sure enough, it was up there on the uppermost level of a storage silo, about a hundred yards away, perched on a cat-walk which joined the silo with the main building. Baum's pulse began to quicken. The more he looked at it, the more he realized it was impossible. The mill was in mothballs, locked up tight as a drum. Besides, nothing of that size could have been hoisted up there anyway. It must have been driven up some unseen ramp or something.

How else could an enormous antique car be perched up there on the top of a frigging storage silo?

Then it hit him: *The silo rises up over the nearby highway. Whoever is in that car, they're fixing to watch the big show out on Highway Twenty-four! The goddamn refueling stunt that Delbert was ranting and raving about! They're up there on that catwalk waiting for the goddamn show!*

Baum flipped on his gum-ball lights. The swirl of blue and red ignited the stillness. He pulled away from the shoulder, sped across the two-lane, and entered the mill's lot. The cracked pavement was whiskered with weeds. Broken glass glinted in the wash of his headlights. But his mind was on the impossible car. Pulling up to the base of the tower, Baum glanced up at the catwalk.

The car was gone.

"What in Sam Hell is—?"

There was a sudden crash. Metal on metal, bursting out-ward, coming from nearby. Baum spun around. The glare of two vintage headlamps exploded in his face.

A moment later, the ancient limo roared past his rear bumper, leaving two battered elevator doors flapping in its wake. Evidently, the car had found an old freight elevator upon which to ride up and down. But within seconds, the limo was on its way to the exit, fishtailing across the de-serted lot, raising a swirl of rock dust and ignoring the sher-iff's lights.

Baum spat a gob of tobacco juice and slammed on the gas. No antique son of a bitch was going to elude him. The cruiser caught up with the limo almost immediately. Baum's headlights washed over the rear of the car. And although its shaded windows obscured the occupants, Baum got a closer look at the vehicle.

It was a beauty. A 1927 Rolls Royce Derby Phaeton limousine. Baum recognized it from his brother-in-law's whiskey decanter collection, though he had never expected to see one in the real world, let alone be tailing it in hot pursuit. Low-slung, trimmed with miles of chrome, it was in mint condition. Its body was varnished a deep green, filmed with dust. From the rear it looked like the delicate spoke wheels might fly off at any minute.

Baum turned on his PA system and spoke into his hand mike. *"OKAY, FOLKS, Y'ALL CAN PULL OVER NOW!"*

The limo responded by speeding up. It hopped the speed bump at the mill's exit and roared onto Gainesboro Road. Baum followed closely behind it.

"Goddamn bastards!" he spat. The limo's license plate was missing. Probably for a reason.

A moment later, the Rolls cut around a hairpin turn that led into a stand of hickories. The limo must have killed its headlights, too, because it vanished behind the trees. Baum stomped on his brakes and skidded past the turnoff. Then he threw it in reverse and scuttled back to the side road.

The instant he entered the forest Baum knew the sons of bitches had gotten away. The dawn had not yet penetrated the woods and the road was still pitch dark. There was no sign of the limo. Baum slowed to a crawl and flipped on his searchlight. He swept the light across the path. Twenty yards away the road was swallowed up by the trees.

Baum continued after them, deeper and deeper into the forest, though he knew he wouldn't find anything.

On their way to the junction, Cody and Guillermo passed through a piss-ant little hamlet known as Sheridan Ridge. The site of a minor Civil War battle, Sheridan Ridge was really nothing more than a few dozen tar-paper shacks, a feed store, two farm implement shops, and a gas station. The surrounding landscape was mostly farmland. Tobacco and corn-fields buckled the neighboring hills like the folds and

wrinkles of a patchwork guilt. Guillermo noticed how the
light was beginning to change. The first blush of sunlight
was starting to color the horizon, blur the shadows, and make
the pavement glow.

At the end of the main drag, Cody pulled up to a stop sign
and paused to read the directions from a battered wooden
signpost. To the south was Highway 79. To the north, the
Pinkney Grain Elevator. "I know a hellacious spot," Cody
said, shifting the Jimmy into low and starting up the northern
slope. "Parking lot of the Pinkney Grain Elevator is smack
dab on a scenic overlook. Interstate curves around below it.
You can damn well see twenty miles or more of highway
from up there. Be able to see the whole goddamn stunt."

A moment later they reached the top of the hill, turned a
corner, and entered the lot.

Guillermo gasped.

There were hundreds of trucks, all shapes and sizes, all
makes and models, lined up along the edge of the lot. There
were tankers, moving vans, reefers, and flatbeds. There were
cackle crates, possum bellies, dump trucks, portable parking
lots, Peterbilts, Kenworths, Freightliners, Diamond Reos,
Marmons, and Macs—every model and make imaginable.
Some of the drivers were sitting on lawn chairs in front of
their rigs, drinking coffee, and gazing out at the distant highway below. Others were perched on top of their cabs, smoking, waiting for the show. It boggled Guillermo's mind.

"Drop your drawers and bar the doors," Cody exclaimed
as he found a suitable spot at the far end of the lot to park the
Jimmy. "Never seen so many rigs planted in one place in my
life."

Guillermo grumbled, "Goddamn carbon monoxide scram-
bles their brains."

They got out, walked beyond the parking lot, and found a
deadfall log to sit on. The edge of the plateau was right in
front of them, revealing the surrounding Tennessee landscape and the ribbon of highway curving around the distant
valley. Guillermo craned his neck slightly to see the junction
of 79 and 24 in the distance to the west about a quarter of a
mile away. It lay silently in the gathering light—a gray con-

crete overpass covered with graffiti and framed by a clover-leaf of ramps.

Not far from the overpass, idling quietly on the shoulder like a sleeping grizzly, was the big Kenworth known to other truckers as The Black Mariah.

Turning back to the crowded parking lot, Guillermo surveyed the gallery of onlookers. Many of the truckers had brought cameras and were loading them, preparing to document the show. Some of them were looking through binoculars. Others were murmuring softly under their breaths. The anticipation was thick enough to cut with a knife.

Guillermo turned to the cook and said, "You feel like bettin' a little money on this thing or what?"

The cook grinned. "Now you're talkin'."

After a moment, Guillermo gazed back out at the overpass. "Kid's gonna get himself dusted out there."

The cook rolled his eyes. "Don't worry, boss. The boy'll be back tomorrow night for more of your abuse."

Guillermo grunted, pulled out his wallet, and started counting bills. At that moment it didn't occur to him that he would never see Angel Figueroa again.

4

Show Time

"There he is!"

A mixture of excitement and relief colored Sophie's voice as she pointed at her side mirror. She had been sitting with the others in the hot, airless cab for over twenty minutes now, discussing their game plan, and the suspense was killing her. Next to her, Lucas quickly rolled down his window, leaned out, and scanned the horizon behind them. Sure enough, appearing in the shimmering heat rays of early morning sun were the first glimpses of Melville Benoit and his supercharged green Camaro.

The threesome sprang into action. Throwing their respective doors open, Lucas and Sophie hurried out of the cab. Lucas ran toward the rear of the trailer. Sophie circled around the front. Angel followed Lucas.

Sophie climbed the metal steps and took her position behind the wheel. Reaching up to the small video screen mounted above the dash, she flipped on the monitor. Within seconds, the tiny screen was filled with a grainy, bluish view of the trailer's rear bumper. The doors were dusty, corrugated iron, latched in the center with a quick-release bolt. Sun-faded decals on either side depicted the tiger logos of the leasing company. Beneath the doors, an iron footrail thrust out over the mud flaps.

On screen, Lucas appeared around the corner of the trailer. He held the fuel nozzle under one arm. His expression was all business. He reached up to the release bolt, threw open the doors, and helped Angel up into the darkness of the trailer. Then he climbed up himself, pausing on the edge of the trailer and gazing up at the closed-circuit lens.

In the tiny square of the video screen, Sophie watched the big black man wink at the camera.

Sophie felt an odd twinge in her gut. For a good chunk of her career she had struggled to prove herself to Lucas Hyde. And in the early years, it hadn't been easy. The big man was set in his ways, a real creature of habit. Along comes this upstart from Reseda who thinks she knows everything in the book about interstate commerce and you've got the makings of a real tense situation. But after a few shaky trips, things began to settle into a groove and Sophie began to see a side of Lucas that intrigued her. Beneath the big muscles, the metal-toed boots, and the streetwise attitude beat the heart of an authentic *mensch*—a real human being. A mensch who would stop for a wounded deer. A mensch who would recite a corny Red Sovine tune over and over again until he got the words right. A mensch who would actually respect Sophie for her skills and intelligence rather than her ass.

Now Sophie was watching this same man begin a dangerous game that she had initiated and it was bothering her a little. No, scratch that. It was bothering her *a lot*. What in the world had compelled her to goad Lucas into this stunt? Was she acting out some childish impulse? Was she reaching for some petty attention, daring him, challenging him, testing his limits like some smitten little valley girl?

In the brief instant that followed, Sophie flashed on a disturbing yet somehow provocative notion. Perhaps this whole charade was the twisted result of her repressed feelings for Lucas, feelings stifled and buried in her subconscious. On several occasions they had discussed the folly of partners having a romantic relationship; and each time they spoke of it, Sophie came away with a flinty bitterness inside her. The fonder she grew of Lucas, the more confused she became. Was he afraid of being trapped in some possessive relationship? Jesus—didn't he know that was the last thing she wanted? Why couldn't two consenting truckers be more than mere business partners?

Suddenly, a wave of panic gripped Sophie and made her skin crawl. She wanted to call the whole damned stunt off right there. She wanted to jump out of the cab, wave Melville on, bring the boys back inside, and cancel the whole damn thing. But then she saw in the tiny blue square of the monitor that it was already too late.

The game had begun.

Jamming the truck into gear, Sophie stepped on the gas pedal and roared out onto the two westbound lanes of Interstate 24.

"Hold on to the side rails!" Lucas called over the clamor. Angel was next to him, trying to gather his footing on the slippery floor of the trailer as the Mariah rumbled and shook through its acceleration gears.

Just under thirty-five feet long, constructed from corrugated aluminum with metal shelves on either side, the empty trailer was like a cavernous boxcar hooked to a runaway train. With its doors open and shelving vacant, it rattled and clattered angrily. The fumes of rotting vegetables and old, wet cardboard permeated the air. Three overhead dome lights illuminated the trailer's length but it was still hard to see through the dusty gloom. The floor was covered with the greasy detritus and cabbage leaves of former loads, making footholds somewhat tentative, especially in transit.

Lucas lifted the gas can and lugged it over to the edge of the rear end. Damn thing felt like it weighed a ton. Four feet tall, the width of a tree trunk, and slippery with grease. Angel grabbed the extension funnel and screwed it on, adding another four feet to its height. Their frenzied movements and footsteps sounded hollow in the empty trailer.

In the distance they could see Melville approaching, now less than a mile away. A sea-foam green '72 Camaro with hood intake and spoilers, the car was a muscle-bound hog.

Its rear wheels were oversized, it had a row of fog lights along the bottom of the grille like incisor teeth, and its windows were tinted so dark they looked like black Lucite. Moving along at a mere forty-five or fifty miles an hour, the Camaro shivered and vibrated wildly like a mad bull preparing to charge.

Seeing the actual car approaching made everything come into sharp focus for Lucas. This crazy dude from 'Bama was no longer just a voice over the CB. Now he was real. The game was real. And Lucas realized he had better get his shit together pronto or he would be eating two hundred clams and a lot of male pride.

"Alright, just like we said in the truck—" Lucas barked over the rumble of the truck "—we'll keep it down around twenty-five miles per, something like that. I'll get his cap off with my jimmy bar."

Angel swallowed air. "What if you slip?"

Lucas thought about it for a moment. "You hold on to my belt—just in case. Alright?"

Angel nodded.

"Stick to the plan and we'll be fine," Lucas continued. "I'll hold the funnel steady, feed it into Melville's tank, and you lift the can."

Again, Angel nodded affirmation. Outside the back of the truck, the Camaro was approaching. It was less than a hundred yards away now. Its blackened windows were gleaming in the rising sun.

Lucas glanced up at the video lens and gave Sophie the signal.

Sophie gnawed her lip. On the monitor, Lucas was giving the thumbs-up sign. Sophie grabbed the mike and said, "Melville? This is Sophie. You copy?"

Melville's voice, tense and thin: "Melville here. Yes ma'am, I hear ya'll loud and clear."

"We got an eyeball on ya, Melville," Sophie said into the mike. "We're about a mile away."

The anxious voice returned. "Whatty'all want me to do?"

"Go ahead and swing out into the fast lane," Sophie instructed, speaking gently, as if to a petulant child. "Pull alongside the back of the trailer. I'll stay in the slow lane. Make sure you keep your tail flush with ours. Understand? Over."

Through the speaker: "I understand."

Sophie downshifted and kept the truck at a steady twenty-five miles per hour. At this hour of the morning, the interstate was mercifully deserted. But there was a palpable tautness in the air, like a silent room filled with people holding their collective breath before a horrible surprise party. Sophie alternated gazing straight ahead at the white lines, into the side mirror, and up at the video screen. By shifting her gaze back and forth, she was able to simultaneously drive the truck while performing the tricky docking maneuver in back.

It took only a couple of minutes for the Camaro to pull out into the fast lane and reach the rear of the truck. But the moment it arrived, Sophie could tell something was wrong. The Camaro was weaving slightly, lurching, speeding up, slowing down.

Thumbing the call switch, Sophie said, "Melville—what's the matter?!"

Melville's voice was hoarse and shrill. "Y'all are going too slow!"

"Lot safer at this speed, Melville."

There was a garbled, crackling burst, then the sound of Melville's anxious cry. "Y'all don't understand! It hurts at this speed! It hurts bad!"

Sophie thought about it for a moment. Each extra mile per hour was increasing the stakes, making it more dangerous for Lucas and the kid. But on the other hand, she reasoned, it would do little harm to create more of an air draft for the car. "Alright, alright, alright," she finally said into the mike. "Takin' her up to thirty-five."

Coaxing the gas pedal forward, shifting to a higher gear, Sophie felt straps of panic tighten her stomach muscles with each bump. The truck had a certain feel at thirty-five miles per hour, a certain needling vibration that seemed to urge a driver to go faster. At the present moment, it was doubly disturbing to Sophie. The last thing she wanted to do was lose control of their speed. The moment she lost control of the speed was the moment they could pack it in, call the meat wagon, order the flowers.

She gazed back up at the monitor.

"Goddamnit!" Lucas cried out in frustration.

They were stumbling all over hell, grappling for purchase on the slimy floor of the trailer. It was like walking the deck of a wind-tossed boat in the middle of a storm. The trailer was pitching and rolling and wobbling furiously. In fact, in all his years of trucking, Lucas had never experienced the displeasure of bumbling around a trailer while in transit.

It was an eye-opener.

As the Camaro hovered in the parallel lane, Lucas searched the Camaro's windows for a glimpse of the elusive young man. The car's passenger-side window was rolled down halfway and Melville's head was barely visible in the shadows behind it. A light-skinned black man with frightened eyes and wild corkscrews of relaxed hair, Melville wore a Saints football jersey and kept his gaze riveted to the road, as if he dared not look away for fear of crashing.

Apparently, the young man was having problems keeping the car even with the truck. Every time the semi would fall in line with the back of the car, the Camaro would speed up and the two vehicles would fall out of line again.

Lucas glanced up at the eye of the video camera, its cylindrical lens canted off the ceiling of the trailer and pointed down at them. It was strapped in place with metal braces and worn duct tape, and a tail of cable wound off its back and across the ceiling. Lucas could feel Sophie's anxious gaze within that lens, her intense brown eyes fixed on the trailer, tracking them nervously.

A moment later, the Camaro finally fell in line with the truck and held steady. Lucas saw the opening and nodded at Angel. Then Lucas pulled the slim jim from his belt. The two-foot piece of metal was designed to slip underneath car windows and jimmy open door locks. But Lucas was about to find a new use.

Taking a quick breath, he stepped out onto the wraparound bumper.

The first thing to strike Lucas was the wind. Even at such a low speed, the wind created a pocket around the rear of the semi that slapped him in the face. The smell of gasoline mingled with the stench of fertilizer and decay blowing off neighboring fields. Lucas squinted and searched for the Camaro's gas cap. He was hoping it would be on the left rear quarter panel, which would give him a better angle. But soon he realized it was under the license plate—a full three to four feet away from the corner of the semi's step rail. Whether he liked it or not, Lucas was about to become a circus act.

He tiptoed out to the edge of the step rail, carrying the jimmy bar. Something began to worry him. It seemed as though they were speeding up. Although the rear bumpers of the vehicles were staying aligned, it seemed that Sophie was stoking the fires. They were already edging toward the speed limit.

Not good.

Lucas reached the corner of the step rail and clamped his free hand around the door hinge. Leaning out into the wind, he slammed the slim jim against the Camaro's gas cap and pried with all his might. At first, the cap wouldn't budge. But then, without warning, it snapped off its threads and jettisoned into the air like a champagne cork.

At that moment, the truck hit a bump and Lucas lurched forward. His left foot nearly slipped off the rail but he grabbed the door hinge just in time to steady himself. The slim jim fell to the rushing pavement below and vanished in a cloud of exhaust. Lucas's heart thrummed in his chest, his mouth went dry.

Turning to Angel, Lucas yelled over the roar of wind and engines, "Gimme the gas!!"

Angel shoved the can out to the edge of the trailer. Lucas grabbed the spout, turned, and muscled it toward the Camaro. Although the plastic spout was nearly four feet long, Lucas had to pull the gas tank out to the edge of the step rail in order to reach the car.

Lucas shoved the tip of the spout into the Camaro.

A gust of wind curled around the truck. Lucas grabbed the door hinge and held tight. The gust buffeted him wildly, then settled. Turning to Angel, the big black man hollered, "Lift the can! Now!"

The boy tipped the can forward. Gas dribbled through the funnel spout and into the car. Angel tried to lift the end of the can but it was too heavy.

"Can't lift it!" Angel yelled over the din.

The truck hit another bump and the rear end bucked. Lucas braced himself on the edge of the rail and held the funnel steady. Gazing back at the boy, Lucas hollered, "Trade places!"

Angel set the can upright, took a deep breath, and stepped out onto the ledge.

The two men awkwardly traded places on the windy precipice. Then the boy crept cautiously out to the edge of the rail. He crouched against the vibrations of the truck, squinted into the wind, and shoved the spout back into the Camaro.

"Hold it steady!" Lucas yelled sharply as he lifted the gas can and began to pour.

"BZZZZZZZZZZZZUHHHT—zzzht-zzht-zzht—zzzzh-htp!"

Sophie watched the monitor pop and crackle with static as she held the truck steady. On the tiny screen, between flashes of interference, Lucas and the young boy were wrestling with the gas can, teetering precariously along the edge of the rail, grimacing at the whipping wind. Sophie glanced at the speedometer. They were climbing past sixty.

Sophie chewed her lip nervously. A sick feeling was gnawing at her insides, a feeling of dread like the warmth of an infection in her belly. She tried to shake it off, tried to grip the steering wheel tighter and keep her gaze riveted, but it was no use. The grim feeling was surfacing in her as it always did during tight situations. But this time it was one doozy of a panic attack, fed by the keening roar of the engine, the tommy-gun rattle of the bearings, and the jackhammer vibrations beneath her. It made her throat feel like it was lined with parchment. But in many ways, it was a nurturing worry, a maternal fear for Lucas.

"ZZZZZZZZZZZzzzuhhhhht!!" The screen crackled again as they traveled through another pattern of interference.

"Damn it!" Sophie slammed her fist against the monitor. The picture sputtered back into resolution. And what it revealed sent a burst of panic through Sophie's fevered brain.

Angel was riding the step rail. His skinny legs pistoned up and down wildly with the bumps and dips. He could feel the cool flow of gasoline beginning to course through the plastic pipe. He could hear the slosh of gas behind him as Lucas hefted the can into the air. And he could feel the dissonance of both engines as the truck downshifted into another turn.

At that moment the truck hit another pothole.

Angel slipped off the rail. The funnel popped out of the Camaro and gas spurted into the wind. Angel caught himself on an iron handle just as his toes met the pavement. His sneakers skidded and bounced convulsively. Gas sprayed all around him, soaking him. He tried to climb back up but the oily fuel made the rail slippery.

Lucas grabbed for the boy. Unfortunately Angel was too far away. Lucas dropped the gas can and crept out onto the rail. With all his might, he leaned out into the wind and swiped at Angel's belt. Once, twice, three times—with no luck. Finally Lucas snagged Angel's shirt and pulled.

The boy scurried back into the van. Lucas fell to the floor of the van, pulling Angel down on top of him. Both men panted and gasped for air, stricken with shock.

"Jesus!" Sophie was watching the video monitor. She felt her heart lurch in her chest. She tried to stay focused on the road, struggled to keep the semi under control. Her mouth had gone dry and she'd bitten her lip so hard a tiny thread of blood had crept down her chin.

"Just then, Melville's panicky voice came through the CB speaker. "Jesus God Almighty—they pretty near—they almost—Jesus—Jesus!!"

Sophie thumbed the mike. "Easy, Melville. Easy does it. Slow down, hear me?! Slow down!"

Slamming the handset back onto its cradle, Sophie sucked in a couple of deep breaths. The anger was seething inside her, threatening to explode. Mostly it was anger at herself for getting everybody mixed up in this idiotic stunt. Again, she pondered aborting the stunt right then.

But for some reason, she couldn't bring herself to do it.

"Fuck me!"

On the back rail, Lucas was buzzing with electricity. The feeling was emanating from the pit of his belly, sending hot vibrations through his bloodstream and making every synapse tingle. It was a rush that could only be generated in the heat of something extremely dangerous. Both mountain climber and daredevil knew of this feeling. So did criminals. The gang members spoke of it often. It was a potent mixture of euphoria, sensory overload, and outright terror that accompanied the execution of a crime.

Lucas shook the fear from his head, spat a coppery wad of phlegm into the wind, and prepared to rock and roll.

For a split instant Lucas thought of his father. The old man used to talk about the inexorable force of a man resolved to action. He used to tell the same story, over and over, of an unknown black soldier in World War II who had been left for dead in the German forest by his racist platoon leader. He had fought alone, all the way back through enemy lines, to Allied territory. The story had made an indelible impression on the young Lucas.

Taking a quick gasp of air, Lucas gently shoved the boy out of the way, lifted the can, and stepped out onto the vibrating step rail. He shuffled out to the edge of the iron and slammed the funnel into the Camaro. Gas sloshed through the funnel. Some of it spilled out the sides of the spout. Tiny tendrils of fuel sprayed out and vaporized in the wind. But soon the gas was flowing into the car.

Lucas opened his mouth and screamed triumphantly into the wind. The sound of his voice was swallowed by the rushing noise of the vehicles. But Lucas kept screaming. His whole body was tingling. His brain was buzzing.

He was going to win this fucking bet after all.

Sophie was glued to the monitor. For a brief moment, she was utterly absorbed. In fact, she was so absorbed, she might as well have been sitting in her apartment back in Frisco, watching the *Ten O'Clock News*. Her gaze was locked on to the tiny smudged screen above her. Her breathing was shallow. Her teeth gritted. In that brief moment, she was completely oblivious to the road ahead.

Which was precisely why she didn't see what was approaching in the right lane less than half a mile away.

Sophie gazed back at the road and gasped. She snatched the handset and shrieked into the mike. *"Melville-Melville-Melville!!!* Get outta there, now! Pull away now!!"

Ahead of them, rapidly approaching in the right lane, was a construction zone. A series of rubber cones directed traffic into the left lane. Beyond the cones, the pavement ended in a swath of black dirt filled with idle construction equipment.

The Kenworth had two horns. An electronic job for city driving, triggered by a button on the steering wheel, and an air horn activated by a cable on the ceiling. The sound of the air horn was a hell of a lot ballsier.

Sophie grabbed the cable and pulled.

Lucas heard the horn blow a split second before the truck swerved and braked. The spout snapped out of his hand, slipped from the Camaro, and broke off at the base of the can. A cloud of gasoline engulfed Lucas as he grabbed for the door hinge, the handle, the corner of the van—anything to pull himself back up. Behind him, the gas can fell to the pavement, tumbling out of sight across the median. Finally, just before falling, Lucas felt a hand grip his pants and pull him back in.

It was Angel. The boy was hauling Lucas back into the van by the belt. Lucas fell into the doorway, breathless, clawing at the floor.

The Camaro slammed on its brakes and plummeted backward into the violent draft behind the truck. The car weaved and fishtailed wildly, nearly overturning. Its right front hubcap spun off into oblivion like a rusty roulette coin. And its engine groaned and complained as Melville ground it into low.

Meanwhile, the truck rumbled past the construction zone, raising a cloud of debris, litter, and exhaust in its wake.

Gazing into her side mirror, Sophie could see the Camaro falling back, slowing down. Thumbing the call switch, she hollered, "Melville?! You copy?! Melville?!!"

No answer. Nothing but static.

She checked the video monitor. On the tiny screen she saw the rear doorway of the semi. Lucas's cowboy boots were visible just inside the door. To his right, Angel sat there catching his breath. Both men seemed okay.

Sophie tried the CB again. "Melville, please respond! Seventy-sevens to ya, pal. Come back! Over!"

Still no reply. The waves of static squelched through the loudspeaker and put a chill along Sophie's spine. She gazed out her window and searched the side mirror for Melville.

The Camaro was hovering a hundred yards behind them, the rising sun glinting magnificently off its roof.

"Melville?! Do you copy?!"

Shifting down, Sophie pumped the brakes and pulled back into the slow lane. Then she waited for the Camaro to pass.

"Melville?!"

Just then the Camaro roared past her, belching black exhaust and vibrating angrily like some wounded bull hissing its last gasp. Its gold-teeth fog lamps sparkled, its tinted windshield a molten blur. It was accompanied by a sudden shriek on the CB.

It was Melville's voice, hollering inarticulately, piercing the static.

For a moment, Sophie thought the Camaro was going to clip the corner of the cab. But the Camaro simply farted exhaust in her face, trailing a spray of gas from its open spout. Within moments the car was half a mile down the road.

"Melville, please respond," Sophie pleaded, then, without

much deliberation, she added in a sheepish voice, "we're sorry."

But the enigmatic young man just vanished around a bend a mile away. No reply. No thank-you. No effort to even acknowledge the attempt.

Nothing.

Five minutes later, Sophie found a wide spot in the shoulder and pulled off. The Mariah came to a hissing stop. Sophie put her flashers on and sat there for a moment, waiting for her heart to finish the Sousa march it had been playing for the last hour. After a moment, she felt calm enough to climb out of the cab and start back toward the rear of the truck.

Lucas met her on the shoulder. He was still breathing hard, his face rigid with tension. "Alright, don't rub it in."

"I didn't say a word."

"How's our psychobabbler?"

"Melville?" Sophie motioned at the distance. "Burned rubber like a bat outta hell."

"Did he say anything?"

"Nope. Just screamed like a stuck pig."

Lucas took a few deep breaths and shook his head. "Strange fucking behavior. . . ."

Angel patted Lucas on the back. "We almo'th did it though—almo'th made it work!"

Lucas knelt down and inspected the truck's undercarriage, making sure nothing was damaged. "Almost, kid. . . ."

Sophie felt strange. Heart hammering, she looked down at Lucas. She couldn't decide whether she wanted to hit him or hug him. Instead, she just gave him a friendly kick on the butt and said, "If you ever scare me like that again I'll fucking kill you."

Lucas stood back up and shrugged. "Thought I had it at the end." Turning to the boy, he added, "But this is one ballsy little hombre right here."

Angel looked at his shoes. "I love truck'th. Gonna take my chauffeur exam next month."

There was a long pause as the three of them got their

frayed nerves under control. Finally, Lucas said, "Tell you what, Amigo . . . in return for helpin' us, you can bust your cherry on our rig."

The boy's eyes lit up.

Lucas started for the cab. "C'mon."

They all piled into the cab. Angel took the driver's seat and marvelled at all the instruments. Lucas sat on the shotgun side. Sophie took a seat in back. The boy looked like a child settling into Santa's lap. His soft brown eyes were filled with wonder. His slender hands were trembling.

"Babie's got thirteen speeds," Lucas said, fishing in his pocket for one of his miniature cigars. "Eleven of 'em are forward. Two are reverse. Pick the lowest one and give her some gas."

Angel carefully put it in gear, checked the side mirror, and slowly rolled back out onto the highway.

"Easy, Amigo!" Lucas hollered over the grind. "She's not a whore. Treat her like a high-school girl on a first date, take your time."

Angel slowly climbed through the gears.

From her perch in back, Sophie watched the Latino boy grapple earnestly with the stick. The kid was a real sweetheart. In the short time since they'd met, Sophie had really grown fond of him. She shuddered at the thought of putting him in jeopardy during their idiotic stunt. Finally, she leaned forward and said, "Live around here, Angel?"

"Yeth, ma'am." Angel kept his eyes riveted to the road as he spoke. "Over by Brummel Creek."

"How long have you worked at the Dixie Boy?"

"Going on three year'th now . . . ever thince my mom got put in the th'anitarium . . ."

"Got any brothers and sisters?"

"No, ma'am."

Wrinkling her nose, Sophie said, "Do me a favor, Angel— call me Sophie. People call me ma'am and I feel like I should be wearing orthopedic shoes with square toes and white socks."

Angel grinned. "Okay, Th'ophie."

From the jump seat, Lucas blew a whiff of smoke, turned

to the boy, and said, "Just you and your daddy living over there in Brummel Creek?"

There was an awkward moment of silence during which Sophie could have sworn she saw the boy's expression change into an ironic smile. "No, thir. Daddy left my mama when I wa' little. Never knew him. I live alone now. Tw'ith a week I go up to Chattanooga where my mama in the th'ani-tarium. Take her chicken and tortilla—I make 'em my'thelf. Take care of my Uncle Flaco, too."

Lucas nodded. "Lots of responsibility for a young buck."

Angel just shrugged.

Through the windshield, Sophie watched an upcoming turn. They were rounding a corner which cut through a rise of ancient granite. On either side of the highway, stands of pine trees climbed the neighboring hills in waves, reaching up into the sapphire morning sky. Rays of sunlight sliced through the pines, dappling the rocky earth. The air seemed as crisp and clear as a diamond.

"Hey, Sophie—" Lucas was grinning at the boy. "Looks like we gotta born trucker on our hands."

Sophie smiled. "Yeah, kinda reminds me of—"

She froze in mid-sentence.

Up ahead, less than a hundred yards away, an American sedan was hobbling off the side of the road and onto the shoulder. It was sputtering, lurching convulsively, as if running on the last fumes of an empty tank.

The threesome recognized it immediately.

It was Melville's sea-foam green Camaro.

5

Behind
the Curtain

Lucas smashed his cigar out in the ashtray. "Pull over, kid! Shift it on down!"

Struggling with the massive shift lever, Angel shoved it through the low gears and applied pressure to the brake pedal. The air brakes hissed. The engine complained and The Black Mariah began to slow down.

Angel steered the truck onto the soft gravel shoulder a few yards behind Melville's Camaro and brought it to a stop. Lucas reached under the dash and flipped on the hazard lights. Sophie grabbed a couple of flares from the seat pocket. They all hurried out of the cab.

The morning air was cool and clean. The sun had not yet heated up and the smell of dew-covered weeds and crab grass permeated the air. Lucas glanced over his shoulder and checked for oncoming traffic. The road was clear.

"Melville?!" Lucas hollered as he cautiously walked up to the car. "You alright?"

The car remained still. Nothing stirred behind its tinted windows. No one answered. As Lucas approached the rear bumper, his footsteps crunched loudly against the gravel. For some reason, his imagination was shifting into high gear. He

imagined Melville trapped inside the car, melting like the
Wicked Witch of the West, his pointy black hat sinking into
a puddle on the seat. Lucas paused a few inches away from
the car and tried to see inside. But he could still only make
out the fun-house mirror reflection of the surrounding landscape and his own uncertain expression in the shaded glass.

Behind him came a snapping noise. Lucas nearly jumped
six inches off the ground. He spun around in time to see Sophie and Angel lighting the emergency flares and sticking
them into the gravel. "Little jumpy are we?" Lucas asked
himself under his breath. "Little twitchy?"

Another noise startled him. It came from inside the Camaro. Muffled and indistinct, it sounded like the whimper of
a wounded animal. Lucas approached the driver's door. He
could smell the odors of old bacon grease and something less
distinct, like an overloading electrical terminal.

The door sprang open.

Taken by surprise, Lucas stumbled backward, landing on
his ass in the gravel. The rocks bit into his rear, perforating
the seat of his pants, stinging, pricking his flesh.

The thing that lurched from the car and darted past Lucas
was no longer an ordinary human being. It was more of a
fluid blur of sweat-soaked agony and writhing limbs. A
piercing shriek sang out of the young man as he rushed toward the truck, arms flailing, strings of drool flagging from
his mouth.

"Ruh—Ruh—ruuuhhhh—

"RUHHHHH—RUH—RRRRRRRRRRRUUUUUHHH!!"

Clambering toward the cab, the young man was trying to
speak but the words were impossible to understand amidst
the garbled cries and convulsions. He collided with the passenger side of the tractor and clawed at the door. His hands
were bleeding. They left wet, sticky stains on the black metal
as he slid to the gravel and shivered in a cloud of dust and
pain.

Stranger still, it seemed that at the precise moment he
stopped running, the pain seized him worse than ever.

"RUH-RUH-RUH—RRRRUUUU—HHHHNNNN
NNNN!!!!"

The young man twitched and jerked helplessly on the ground. His hands curled into claws and reached up at the heavens for deliverance. His lungs heaved and he gasped for air. His eyes were shocked wide open, electrified with pain. His drool was mixing with blood, trailing down his chin and across the front of the Saints jersey like sloppy remnants of a raspberry pie.

"Ruh-ruh-RRRRRUUUUUUHHHHH!!!!"

A few feet away, crouched behind the grille of the cab, Sophie and Angel watched. They were transfixed by the spectacle unfolding before them. It took the sound of Lucas's voice to snap them out of it.

"Call an ambulance!" Lucas was struggling to his feet near the gaping door of the Camaro, hollering above the noise. "Call an E-Unit! Something!!"

Another piercing shriek erupted from Melville. It was as if he'd been goosed by an electric cattle prod. He crawled away from the cab in fits and jerks, crossing the shoulder and entering a marshy stand of weeds and cattails. A moment later, he collapsed in a heap, squealing in agony. His voice sounded feral and unborn.

Lucas rushed through the weeds and approached the young man. "What is it, bro?! What's wrong?! What happened?!!"

But Melville couldn't answer. The unseen tormentor was working inside him now. He tried to stand up but could only rise to his knees. Reaching up to his face, the young man dug his fingers into his eye sockets as if trying to uproot a pair of throbbing, infected teeth. His eyeballs sklurched and sucked noisily above the sound of his anguished cries. His blood ran down in rivulets across his cheeks. His mouth opened to express a pain beyond expression.

"Melville?!" Lucas was edging closer. "What is it?!!"

But it was futile. The young man seemed unable to communicate anything but the most involuntary agony. It almost reminded Lucas of the time he had accidentally backed over the German shepherd at the Eagle Foods warehouse in Santa Monica. The rear wheels had instantly crushed the animal's skull, but the dog had kept whining and crawling around the lot for nearly three minutes. The longest three minutes Lucas could have ever imagined . . .

That was, until now . . .

Lucas decided to act. He knelt down and tried to pull the young man's hands away from his eyes. But upon touching Melville's wrists, Lucas found them as hot as a pair of branding irons. Reaching down to Melville's waist, Lucas tried to help him up. But it was hopeless. Melville was going into seizures, ripping at his face, his neck, his clothing. All the poor guy could manage was a trembling, garbled cry—

"Ruh-rrrrruuuuh—RRRRRRUUHHHHHHH-HHNNNNNNNNNNNNN!!"

Then the fire came.

It erupted from Melville's eyes, bursting forth like two orange jets of cooking gas. The blast of heat startled Lucas and sent him falling backward. It almost felt like the discharge of the Mariah's vertical exhaust stack. An instant puff of supercharged flame, hot enough to singe the eyebrows off your face and knock the wind out of your lungs.

The young man yelped, more like a garbled infant's cry than a man's. Tiny flames were licking up the top of his forehead and igniting his hair. Boiling mucus gurgled from his flaring nostrils. Rows of blisters swelled along his neck and cheeks and forehead, his skin bubbling like buckling strips of wallpaper. His shoulders hunched, his back arched and spasmed wildly, but his body remained upright for a moment, shivering with the pulse of the flames.

Lucas gagged. The odors of sizzling gristle and burning fat were wafting up from the poor bastard. Indescribable sounds farted deep within the young man's anus. The sick furnace rose all around.

The young man's last act was the yawning of his mouth to scream. The sound that emerged was unlike anything Lucas had ever heard. A keening death shriek, starting out high and shrill, then spiralling upward into a primal falsetto. It was like the touch of a cool razor on Lucas's spine.

Then the scream was consumed by flames. Fire exploded from Melville's gaping mouth, from his nose, from his ears, from his belly button, from his crotch, and from his fingertips like deadly, glowing ectoplasm. It swirled around his shirt, snaked up his trousers, and curled around his head. It wrapped him in a cocoon of horrible brilliance. He was burning from the inside out and there was nothing anybody could do about it.

Lying prone a few feet away, Lucas watched, helpless, like a man suspended in molasses dream time. His arms and legs felt weak. The stench of burning flesh was making him lightheaded. But the worst part was the sound; the sizzling, crackling, searing sounds mingling with the guttural gurgling and bubbling noises issuing forth from Melville's body.

For another moment, a moment that seemed to stretch into eternity, Melville managed to remain upright, a human torch, crisping in the Tennessee breeze. Then he collapsed into a flaming heap of charred flesh, smoldering cloth, and leather.

Swallowing back the bile and terror, Lucas slowly rose to his feet and scanned the area for Sophie and Angel. The kid was hiding behind the front bumper of the truck, his eyes as wide as half dollars. Sophie was inside the cab, frantically giving their coordinates to someone over the radio. A sound was rising in Lucas's head, a ringing sound. At first, he thought it might be one of his migraines or an ear infection or simply the shock of what he had just witnessed. But the ringing grew until it was piercing the early-morning air around him and Lucas realized it wasn't in his head at all.

It was a cop siren approaching from the east.

Lucas turned back to the corpse. It was nearly extinguished now, save for a pile of smoking embers wrapped around a husk of human being. Lucas stared down at it and felt his chest turning icy cold.

The poor dude never had a chance.

Behind him, Sophie approached and gawked at the body, her eyes were bright with fear, her lips were trembling. "It was gas . . . wasn't it . . . he was covered with gas . . . and a spark touched it off . . . right?"

Lucas didn't answer. He was too busy staring down at the smoldering body, turning the phenomenon over and over in his mind. His eyes and nostrils stung from the rich odors rising around him, the smoke and the stench of roasting meat.

The shriek of the cop siren was looming closer and closer. He absently gazed down and saw that his arms were covered with a fine layer of ash. Along the top of his beefy forearms, inside his elbows, his ebony skin had virtually turned white. The sight of it made his mouth water and tiny hairs on the back of his neck stand up.

Lucas turned away and vomited into the grass.

His bile was dark, a mixture of coffee and half-digested chili from the night before. But it burned as if concocted of molten steel.

Sophie wheeled around. "Lucas—are you—?"

"It's okay, I'm alright," he said, wiping his mouth and waving her back. He turned toward the Camaro. It sat baking in the sun less than ten yards away. Angled downward, its nose pointed toward an adjacent drainage ditch, it looked like an anesthetized dinosaur.

Lucas strode over to the car and peered inside.

What he found could only be described as another world. The car was filled with trash. Empty fast-food containers congealed with old sauce, crumbled newspapers, greasy grocery bags, and sticky discarded bottles of soda and wine were scattered across the floor mats. The smell of urine and feces and rotting food poured out like an invisible alkaline demon. But there was also something grotesquely stunning about the interior of the car, something irresistible. It was like looking behind the curtain of a freak show.

Holding his breath, Lucas leaned inside.

On the floor next to the gas pedal was a rusty pail filled with urine. Strewn across the passenger seat were crumpled candy wrappers and junk-food containers. Amidst all the detritus were dark crimson slash marks. They ran across the length of the seat, over the dash, up the side windows, like finger paintings the color of deep red motor oil. Large interlocking squares. Inside the squares were esoteric words in some unidentifiable language. *Alimuz. Delios. Zizimuth.* Lucas reached out and touched the slashes. They were as sticky as tar.

"What the fuck—?" Lucas noticed something odd hanging from the rearview. A delicate cable of twine. Fuzzy brown twine. Upon closer inspection, Lucas realized it was made of hair. Human hair that was just beginning to gray.

"Jesus—!"

At the end of the hair was a small gold jewelry clasp. Its bottom ring had been twisted off, perhaps with the weight of some missing amulet. Then something caught Lucas's eye on the floor mat beneath it. Something had fallen there, something exotic and shiny. Lucas knelt down and took a closer look.

It was a very ornate, jewel-encrusted ornament in the shape of a hand. About six inches in diameter, attached to the missing jewelry clasp, it looked as though it was made of dark-brown Lucite or marble. Probably an antique heirloom, probably very rare. . . .

At that moment, two things happened almost simultaneously.

First, a panicky voice rang out behind Lucas. It was Angel. He was yelping something Lucas couldn't quite understand. The sound of the police siren was so close now that it was drowning the kid's startled voice.

Second, Lucas noticed a newcomer arriving on the scene.

The old man had emerged from the adjacent forest. Lucas could see him through the passenger window. Well over six feet tall, lanky and big-boned, the old codger appeared to be in his late sixties or early seventies. He wore a strange moth-eaten uniform. Gray epaulets, jodhpurs, captain's cap like an old chauffeur. What the hell was this geezer coming straight for the Camaro for?

"Jesus Christ! Lucas!" Now Sophie's voice chimed in behind Lucas, urgent and shrill.

The old chauffeur froze like a deer in the lights of an oncoming truck. He noticed Lucas inside the car. Then the geezer noticed something else, did a quick about-face, and ran like a son of a bitch for the woods.

"LUCAS!!" Now Sophie's voice was just outside the car and there was real terror in it. "LOOK OUT!!"

Lucas climbed out of the car and saw the problem.

He grabbed Sophie and ran.

For a big man, Lucas was fast. Damn fast. In fact, back in

high school, as a fullback for Torrance Central, Lucas was being groomed for the Big Time. Full ride scholarship. His specialty was the kamikaze slant play where the QB would drop back and send every eligible receiver downfield to draw the defense into pass coverage. Then the QB would simply hand Lucas the ball. Lucas would drop his face guard and barrel up the middle, grinding, churning, often carrying three or four defenders along for the ride. Odds are, he would have played for USC had he not developed a glass joint in his left knee.

But this time, dragging Sophie across the gravel shoulder, Lucas was reaching for deeper inspiration.

This time it was sudden death.

Dick Baum was approaching the scene just as all hell was breaking loose. Thank God the sheriff had a keen eye for observation because there were things happening so quickly he could barely register them in his mind. First, he saw a white woman and a big black guy hightailing it across the shoulder. The twosome lurched behind a nearby semi truck as if someone was about to take a shot at them. Behind a ditched Camaro a smoldering body lay in the tall grass. A tendril of flame was creeping along the ground toward the car, feeding off the spilled fuel and fumes leaking out of the car's rear end.

Slamming on his brakes, Baum skidded to a stop about twenty yards away.

Then came the blast, a sonic boom deep enough to rattle bones. Baum ducked behind the dash for an instant, instinctively shielding his face. He felt the heat through his open window on the side of his face, on his ear and his cheek. Then a flash of light burst around him. Magnesium bright, it lit up the highway like a photographer's bulb. The shock wave rattled the hood of the cruiser.

After a moment, Baum peered through his windshield. In the early-morning light, the Camaro had become an angry inferno. It was spewing flames over forty feet in the air. It sounded like a roaring river, twisting and curling angrily. Above it, a column of black smoke and debris rose and mushroomed while tiny flakes of burning upholstery and paper snowed to the ground.

Baum took another moment to check his cruiser for any damage, then he got on the radio. He called the dispatcher and ordered a fire truck from Sadlersville, an ambulance from St. Frannie's, and a backup. He also read The Black Mariah's license plate number over the air for any outstanding warrants. Then he unsnapped his holster and made sure his good old chrome .357 was readily accessible.

Out of the corner of his eye, Baum saw movement behind the semi truck. Two, maybe three people, crawling along the ground. Baum grabbed his PA mike and barked into it. *"OVER BY THE TRUCK! Y'ALL JUST STAY ON THE GROUND FOR A SECOND—YOU HEAR?! STAY PUT!!"*

Baum pulled his gun and got out of the cruiser. Circling around the trailer, he crept along the back of the truck with his weapon poised. He didn't know what the hell he was dealing with here. He didn't know exactly what these people had done. He had been too busy chasing down a ghost of an old Rolls Royce through the woods outside Hawkshaw Mill. And the worst part of it all was that Delbert Morrison had been right: They probably should have nipped this damn thing in the bud before anything had happened. But now it was too late. Baum had one casualty, a small inferno, and a group of twitchy truckers on his hands.

"Told you folks to stay down!" Baum hollered at them as he approached. There were three of them. A black guy, a woman, and a young boy with girlish hair.

The black guy was rising to his knees. "Gotta get my rig outta here before it catches!"

"You just stay put, son. Hands on your head." Baum approached and gestured with his gun. The big guy lowered himself back to the pavement. They each put their hands on their heads. Baum stood over them for a moment, checking for any weapons or anything out of the ordinary. In moments like these Baum knew the secret was control. You grabbed as much control as possible, as soon as possible, and you assessed the situation.

Baum scanned the area. On the other side of the truck, across the shoulder, the fire was beginning to dwindle. The flames had died down to a steady burn.

Pulling his walkie-talkie off his belt, Baum pressed the call switch. "Three-twenty—this is three-nineteen."

The voice of the dispatcher crackled through the radio. "Three-nineteen, go ahead."

"Anything on the California plates yet?"

"Not yet, Sheriff."

"Well, try tapping in to the—"

The sheriff paused. Thank God his ears were just as keen as his eyes, because he had heard something familiar beneath the sound of the flames, drifting on the breeze. It sounded like a faulty washing machine. Rattling faintly somewhere up in the nearby hills, it raised hackles on the back of Baum's neck.

It was the clocking of an antique limousine engine.

The sheriff just shook his head and said under his breath, "Must be hearin' things. . . ."

6

Kaleidoscope
of Words

The limousine was idling right where Eric Kelsinger had left it, at the edge of scenic turnoff above the highway, buried in the shadows of an ancient willow. Shrouded from the light of day, the car looked almost spectral. An armored leviathan dredged up from the depths.

The chauffeur hobbled up to the limousine, gasping for air, legs throbbing. He hadn't run this much in ages. His lungs felt as if someone had doused them with kerosene and set them on fire.

The limo's rear window was vented a couple of inches in order to provide an unobstructed view of the highway below them. The thick odors of mentholatum rub and Eau de Beau Monde wafted out of the window. The perfume was masking another scent. Lingering faintly beneath the mélange, it was an acrid smell. Hot and milky. The smell of infection.

Her smell.

The chauffeur opened the driver's door and climbed inside. His brittle bones creaked as he slid into the seat and slammed the door. At seventy-two years old, Eric moved quite a bit slower now than he used to. Quite a bit slower. In the old days, of course, he was very nimble. Nimble enough to win six consecutive titles on the World Wrestling Circuit. They called him The Teutonic Titan. Of course, that was back in the sixties, before he had become Madam's servant.

The years were etched in his face. His faded blue eyes were deep set in his long craggy visage. Sparse blond stubble rimmed the base of his neck, which was as loose as turkey skin. His body barely filled his uniform anymore. The barrel chest, washboard stomach, and iron biceps had all withered away to fat and gristle. What a shame. . . .

The screen lit up next to him.

DID—YOU—

The tiny remote computer screen was mounted on the dash above the police scanner. The LED letters glowed bright yellow across the monitor. Eric watched them with mounting dread. He knew what was coming next. He knew what the question would be before it was even posed . . .

DID—YOU—FIND—IT—????

Eric swallowed hard. He had been driving Madam on these strange excursions for nearly ten years now. Ten years of following the poor doomed Negroes so that Madam could watch them self-destruct from her perch in the back of the Rolls.

Ten years, and Eric had never once made a mistake.

Certainly there had been plenty of opportunities for errors. There was the time in Baton Rouge when the Negro politician had stumbled into the emergency room and had nearly set the entire hospital on fire. Then, there was the time down in Panama City when the black attorney who had sued Madam had perished in the crowded motel lobby. Several innocent bystanders had been killed on that particular outing; but Eric had still managed to retrieve the talisman.

No, there had never been a mistake.

That was, until now.

DID—YOU—FIND—IT—DID—YOU—FIND—IT— DID—YOU—FIND—IT—DID—YOU—FIND—IT—DID— YOU—FIND—IT—?????????????

The screen was filled with a kaleidoscope of words, more and more desperate with each repeated phrase. Just for an instant, Eric imagined the screen fracturing under the sheer pressure of her emotion, a ripe melon splitting apart to reveal the maggot-ridden rot inside.

Sometimes Eric wondered why he continued working for Vanessa DeGeaux. He bore no particular grudge against her victims. He did not have the talent for hating that Madam did. Besides, her magic sometimes frightened Eric. The magic was unpredictable and dangerous and unfathomable to him. But perhaps, in some strange way, that was the very reason he had stayed loyal to her all these years. She was as mysterious as her magic. Powerful and magnetic.

He turned and prepared to push open the partition window so that he could give her the bad news.

He paused. He wasn't quite ready to tell her just yet. His heart was thrumming too painfully in his chest. It worried him. All the years of lager and bratwurst and sauerbraten had taken their toll on his arteries. The doctors in Mobile had told him that he had a blockage and that he would require surgery soon. But when Madam caught wind of this she insisted that he cut off his visits to the clinic immediately. She preferred Eric to treat his angina by wrapping the sting of a scorpion in a deer's skin and hanging it around his neck. But Eric was too frightened to complete the charm and had instead called in his prescription behind Madam's back.

Digging in his coat pocket, Eric found his bottle of nitroglycerine pills. He quickly swallowed one and closed his eyes. Perhaps he was getting too old for these adventures.

Of course, this current excursion had proven exceptionally difficult. The worst part was kidnapping Madam DeGeaux's grandniece. Samantha Mosby was a bright young girl from New Orleans with a promising future ahead of her. A quick smile, beautiful complexion, strong athletic body, she was a complete innocent. Unfortunately, she was also heiress to the DeGeaux fortune and was foolish enough to fall in love with a Negro. Madam had decided to teach the girl a lesson. Two nights ago, Eric had abducted Samantha from the parking lot of a Winn Dixie. He had used a Pentothal-soaked rag to knock her unconscious. The plan was to take the girl back to the DeGeaux house on Egg Island for safe-keeping until her fiancé was dispatched. But on the way, the girl's system went into shock. Either she had absorbed too much Pentothal or she had swallowed the rag or both.

By the time they had arrived in Mobile, Samantha Mosby was dead.

Unfortunately, the incident only seemed to spur Madam on. She insisted they proceed with the curse. Eric reluctantly obliged. But after capturing the Negro boy and preparing his vehicle, the young man had proven himself more resourceful than they had expected. It took nearly three days to see the boy perish.

The final indignation, however, was the comedy of errors on the highway today. The appearance of the truckers. Their botched attempt to save the boy. And worst of all, Eric's inability to retrieve the talisman before the authorities arrived. The sacred talisman. The dark heart of Madam's magic. Adrift out there somewhere among the unwashed.

The screen began to buzz.

PLEASE—ERIC—ANSWER—ME—DID—YOU—FIND—IT????? PLEASE—DID YOU???? DID YOU???? PLEASE ANSWER ME!!! PLEASE!!! ANSWER!!! ME!!! DID!!! YOU!!! FIND!!! IT??????!!!!!!!!!!!!!!!!!

The words reflected Madam's weird blend of Old South gentility and volatile emotion. To Eric, she was a strange exotic bird imprisoned in the gilded cage of her body. The raw passion and hate and dark magic that ran through her veins kept her alive.

Swallowing back his fear, Eric pushed the partition window open and told her the bad news.

Then he braced himself for the storm.

7

Antsy

Meditating on trivial detail can drive a person insane. But Sophie's mind was like that. Obsessive and compulsive. Actually, it was a lifelong curse that often found her latching on to the most insignificant little details around her until she nearly went cross-eyed.

Her latest subject was the plaster ceiling in the lobby of the Pennington County Courthouse. Sitting on a ratty, green vinyl sofa outside Sheriff Baum's office, Sophie was staring up at the ceiling, pondering the texture of the paint, counting the strokes in the plaster, noting the number of repeating patterns. . . .

"Stop it," she whispered under her breath. She looked away from the ceiling and tried to think about something else. But she knew it wouldn't work. She knew it was only a ploy to avoid thinking about what had happened out there on the litter-strewn shoulder of Interstate 24.

"Stop it, already!" she said again in a hoarse, uncertain voice. Her stomach was tied in knots and her lower back was taut with tension. She couldn't get the image of Melville's death out of her head. She had seen it with her own eyes. She had witnessed the damn thing for herself and now she had to deal with it. Like a newborn photograph coming out of the chemicals, a newspaper headline still warm from the press, an obscene splash of graffiti across a virgin church wall, there it was, indelibly burned into her memory.

She reached into her purse, found a fresh cigarette, and lit it up. The smoke brought her back to life. "Alright, genius," she whispered to herself, "let's get a grip."

Sitting back, taking another drag, she tried to get things into perspective. What had she actually seen? A young man in a muscle car runs off the road and then bursts into flames. There were so many valid explanations. He had probably gotten soaked with fuel during the exchange. He had probably been around gasoline numerous times during the course of his lunatic escapades. Melville was an accident waiting to happen. Totally insane. Schizo City.

But what about the complexity of his rant? A voice inside Sophie's head was prodding at her.

Granted, the guy's story was complex and textured, with a line of logic running through it that sounded unlike that of any mental deficient Sophie had ever seen. And she had studied enough abnormal psychology in school to recognize the ramblings of a head case. But no matter how compelling his rant had become, it didn't prove anything. It merely suggested that Melville had incorporated truth into his fantasy. Perhaps there truly was a Samantha Mosby and a Vanessa DeGeaux. The old gal may very well be a racist. But the rest was purely Melville's invention.

Okay, but what about the fact that Melville really did die—very dramatically, one might add—once he came to a stop?

It was undeniable that Melville had perished just as he said he would. In fact, in a court of law, this would verge on being evidence—albeit circumstantial—in favor of his delusion. But Sophie was well-read in the area of mind/body dynamics. She knew how powerful the seed of suggestion could become when nourished with a wild imagination. Because Melville *believed* he was cursed, he found a way to fulfill the prophecy.

Yeah, right, you're having such a good time with your

pseudo-science and smug conclusions, but what about the thing you saw with your own eyes? What about that, boopie?

Sophie didn't want to think about this last little tidbit at all. She was tired of thinking about it. She was tired of re-living it. She much preferred to look up at the ceiling and study the plaster patterns and trace the smoke stains and count the air-conditioning vents and listen to the Muzak and—

What about it? What about the last thing you saw?

The last thing she saw was so simple, yet so horrible, it seemed like a fun-house hall of mirrors in which she could lose herself and never escape. It defied explanation. It transcended fact. It eclipsed everything else in her mind like a hideous ink blotch spreading across her consciousness. . . .

You saw a man burn from the inside out.

Alright, there it was, inexorable and malignant. And the chances it had happened because of gasoline fumes or sparks or any other banal cause were remote to say the least.

The memory made Sophie feel like a member of the Flat Earth Society who had just been shown that the planet is a sphere. All her paradigms, all her notions of reality, all her concepts of the physical universe had been heaved out the window. Now she found herself thinking back to esoteric courses she had taken at Berkeley, courses on paranormal phenomena, shamanism, frontier sciences. Little did she know back then, coasting through her studies, that one day she would consider applying the stuff to real life.

She took a last drag off the cigarette and ground it out in the ashtray next to the sofa.

Gazing across the lobby, she pondered the door to the sheriff's office. At this very moment, Lucas was back there getting grilled by the constable. Would Lucas be fined? Would they throw him in jail on some kind of trumped-up charge? There was no telling with these backwoods lawmen.

Sophie wondered what Lucas would say about her little internal dialogue. He'd probably just laugh his big goofy laugh and call her a neurotic egghead. Lucas had a wonderful way of keeping Sophie grounded. Whenever she would go off on some wild diatribe, he would always bring her back to earth. *You're thinking too much again, girl,* he would say, and he was usually right. Lucas believed in going with his gut. Sophie liked that about him. He lived more by his heart and his balls than his brain. Which was precisely why, in Sophie's mind, they made such perfect partners.

The only complaint Sophie had about Lucas was that weird attitude he had toward their relationship. It had always seemed to Sophie that there was an odd barrier between them, a glass wall, an unspoken limit to their friendship that Lucas dared not breach. And whenever Sophie joked about it, Lucas just dragged out the old excuse that it was bad business to get too close to your partner. But the more Sophie thought about it, the more she began to suspect it was something deeper than conventional trucker wisdom, something deeply ingrained and thorny and personal. Perhaps it was something best left unchallenged.

After another moment of gazing at the sheriff's door and thinking about Lucas, Sophie picked up a magazine and pretended to read.

Tap-tap-tap-tap-tap—

There it was again. During the interrogation, Baum kept hearing the strange metallic noise coming from somewhere inside the office but he just couldn't place where the hell it was coming from. *Tap-tap-tap-tap-tap-tap*. It was bugging the shit out of him. Ever since the black trucker had sat down on the folding chair across from Baum's big metal desk, it had been intermittently clicking inside the sheriff's ears like a bad piston.

"Whoa there, Tonto," Baum interrupted the trucker for the third time. "You're losing me with this cockamamie story about a voodoo curse. Just gimme the skinny about pulling such a dangerous stunt on a national highway."

Lucas wiped his mouth with the back of his hand. He was perched on a wooden swivel chair, his massive black hands rubbing the edge of the sheriff's desk nervously. "Look, I know it sounds ridiculous, but this kid told us he would die if he stopped. My partner thought he was being sincere."

"Run that by me again . . . you thought this kid was telling the truth?!"

Lucas shrugged. "Not saying I believed him. Just saying we thought the kid might be sick enough to believe it."

Tap-tap-tap—

The sheriff grunted and pulled out his tin of Copenhagen. "Because of that you decide to endanger the lives of a whole messa people?!"

For a moment, Lucas stared at the sheriff like he was sizing the lawman up, which made Baum more than a little uncomfortable. Then, the black man lowered his voice and spoke confidentially, like he was letting Baum in on a little secret. "To be honest," Lucas began, "it was all because of a little gentleman's bet I had with my partner."

The sheriff put a pinch of tobacco behind his cheek. "You don't say."

"Yeah," Lucas continued, "I admit, I've gotta real weakness for the wager."

A tense pause fell upon the room as Baum picked a speck of tobacco from his lower lip. He didn't like this story much at all. In fact, he was running out of patience for this burly trucker from the west. While he sat here making lame excuses, a couple of coroner's assistants were hauling a charred stump of a human being into the morgue across the street and nobody knew exactly why. "Alright, you listen to me, bubba," the sheriff began. "I don't give two rats' asses for your gambling habits. I got a young kid dead and a freak accident nobody can explain and I don't like it one little bit! Hear?"

"I'm as confused as you are," Lucas said, raising his hands in an odd gesture of surrender that Sheriff Baum couldn't really read. "I admit we did something stupid and dangerous, but the fire came outta nowhere. I swear to God we tried to save the poor kid."

Tap-tap-tap-tap-tap-tap—

Frustrated, Baum turned away and gazed across the room. His office was located in the bowels of the Pennington County Courthouse, one level below the jail. A twenty-five-foot-long cubicle choked with the odors of stale coffee and smoke, the room was bordered by a series of narrow windows near the ceiling. Through these windows came rays of afternoon sunlight, slicing though the dust motes and gloom. Along the far wall were rows of old wooden file cabinets, framed diplomas and awards. A couple of braided rugs and paper-shaded lamps completed the homey effect, completely belying the cinder-block institutionality of the place. This was Baum's sanctum sanctorum, a space that had over the years literally absorbed the sheriff's essence.

Across the room, leaning against a file cabinet in the corner, was Deputy Delbert Morrison. Rail thin, freckled, earnest as hell, the deputy held a beaver-felt hat in his hands and fiddled with it thoughtfully as he listened to every word. Eyebrows furrowed, lips pursed delicately, Delbert seemed to be turning Lucas's story over and over in his mind.

Baum's irritated voice boomed across the room. "Delbert, for Christ's sake, what the hell is that *sound*?"

Delbert snapped out of his ruminations. "Sound?"

"Goddamn infernal tapping noise! Is that you?!"

Delbert stiffened. "No, sir."

"Then where the hell's it coming from?"

Tap-tap-tap-tap-tap—

Baum turned back to the suspect. "Is that you?!"

Lucas stared at the sheriff for a moment, uncomprehending. "Excuse me?"

"That sound," Baum barked, "that tapping noise, where the hell is that—" Suddenly Baum shoved himself away from the desk, bent over, and scanned the darkness underneath. On the tile floor, only inches away from the caster of his chair, something gleamed in the shadows. The metal tip of Lucas's left cowboy boot.

It was tapping restlessly against the leg of the desk.

Baum straightened back up and smiled at Lucas. "You got ants in your pants, Mr. Hyde?"

Lucas blinked, still a trifle vexed. " 'Scuse me?"

"Your toe—tapping against the desk."

Lucas glanced down at his feet, then shrugged. "Oh."

"Gotta take a leak?"

"No sir, I'm fine."

The sheriff leaned over, spat in his wastebasket, and then

straightened back up. "Suppose you tell me what's the matter?"

Another pause. "Guess I'm just a little anxious to get back on the road," Lucas finally said. "Due back on the coast in a couple days."

Sheriff Baum nodded. "Y'all are a little antsy to hit that superslab again."

"Yessir, I suppose so."

Moving the tobacco around his cheek with his tongue, Baum pondered what to do with the black trucker and his girl partner. Seemed like a clear-cut case of manslaughter; but then again, the girl had called in the emergency crew before the boy burned to death. If he threw these yay-hoos in the cooler, he'd have to come up with a charge and do all that goddamn paperwork. Besides, he wasn't sure if he wanted to complicate this whole thing any more than necessary.

Tap-tap-tap—

Baum rolled his eyes and grunted sourly. "Get outta here."

Lucas seemed surprised. "What?"

The sheriff repeated it.

Lucas smiled. "You're saying we're free to go?"

Baum glared at Lucas and pointed at the door. "If I hear you've been playing any more of these goddamn road games, I'm gonna come after you personally. You hear? Now get the hell outta here before I nail that boot to the floor!"

Springing to his feet, Lucas thanked the sheriff and headed for the door. In the blink of an eye he was gone. Spitting again, Sheriff Baum straightened up and stared at the empty doorway for quite a while. Suddenly, a voice sounded from across the room.

"You sure that was a good idea?"

Baum turned to his deputy. "Delbert—shut up."

Lucas found Sophie in a waiting room outside Baum's office. She was biting her nails and staring at an old dog-eared copy of *People* magazine with Rosanne Arnold on the cover. Sophie's cigarette pack was empty, crumpled next to her. A nearby ashtray was overflowing with butts.

Pulling on his jacket, Lucas nodded at her. "We've been given a stay of execution. Let's blow this pop stand before they change their minds."

Sophie threw the magazine down and gathered her purse and logbook. "What happened? What are they saying about Melville?"

"I'll tell you in the truck."

Lucas hurried toward the door. Sophie rushed after him, jogging slightly to keep up. "What's the big hurry?"

"Just want to put some miles behind us."

Shoving the glass door open, Lucas strode out into the sunny afternoon. The truck was parked on the edge of an adjacent parking lot, behind a pair of paramedic vehicles. Lucas marched toward it, taking big strides, moving with a real purpose. "Slow down, Lucas," Sophie pleaded. "Highway's not going anywhere."

"Just anxious to get back on the road."

PART II

Coffin Box

"Hatred is by far the longest pleasure."

—Byron
Don Juan

8

Skeletons
on Bicycles

Flaco Figueroa was mixing paint in his tool shed when the feeling came. It hit him like an ice pick through the temple. Rearing backward, staggering at the sudden pain, he dropped the can. The red Rustoleum paint splashed across the floor of the shed, spreading across slatted boards and seeping into cracks.

Wincing, Flaco fought the urge to cry out. A tiny Hispanic man in his late seventies with a deeply lined face, skin like charred leather, and obsidian hair dusted with gray, Flaco was no stranger to pain. Over the years he had developed arthritis, bleeding gums, high blood pressure, a swollen prostate, and psoriasis. But nothing compared to the pain he felt when he got one of his feelings.

He fell against a nearby shelf and braced himself. The contents of the shelf—a row of baby-food jars filled with little rusty screws and washers—trembled with his weight, making a soft tinkling noise like wind chimes. But Flaco didn't hear anything. He was too busy fighting off the nausea and dizziness that was accompanying this sudden feeling of dread.

The feelings were nothing new to Flaco. They had started

when he was a ten-year-old back in Tampico, Mexico. They usually found him late at night, seeping into his sleep like a tincture of poison clouding a clear stream. They were sudden, brief moments of pure terror, accompanied by indistinct visions. His mother had attributed the spells to the flu, *la fiebre,* and had administered cold cloths and olive leaves. But the spells had continued, nearly half a dozen per year throughout Flaco's young adulthood. By the time he had married and had immigrated to America, the feelings had dwindled somewhat. But then, late in life, after Luisa had passed, they had started up again, more potent and frequent than ever.

Tonight the spell was exceptionally strong.

Flaco gasped. He sucked in breaths of air and tried to get his bearings. His chest was frozen with panic. His mind swam. The walls of the little tool shed began closing in on him. Shivers traveled up his spine. Cold, clammy perspiration had broken out along his arms and face and neck. He tried to regain his balance but his feet were slipping through the spilled paint.

"Por qué! Dios mío, por qué amí!" Flaco pleaded for it to stop.

The images were flooding his brain. As always, he couldn't get a handle on the shapes that were looming hugely before his mind's eye. They were nebulous shadows, spilled like Rorschach patterns across the canvas of his brain. Bloated, diabolical, cancerous, they rose and grew and multiplied.

"Cuando?!" Flaco hissed through a grimace, a pained utterance delivered to no one in particular. *When?* That was the question. When will it happen? Ever since Flaco was a teenager and the Franciscan missionaries had come through his village teaching *Revelations,* he was convinced these spells were omens. Portents. Signs of some apocalyptic event. He didn't know why for sure. He didn't know any of the details. He merely felt in his heart that throughout all these years God had been communicating something to him.

Something important.

"Sweet Jesus . . . !" Flaco brought his palsied hands to his mouth.

Something was happening. It brought tears of panic to his eyes. It made his flesh crawl and his stomach turn to ice. The shadows in his mind were coalescing, melding together. Like swirling eddies of smoke, they were forming a cloudlike monolith in his imagination. It was a huge, boiling girth with tendrils of darkness splaying outward. And soon Flaco realized what it was.

A hand.

Flaco's heart began to race. For the first time in his life his spell had brought on a clear image. A vision. A dark, sinister human hand, palm open, signalling some kind of apocalyptic gesture. It was accompanied by a rising peal of whispers, inarticulate and frenzied.

Then the hand closed around Flaco's mind.

Flaco opened his mouth and let out a terrified wail.

Almost simultaneously, with an abruptness that sent the old man's head whiplashing back against the wall, the spell ended as if someone had flipped off a switch.

Calm returned to the shed like a slap in the face. Only the faint sound of spilled paint bubbling down through the floorboard slats and distant bird calls outside could be heard. Taking a pained breath and lifting himself to his feet, Flaco tried to regain his equilibrium. The back of his head was bruised slightly and his arthritic knees throbbed.

But for the most part, he was okay.

Brushing a strand of thinning hair from his eyes, he turned and searched for a rag to clean up the mess. Next to the door, he found a plastic pail filled with old moldering T-shirts and stiff terry-cloth towels. He fished one out. Then he turned back to the center of the shed and gazed down at the stain that was seeping into the floorboards.

Another involuntary gasp escaped Flaco's lungs.

The stain had materialized into a recognizable object. Like some bizarre stencil, it had formed a pattern across the length of the shed, its tributaries forming a ghostly illustration of outstretched fingers. An opposing thumb. The meaty palm of a huge, human hand.

Kneeling down by the stain, softly praying under his breath, Flaco reached out with trembling hands and began to wipe away the evidence.

An hour later, Flaco emerged from the ramshackle tool shed and struggled across his property. His knees were screaming with pain. His overalls and linen shirt were soaked with sweat. But he kept hobbling bravely along. He was on a mission now. He carried a couple of cardboard boxes, one under each arm, filled with paint and balsa-wood scraps.

Flaco's tiny plot of crab grass sat on the edge of an access road that dissected two soybean fields about ten miles outside of a little village called New Deal, Tennessee. At the edge of his plot sat an ancient school bus. Riddled with dents, chipped paint, and graffiti, the yellow monstrosity was Flaco's self-styled mobile home. Back in the good old days, he had commandeered the bus for Nackashaw Grade School, taking screaming broods of kids to school each morning for a hundred and ninety dollars a week. Combined with a small pension from his days in a shoe factory, it had been enough to keep Flaco and Luisa comfortable in a small retirement village.

But in the spring of 1981, Flaco was hit with a double whammy: He lost his sweet Luisa to throat cancer and he flunked his semi annual driver's exam. His job at Nackashaw went away and he was forced to move out of the retirement home. His only option was this small notch of farmland—which had been in Luisa's family for years—and an offer from the school system to sell him the bus for a song. He decided to make the best of a bad situation and turn the farmland and the school bus into his home.

Climbing the homemade porch of cinder blocks and shoving open the door, Flaco went inside the bus.

The interior was a dim, cool rectangle strafed with sunlight. The air was thick with the odor of old bubble gum, worn leather benches, and dried chiles and cumin from Flaco's lunch. Flaco dropped the boxes by the driver's seat and gazed down the length of the vehicle. Augmented by an ancient diesel farm generator, the bus had full electrical service, yet it still was roadworthy, as Flaco never knew when he might want to pack up and return to Mexico. Along one side, Flaco had removed an entire row of seats and installed a small cot, reading lamps, hot plate, camper sink, and mini-refrigerator. Some of the windows had been boarded over. Old Venetian blinds covered others.

At the back of the bus, beneath the EMERGENCY EXIT sign, was his shrine. It rose to the dome lights, a mammoth conglomeration of dried flowers, loaves of pink and blue finger-bread, shelves of figurines, and rows of old photos. It was bathed in a pool of purplish light from a single 40-watt growlight clipped to the ceiling. The only other illumination came from a shaft of sunlight slicing down through a crack in the roof vent which gave off a soft membrane of light.

Most of the photos in the shrine were of Luisa, captured in various settings, at various ages. In youth she'd been a caramel-skinned beauty with a tangle of wild inky curls. Later in life, she became a plump Mexican matron with twinkling eyes the color of mahogany. The only other figure honored within the shrine was Jesus Christ Himself. Nestled in the heart of the altar, framed by multicolored beads and *tejocote* fruits, was an eight-by-twelve portrait of the Lord in all His charismatic glory. Hands folded reverently in His lap, face back-lit by soft light, He gazed out beatifically from the womb of flowers.

Flaco approached the shrine and knelt down before it. His arthritic knees complained sharply as he shifted his weight from one leg to the other. His forehead drummed with pain. His stomach churned. Reaching into his breast pocket, he pulled out a pack of Camel filterless cigarettes. In life, Camel was Luisa's favorite brand; and ever since she passed away, Flaco had made it a point to place a fresh package on the shrine at least once a month. But tonight, in the wake of his terrible vision, he felt a heightened need to pray to his late wife.

Gently laying the cigarettes on a small wooden pedestal, Flaco bowed his head and began to pray. Although the fearful vision of an hour ago was still haunting him, he wasn't praying for himself, for he was unafraid of death and suffering. Instead, he was praying for the living.

For Flaco, life was always more terrifying than death. As an elder Mexican, he belonged to a culture based on ancient Aztec reverence and fascination for death. To the Aztecs, death was a catharsis—a way out of this life of pain and poverty. And Flaco's childhood in Mexico had been steeped in this tradition. Every autumn, his family would prepare for *El día de los muertos* with great gusto. In this lively festival, Mexican children would fashion ornate plaster skeletons and death masks for nighttime parties in graveyards. Bakers would create beautiful breads and pastries in the shape of skulls. Store windows and flower shops would overflow with images of skeletons—skeletons on bicycles, skeletons playing guitars, skeletons doing dentistry. Whole neighborhoods would gather in graveyards to clean and paint and decorate the grave sites of their loved ones. Entire towns and villages would come alive with images and icons of death. And the underlying message was always to celebrate death, laugh at it, enjoy it, because it is a part of life.

Today, this tradition was woven through every fiber of Flaco's being. He did not fear the day he would join Luisa and all the other generations of Figueroas in heaven. Instead, he feared meeting up with the kind of wickedness that could make subsequent generations here on earth suffer.

Pausing from his silent prayers, Flaco glanced up at the shrine. Something was wrong. He felt it in his gut. A change. Something within the portrait of Christ.

Flaco struggled to his feet and took a closer look at the main portrait in the center of the altar. Were his eyes playing tricks? Flaco leaned closer. The portrait was at least twenty years old and covered with a fine layer of grime. He wiped the surface and studied the picture. Sure enough, the portrait had changed ever so slightly. There was a flaw, a discoloring in the lower third—so subtle, the casual eye would most certainly miss it. But to Flaco, a man devoted to tending the shrine, it was glaring; somewhat akin to waking up with your head on backward.

The old man collapsed to his knees again. He felt like cry-

ing, like curling into the fetal position, like calling for his
Luisa, like running away, like disappearing into the forest
forever. But somehow he knew that he could do none of
these things. He knew he would never be able to run away
again because this was most certainly a sign. The change in
the portrait of Christ was surely a sign meant only for him.

Flaco began to pray.

The sound of footsteps outside the bus startled Flaco out
of his prayer.

"Who's there?"

"*Tío?*" A voice called through the front door of the bus.
"*Tío* Flaco?"

It was Angel.

Flaco turned and hobbled toward the front of the bus. He
shoved the trip lever forward, threw open the door, and
found Angel standing on the edge of the front stoop, his
clothes reeking of gasoline, his deformed face ablaze with
excitement. Behind the boy, across the yard, a police cruiser
was backing down the dirt road and heading back toward the
highway.

"Ángel, good God!" Flaco gazed down at the boy, then
glanced off into the distance at the retreating police car.
"You're in trouble with the police now?"

"Not exactly," Angel said and pushed his way into the
bus.

Flaco followed. "Are you alright?"

"Yeah, I'm okay." Angel sat down on the cot and took a
deep breath, rubbing his eyes and trying to get his nerves
under control. "You got any ithe tea?"

The old man got some ice tea, gave it to the boy, and then
sat down on a bench across from his nephew. "You stink of
gasoline," Flaco said and gestured at Angel's shirt. "What in
God's name happened?"

Angel took a gulp of tea and wiped his scarred mouth. He
was still trembling slightly. "I thaw the wor'th thing I ever
thaw in my life today."

For an awkward moment, the old man stared at his
nephew. Then Flaco gazed over at the shrine where the defaced picture of Christ sat in the soft glow of purple lamps.

Flaco was worried that Angel would see the picture and become even more frightened. Perhaps the boy would think it was a sign meant for him.

Flaco sprang to his feet and blocked the boy's view of the shrine.

"Wha' the matter, Uncle?" Angel said, trying to see over the old man's shoulder. "What ith the matter with the altar?"

"Nothing's the matter with the altar." Flaco's hands were trembling. He couldn't get the horrible image of the defaced picture out of his head.

Angel sensed the old man's uneasiness. "Wa'th wrong?"

"Nothing."

"Come on, Uncle." Angel craned his head to see over the old man, but Flaco was carefully blocking the way.

"The altar is perfectly fine." Flaco backed toward the shrine. "Perfectly fine."

Turning around, Flaco found a blanket on an overhead shelf and pulled it over the altar, making certain that Angel would not be able to see the portrait. Unfortunately, while pulling the blanket down upon the shrine, Flaco couldn't help catching another fleeting glimpse of the place in the picture where Christ's left hand had turned black as pitch.

9

Leads

The scream came a few minutes before noon. At first, it sounded artificial and metallic, like the screech of an air horn. Lucas jerked forward and instinctively pumped the brakes. The cab shivered slightly. Then, the scream came again. This time Lucas recognized the voice.

It was Sophie.

She had been dozing in the rear compartment for several hours and was just now emerging from a nightmare of her own. As her scream dwindled into soft mutterings, Lucas turned down the radio and yelled back at her. "Cohen! You alright?"

A long moment passed. Then came Sophie's reply. "Holy Christ, what a pisser!"

"Nightmare?"

"Yeah." Sophie's voice could barely be heard above the rumble of the engine. "In technicolor, too."

Lucas rubbed his mouth. He had been brooding for the last two hours about his queasy feeling outside the sheriff's office, his urgent hunger to get back on the road. Although he felt physically fine at the moment, the memory still gnawed at him. "Seems to be an epidemic of that shit going around."

"Yeah, well . . . I probably caught it from you."

"Don't pin that shit on me, girl."

"Who else can I blame it on?" Coming through the half-drawn accordion door that separated the sleeper from the cab, Sophie's voice was hoarse and wrought with tension. "Besides, you're usually guilty of something."

Lucas smiled wryly. "Come on out and I'll analyze your dream."

The sound of fabric rustling, the splash of water from the Hinkley and Schmidt jug, and the soft skraffle of Sophie's toothbrush came drifting up from the back. A moment later, she emerged from the sleeper and climbed into her seat. Her hair was pulled back in a tight braid and she wore a fresh T-shirt adorned with a garish silk-screen from *The Texas Chainsaw Massacre*. Her eyes looked weary and strained. "Have you seen my Marlboros?"

"Nope."

"Shit."

"You smoke too much anyway." Lucas kept his gaze on the road. They had put over a hundred miles between them and Pennington County. And now they were halfway across Kentucky. The landscape was flattening out, fading to a lighter green. They were descending into a gently rolling valley.

Digging in her pocket, Sophie found a straggler. "Hot damn! One left." She carefully perched it between her teeth and sparked it with her Bic. Her hands were still trembling.

Lucas grunted. "Tell me your dream."

Sophie blew smoke rings and stared out the side windows. "Nothing to tell, really. Just one of those stupid anxiety dreams."

"Come on, spill it," he pleaded.

Over the years, Lucas and Sophie had gotten into the habit of sharing their dreams. Not only was it an effective time-waster, but it also allowed them to understand each other's background a little better without seeming nosey. Each dream revealed much about the dreamer—hopes and quirks and hot buttons. Each dream was a fingerprint.

"Okay, you asked for it." Sophie shrugged and began recalling the dream. "It was a weird mix of what happened this morning and other bizarre stuff I can't quite place. I dreamt I was trapped in the Swingline warehouse—the one in Bakersfield."

"The pallet place?"

"That's right." Sophie took a shallow drag and exhaled. "I was trapped inside the warehouse and it was filled with water. And not just a couple feet of water, but clear to the ceiling. Dirty, oily, polluted water. I was swimming through a warehouse filled with water—"

"—and the level was rising," Lucas interjected. He had a morbid feeling that he had dreamt something very similar to this not long ago.

"No," Sophie said sharply, "not at all. It was just stagnant, polluted water. And there were tiny spots of flames burning here and there, like an oil slick that was partially on fire. They were throwing weird, dancing shadows. And somehow I knew I was trapped. It was like an M.C. Escher staircase that goes neither up nor down. Like a maze. And all I could do was dog paddle around like an idiot."

She paused and took another drag, shuddering slightly at the memory. "Then I noticed the others."

Lucas glanced over at her. "The others?"

"People," Sophie replied, "moving through the murky water beneath me. All the Swingline people, the secretaries, the warehouse stock boys. They were all beneath me in the bluish light, at their desks, on the phone, doing paperwork. They were all pale and bloated and dead like they'd been in the water for years. But they were still working diligently. And in that insane kind of dream logic, I started to worry that they would see me, that they would see me and think I was shirking my responsibilities. You know—floating around above them and not doing my duties."

Sophie paused again and laughed nervously. "So I started swimming toward this object floating in the water. Figured I could grab hold of it and float away."

"Object?"

"Yeah," she continued, "this thing was floating in the water about twenty feet away from me. Dark, shiny, oblong . . . at first I thought it was a piece of driftwood or a tree limb or something. . . ."

She took another drag. Lucas sat forward. "What? What was it?"

"It was a hand."

"A hand." The word felt strange in Lucas's mouth.

She turned to him. "A big, black, petrified human hand. The wrist was a bloody stump. The fingernails were dirty and long. And I grabbed hold of it."

She swallowed hard. "And it grabbed back. It wrapped around my hand like a vise. . . ."

After a long, noisy silence, Lucas said, "And that's when you woke up."

"Yeah."

Lucas shook his head. "Nice little dream."

Snuffing out her cigarette, Sophie shrugged again. "You asked for it."

They drove in silence for several times. Something was eating at Lucas about the dream, something about a hand. A petrified black hand. Somewhere deep in the recesses of his mind, a feeling of uneasiness lay festering like a rotting molar. "Wait a minute . . . speaking of hands. . . ."

Lucas dug into the pocket of his faded denims. Nestled between a Swiss Army knife, a pack of Juicy Fruit, and thirty-two cents in change, were the cool, puckered fingers of the ornamental hand from Melville's car. Lucas rooted it out and held it up into the light. The mere contact with it made his fingertips tingle. It was as if the thing was charged with electricity.

Sophie stared at it. "What the hell is that?"

Keeping his eyes on the road, Lucas gently waved the jewel-encrusted extremity back and forth so the daylight played off the edges. It glimmered magically. "Wanna hear something weird?"

"Stop bullshitting me, Lucas."

"I got this thing off Melville."

"You stole it?"

"Fuck no, I didn't steal it. Not on purpose, anyway. Picked it off the floor mat and had it in my hand when you pulled me away." Lucas paused for a moment and thought about it. He hadn't really meant to steal the hand. As a matter of fact, he had a thing about larceny. As a kid he had shoplifted compulsively, either as a cry for attention or a way to assert control over his oppressive environs. But late in his teens, he did a complete one-eighty on the subject. He came to see theft as a weakness, a cancer eating away at the heart of the underclass. In fact, during the infamous L.A. riots of recent years, Lucas could not bear to watch the TV reports of his own people looting from each other. It had made him physically ill.

So what had compelled him to hang on to the trinket back there? What had compelled him to break his personal commandment? "Guess I just wasn't thinking," he finally said, concentrating on the road ahead.

Sophie was gawking at the hand. "You gotta be shitting me—you copped something from the poor guy while he was roasting?"

"I said I didn't cop it!"

"Damnit, Lucas!" Sophie was mortified. "You have any idea what the cops could do with something like that in our possession?!"

"Who's gonna know?"

"Jesus Christ, Lucas! You know how close they came to booking us for manslaughter?!"

"Look," Lucas said, a conciliatory tone creeping into his voice, "I feel horrible about what happened. The poor bastard never had a chance. And I'll live with the memories of seeing him die for the rest of my life. But the dude was a couple sandwiches short of a picnic. Know what I mean? Nobody's gonna miss this little trinket. . . ."

Lucas paused and glanced at the hand. In the brightness of the midday light, the hand looked even blacker, a shriveled prune of an appendage, shrunken and cured like a dark knot of leather. It was about four inches long. Its wrist terminated in a ragged stump sealed with some sort of clear shellac. The jewels had been set into its knuckles with precision craftsmanship. And upon closer inspection, Lucas could see it had delicate nails, cuticles, and ridged prints across the pads of its fingers. Very realistic. Almost too realistic.

"I can't believe we're sitting here with a piece of jewelry

from a dead man." Sophie was looking askance at the hand like it was some sort of sacrilege.

Lucas offered it to her. "Take a look at this thing. Look at the detail."

Sophie shook her head. "Get it away from me."

"What?"

"I don't want anything to do with it."

Lucas rolled his eyes. "It's just a piece of marble, for Christ's sake. It's not gonna bite."

Licking her lips, Sophie stared at the icon. Her mouth curled into a sour frown. Then, she grabbed it and took a closer look. She turned it over and studied its puckered palm. Her expression changed slightly. Her eyes widened. Then she immediately tossed it back at Lucas with a flip of her wrist, as if the thing had literally shocked her.

"Jesus Christ!" She yelped the words as if she'd been slapped.

The hand landed on the dashboard above the steering wheel. It slid down the defrost vent and sat wedged between the glass and the dash. Lucas held the truck steady, leaned forward, and fished the hand back out of the vent. "What the hell's the idea!?"

Sophie was staring at the hand like she'd seen a ghost. Her expression was frozen in a mask of horrible recognition. Her eyes were burning with dread.

"Jesus." She was muttering now.

"Sophie, what's the matter?"

At first Sophie didn't answer. The engine bellowed beneath them. The tires whined. A steady whisper of air came rushing through the side vent, adding to the frozen quality of the moment. Then Sophie broke the silence. "That thing's not made out of marble at all."

At about noon, Sheriff Baum went to get some coffee. The sheriff's office was connected to the offices of the county assessor, records bureau, treasurer, and county clerk. Much to Baum's chagrin, all these offices shared the same ancient stainless-steel coffee urn in the northeast corner of the courthouse basement. The urn had been a fixture there since before Christ left Chicago. Through the years, the coffee produced by the urn had gotten gamier and gamier, until now Baum could barely stomach the stuff.

The sheriff poured himself a cup, took a sip, and grimaced. It tasted like rancid diesel.

A voice came from behind him. "Dead-ends all over the place."

Wheeling around, Baum nearly spilled his coffee. Delbert Morrison was standing behind him, waving a computer printout and looking frustrated. Baum rolled his eyes. "Delbert, what the hell are you talking about?"

"The Rolls, the old Rolls Royce limo you saw. Checked it out on the computer and came up with zilch." The deputy's eyes were filled with anguish. Baum could see the kid had been hoping for some intrigue.

"Did you check the stolen vehicle bulletin?"

"Yessir."

Baum took another sip of coffee and winced. "How 'bout the stiff? Any luck with the next-of-kin?"

"Parents are deceased. Girlfriend don't seem to be at home. Girlfriend's parents are outta the country."

"What about the old lady? The wicked great-aunt—what's her name—?"

"DeGeaux," Delbert said, holding the printout aloft. "Nothing much on her. No record, nothin' outta the ordinary. Found her name listed in the Mobile Historical Registry. Home's a landmark. Tried to reach her. No answer."

"That right?"

The deputy looked glum. "Yessir. Guess there ain't too many more fish to fry on this one. Looks like accidental death, cut and dried. 'Least till we get the autopsy report."

There was a long pause. The young deputy stood there looking like a little boy who just got a lump of coal for Christmas. For years, Baum had been mildly amused by the fact that Delbert had developed a hard-on for investigative work. Ever since the kid had started with the force, he talked about nothing but his favorite television program, *American Detective*, or his favorite reading material, *True Crime Magazine* and *Real Detective Stories*. It was pretty pathetic to

Baum, considering the fact that the kid needed a road map to find his own pecker. But there was also something about Delbert that tickled Baum, a kind of eagle-scout earnestness. Perhaps it was because Baum and Gloria had never had a child . . . or maybe it was merely because Delbert reminded Baum of his own apprenticeship with the Memphis Highway Patrol a million years ago. . . .

"Wait a minute, Delbert." The sheriff had an idea. Even though the whole fuel stunt was probably nothing more than an unfortunate freak accident, Baum couldn't resist throwing Delbert a bone. "Did you try plugging the names into LEADS?"

The deputy nodded. "Yeah, searched under priors, warrants, records. The usual stuff. Why?"

"Follow me."

The sheriff led Delbert down the hallway to the operations room. A narrow cubicle drenched in fluorescent light, the room housed the sheriff's data processing equipment. Maps, bulletins, and FAX sheets covered the walls. Computer desks crowded the floor. Baum ushered Delbert over to the main computer and said, "Try punching in the boy's name again."

Delbert took a seat and entered the letters B-E-N-O-I-T. After a moment, the computer spat out an empty list. "See," Delbert said, "comes up clean."

"Try the old lady's name again."

Delbert typed D-E-G-E-A-U-X. After another instant, another empty list appeared. "Nothing."

"Alright, hold on—" Baum licked his lips thoughtfully. He knew the LEADS program was not the only source. Another one of those cutesie cop acronyms for Law Enforcement Agency Data System, LEADS was the best bet for priors in Tennessee. But for Alabama they would need to plug into the National Crime Information Center. "—try the NCIC."

Delbert typed both names into the national data base. Again with the same results.

Baum pondered the green glow of the computer screen for a moment. "Try searching under complaints."

"Complaints?"

"Yeah."

Delbert told the computer to search the last twelve months for any complaints brought by BENOIT, M. After a moment, the computer came up negative. Baum told the deputy to try the old lady. Delbert typed it in and pressed RETURN.

The screen lit up.

"Bingo!"

Baum dug his bifocals out of his breast pocket and read the display. Evidently, the DeGeaux family had filed a formal complaint against one Hawkins Nocturne Memorial Park of Point Siren, Alabama. According to the NCIC files, the complaint, which was ten years old and unresolved, dealt with negligent custodial services. Although the details were vague, it seemed someone had vandalized the DeGeaux family crypt.

"Look at that—" Delbert stared at the screen. At the bottom of the display a line of text explained there was a security gag on the case. Presumably, the facts of the vandalism were not well-suited for public consumption.

"Calm down, Sherlock," Baum said all of a sudden. He could tell the young deputy's dander was up. In the blink of an eye, the case had gone from a dog to something fairly interesting. Out there on the highway, before getting barbecued, the Benoit kid *had* been babbling something about stuff taken from a grave. Here was a clue that there might have been some truth mixed in with the poor kid's paranoid bullshit. There might also be some valuables still in the wreckage that should be recovered and returned to their rightful owners.

"You know, those Alabama boys probably won't release every last detail of this thing over the phone," Delbert said, hopefully glancing up at the sheriff.

Baum looked down at the deputy. "Lemme guess—you're thinkin' you want to go down there to that little old town and do some serious sleuthing."

Delbert looked like a puppy about to get scratched. "I got the afternoon off today."

"That right?"

"Yessir. I could be down there and be back by nightfall."

Baum just shook his head and tried to stifle his grin.

"All I'm saying is we should just get rid of it as soon as possible." Sophie Cohen was sitting in the jump seat, chewing her lower lip. She always chewed her lip when she got nervous. "That's all I'm saying."

The Black Mariah was skirting along the western edge of Kentucky. The sun had risen high in the sky, warming the afternoon. The landscape had evolved into a rolling gallery of pine trees and hills. Every few miles the highway would slice through a granite pass, bordered on either side by endless strata of chocolate stone and ancient sediment. But Sophie noticed none of the natural beauty. She was consumed by the grotesque implications of the ornamental hand.

"Don't gimme any more shit about the hand," Lucas said over the rumble of 750 horses. "It's just some stupid good-luck charm the poor dude picked up along the way."

"I believe it's a charm. Question is, whether it's good luck or not."

Lucas sighed. "Since when are you so superstitious?"

Gazing out the window, Sophie looked at nothing in particular. Maybe Lucas was right. Maybe she *was* being a tad silly. But that flash-frame horror was still burned into her middle brain, still doing its work, still reminding her that even in the prosaic light of day the inexplicable can turn things upside down.

Her mind began to race back over the limited number of encounters she'd had with the unexplained. Of course, there were the esoteric classes at Berkeley, the eccentric professors, the ritual studies. She had done all the standard New Age field work. She'd done mushrooms with Native American shamen. She'd gone on vision quests loaded to the gills with laboratory-grade acid. At one point in her early twenties, she had even struck up a friendship with a particularly hip rabbi in Oakland named Milo Klein. In addition to being a hell of a macrobiotic cook, Milo was a walking encyclopedia on obscure Hebrew texts and Jewish folklore. Milo had turned Sophie on to the strange and hidden worlds of her Judaic heritage.

But ironically, none of this adult stuff had impressed Sophie as profoundly as one odd experience with a Ouija board back when she was twelve.

It was late one Saturday night. Sophie's cousin Jennifer was sleeping over and the two girls were sharing ghost stories. Eventually, they decided to goof around with Sophie's Ouija board. They chose to communicate with the ghost of Buddy Holly. They started softly humming his songs— "Peggy Sue," "Not Fade Away," "That'll Be the Day," "Maybe Baby"—and concentrated on evoking the Texas troubadour's spirit. For nearly an hour, nothing happened. But then, just as they were getting bored and preparing to give up, the plastic stylus took off in a convulsion of epileptic movement. For several minutes, the planchette wildly scratched back and forth across the cardboard surface of the toy. Then, in a screaming, giggling fit of hysteria, Jennifer kicked it off the board and onto the floor.

But it wasn't until minutes later, after picking the board up and putting it back on the coffee table, that the girls realized what had happened. The Ouija needle had scratched messages into the board. Very faintly, over and over again, the needle had written *no—no—no—no—no*.

The following day, Sophie's father had explained that it was called automatic writing. But for the rest of the night, the two adolescent girls lay wide awake in their sleeping bags in that darkened basement, unnerved by the knowledge that they had touched the other side. And now, almost twenty years later, Sophie felt a strange identification with that redundant warning—

No—no—no—no—

Turning back to Lucas, she finally said, "You want to know how long I've been superstitious? Ever since I saw a poor bastard in a Saints football jersey burn from the inside out."

"We've been through this over and over again," Lucas opined. "The kid got soaked with the gas, his clothes were soaked. Kid was an accident waiting to happen."

"Jesus Christ, Lucas! He had flames coming out his nostrils."

"I was there."

"Then you know what I'm talking about."

Lucas shook his head. He looked exasperated as hell. "Girl, don't *you* start giving me this mumbo jumbo. You're smarter than that. Goddamn world's hard enough to understand without believing in voodoo bullshit. Gimme a break. Only boogyman I know is the motherfucker who screwed us out of our full transport fee back in Jacksonville."

Sophie looked at her partner for a moment and thought about what he was saying. There was something in Lucas's voice, something brittle and tenuous, something belying the pragmatic rant he was laying down. Finally Sophie said, "I just think we should get rid of the thing."

Lucas grunted and cracked his window. He dug in his pocket for a moment and came up empty. Cursing under his breath, he turned back to Sophie. "Gimme a cigarette."

Sophie shrugged. "I'm out."

"Shit."

Sophie pointed at the gauges beneath the sunshade of the dashboard. The fuel gauge was edging toward empty, the reserve tanks were low, and the oil gauge was on the lighter side. "Better think about stopping soon. We can refuel, get a bite to eat, and maybe call Bakersfield for job prospects."

Lucas stared straight ahead. "Not ready to stop just yet."

"Lucas, c'mon—we've been red-lining for over three hours. You can buy some more of your stinky cigars."

"Not ready yet."

Sophie rolled her eyes and decided to figure out their location. She pulled open the glove box, fished out a bundle of maps, and found Kentucky. They were currently westbound on Highway 24 outside Paducah. The plan was to get within range of some of the bigger Midwestern metro areas—St. Louis, Kansas City, or Des Moines—with enough daylight left to make a pickup. With the Bakersfield guy calling stockyards and warehouses and foundries along the way, something had to pop.

Glancing up at the passing shoulder, Sophie saw a sign approaching on the right. It said WEST PADUCAH—2 MILES. Folding up the map, she stuck it back in the bundle and returned it to the glove box.

Their location told Sophie several things. If they were nearing West Paducah, it meant they were closing in on the Ohio River. If they were closing in on the river, it meant they were nearing the Illinois border. And if they were nearing the border, it meant only thing.

"Gotta stop at a weigh station soon."

Lucas responded as if something else was on his mind. "What?"

"Illinois chicken coop coming up." Sophie gestured into the distance. "Smokie wants us to sit on his face so he can guess our weight."

Lucas wasn't buying it. "Can't stop yet."

"Tell that to the bears."

"Fuck the bears."

Sophie sat up straight. "You're not thinking about blowing-off the chicken coop—"

Lucas rolled down his window, choked up a wad of phlegm, and spat into the wind. "I want to put some heavy-duty miles between us and Pennington County."

Staring at Lucas for a moment, Sophie tried to let it sink in. The weigh station had always been a minor irritant to cross-country truckers. Operated jointly by the department of transportation and the state police, weigh stations were positioned both at the entry points and key junctions throughout a state's interior. Using giant scales embedded at the top of exit ramps, stations were designed to simply weigh each axle and make sure a truck was under the legal limit. Usually, they were manned by weight inspectors from the state, who might or might not notice somebody skipping by without stopping. But occasionally, a state trooper would be lurking in the scale house. In that case, it was extremely unwise to pass.

Sophie finally said, "Lucas, we're already on thin ice with the smokies. You think it's a good idea to blow past a weigh station?"

Lucas shrugged. "What are they gonna do? Chase us? We're empty."

Chewing her lip some more, Sophie gazed out the window and watched the exit sign for West Paducah zoom past them.

The road was winding gently toward the river. The afternoon sun was glinting off the upcoming suspension bridge and the sparkling waves below it. The wind stank of rich bottom land and rotting fish.

Turning back to Lucas, Sophie said, "You ask me, I think we oughtta stop."

"Sorry, gotta keep rollin'," Lucas said and kept his eyes locked on the horizon, his meaty palm wrapped around the shift knob. His expression was implacable. A big burly Buddha in black leather and cowboy hat, his beefy arms protruding through the oily vest, Lucas reminded Sophie of a mountain. Immovable, rooted in the iron frame of the huge truck.

She knew better than to argue with him when he got like this. "Okay, but don't come crying to me when they lay the green stamps on us."

Lucas shifted the truck down into the lower register as they approached the steel bridge. The tires hit the corrugated pavement with a bump and began to sing. Sophie gazed out her window at the water below them. Fifty feet down, the dirty currents roiled and swirled in whirlpools of silt. The river was high for this time of year. Active, too. Violently active.

No—no—no—no—

A minute later, they were on the Illinois side. The landscape seemed to immediately change. The trees got older. The leaves turned a lighter shade of green. And the land flattened into corn and soybean fields as far as the eye could see.

On the right side of the interstate, less than a mile away, was the weigh station. It sat baking in the afternoon sun, a modest little scale house planted at the end of a ramp. A department of transportation decal was plastered on its roof. An empty state police car was parked out behind the building.

As they approached the turnoff ramp, Sophie tried one last time to change her partner's mind. "Last chance to be a model citizen."

Lucas turned to her and winked. But there was no humor in his eyes. Only a look of intense, white-hot purpose.

"Don't worry," he murmured, his voice colored with a strain of tension. "They'll never catch me."

Sophie gazed through the window. The truck roared past the weigh station in a gust of exhaust and noise. She looked in the side mirror and saw the little Quonset hut receding into the distance. Then she turned back to her partner and saw something that gave her a feathery chill along the back of the neck.

Peeking out of the pocket of Lucas's vest, its delicate nails gleaming, was the shriveled little hand.

It seemed to be pointing at her.

10

Forever Car

Praise God in His sanctuary . . . praise Him in His mighty firmament . . . praise Him for His mighty deeds . . .

Delbert Morrison gripped the armrests with his sweaty palms and praised God like crazy as the Cessna took another yawing dip into turbulent air, three thousand feet above the marshlands of Dauphin Bay. Delbert wore his standard-issue police windbreaker. Beneath the jacket he wore a crisp dress shirt, rep tie, plastic pocket protector with pens and notebook, and his immaculate .38 caliber tucked snugly into its body holster.

Tucked beneath his seat was a small leather case about the size of a doctor's bag. Inside it were the investigative tools which Delbert had purchased with his own money over the course of the last year. Among the items were magnifying glasses, tweezers, evidence bags, I.D. tags, latent print powder, makeup brushes, and a Polaroid 600 camera with extra film. Everything was clean, oiled, and organized. Everything was ready.

"Son of a bitch feels lame today!" the grizzled old police pilot named Scanlon barked over the soprano howl of the airplane. "Feels like somebody put her away wet."

Scanlon fiddled with his headset and spat tobacco into a can rattling around the floor of the cockpit. A wiry little man with a tuft of steel wool on his chin, Scanlon wore a tattered hunting vest over a loud Hawaiian shirt. He was an old fishing buddy of Sheriff Baum's from the Franklin Police Department. The boys in Franklin were the only squad for miles who had a single-engine plane to lend out; and the sheriff had called in the favor a couple of hours ago so that Delbert could get down to the Gulf and back in a day's time.

"Officer Scanlon!" Delbert called out from the passenger seat. "How much farther is the Point Siren airport?"

"Call me Jerry," the pilot said.

"How much farther, Jerry?"

The pilot laughed above the sound of the engine. "First of all, Point Siren ain't really much of an airport. More like a low-rent, shit-heel landing field. Second of all, we been circling it for ten minutes now."

Delbert looked out the window. Down below them, through the rushing airstream of clouds, were patchwork swaths of brown grass and cracked pavement. Faded directional lines like childish strokes of a pencil bisected the landing strip. The roof of an office complex stood off to the north—at this altitude it appeared to be no bigger than a matchbox. And scattered throughout were unidentifiable objects that looked like the carcasses of huge tires. They appeared to be moving.

Straightening back up in his seat, Delbert asked, "Some reason we're not landing?"

"Just waiting for traffic to clear."

"Pardon me?"

The pilot gestured downward. "Goddamn gators wanderin' around the field again. Takes a few minutes to herd 'em off."

Just then, the plane lurched on a gust of turbulence. Delbert levitated above his seat for a moment, then slammed back into the torn upholstery. He felt his lunch high in his stomach, threatening to make an appearance. His scalp crawled.

Let everything that breathes praise Him . . .

"Shoulda landed an hour ago, but the department's got these new computerized flight plans," Scanlon hollered, pointing to a laminated pouch clipped to the instrument panel. "Captain thinks it's the latest thing in state-of-the-art tactical. You ask me, it's a bunch of hog shit!"

The pilot spat another projectile into the can beneath him. Then, reaching up to the panel, he rapped his fist against the altimeter. The needle bobbed.

Delbert gazed back out the window and practiced his deep-breathing exercises. This trip was going to be his big opportunity. He was going to prove once and for all that he had the mettle to be an evidence technician. In preparation for this moment, Delbert had studied hard. Over the past two years he had read and reread the *ARCO Police Detective Manual*, the *U.S. Department of Justice Handbook of Forensic Science*, and Conrad Cornbluth's *ABC's of Evidence Gathering*. He had forced his mother to quiz him daily on the various types of hair follicles and carpet fibers and skin oils found at crime scenes. He'd experimented with his dad's 12-gauge out behind his family's garage to learn burn patterns and ballistics. He'd even taught himself how to plant a wire on somebody with a few parts from Radio Shack and his daddy's old Heath Kit crystal radio. Now it all boiled down to this one mission. God willing, Delbert would finally show the department—and especially Sheriff Baum—just what Delbert Morrison was made of.

Suddenly, across the cockpit, the goateed pilot nodded. "Here we go! Drop your socks and grab your cocks."

Delbert closed his eyes and gripped the edge of his seat like his life depended on it. The plane lurched forward and began its descent.

Praise Him . . . praise Him . . . praise Him . . .

"There it is again—"
"There what is?"
"The voice." Lucas was holding the truck steady at about seventy miles an hour, listening to the garbled bursts of static on their CB. They were cutting through a sea of soybeans along the southern shank of Illinois. For the last thirty miles

or so they had been hearing intermittent bursts over the air. At first, Lucas thought it was the Latino kid, Angel, speaking in Spanish, trying to reach them through waves of interference. But then he wasn't so sure. It sounded like broken English, but that was as much as Lucas could decipher.

To make matters worse, Sophie was getting more and more unnerved over the grotesque little charm Lucas had found in the detritus of Melville's Camaro.

"I'm serious about this hand thing, Lucas . . ."

"Alright, you win!" Lucas glanced at a passing mileage sign. "I know a little place around the fifty-first mile marker. Little pawn shop that's catty-corner from a gas station."

"Whatever," Sophie said from the gunshot seat, twisting the back of her punky hair into a tight ponytail and wrapping it with a rubber band. "Just so we get rid of the thing as soon as possible."

"Jesus, I told you I'd get rid of it. Damn thing's probably from some New Orleans dime store."

"I don't care."

"What the hell is it with you?!"

"I'm a little freaked, Lucas."

"Calm down."

"I don't want to calm down."

"Jesus Christ." Lucas rolled his eyes and gazed back through the windshield. They were cruising along at about sixty miles an hour, approaching the Shawnee National Forest that covered the southwestern thumb of Illinois. The ocean of pine trees spread off to the right as far as the eye could see. It was nearing 4:00 P.M. and the sun was just beginning to descend, the shadows beginning to lengthen. "I know what it is," Lucas suddenly offered. "You're hungry."

"I'm not hungry."

"Christ, we haven't had anything but Ritz Crackers since dinner last night."

"I said I'm not hungry."

"C'mon, Cohen," Lucas said with a smirk, trying desperately to cheer her up. "Don't tell me you wouldn't like to dive into a pile of your rabbit food right now."

Sophie rubbed her tired eyes. "Cut it out, Lucas."

"Big plate of stinky asparagus . . . maybe some delicious soybean mush . . . perhaps some of those steaming hot tofu turds smothered with seaweed . . ."

"Lucas, I'm warning you—"

"Shit, girl, my mouth is watering just thinking about it," he continued teasing. "Maybe we could even find a couple pints of that wonderful beet juice I love so much—"

"Lucas, stop it!" Sophie shot him a razor glance. Her temples pulsed as she clenched her jaw. Lucas studied her face for a moment. He had never seen her look so old. The lines around her eyes had deepened, the corners of her mouth cleaved grimly. She was terrified.

"Take it easy, woman." Lucas felt a sudden pang of sympathy for his partner.

"Lucas, I'm scared." Sophie was biting her lip again, vigorously.

"Alright, let's talk."

"It's just too weird." Now she was picking at her lip too, biting and picking and chewing compulsively. In a minute her mouth would be bleeding. "The fire, the kid burning to death, the nightmares, and you know—the fickle fingers of fate in your pocket. It's just too fucking weird."

"Look, I'm sorry. I'm being an insensitive motherfucker as usual."

Sophie glanced at him. "You can't help it—you're a man."

Lucas winced. "You got me. Another mile and we'll get rid of the thing once and for all."

Sophie nodded sharply. "Fair enough."

Lucas shot another sideways glance at the woman. After nearly four years, she was still as enigmatic as ever. All hard and punky and cynical on the outside—yet vulnerable as hell on the inside.

The paradox was most apparent in Sophie's eyes. Upon first glance, Sophie's dark-brown eyes appeared keen and intense, with an edge of anger glinting behind every look. But upon closer examination, the spark was revealed to be something else entirely, something deeper, something more passionate. It was as if the spark was a perpetual glimmer of feeling. A cinder of emotion playing behind every gaze. It was everything Lucas found mysterious and fascinating about Sophie.

Lucas remembered seeing that emotion bubble to the surface two summers ago during the L.A. riots. At the height of the troubles, Sophie had come down to visit Lucas at his place in Santa Monica. As she pulled up in front of the apartment, a group of kids had surrounded her car, throwing rocks and shouting at her. Lucas had managed to quickly chase them away and afterward Sophie seemed as cool as a cucumber, even philosophical about the whole incident. But later that night she excused herself and went into the bathroom and spent a long time by herself. Lucas had heard her softly sobbing in there. Sobbing out all the fear and anger and shame over the rushing tap water.

"What's the matter?"

Sophie's voice snapped Lucas out of the memory. He rubbed his eyes and looked across the cab at her. "Whattya mean?"

"You were staring at me like a zombie."

"Was I?" Lucas pondered Sophie's anxious expression. Then he did something that violated his unspoken code of conduct. He reached over and softly touched her shoulder. Just a friendly, reassuring squeeze. But at that particular moment, it had enormous symbolic power. "Listen, I'm sorry about this business with the hand. I'm sorry I came down on you for being scared. You think you'll ever forgive me?"

Sophie stared at him for a moment, then grinned and said, "Never in a million years."

Lucas smiled, then turned away. A surge of sadness had risen in his chest powerful enough to bring a lump to his throat. If only they were something other than business partners. If only it was another time, another place, another situation . . . then perhaps he would be able to reach over and touch the soft fringe of her hair along the back of her neck. . . .

The mystery voice crackled through the speaker again.

"There! There it is again!" Lucas reached down, fiddled with the squelch, and tweaked the treble. The voice sounded as though it were coming from under water during a hurricane.

Sophie watched. "Lucas, it's nothing. Just bleed from some other channel."

"I'm telling you, it sounds like somebody trying to break through with a bad transmitter."

Lucas concentrated on driving for several more noisy moments before the voice faded away.

A sign loomed on the right. A green reflective square announcing the upcoming exit for Round Knob, Illinois. Lucas silently thanked God. In a few minutes they would be able to unload the little hand and be done with this whole charade once and for all.

Lucas reached over and flipped on his blinker. Glancing in his side mirror, he noticed something interesting behind them, about a half a mile back. At first, the sun glinted brightly off its roof, then flowed over it like mercury as it approached from behind.

A limousine. An old antique limousine, gliding along buoyantly in the late afternoon sun. Although a completely different color and type of car than the hearse from Lucas's father's funeral, its sheer size and bulk was familiar enough to raise chills along the base of Lucas's spine.

Lucas squeezed the steering wheel, hard enough to whiten his knuckles. For years he had been spotting cars along the highway that reminded him of that horrible day. Old station wagons, stretch limos, dark-colored Jimmies, it didn't matter. Whenever Lucas saw a vehicle that was even remotely like the hearse, he flashed back to that terrible moment.

Today was no different.

On a sudden surge of dread, the memory strobed through his mind again.

The rain had been coming down in sheets. Inside the sanctuary it sounded like marbles rolling across the roof. Sitting in the front row with his mom and sisters, Lucas had begun to go out of his mind with restless tension. He began fidgeting against his older sister. Reaching down to the boy with trembling hands, the grieving girl urged Lucas toward the exit, whispering something about waiting near the hearse for Mama.

Outside, the rain had just begun to lift and turn the sky to a featureless shroud of gray. Wandering toward the street, Lucas found the hearse at the end of the church's circular drive. It was an ebony Dynaglide version of a stretch Caddy, with landau rear panels, opera windows, and an angular back. Low-slung and oversized, the vehicle seemed to radiate a certain dark gravity, as if all other cars were merely toys and this was somehow the real thing. The automobile for eternity. The forever car.

At that moment, a twinge of anger and grief twisted in Lucas's gut. Realizing that his father, a man who had once lifted an entire pallet of canned beets with his bare hands, would soon be a rag doll inside this giant car, Lucas fell against the hood and wept. Tears burned in his eyes. His body convulsed. His mind reeled with chaotic thoughts and emotions. And before he even realized what he was doing, he began slamming his fists against the hood.

"Hey!" A voice bellowed up from behind him, shocking him out of his grief. "Hey, kid!"

Lucas wheeled around quickly and glimpsed the hearse driver approaching from the parking lot. Dressed in a navy-blue uniform, the man was holding a newspaper under one arm and was adjusting his mirrored sunglasses with the other. To Lucas, he appeared to be about ten feet tall.

"Easy on the jalopy," the driver murmured as he approached and gazed down at Lucas with his silver eyes.

Sniffing back his tears, wiping snot from his mouth, Lucas just stared up at the man for several moments. Then, taking a deep breath, Lucas nodded a silent acknowledgement.

At that moment, Lucas expected the driver to apologize or offer condolences or simply go away. But the driver lingered. His mirrored visage remained locked on Lucas for what seemed an eternity. It became nearly impossible for Lucas to read the expression behind those sunglasses. There was only that crooked, nondescript smirk.

*Then, moving around to the driver's-side door, the tall
man paused and added something so softly that no one else
could have heard it but Lucas.*

"Your dad's a good nigger."

"What—?!" Lucas was stricken.

*"Only good nigger's a dead nigger," the driver explained,
"and since your daddy's deader than a two-penny nail, that
makes him pretty goddamn good."*

*Then the man with the silver eyes had a good laugh. He
laughed and laughed and laughed and his voice was like flint
scraping flint.*

*For a moment, Lucas was stunned. Then the poison rush
of anger came. Instantly stepping back, clenching his fists,
breathing quickly, Lucas looked around for someone—someone from whom he could seek help. But there was nobody. It
was just Lucas and the smirking man in the polarized sunglasses.*

*Then came the worst part of the memory. The part that al-
ways awakened Lucas from the nightmare or stabbed him
out of his memory or brought acid up his gorge. The part he
dreaded most.*

The silence.

*Lucas couldn't make a sound. He couldn't scream or tell
the driver to shut up or call him a bigot. He couldn't stand
up for himself. He couldn't even run away. He was paralyzed.*

*He could only stand there biting his lower lip and clench-
ing his little fists, the rage coursing through his veins like
acid, binding him to the pavement as if his feet were encased
in cement. . . .*

"Fucking paralyzed . . ."

Lucas didn't even realize he was talking to himself.

"What?" Sophie was staring at him. "What did you just
say?"

"Nothing . . . just . . . something I remembered from a long
time ago."

In front of them the right lane split off toward the exit ramp.

Lucas tapped the brakes and eased The Black Mariah onto the ramp. He wiped a bead of sweat from his brow. "Here we are—the sprawling metropolis of Round Knob, Illinois. Home of the best pawn shop this side of the Mississippi."

Sophie let out a breath. "Finally."

11
Symphony of Tears

Just what the fuck was Dirk Touy thinking when he got the big idea back in the joint to return to the little shit-hole town he grew up in? What the fuck was he thinking? Did he think he was going to get rich burglarizing pig farms? *Judas H. Priest*, he was one stupid son of a bitch.

Wiping a greasy strand of hair from his eyes, Dirk hollered over the roar of his GTO, "Fuck me!"

He was speeding through an alley that cut between the loading docks of Round Knob Farm Implements and Simkins's Body Shop. His Kentucky Headhunters T-shirt was sweaty with rage and restlessness. He had just beaten up his sixty-year-old daddy for the third time this week and it wasn't sitting too well with him.

"What the fuck was I thinking?"

Dirk had been out of the joint for less than a month. He'd done a nickel's worth of time at Marion for armed robbery and while he was inside, the gangs had tried to make Dirk their butt-hole boy. But Dirk showed them what's what in a hurry. He showed them he was willing to die before he'd take a John Henry up the poop chute.

He skidded to a stop at the mouth of the alley and took a

look around. He was close to the highway. He could smell the diesel fumes. He could hear the distant whine of semis. Reaching into his pocket, he searched for a smoke.

"Shit!" He was out of cigarettes.

He turned south and burned rubber toward the Stuckey's down by the overpass. It was the cultural nerve center of Round Knob, Illinois. The only place for miles that Dirk could find a fresh box of Viceroys, a six-pack of Mickey's Big Mouths, and a bag of pork rinds. Then he could figure out his next move.

He rounded the turn at the bottom of Rainey Street. The Stuckey's was off to the right. A row of store fronts were off to the left—DeForest Feed and Seed, Swifty-Wash Laundromat, Henniman's Barber Shop, and Round Knob Pawn Brokers.

Place was pretty crowded for a Friday afternoon. A cluster of old-timers sat on a bench outside the barber shop. The laundromat was busy. The Stuckey's parking lot had two mini-vans gassing up and a slew of foreign jobs outside the restaurant. Over by the diesel island there was a big old deluxe Kenworth getting fueled. Dirk had never seen such a fancy-ass rig. Shit-loads of chrome. Custom paint job. Damn thing looked like a fucking space ship.

There was a special moniker hand-painted across its cab. *The Black Mariah.*

Dirk spat out his window as he pulled into the Stuckey's lot. "What the fuck is a Black Mariah . . .?"

Off to the left, something else caught his attention.

"Hold the fuckin' phone!" He pulled across the lot and circled around the rear of the restaurant to get a better look at it. "What do we have here?!"

Stuckey's had a small dog-run out behind its restaurant. There were about a hundred yards of deserted lawn, a couple of spindly maple trees, and a few empty picnic benches. At one end, behind a row of Dumpsters, were the rest rooms. A vintage limousine was sitting in front of the rest rooms. It was angled toward the store fronts as if someone inside was keeping tabs.

"Holy shit," Dirk whispered to himself, "a Rolls-fucking-Royce with the original door locks I bet."

His mouth watered as he slammed the brakes, did a U-Y, and pulled the GTO out of the lot. He parked his wheels on Rainey Street behind a rusted carcass of a tractor. Then he grabbed his tools out of the trunk, shoved them into his jeans, and crept back across the vacant lot behind Stuckey's. His head was buzzing. If he could score a classic in mint condition, he could fucking retire. Chop shops up in East St. Louis would pay a king's ransom for a vintage Rolls. This was just too fucking lucky.

He approached the limousine from the rear and peered inside. Through the shaded opera window it was tough to see anything, but it looked like the car was empty. Owners were probably inside the rest rooms, taking a piss.

Dirk knew he had only seconds to rip the car off.

Glancing around the lot, he made sure nobody was watching. Then he quickly crabbed along the driver's side of the Rolls, reached up to the door, and slammed his slim jim into the gap between the door and the window. The antique lock gave way like a ripe walnut.

Dirk grinned and opened the door.

The stench hit him like a slap in the face. It was a rich mixture of musty, cheesy odors that reminded Dirk of the old folks home in which his granny had wasted away a few years back. And there was something else beneath it, something sharp and tinny that he couldn't quite place.

He quickly slipped behind the wheel and reached under the steering column for the ignition wires. Fumbling with the wires, he scanned the front seats for any valuables. The wood-grain dash was in mint condition. The original leather bench was worn and puckered with age. A few items sat on the passenger side—binoculars, leatherette pouch, nitroglycerine pills.

Something was buzzing softly to his right.

D—

Dirk looked up and saw the monitor. It was mounted just above the radio. It looked like one of those cheap Radio Shack laptop computers with the yellow LED screen. The little cursor was creeping across its screen.

D I E—

Dirk felt something behind him. It wasn't exactly the sound of someone breathing or the warmth of another body. It was more of a presence. As if eyes were suddenly boring into his back, making the tiny hairs on his neck stand at attention.

The computer screen went berserk.

DIE—DIE—DIE—DIE—DIE—DIE—DIE DIE DIE !! DIE !! DIE !! DIE !! DIE !! DIE !! DIE !!!!!!!!

Dirk turned around.

Something popped in his face. It came from the shadows of the rear and happened so quickly that Dirk thought at first somebody had snapped a rubber band against his cheek. He felt a stinging sensation in his left eye and a pocket of cold, growing, spreading down the side of his face.

Dirk realized his left eye had been gouged and suddenly bleated like a pinched lamb.

The second blow hit his neck. The knitting needle pierced his carotid and a geyser of blood ejaculated across the seats. Dirk convulsed backward against the dash, his cry corrupting into a gurgle as he clutched his throat. All at once, blood was everywhere. It sluiced between his fingers, it pulsed and spackled the leather, it spattered the inside of the windows.

Dirk slipped to the carpet, which was now absorbing his life stream. He fumbled in his coat pocket for his hunting knife but his fingers were too clumsy, too slippery with gore. His lower half was going numb. His vision was swirling away as if a dark tide was flooding the interior of the limousine.

Gazing up through the veil of pain, through his one good eye, Dirk Touy saw his assailant.

The hag had inched forward through the gape in the partition to ogle Dirk's death throes. Nine decades of lunacy were deeply etched in her wrinkled face. A wild nimbus of steel wool framed her liver-spotted skull. Her eyes were the color of ashes. Her bloodless mouth curled into a lopsided sneer as she gazed down at Dirk.

Dirk tried to say something but his awareness was flickering away.

The old crone drank in the suffering as if sampling a fine vintage. Then, with great effort, summoning all her strength, she took a pained breath and whispered, "Please die . . ."

Dirk Touy obliged.

A moment later, Eric returned. Vanessa watched him survey the carnage.

"My God . . ." The chauffeur hovered in the doorway of the limousine for a moment, gawking at all the blood. The limp corpse of the thief lay on the floor, arms and legs akimbo like a broken doll. Eric wiped his mouth with the back of his hand and turned to the back.

"Madam?! Are you alright?!"

Vanessa turned toward him and tried to answer. The attack on the thief had taken all her energy. Speaking was exceedingly difficult. All she managed was a sibilant wheeze.

"Madam—?!!" Eric leaned in the back and frantically examined her withered form. Her dress had a light spattering of blood on it. Her shrivelled legs curled out from the bottom of her skirt, inert as ever.

"Eric, please . . ." Vanessa uttered the words. She didn't have time to use her CompuTalk pad. Her good arm hung limply over the edge of her safety seat, the Arthwriter ball still gripped tightly in her right palm. From the center of the ball thrust the knitting needle, its point still slimy with blood, dripping softly.

Eric reached in and took the Arthwriter from her grasp. Then he helped her lay her good arm back on the padded rest beside her. "What have you done?" he whispered to himself more than to Vanessa.

"Eric—" she whispered weakly, "please . . . clean this mess up directly . . . before something happens . . . and don't forget the man's eyeball. . . ."

The chauffeur stared at her for a moment, his brow furrowed. "Please, Madam—"

"Don't argue with me, Eric . . . just hurry . . ."

Vanessa was worried they were going to lose the Negro who had taken the talisman. Only minutes ago, the trucker and his partner had disappeared inside the pawn brokers' shop across the street. Now Vanessa was concerned that this little dalliance with the thief would distract her long enough to lose the trucker. And Vanessa just couldn't let that happen. She couldn't bear to lose track of the talisman. She couldn't bear to miss the suffering of the mongrels who had stolen it. The sweet odors of burning flesh. The symphony of tears.

Eric followed her orders quickly and dutifully. He dragged the body across the deserted picnic ground and deposited it into the garbage Dumpster. Before slamming the lid, he reached in and uprooted one of the man's eyeballs. It was like scooping the yolk from a hard-boiled egg.

The chauffeur returned to the limousine with a sour look on his face, dropped the eyeball in a container at the old woman's feet, and quickly cleaned the interior with a box of Bon Ami that he had stored in the trunk. Though his hands were trembling, Eric was able to restore the seats to their well-oiled sheen within a couple of minutes. The carpet was another matter; it was destined to be stained.

"You're sure you're alright?" Eric asked Vanessa after stowing the bloody rags in the trunk and climbing back behind the wheel. He was breathing raggedly. It was obvious his heart was on borrowed time. Fear and repulsion burned in his eyes. He was afraid of being caught. Afraid of going to jail. Afraid of going to hell.

Foolish old dear.

Vanessa tried typing her answer on the CompuTalk but stopped herself. Though her voice was weak and slow, she despised talking with the infernal keypad. "Eric . . . please . . . get us closer . . . I want to see everything . . ."

The chauffeur nodded quickly, started the limousine, and pulled away from the picnic area.

The Stuckey's parking lot had thinned. Only a lone pickup remained near the front entrance. Over by the entrance ramp a couple of buses were disgorging passengers. Eric crossed the lot slowly and pulled up in front of the pawn brokers' shop, parking next to the curb. Vanessa shoved her good hand into the grip of her folding reacher. A three-foot metal arm with plierlike jaws on one end, the reacher enabled Vanessa to grasp objects on the rear seats with a minimum of effort.

She swung the reacher over to her Green Scope opera glasses mounted by the window and pulled them into position against her face. The glasses were Vanessa's window on the world. Through them she could see the ramshackle front entrance of Round Knob Pawn Brokers. The scarred metal door undulated in rays of afternoon heat. Somewhere inside were the Negro trucker and his white partner.

Vanessa glanced to her right. An empty teak box sat on the seat next to her. The lid was ajar. Inside, the empty velvet lining was shiny in spots, worn down to the nubs, and pressed into the shape of a hand.

Vanessa swore to herself that she would get her talisman back into the box before nightfall. Whatever it took, she would get the talisman back.

"Do you need anything, Madam?" Eric asked her from the front seat.

"No thank you, Eric," Vanessa said, taking one last look at the empty box.

Vanessa sat in a mechanical chair. Dressed in a faded cotton dress and pinafore, her matted gray hair spiralling off her skull in thin tufts, she looked all of her eighty-nine years. Crippled from a childhood injury, her legs and left arm had deteriorated even further from osteoporosis and rheumatism. They were now shrivelled, twisted husks shooting out from under her skirt. The pain was manageable, as long as Vanessa remained still. Still as an old marble sculpture.

The devices helped. The limousine was equipped with the latest in prosthetic technology, purchased with the bottomless well of DeGeaux trust funds. In addition to her safety chair, which slid along metal brackets mounted on the floor, she utilized a whole battery of electronic mobility machines. A lightweight porta-ramp was tucked inside her door. Reaching devices were holstered beside her chair like six-guns. The bench adjacent to her seat was motorized and could reveal the toilet facilities underneath. An electronic keypad near her good hand enabled her to communicate with the chauffeur, dial phone numbers, or engage the police scanner. Video screens were hot-wired at her feet, reporting the status of everything. In fact, if it wasn't for the tools of her magic, the rear of the limousine would resemble a medical supply closet.

Vanessa used the reacher to pluck the thief's eyeball from the glass jar at her feet. She put the wet organ in a metal box above her. Scrawled with obscure insignias, the box sat on a shelf brimming with magic esoterica. Organ-filled apothecary jars, tangles of dried nightshade and herbs, tiny skulls with bejeweled eye sockets, and obscenely rearranged anatomies.

She repositioned the opera glasses and returned her gaze to the front of the pawn shop. The waiting was killing her. Pain radiated through her heart. Ghostly ripples of pain penetrated her frozen limbs. But she couldn't move. As always, she couldn't move.

The pain made the magic work. Her father had taught her that many years ago.

It was a pity that Vanessa could barely remember those days before her injury, before the crippling time came. It was back around the turn of the century. In the gardenia-scented womb of Mobile. Vanessa had grown up the eldest child of a family of wealthy southern aristocrats. Her early days had been normal and healthy and full of galloping like a skittish colt along the banks of the Gulf with her sister Helen. But Vanessa was destined to fly too close to the sun. Her father had been the catalyst.

An infamous faith healer, volatile, mysterious, Maurice DeGeaux had been an enigma to all who knew him. Some said he had run with the Grand Dragons of the newly formed Klan. All Vanessa knew was that she alternately adored and hated the man, desired and feared him. After Vanessa had been crippled in a freak accident—an accident that was excised from her memory like some shrinking malignancy—

she had become obsessed with her father. From her wheelchair, she spied on him every hour of every day. She fought with her sister over who would bring the man his dinner each night. She followed the man everywhere. When she finally discovered that he was a practitioner of black magic, she was transformed.

She learned his craft well.

Now, Vanessa was the last surviving DeGeaux. Her father was gone. Her sister, too. And Vanessa had dedicated the rest of her days to the Cause—using her pain to bring pain to others. From her frozen vigil she conjured and tormented and hexed. Her stoney limbs were the source of her power now. The hate. The hate and the rage and the pain. It flowed from her bodily prison . . . radioactive, insidious . . .

The curse . . .

. . . tendrils of black rage shooting out from her cold motionless heart . . . showing them . . . showing the savages what it's like to move . . . move . . . move you dirty savages forever until you die move die move die move. . . .

. . . die . . .

12
White-Hot
Stars

"Yo, Amigo! Can we get some service here?!" Lucas was tired of waiting. He had been fidgeting in the airless little pawn shop for nearly ten minutes now.

"Be with you folks in a second." The head clerk and sole proprietor of Round Knob Pawn Brokers was standing behind a glass counter covered with decades of fingerprints, scratches, and oil from the hands of small-town commerce. A pear-shaped man in a Ban-Lon golf shirt stretched to the limit by rolls of flab, he wore a jeweler's eyepiece over his balding head and was muttering under his breath into the telephone. His shop smelled of musty books, damp cardboard, and machine oil.

"You tell Rilla I said it ain't real 'cause Corkie's dachshund tried to bury it and the ground turned the damn thing green as a booger."

"Excuse me, sport! We're on a schedule here!" Lucas's voice was stretched taut with tension. He felt like an army of ants was crawling up his spine.

Sophie stood behind him. She was periodically glancing over her shoulder, through the front window, at the Stuckey's across the street. The Black Mariah was parked between two fuel islands. A gangly teenage attendant in overalls had just plugged a fuel nozzle into the truck's belly.

Turning back to the counter, Sophie nudged Lucas and spoke under her breath. "Can we do this today?"

Lucas rapped his knuckles on the counter. "Hey, man—you gonna help us or not?"

The clerk cupped his hand over the phone. "Just one more second, folks."

"No, goddamnit! Now!" Lucas slammed his fist on the glass.

The clerk jerked backward slightly and stared dumbly at Lucas for a moment before muttering into the receiver. "Call you back, Shaver." Hanging up, the clerk's gaze turned cold. "Can I help you?"

"Goddamn straight, you can help me." Lucas reached into his pocket and produced a wadded handkerchief. He set it on the counter and uncovered it. Nestled in the cloth like a desiccated spider was the hand.

"How much for this?"

The clerk squinted at it. "What in hell's half acre is that?"

Lucas glanced over at Sophie for a moment. The longer he stood in this little musty shop, the more he felt like his teeth were going to vibrate out of his head. He wondered if it was his allergies acting up. "It's a very rare French Cajun ornament."

The clerk reached up, lowered his jeweler's scope over his left eye, and took a closer look. "French what?"

"Cajun, Cajun, French Cajun. You know, like down in Louisiana." Lucas's voice was growing increasingly shrill.

Pulling a ballpoint from his pocket, the clerk prodded the hand, turned it over, pondered it. He seemed reticent to touch it with his bare fingers.

Lucas fidgeted. His stomach was churning. "The stones are real."

"Real what?" The clerk was becoming uneasy.

"Emeralds, turquoise, you know."

Replacing the pen in his pocket, the clerk stiffened and looked askance at the object. "Where did you get this?"

"What difference does it make? How much?!"

"Ain't sure I want to buy this thing."

"What?!"

The clerk wrinkled his nose. "Put it this way—I ain't sure I want this thing on my shelf."

"What the fuck are you talking about?!" Lucas felt a wave of nausea rising in his belly, a burst of acid gurgling up and burning his gullet. It was bothering him, too; because he rarely got sick. He had a cast-iron stomach, impervious to the worst diner chow the highway had to offer. But now he was beginning to feel miserable.

Sophie stepped forward and grabbed Lucas by the arm. "Just leave the damn thing for the trash man."

Lucas belched and fought the nausea. "No fucking way."

"C'mon, let's get outta here." Sophie was pulling him toward the door. Her eyes were wide with panic. She seemed clammy herself, sick and racked with chills.

Lucas slipped from her grasp and lurched back toward the counter. Reaching up, angrily shoving the object toward the clerk, he barked, "Touch it! Goddamn thing won't bite!"

The clerk raised his hands. "I don't want no trouble."

"Touch it!"

"I'll call the cops."

"Touch it, goddamnit!" Lucas suddenly winced at the hot pokers in his belly. It was as if someone were trying to tie his intestines into a knot. He staggered backward, slamming into a nearby rack of merchandise and gasping at the pain. Several dozen small kitchen utensils wobbled off their shelves and crashed to the floor, shattering, sending plastic shards skittering across the tiles.

The clerk reached under the counter for something. "Told you I don't want no trouble!"

Sophie grabbed Lucas and tried to wrench him toward the exit. But Lucas staggered back toward the counter, gasping at the shooting pains. "Fine! Fuck it! I'll sell the thing down the road in two seconds!"

The clerk pulled out a six-inch stainless-steel .357 Magnum revolver from under the counter. He snapped the hammer back and trained it on Lucas. "Out!"

"I want my merchandise back." Lucas reached up, swiped

the hand off the counter, and stuffed it back in his pocket. A
sudden rush of chills gripped his body, icy hot, seething.

With all his might, Lucas made for the door. His head was
spinning, ringing with fever. His knees buckled beneath him
and he almost collapsed, but he kept on hobbling along, past
the old electric guitars, past the cheap radios, past the faded
lampshades. Finally, as the heat in his belly swelled to an unbearable level, his legs folded and he tumbled to the floor
near the door, knocking over a metal tree draped with old
ties.

Lying still for a brief moment, he felt a new rush of pain a
thousand times sharper than a few moments earlier. It started
at the soles of his feet and rolled over him like a wave of
molten lava. When it reached his lungs, Lucas opened his
mouth and shrieked.

Sophie appeared above him. Through the curtain of pain,
Lucas could see her reaching down and pulling him up. Her
voice sounded as if it were coming through cellophane
paper. "Gotta get back on the truck."

Lucas struggled back to his feet. Sophie urged him
through the door and into the afternoon.

There was a dusty four-lane that ran between the pawn
shop and Stuckey's. Tattooed with skid marks, cracks, and
oil spots, it now seemed like an impassable moat that separated Lucas from the sweet deliverance of his truck.

"Get back ... on the highway. ..." The words came out
of Lucas on gasps of excruciating pain as he staggered
alongside Sophie toward the truck. Every step sent shock
waves of feverish chills and nausea up Lucas's spine. But he
kept going, steadfast in his inexplicable certainty that getting
back on the road was the only cure.

I been cursed ...

Sophie hobbled along next to him. She didn't seem to be
feeling too wonderful herself. Her skin was oily with perspiration and she was shivering convulsively.

A piercing honk erupted behind them. They turned just in
time to see a pickup truck bearing down on them, swerving
at the last minute and barely missing them. The pickup rattled on, its rusty bumper fishtailing wildly. An angry fist jut-

ted out of the driver's window as the truck vanished into a distant cloud of dust.

Reaching the other side of the street, they staggered across the blacktop lot toward the truck. By now, pockets of towns-people had come out of their shops and offices to watch the commotion. Even the acne-faced teenager pumping diesel into The Black Mariah looked up from his work to check out the two lunatics cobbling toward the truck.

Lucas fell to his hands and knees about fifteen feet from the truck and vomited into the gravel. His back arched and heaved. There wasn't much in his stomach, so he mostly ex-pelled acids and white strings of saliva and mucus. White-hot stars of feverish hallucinations exploded in his brain as he upchucked. Like fireworks, they sparked brilliant and sharp.

Sophie clutched at Lucas's vest and tried to pull him back to his feet. But Lucas was going into convulsions of chills.

In his delirium, Lucas began to wonder what it would be like to puke his entire innards out. What a sight that would be. To see a man spew himself completely inside out. Then, through the blur of pain and sickness, Lucas gazed down at the pavement and saw that his vomit was boiling.

I been cursed . . . cursed to never stop moving . . . never in a million years . . . never stop . . .

The voice of the late Melville Benoit rang in Lucas's fevered brain as he convulsed on the ground. And in that one instant of monumental pain, Lucas realized how easy it would be to surrender to the conclusion that it was voodoo that was making him sick. That it was some evil machina-tion, some backwoods spell. But as he crawled toward the truck, fighting the raging pain, he refused to give in to the notion that it was black magic. There had to be some logical explanation for why he knew intuitively the only way to stop the pain was to get back in the truck and hit the road.

Sophie fell to her knees next to him. She doubled over, wincing and cradling her stomach like a woman having a miscarriage. Lucas tried to reach out to her, tried to help her, but he couldn't find the strength. His arms and legs felt as though hot pins of molten steel were piercing them.

Things began to go out of focus. The image of Sophie next to him began to fade and distort as if under water.

"*So—phie—get—uuuhhhh—*"

Lucas managed to crawl another ten feet and then collapsed next to the cab.

He could taste the oil and grit in his mouth, the acid rising in his throat, the coppery tang of blood. His vision was almost completely gone now. The daylight was going hazy and silver. Endorphins were taking over. Shivers of shock were flooding through him and he was going to pass out and that would be all she wrote.

Looking up through the gauzy light, the fever screaming in his brain, Lucas saw the driver's-side door.

It might as well have been a million miles away. Sealed up tight. Engine cooling. It was as if the cab were taunting him. Lucas tried to crawl closer but his legs were dead wood now. The pain was paralyzing him. He was inches away now. Close enough to smell the diesel fumes and the grimy running board. His strength was dwindling rapidly. He reached up and tried to claw open the door but his arm would not work for him.

"*—hhheh—help—!!*"

As if on cue, the driver's-side door suddenly burst open.

Lucas froze. Somebody was inside the cab, slamming the clutch home, twisting the key. The engine exploded into life. Smoke belched from the stack. The figure inside the cab reached over to the passenger door, threw it open, and then slipped away without a word.

Lucas found enough strength to cobble up the stepladder. With a yelp of pain he pulled himself into the cab. Falling across the swivel seat, Lucas slammed his throbbing foot down on the accelerator. The power plant erupted. Beside him, Sophie hurtled inside. Her mouth was open, her eyes pressed painfully shut. But no sound came out of her mouth. Only a thin string of bubbling saliva looped off her lower lip.

Lucas howled and threw the shift lever forward.

Outside the cab, the truck-stop attendant jerked back away from the truck. "Fuckin' son of a bitch! What the hell are you doin'?!!"

The Mariah blasted off with the diesel nozzle still lodged in the back. The drive axle moaned like an angry dinosaur. Exhaust plumed from the stack. The rear wheels screeched against the pavement, raising dust and gravel over thirty feet into the air as the truck lurched out of the lot. The nozzle snapped off at the base of its hose, leaving a fountain of diesel spewing from the pump and a ragged piece of hose flagging from the truck's gas tank.

Inside the cab, Lucas tried to catch his breath. For a moment, he thought he was going to burst into flames just like Melville. But as he swerved across oncoming traffic toward the entrance ramp to the highway, things began to swim back into focus. His stomach began to cool. He rolled down his window and let the air blow across his moist face.

For an instant, Lucas felt like a junkie who had just shot up with a big blast of smack. It happened so fast—the soothing, recuperative powers of the truck—that it was almost as if the drug of motion had just hit his bloodstream, sending the cooling waves of a high straight to his central nervous system.

Lucas turned to Sophie and scanned the woman's face. "You alright? Everything okay?"

Sophie was hyperventilating, wiping her mouth with the shank of her T-shirt. Her face was flushed as red as a radish. Her eyes were watering. "I dunno." She turned and gazed through the window. "Did you see . . . who it was? Who helped us?"

Lucas took a series of deep breaths. He wiped the back of his hand across his sweaty forehead and checked his side mirror. "I didn't get a good look."

"Oh, my God." Sophie swallowed back the fear and rolled down her window. They were just beginning to descend the entrance ramp toward the highway but the truck stop was still visible behind them, giving Sophie a good view of their allies.

"Who was it?" Lucas strained to see through the side mirror. In the reflection, receding into the dusty distance behind them, he could see dozens of townspeople gathering on the apron of the Stuckey's parking lot. They were pointing and gawking at the Mariah. Behind them, the attendant was madly stuffing rags into the breached pump, sopping up all the leakage.

But soon Lucas saw two other figures rushing across the short distance toward an idling school bus parked on the shoulder. It was an elderly man dressed in a faded tunic, linen pants, and sneakers, and a young teenage boy with long, unruly hair and torn denims. Lucas recognized the boy immediately.

It was Angel Figueroa.

13

Walls Exploding

"Hello?!" Delbert rapped on the edge of the iron gate a third time. "Anybody home?!"

Something was wrong. In fact, from the moment Delbert had pulled his rental car off the main highway and had descended into the marshlands, things were going to hell in a handbasket. First of all, the directions that the Point Siren Police sergeant gave him had been impossible. For nearly twenty minutes Delbert had circled a deserted nature preserve on the wrong side of the bay in search of the proper turnoff. Second of all, when he finally managed to locate the remote bayou cemetery, he'd found the front gate locked up tight as a drum.

Delbert knocked a fourth time, his knuckles turning orange from the rusty wrought-iron. "Official police business! Is anybody there?!"

Only the drone of frogs and the distant bray of Gulf pelicans were his answer.

Delbert stepped back and scanned the mouth of the cemetery. Enormous oaks and cypress trees stood guard at the gates like palsied old men, their long beards of Spanish moss softly swaying on the humid breeze. The air was pungent as a bowl of gumbo, ripe with the odors of swamp gas and rotting fish. The light was deep green from the afternoon sun filtering through the foliage. He looked up at the gates. Choked with vines and moss, the huge archway towered above the trees. Embedded into the top of the arch, a frieze of crumbling letters said: HAWKINS NOCTURNE MEMORIAL PARK.

Marching back up to the gate, Delbert rapped again and hollered, "Damn it, somebody answer me! This is official police business!"

From behind him came a voice.

"Git yer hands up, piss-ant—!!"

Delbert started to turn around when a gun barrel was shoved against his neck. The cold steel forced his head forward. Delbert dropped his tool case and yelped, "Hold it a second!"

Reaching into his jacket for his shield, Delbert turned around, but before he could produce his I.D. or even catch a glimpse of the intruder, a heavy steel-toed boot slammed against his chest, driving him backward. Delbert staggered and fell on his ass, landing by the gate. Through the dust and confusion he gazed up and saw his accoster.

She was the largest woman he had ever seen.

"Told ya to git yer hands where I can see 'em!" Bobette Dudley snapped back the cocking mechanism on her pump shotgun. It clanged menacingly. Dressed in soiled engineer overalls that strained with the girth of her rotund belly, she was a gargantuan black woman with glistening caramel skin and wild dreadlocks. African jewelry adorned every available inch of her arms and earlobes. Dark oval sunglasses covered her eyes. She stuck the shotgun in Delbert's face and inquired, "You got wax in your ears?"

"Pennington County Sheriff's Department!" Delbert waved a trembling hand in front of the shotgun. "Chief Taggart was supposed to tell y'all I was comin'."

For a moment, Bobette just stood there, regarding Delbert suspiciously. Then a huge ironic smile broke out across her portly brown face. She averted the shotgun. "Damnit, I'm

real sorry, bubba. The name's Dudley . . . Bobette Dudley.
I'm caretaker 'round this here Godforsaken place."

Bobette reached down and gave Delbert a hand. It was like
being helped up by a forklift. Delbert staggered to his feet
and brushed himself off, his face hot with embarrassment.

Then he followed the fat woman through the entrance.

"This is the crypt?" Delbert was standing on the threshold
of a miniature temple, hewn from cracked marble, disguised
by weeds and shadows.

"Yessir . . ." Bobette nodded and strode past the entrance
of the sarcophagus. She approached a smaller side door partially obscured by a spray of weeds off to the left. She fished
in her pockets for the proper key. " . . . Hotel DeGeaux."

Delbert stood behind the woman and motioned at the mausoleum. "Get many cases of people breakin' into places like
this?"

"Not hardly."

"How many times has something like this happened?"

The woman paused and pondered the question. "Since I
been working here—just the one time back in eighty-three."

"You're kidding."

"Swear to Christ it's the truth."

Delbert glanced around the periphery of the tomb.
Shrouded from the late afternoon sun, the place was colored
with perpetual gloom. Giant, naked, arthritic cypress trees
grew up between the decaying mausolea, their bare branches
clutching at the sky. Vines and weeds whiskered the grave
markers. Odd statuary of animals rose up here and there on
pedestals, their marble faces chipped, their appendages withered away, their torsos stained and pocked with age and sea
breezes. Delbert turned back to the fat woman. "Can you tell
me how it happened?"

The woman continued fishing through her keys. "Nothin'
much to tell. One evenin' I left the cemetery 'bout midnight.
Came back the next morning and the DeGeaux crypt was
standing wide open."

Delbert glanced up at the roof of the mausoleum. "How
easy is it to break into this place?"

"Pretty dirn easy." Bobette finally found the appropriate key. "Here it is!" She turned and inserted it into a deadbolt just above the iron doorknob. Then, she opened the DeGeaux sarcophagus. "Watch your step, Deputy. Ain't real bright and cheery inside."

The caretaker vanished inside the mausoleum.

Delbert froze in his tracks. His palms had gone all clammy. His stomach had tightened into a knot of steel cable. And he stood on the threshold of that crypt for several moments, thinking about the wisdom of becoming an investigator. Maybe he was pushing it. Maybe he was taking this detective thing a little too fast. The health insurance and dental benefits weren't all that great. You got less vacation time and the hours were horrible. Maybe he should consider some of the other fine career paths open to a young man in law enforcement. Traffic guard, for example, could be a very rewarding—

"You gonna stand out there all day?" Bobette's voice blurted out from the darkness of the crypt.

Delbert gathered himself. He thought of his father, he thought of his old man's pride in having a son in law enforcement, and Delbert thought of the scripture. *Thou art with me . . . thy rod and thy staff . . . they comfort me . . .*

Taking a deep breath, clutching the handle of his evidence case, Delbert went inside.

The first thing that struck him was the complete and utter blackness. The tomb was immersed in pitch. And if it wasn't for the thin shaft of daylight slicing through the airless crypt from the half-ajar door, Delbert would have been blind as a bat. Thankfully, there was enough light to see a patch of dusty granite floor and a pair of crumbling Doric columns bisecting the center of the room.

Delbert took a few tentative steps. His shoes crunched against a fine layer of dust and gravel. The place smelled of ancient, dry stone and something else, something like the odor of very old spices.

"Over here." The woman's voice wheezed through the darkness. There was a click and a sudden burst of light from Bobette's flashlight ignited the room.

The walls exploded with symbols and words. Hastily

scrawled in blackish tar, the graffiti had dried indelibly over the years. Some of the words were faded in patches where Bobette had rubbed the moist stone with cleaning solvent but many were still legible. Bizarre cants such as *Accon Dri, Dalimus, Zizumuth*, and *e yuhl* were joined by crude penta-grams and splashes of cryptic Arabic letters. Although none of it made any sense to Delbert, it made his skin crawl nonetheless.

He moved over to one wall and took a closer look. He fumbled with the latch of his evidence case. He figured he probably should take some pictures, but when he brushed a fingertip across one of the letters, his mouth went dry.

"Is that dried blood?"

"Yessir," Bobette replied. "Mobile police said it was prob-ably sheep or cow. Figured it was some smart-ass kids tryin' to scare the locals."

Following the beam of the flashlight, Delbert joined Bo-bette in the small alcove at the end of the main chamber. The woman swept the light around the tomb. "Little bastards van-dalized everything, took all sorts of booty. Family heirlooms, markers, bronze statuary."

Delbert looked over the woman's shoulder, beyond the al-cove, into a narrow tunnel housing individual compartments. "Were any of the bodies disturbed?"

"No, sir. Seems like they just went after goodies in this outer room."

Heart racing, Delbert gazed into the antechamber. Nestled in the compartments like objects from an archaic museum display were individual coffins. At the end of the passage, embedded in the far wall and lodged in the largest berth, was the most ornate coffin. Covered with a patina of age, it was a gray monstrosity, every inch of it blanketed with religious carvings and symbols.

"Wait a minute—" For just a brief instant, Delbert saw something off-kilter at the end of the passage. It made his sphincter muscles contract. "Shine your light over there, at the last coffin—"

The big woman obliged. Her light swept past the other

coffins and landed on the gray king. For a moment Delbert couldn't tell what was wrong.

Then, he saw it.

"Looks like the top's been moved."

Bobette stared at the coffin for a moment, grunted, and said something Delbert couldn't quite understand. Then she strode down the passage toward the last berth. Delbert swallowed a mouthful of fear and followed.

They reached the end of the passage and Bobette shone her light down upon the biggest casket embedded in the wall. The top was slightly ajar. At the uppermost corner, where the lid had separated a couple of inches from the body of the coffin, there was a fresh series of scratches suggesting the lid had been forced open.

"This here is Maurice DeGeaux's box," Bobette grumbled. "Better check the interment."

She shoved the lid back and revealed the remains of Maurice Michel DeGeaux.

Delbert dropped his evidence case. On impact, the bag snapped open and spilled its contents across the floor. The magnifying glass shattered. Latent fingerprint powder blossomed across the stone. Film cartridges burst open. The camera shattered and empty pill vials rolled in all directions.

"Sweet Jesus—" Bobette was murmuring, holding her hands to her mouth, gawking down at the body.

Backing away through the fallen items, Delbert found he had no power over his own movement. His body was numb with terror. He could only think about getting out of this horrible room. He could only think about escaping this terrible place. But he could not move. He could not tear his eyes away from the contents of the coffin.

There were two problems.

First, in his investigative studies, Delbert had learned the way most corpses decay is through a process called adipocere formation. Over the years, the skin goes away and the remaining tissue changes to a soaplike texture from all the natural sodium and moisture. The result is a grayish-white film that makes the body look like it's made of wax.

This particular body had decayed differently.

The remains of Maurice Michel DeGeaux had shrunken into a little brown doll. His face, a leathery caricature of a man at peace, poked out from the oversized collar of his pin-striped burial suit. His arms, shrivelled into a pair of emaciated twigs, protruded from their billowing suit sleeves and pretzeled across his chest.

Bobette shone her light a little closer. Her words were clipped, taut. "The seal in this place . . . it . . . keeps 'em well preserved."

Delbert couldn't hear a thing she was saying. He was too busy pondering the second problem with the corpse. He was too busy trying to make his legs work so he could get the hell out of this horrible place. He felt the bile sizzling in the back of his throat. The Coney dog he had gobbled at lunch was coming back to haunt him. Trembling fingers found his lips and covered them.

Then Delbert turned and staggered out of the crypt.

Bobette lingered by the open coffin for one last moment, turning things over in her mind. She just couldn't figure why kids would do something like this. Sure, the DeGeauxs never won any popularity contests among the black folks in the area. Sure, old man DeGeaux was a notorious bigot. But to desecrate a grave like this . . .

"Shameful is what it is . . ."

Before closing the lid, Bobette marvelled one last time at the way the right hand had been snipped off, leaving a surgically clean stump.

Must have been a goddamn big set of pruning shears.

14

Article
of Faith

"—come in—*ffffzzzhht*—the channel won't—*fffssshhtt*—*zzzht-zzzht-zzt-zt*—!!"

Sophie was trying every trick in the book to tune in the garbled broadcasts coming over their radio. Nothing was working. She grabbed the handset and pressed the switch. "Break one-nine for Angel . . .can you hear me one-nine? Come back."

A splash of static filled the cab. Somewhere beneath the noise, the voice of the Mexican boy crackled through in fits and bursts. "—*fffssstt-fht-fht*—trying—*shhhhwwwwhht*—ya'll on the—*ffffffffssshhht*—"

"Try channel thirteen," Lucas said, craning his neck to see the bus in his side mirror.

Sophie nodded and shouted into the mike. "Breaking for Angel Figueroa—come back on channel thirteen! Repeat—come back on channel thirteen!"

"—*ssssshhhffftftttffft*—can't get—*ffffhht*—*fht-fht*—"

"Wait a minute." Sophie had an idea. She dug in the glove box and found a marker pen. Then she reached under the jump seat and found a bundle of old logbooks and maps. She tore a cardboard cover off one of the books and wrote in big letters C-H-A-N-N-E-L T-H-I-R-T-E-E-N. Then she handed it to Lucas. "Show 'em that."

Lucas held the placard out his window.

A moment later Angel's voice came over the air. "Hello? Th'ophie—can—hear me?"

Sophie pressed the call switch. "Receiving poorly. Speak a little louder, Amigo."

"How 'bout now?!"

"Ten-Roger, Angel. That's better. How in the world did you find us?"

After another spray of static: "You told me you were headed to St. Louis. My Uncle Flaco—he drove a bu'th for the element'ry thcool for a long time—he know the highway like the back of hi'th hand. Been followin' you for over a hundred mile' now. Over."

Sophie glanced over at Lucas, who had his eyes glued to the road. Sophie could tell the big man was still recovering from the sudden hot spell. His teeth were clenched, the specks of sickness still clinging to the corners of his mouth. His temples pulsed with nervous tension. His ebony skin was dry and caked with grit. But beneath the frazzled exterior, Lucas's strength still amazed Sophie. He was still as stubborn as an ox, with his ham-hock forearm gripping the stick. Unfortunately, at the present moment his strength was tempered with fear. And it was that fear which bothered Sophie more than anything else.

She turned back to the microphone. "But Angel—why didn't you try to reach us earlier on your CB?"

The voice returned. "Been tryin' to get ya'll for hours now—but our thee'-bee radio don't work too well—and I couldn't figure out what channel to talk on—*over*."

There was another wash of static. Sophie glanced out Lucas's window at his side mirror. She could see the school bus hovering a couple of car lengths back. Pocked with primer spots and patches of rust, the ancient yellow bus was getting buffeted by the wind, weaving and shimmying back and forth as it trailed the Mariah. Sophie found it hard to believe that she hadn't noticed the bizarre modified bus rattling after them before now. Of course, over the past couple of hours, she *did* have other things on her mind.

She pressed the call switch. "Angel, just why exactly did you follow us in the first place?"

There was a long stretch of sputtering interference. Sophie reached up and adjusted the squelch. Brief snippets of frenzied voices speaking in Spanish crackled through the speaker. Finally, the boy's voice returned. "Lemme introdu'th my Uncle Flaco—hold on a minute—"

There was a rustling sound as the microphone was passed from one person to another. Then, after another squirt of interference, the soft wheeze of the old man came over the air. *"Buenos días,* my friends. My name's Flaco Figueroa and I'm the boy's uncle. I am sorry about the—*sshsssshhhhh-fht-fffffffht—"*

Static drowned the old man's voice. Sophie pressed the call switch. "Mr. Figueroa? Could you repeat that last break? Lost you for a second there."

Through the static: "I said I am sorry about the awkward—the awkward way we are meeting—it's just that—when my nephew told me what had happened I knew I had to help somehow."

Sophie thought about it for a moment, then thumbed the switch. "Not sure I understand what you mean."

"It is hard to explain—in simple terms."

"Meaning what?"

"The situation—which we find ourselves in."

A shiver crept over Sophie's back. "Just what situation is that?"

Flaco's voice returned. "You must forgive me if I do not communicate in English well enough—after close to thirty years in this country I've—*ffffhhht-fht-sshhhhhfff—"*

Another burst of static obliterated the old man's voice. Sophie glanced over at Lucas. He was frowning, fidgeting in his seat. It seemed this whole conversation was making Lucas very uncomfortable. Lucas grabbed the handset from Sophie and said into the mike, "Mr. Figueroa, this is Lucas Hyde. My partner and I appreciate your help back there. We really do. But we're okay now. Believe me, we're fine."

Static. Then, the old man's voice croaked through the speaker. "Tell me what happened back there, Mr. Hyde."

"Outside the pawn shop? Nothing. We got a little sick—too many little white pills, you know—too much coffee."

Through the speaker came another burst of static and voices speaking in Spanish. Then, the old man's voice said, "My nephew says a boy burned to death."

Lucas answered quickly. "Yeah, a freak accident."

"It was an accident?"

"That's correct."

"There was not a curse involved?"

Sophie watched Lucas mull it over. The big man was getting progressively twitchy, restless. Clenching and unclenching his meaty fists around the wheel, he tried to control his temper. "Okay, here's the deal—we're not gonna talk about this crap on the air anymore. I came real close to getting busted once today and I don't need any more smokies listening in and thinking that we're a convoy of psychos endangering the American roadways. Comprendo?"

After another staticky pause, the old man's voice sputtered through the speaker again. His tone had changed, become haunted. "Mr. Hyde, I do not want to get you in trouble. I am a simple man. Not too smart. But I love my Saviour—"

Lucas cut in. "I didn't mean to offend you, amigo. I'm just saying—"

Sophie reached over and grabbed the handset. Her heart was racing. She felt deep down in her belly that they should listen to what this old man had to say. They should listen carefully. "Mr. Figueroa, this is Sophie Cohen. Go ahead and speak your piece. Go ahead—we're listening."

Lucas shot her an angry glance and was about to say something when the old man's voice returned.

"Best way for me to explain, is to tell you why I am here . . ."

Sophie pressed the switch. "Fair enough."

"I had a vision last night. I believe it was from God, a sign you might say—*fffffffht-fht-fht*—*ssshhhh*—when my nephew showed up on my doorstep this morning, I knew I was right . . ."

"You're breaking up a little bit," Sophie said into the mike, her mouth dry with panic. "You said you had a vision . . .what does that have to do with us?"

Lucas slammed his fist against the dash. "Fuck this shit, Sophie—you're smarter than this!"

"Lucas, please . . . !"

Through the static: "—cannot tell you why for certain, but I believe it was a warning—I believe it was a warning meant for all of us."

Into the mike Sophie said, "What was the vision?"

"The vision was a hand."

Sophie's throat constricted. "A hand—?"

"A black hand," the voice said, before being consumed again by static.

Lucas was about to say something when Sophie raised her hand to shush him. Then she said into the mike, "You saw—a black hand?"

Static was saturating the air. The back of Sophie's scalp was prickling. She could hear her heart thumping in her ears. And in that brief instance of uncertain terror, as the wash of static filled the cab, Sophie flashed back to her days in San Francisco with Milo Klein.

Open thine eyes, the mysterious rabbi used to say to her when he got a little inebriated, *and you'll see wondrous and frightening things just beneath the surface of this pitiful little world.*

Sophie had first met Milo in 1982 at a health-food market. Though not traditional kosher fare, the macrobiotic ingredients had appealed to the hipster rabbi's sense of postmodernism. No blood, no winged insects, no creeping things, only sweet, sweet roughage. Sophie instantly befriended the man. She began hanging out at his funky loft apartment on Russian Hill, spending long drunken evenings talking metaphysics with the man. There was never anything sexual between the two friends. In fact, Sophie had always suspected Milo was gay; but it didn't matter. The compact little rabbi with the Woody Allen glasses and Jerry Garcia hair had always fascinated Sophie.

Most important, Milo was an avid student of the Kabbala—the esoteric system of Judaic mysticism. He would talk endlessly about the Kabbala's rich tapestry of magic, the wonderful wisdom and self-actualizing power in its texts. He would spout dizzying scripture from the Zohar, the ancient books, on subjects such as ghosts and reincarnation and psychic energy. But the most frightening part of the Kabbala was the complex demonology which Milo had never quite elaborated on . . .

Open thine eyes, lady . . .

The static suddenly broke and snapped Sophie out of her memories.

"In Mexico," the old man's voice continued through the speaker, "Gypsies used to talk of Los Mano de la Maldad—The Hand of Evil. It is a very old story. Very old. I learned it as a muchacho—*sssssshhhh-fffht-ffht*—"

Sophie frantically tweaked the knobs on the CB. "Flaco? Flaco, can you copy me?!"

Through the hiss, Flaco's voice said, "I am here."

"See, the thing is . . ." Sophie was measuring her words carefully now. "Lucas and I found a charm—a little trinket—it was near the dead man's car." Sophie swallowed back her panic. "It was—well, it's a—it's sort of a—"

Lucas grabbed the mike. "It's a motherfucking black hand! Big fucking deal! Doesn't mean a fucking thing!"

Over the air, static squirted and muffled voices spoke in Spanish.

Lucas shook his head and said into the mike, "Okay, kids, I can see where this thing is going and it's bullshit."

He dug in his vest pocket, found the wadded handkerchief, and rooted out the shrunken hand. Then he angrily rolled down his window. The furious rush of air invaded the cab with the odors of hot tar and manure.

Sophie watched him. "What are you doing, Lucas?"

"Something I should have done hours ago."

He tossed the hand out the window.

Sitting on a footstool at the front of the bus, Flaco was about to press the button on the CB mike when he saw the tiny object hurtling out of Lucas's window and hitting the draft of wind alongside the truck. The moment the hand struck the pavement, it burst into flames.

Now the little fireball was bouncing toward the school bus.

"*Mucho ojo!* Look out!" Flaco cried at Angel, who was sitting only inches away, hands gripped tightly on the steering wheel.

Angel swerved. The flaming hand struck the bus's front grille and bounded up the hood toward the windshield. Flaco shielded his eyes as if the thing might penetrate the glass. Instead, the hand struck the windshield and burst like a fragmentation bomb, sending magnesium-bright tendrils exploding outward. For a brief instant, the tendrils formed the digits of a ghostly fire hand. The hand from Flaco's visions. Then, in a flash of blinding white light, the thing imploded out of existence.

"*Mi dios, mi dios*, sweet Christ." Flaco felt his chest heaving and tightening, his lungs burning. But he struggled to ignore the pain and fear and the doubt. He was not going to let the evil get the better of him. Too much riding on this thing.

Angel held the bus steady. "Uncle! You alright?!"

"Fine, I'm fine—just shook me a bit, that's all." Flaco sat back in his seat, brushing the gray hair from his eyes and wiping his brow. He was wearing his favorite denim shirt with the needlepoint lassos that Luisa had sewn on the breast pockets years ago. It was his lucky shirt. He figured he would need it today.

"What the hell wa' that?" Angel asked, struggling to keep up with the barreling semi truck. Long hair pulled back in a ponytail, the boy's lopsided face was set in a stern, determined expression. Although it was his uncle's idea to follow The Black Mariah across two state lines, the boy was becoming exceedingly worried about his two trucker friends. "Wha' happened?"

"I don't know but I have a pretty good idea." Flaco fiddled with the CB mike. "Hello, Mr. Hyde. Can you hear me?"

Lucas's voice came through the faulty speaker. "—copy you—the evil hand is history—"

"What did you just do, Mr. Hyde?"

Flaco waited for a reply.

Through the crackling static came Lucas's voice. "File it under road kill—"

Flaco rubbed his grizzled chin before speaking into the mike. "I'm not sure that was the best thing to do."

"—sshhhhhh—ffffht—it's all over, old man. It's all over now. We really appreciate you helping us out back there but now it's over."

Pressing the button, Flaco said, "I don't think it is over, Mr. Hyde."

Through the faulty speaker, Lucas's voice sounded like the rumblings of a caged animal. "I'm sorry, Amigo—I don't mean to offend you but I just don't buy all this mumbo jumbo—sssshhhh-ffffht-fht—never have and never will—"

"Wish I could explain it better," Flaco said into the mike, "but it's . . . cosa de fe—how do you say it in English?" Flaco cupped his hand over the mike. "Angel, what is the phrase in English?"

After a long moment, Angel told him, "Article of faith."

Flaco continued into the mike. "It's an article of faith, Mr. Hyde. You just have to believe me. It was in my vision. There is something important happening here."

Through the speaker: "—only thing that's happening now is you're giving my partner the willies."

"Mr. Hyde, do you believe in God?"

"This conversation is getting old."

"Do you believe in fate?"

A moment later, the trucker's voice said, "I believe that people can talk themselves into a lot of things—"

Flaco pressed the button. "I believe it is no coincidence that my nephew and I are here today . . . that these things have happened . . . that we are struggling together on this road. Do you understand what I am saying?"

There was no reply.

"Mr. Hyde? Can you hear me?"

Static crashed over the air. Riotous interference, sizzling through the hiss, popping and crackling convulsively. Other voices bled through. Fragments of other conversations, swirling and oscillating like a mad aria.

"Mr. Hyde?"

Angel hollered over the noise, "Try adjusting the squelch—"

Flaco fiddled with the knobs but the interference was swelling. A sudden chill crept up the old man's spine. There was another sound emerging through the cacophony, a razor-sharp sound, distant at first, but wavering in and out of the din. It sounded like an animal howling.

Flaco smacked the side of the radio. "Come in, Mr. Hyde! Please come in!"

Through the noise, the sound of Sophie's voice came back in fits and starts. "—aco—*sssshpt*—hear me? It's Sophie— can you—*fffht*—hear me?"

"I can hear you, Sophie."

"—*fffffht*—*fffht-fht-ft*—your visions tell you? Repeat— what do your visions tell you?"

Before answering, Flaco glanced over at his nephew. The boy held a vise grip on the steering wheel, his deformed face earnestly trained on the road. He was such a noble soul. Smart as a whip. And he always stood by his crazy old uncle, through thick and thin, always there when Flaco needed him. For a brief instant, Flaco felt guilty for pulling the boy into this insane dance.

But then Flaco realized it was meant to be, just as it was meant to be that the two of them were hovering two car lengths behind this massive black truck.

Flaco squeezed the call switch. "In all honesty I don't know for sure what they mean."

"What is your best guess?"

It was a good question and Flaco felt that familiar wave of dread wash over him, the cold sweat on the back of his neck, the sick, burning sensation in the pit of his stomach. It was a question he had avoided for most of his adult life. But now, as the strange clockwork of destiny began to engage around him, he realized he must face it. Pressing the switch, he said, "Give me a moment, Miss Cohen."

It was time.

It was time to look at the words again.

Flaco rose from his stool. "Hold her steady, Ángel. I need to check something in the back."

On wobbly arthritic knees, the old man hobbled back to his shrine. He knelt down by the base of the altar. Hewn from plywood and chicken wire, the foundation was covered with green felt and bordered by shoe boxes. Each box was carefully sealed with ancient, yellowed masking tape. Each held memorabilia that was sacred to Flaco.

He opened the oldest box.

At first, all he could see was yellowed newsprint. It was wrapped around everything, held together with old cellophane tape the color of chicken gravy. When Flaco pulled the paper apart it crumbled in his hands.

Inside were secret things. A white toucan feather his Uncle Ramon had given him on his thirteenth birthday. Faded photographs of his mother, his aunt, his grandmother. A tarnished copper skeleton on horseback, a gift from his father on the occasion of *El día de los muertos*. An old length of chipped rosary beads. And at the bottom, wrapped in crinkled tissue paper, the item he dreaded opening most of all— the blackened husk of a small pocket-sized Bible.

Flaco gently lifted the charred Bible from its nest, held the brittle volume tenderly, and remembered what had happened so many years ago . . .

The fire had started in the kitchen. Probably set off by embers lingering in the belly of the stove, it spread quickly through the tiny cabin.

Flaco was the first to smell the smoke. He stirred from his bed and glanced across his tiny room. There was a bruise of orange light falling across his doorway, a veil of haze hanging in the air. Flaco could hear the faint crackle of flames coming from somewhere nearby.

At first, the ten-year-old boy was paralyzed. Panic filled his veins like ice water and he couldn't find his voice, couldn't move his legs, couldn't budge. His blanket felt like it was made of stone. He lay there for several agonizing moments, thinking he was going to die, thinking the devil was keeping him frozen and there was nothing he could do about it.

Then he thought about the rest of his family. His father and mother sleeping down the hall, his sister in the next room. He thought about never seeing them again.

He found the strength to move.

Springing from his bed, Flaco pulled on his pants and ran out of his room. The heat punched him in the chest as he entered the kitchen. Flames were licking up the timber walls like brilliant snakes. Smoke was roiling across the ceiling. He grabbed a cloth from the basin, held it to his mouth, and ran out of there like a shot.

In a flash he got everybody out of the cabin. His father took the pony into town for help and the rest of the family gathered on the hill next to the house to watch their belongings go up in smoke. The neighbors assembled with lanterns and blankets. His mother cried. His sister just stood there, silent, mouthing a prayer.

Then the feeling came.

Flaco had never experienced anything like it before. It struck him like an icicle through his brain. Something important was still in the house, something in the heart of the rising inferno. It was as if columns of smoke and shadows were rising up and coalescing and curling around the old pine shelf in the corner of his room.

His Bible!

Tearing himself away from his mother, Flaco ran back into the cabin. The flames were everywhere. He held the cloth over his mouth and held his breath. The horrible light and heat weighed him down but he kept going, toward his room, toward the corner shelf, toward his Bible.

He pulled the book from the flames and rushed back out into the night. He collapsed in the cool grass of the hillside, patted out the cinders along the book's binding, and began to cry. It was too late. The Bible had been consumed. It was charred black and crisp as dead leaves.

But when he opened it, he let out a tiny gasp.

Many of the pages were fused together from the heat. Other pages were completely burned away. But in the final section, The Revelation to John, *one page was untouched by the fire. One page was still pristine and perfect. One page . . .*

The page on the Beast . . .

"Who is like the Beast, and who can fight against it?" Flaco was murmuring to himself.

"Uncle?" It was Angel's voice, echoing down the length of the bus and piercing the rumble. Flaco could feel the boy's worried gaze burning the back of his neck. "Wha' the matter, Uncle?"

"Nothing." Flaco slipped the scorched Bible into his shirt pocket, rose, and struggled back to the cab. He took a seat on his stool and rubbed his hand through his hair. "Just an old man shuffling through memories."

"Wha' going on, Uncle?" Angel asked. "There' th'omething that i'th bothering you."

"It's nothing," Flaco replied.

Angel thought about it for a moment. "That thing Luca'th destroyed—that hand—it was powerful . . ."

"I wish I knew—"

At that moment, the crackling sound of Sophie's voice came through the CB speaker. "Hello? Mr. Figueroa? Are you there? Come back, please."

Flaco picked up the mike. "Please, call me Flaco."

Through the speaker, Sophie's voice returned, papery-thin and tense. "Okay, Flaco . . . but you didn't answer my question. What do these visions mean to you?"

Flaco pressed the button and started to answer but stopped short of speaking.

The sound had returned, that razor-sharp sound riding the airwaves just beneath the riot of static. It sounded like the falsetto howl of a wounded predator.

Gooseflesh spread across Flaco's arms and his legs and the back of his neck. He tried to speak but the chills were gripping him and making the words stick in his throat. He had realized that the sound—the awful caterwauling wail—was not coming over the airwaves after all.

It was within his own mind. The same sound that had

haunted his dreams as a boy. The same inhuman wail that had accompanied his shadowy visions. He knew what it was now.

The sound of the Beast . . . coming after them.

Taking a labored breath, squeezing the switch with his palsied fingers, Flaco said gravely, "My friends, things are not what you would call great . . ."

15

Canticle

"SAVAGES!!!"

"Madam, stop!"

She flailed the reacher across the seat backs and brought down another jar. Glass shattered against the side door. Gouts of ox blood and dandelion essence spattered the carpet. The limousine swerved.

"Madam, your throat—!!"

"SSSSSSaaahvuh . . . sssssssavages!!"

"Please calm down!" Through the partition window the chauffeur was trying to get the reacher away from her with one hand and hold the limo steady with the other. "Madam, please . . . !"

"Dirty . . . filthy . . . !!"

"Please, you're going to—!!"

Another tumbler of animal organs collapsed under the fury of her spring-loaded arm. Gore streaked the ceiling and splattered the inside of the windows.

"They've—destroyed—the—!" She couldn't bring herself to even say it. Only minutes earlier, she had seen the Negro toss the talisman from the window of the truck. It had hit the pavement and burned up under the weight of its own incandescence. The sacred talisman. Destroyed on this filthy high-way. It was almost more than Vanessa could bear. It was like someone had injected a cattle prod down the core of her frozen spine and filled her with electric rage.

"—the talisman." Eric completed her thought from the front seat, his voice weak, hoarse, filled with gravel. "Yes, I saw it, I saw it happen . . ."

"Eric . . . the savages . . . destroyed . . . my talisman." Vanessa's throat was seizing up on her. Her vocal chords could not withstand much more punishment.

"Madam, you must try to calm down."

"THEY—WILL—PAY!!"

"Madam—!"

Vanessa swallowed acid. Her jaw felt as if metal bolts were being driven into the bone. Tightening, tightening, until the pain was seeping into her thoughts like ink clouding the icy water of her rage. She tried to breathe normally. She tried to think. Think.

A moment later, Vanessa clutched at her CompuTalk key-pad. Palsied fingers jigged furiously over the keys. The pain was swirling through her brain but the rage kept her focused.

ERIC—PAY—ATTENTION—

Through the window Vanessa could see the chauffeur grow still. He kept one eye on the road and one eye on the monitor.

Vanessa continued typing.

DO—NOT—LOSE—THEM—REPEAT—DO—NOT—LOSE—THEM—NO—MATTER—WHAT!!!

Eric nodded.

Vanessa thought for a moment. Icy fire shot up her good wrist. Daggers of pain sliced the good side of her face. But the rest of her remained inanimate, motionless as lead. A whisper of gray hair dangled in her face but she didn't even feel it. The chauffeur said something else but Vanessa couldn't hear him. The alchemy was ancient. Pain into hate, hate into rite, rite into vengeance.

"Madam—?"

Vanessa didn't answer. She was scanning the length of the rear seats with her one good eye, taking inventory, assessing the damages. In the heat of her tirade she had destroyed most of her magic fumes and organs. But there were plenty of supplies left. At her feet sat a bucket of fingers, fingers of all shapes and sizes, mummified in nitrate. Beside the bucket, a shoe box contained a large desecrated crucifix. The tiny eyes of the Christ figure had been scooped out and blackened with jet.

"Madam, what are we—?"

Eric's voice was a million miles away now. Vanessa's mind was swimming in hate. She clawed at the reacher and pulled herself over to the opera glasses. She peered through the glasses and found the big black truck in the distance ahead of them, about a half a mile away. The school bus was hugging its wake. Coursing through the heat rays, two ships, crawling with vermin . . .

The black truck driver . . . behind the wheel . . . his coarse, rough, black face . . . skin like caramel . . .

. . . *the odor of bougainvillea . . . the chill of dew on Vanessa's bare feet . . . heart pumping . . . syncopated with church bells . . . chiming midnight, midnight, midnight . . .*

Vanessa couldn't breathe. Something was carrying her away on a tide of emotion. A memory. Flooding back on a wave of sights and sounds and scents . . . pealing like a church bell . . . a horrible canticle . . .

Running . . .

She was able to run again . . .

Running through the shadows of the town square . . . running in her bare feet . . . hand in hand with Thomas. They knew it was midnight because the bell was ringing. They knew they were being naughty.

Thomas led her toward the deserted bandstand. "Now be real quiet."

She giggled and raced up the steps with him. They tiptoed across the floorboards. Thomas took her in his arms and they danced, the faint echoes of the band lilting in their memories. The fiddle, the coronet, the cymbal keeping three-quarter time.

They danced the old-fashioned waltz.

The boards felt cool on Vanessa's bare feet. Her face was blushing. Thirteen years old and she had never even talked to a Negro boy before. Let alone danced with one. But Thomas was different than the others. He was kind and smart and funny and he had helped Vanessa with her broken bicycle chain last week near Abbotts Landing.

"Shush." Thomas put his fingers to her lips and pulled Vanessa tighter. They fell against the trestle of bougainvilleas. The aroma of flowers and the warmth of his touch sent shivers over Vanessa. The boy had such lovely eyelashes. Skin the color of caramel butter.

She kissed him squarely on the lips. "I love you, Thomas Nelson!"

Then she giggled and ran.

He chased her. Together they ran through the dark streets, giggling with desire and shame of blissful confusion. Down by the mill house. Up Tassiter Hill. Across the bean field and down Vanessa's own street.

Eventually they came to the farm. The DeGeaux farm. Circled around to the old dairy barn out back. Dark inside. Dark and quiet and empty.

They went inside. Found a soft secret place. A moment of silence.

Something wrong.

Fear shrieked in Vanessa's head all of a sudden. She tried to speak but the words were like razors in her throat, razors stabbing, suffocating . . .

"Madam—!?!"

From the front of the limousine the chauffeur's frantic voice pierced the memory.

"Madam, what are we going to do!?!"

Vanessa gasped for air. She gripped the reacher until her jagged psoriatic fingernails drew blood. The hate was everywhere now. It cocooned her like a sheath of magnesium-bright poison. It made her brain blaze with voices. The bellowing voices of dark gods.

"Madam, please answer me," the chauffeur pleaded, "what are we going to do!?!"

Vanessa pulled her leaden form back to the CompuTalk pad and furiously pecked out her answer. The screen in front seemed to glow a brighter shade of yellow.

MAKE—THEM—PAY—

16

No Cure

"Huge chunk of the right posterior cerebellum missing."

"Sounds like Kennedy."

"Bobby or Jack?"

"Jack."

"Correct."

"Jesus—that was real tough. Why don't you gimme something challenging?" The coroner's assistant with the blond flattop was getting bored. He was sitting at a card table in a basement corridor of the Pennington County Morgue. The table was cluttered with empty coffee cups, playing cards, and stray autopsy notes. His pal, another assistant with a scraggly beard and thinning hair, was leaning against a nearby waste can, playing with a rubber glove and quizzing his pal on celebrity autopsy lore.

"Alright, for twenty points, here's a bonus question," Scraggly Beard said, snapping the glove like a birthday balloon. "Six-centimeter bruise on the left ankle, superficial lesions on the posterior of both thighs."

Flattop frowned. "Gimme more. Histology, toxicology, something else."

"Alright, blood alcohol content was one-eight. That's it. That's all you get."

Fiddling with the ace of diamonds, Flattop thought about it for a moment and snapped his fingers. "Elvis!"

"Wrong!" Scraggly Beard let the rubber gloves sail across the hallway. "It was Harlan Steagall."

"Who the hell is Harlan Steagall?"

"Town drunk. Drowned last spring up at the barrens."

"Fuck you." Flattop went back to his solitaire game. He had been sitting there playing cards with himself and chatting with his colleague for over twenty minutes, ever since Dr. Gibbons had sequestered himself behind the metal door of the central autopsy room a few feet away. As an assistant doing his residency at the Pennington Medical Examiner's Office, Flattop knew all too well the eccentricities of his boss. Gruff and demanding, Gibbons worked alone. And it was only when he needed help flipping a bloated subject over or moving stainless-steel vats of human organs that he called in reinforcements.

Scraggly Beard pulled on his whiskers and nodded toward the metal door. "Who's the customer today?"

"Burn victim. Late twenties, male. Happened earlier this morning on the interstate."

"Sounds boring."

Flattop nodded. "Yeah, well, the old man's been in there long enough to do the stiff's tax returns."

Scraggly Beard shrugged. "At least he's not busting our balls, know what I mean?"

"Okay, it's my turn. Lay one on me."

"Alright, for ten points," Flattop grinned. "Submucosal hemorrhaging, colon all fucked up, discolored, marked congestion in the upper tract."

"Stomach volume?"

" 'Bout fifteen to twenty cc's. Pretty empty."

Scraggly Beard pondered for a moment. "Esophagus?"

"Pretty messed up."

Scraggly Beard broke into song. "Goodbye, Norma Jean . . ."

Just then, the sound of a metal latch opening echoed down

the corridor. Both assistants glanced up. A figure was coming through the glass door at the far end of the hallway. A big man in uniform with a ruddy sun-tanned face. Flattop recognized him immediately and whispered, "Oh, Jesus—look who's here."

"Old Iron Balls," Scraggly Beard whispered.

"I feel safer already," Flattop added.

Scraggly Beard waved at the approaching lawman. "Sheriff Baum! How the heck are you?"

The sheriff walked up to them and stuck a gob of chew behind his lip. "Howdy, boys."

Flattop shoved his cards aside and smiled. "What brings you to our humble little lab this afternoon?"

"Nothing much," the sheriff said. "Doc Gibbons called a few minutes ago. Said I should take a look at the Benoit stiff."

The two assistants looked at each other. Flattop motioned at the metal door. "The crispy critter from the highway?"

"The very same."

"That right?"

"Yes, sir," Baum said, then walked over to the metal door, opened it, and turned back to the assistants. "Now, if you boys will excuse me—"

The sheriff closed the door behind him, leaving Flattop and Scraggly Beard standing in the fluorescent corridor with their hands on their hips, wondering just why the hell Old Iron Balls had to see some garden-variety burn victim.

Lucas jammed the shift lever forward and tweaked the gas pedal. The Black Mariah crossed the center line and roared into the fast lane. There was a slow-moving mobile home on the right and Lucas couldn't wait to get around it. Next to him, Sophie was staring at the CB radio as if it held all the secrets to the universe.

Lucas grabbed the mike from Sophie and barked into it, "Jesus Christ—you guys are telling us we picked up some kinda curse by touching a dead hand . . . and now we're not only doomed to never stop moving—but now you're telling me you've been seeing visions about this thing your whole life?"

After a long staticky pause, the old man's voice crackled through the speaker, "More or less."

Lucas slammed his meaty palm on the dash, spitting his words into the mike like bullets. "Been in the trucking business for almost two decades, folks! Heard every cockamamie tall tale in the world . . . but this takes the motherfuckin' cake!"

Sophie was saying something, under her breath, so softly that at first Lucas didn't even hear it.

"What was that?" Lucas glared at her.

"Pull over."

"What?"

"Pull the truck over." She looked up at him and there was real terror in her eyes. It put a fine layer of gooseflesh on Lucas's arms.

"Whattya mean—pull over?"

"Just do it, Lucas."

"No."

"Why not?"

Lucas shook his head. "Don't need to."

"You're as scared as I am."

"Fuck you."

"Pull over, Lucas."

All at once Lucas realized what she was getting at. "Okay . . . fine. That's a good idea . . . we'll just pull over for a second." He pressed the call switch. "Fellahs—we're gonna pull over for a second."

Static sizzled through the speaker. "Mr. Hyde—what are you doing?"

Lucas pumped the brakes and yanked the shift lever backward. The engine complained noisily for a moment. Then the truck began to vibrate and slow down.

Through the speaker: "Mr. Hyde—?!"

Lucas nodded to himself as he watched the needle sink to forty miles per hour. "Don't know why I didn't think of this—"

The feeling started in his chest. At first, it felt as though he had eaten something that had suddenly disagreed with him. Just a mild twinge of heartburn.

"Should have done this—"

Thirty miles an hour. The pain grew, a seething hot poker in the pit of his stomach. It rose up his gorge. It spread through his lungs, his face. A film of sweat broke out on the back of his neck and across his forehead. He felt dizzy. Chills crawled over his limbs. It was as though he had a terrible sunburn.

"Fucking power of suggestion—"

Twenty miles an hour. The pain was beginning to throb again. Bile rose in his mouth. Hot bile. Acid hot. His stomach heaved and threatened to expel the dry emptiness down there. The tips of his fingers tingled. His ears rang.

"No, goddamnit!" He slammed his fist against the dash again. "Fuck!" He continued to slow down. "Fuck!" He slammed it again. "Fuck!!"

He would have continued had he not glanced over at Sophie. She was hunched forward, mouth agape, drooling, trying to say something. Her face was flushed, her eyes blazing with pain, her body trembling convulsively.

"FUCK IT!!"

Lucas put the pedal to the metal. The truck growled, then erupted back into motion. The cab filled with a fluid, rushing sound. The healing wind of motion.

The cure.

With each gear, Lucas let out a groan of relief. Third and fourth gears found the feeling coming back into his hands, the searing pain drifting away from his limbs. Fifth through seventh made his stomach settle and the sweat dry on his neck. Eighth through tenth brought his vision back into focus, cleared his mind, calmed his feverish brain.

Through a splash of static came the old man's voice. "Mr. Hyde—can you hear me?"

Lucas looked over at Sophie. She was taking deep breaths, wringing the pain out of her hands. Her face was flushed and her eyes were welling with tears.

She had made her point.

Lucas took the Mariah back up to sixty-five. He looked

out his window and into his side mirror. The school bus was still hovering less than three car lengths away. He turned back to the road ahead. The vibration of the truck beneath him seemed to seep up through the Cushion-Air seats, penetrating his ass, soothing him down to his marrow.

After another endless moment, Lucas uttered, "Jesus Christ Almighty."

The old man's voice blurted through the speaker, "Mr. Hyde, are you alright?"

"Yeah—just a little—experiment, you might say—"

"What happened?"

Lucas paused before answering. He turned to Sophie. She was watching him, chewing her lip, waiting for his verdict. Lucas started to say something but then thought better of it. He was wrestling with the feeling of dread that was rising in his stomach like a tide of ice water. All his life he had operated by the law of the jungle. He had fought his way out of the ghetto on pure street smarts. He had built his own business through sheer determination and desire. He had stayed out of the poorhouse by being sharper and quicker to the punch than the next guy. And even in the face of racism, Lucas had risen above it because he understood that it was based on ignorance. Bigotry was just plain ignorance. And it was through this unflinching brand of pragmatism that Lucas had been able to demystify the evils of the world.

But now, in a single cauterizing moment of pain and confusion, the world had turned mystical again and Lucas had no idea how to handle it. His heart was still racing so fast he thought it might explode. His ears still rang. All he could manage was a feeble flip of the switch and the muttered words, "Flaco—you copy? Mr. Figueroa?"

The voice replied through the speaker, "I am here."

"I'm not saying I'm going along with all this stuff—all this voodoo stuff—"

"Yes?"

"I'm not saying I'm buying it—"

"Yes?"

Lucas paused and thought about the violent illness that had just afflicted him as he flirted with stopping. He thought about disease. He thought about airborne contagions and plagues and AIDS. He thought about all the crackpot theories—how God wrought the AIDS epidemic upon the gays of the world or how the shuttle astronauts brought back some new space virus. It was obviously ludicrous. But then Lucas recalled the first moment he had seen the little black hand on the filthy floor mat. He remembered touching it and the grainy peach-fuzz texture of it. He recalled the subtle little charge of static electricity that sang off his fingertips when he snatched it up.

Lucas looked over at Sophie and then pressed the switch. "I think we're in trouble."

Flaco's voice crackled through the speaker. "Whatever we can do to help—my nephew and I will do it . . ."

"You were telling us about your visions—your feelings—what they have to do with us . . ."

A staticky pause, then: "—*sssssshhhh-ffffffht-fht*—has to do with—east—"

Squeezing the switch, Lucas said, "Say again, Flaco, you're breaking up."

Another moment of bleed and garbled interference. Then, "I said the visions have to do with the Beast."

"The Beast?"

"The Beast—the Bible says, the Beast can work great signs—make fire come—*ffffffffht-ffht-ft*—deceive those who dwell on earth—"

Lucas glanced over at Sophie. Her gaze was riveted to the CB speaker. Fighting a wave of chills, Lucas pressed the call switch. "You're talking about the Devil now? Satan?"

After a splash of static, "The Beast has many forms—Lucas, I do not know any other way to put it . . ."

"What do you suggest we do about it?"

The reply was prompt. "The only way to fight the Beast is with your heart. Your heart, Mr. Hyde."

For several awkward moments, Lucas thought about what to say. He could sense Sophie's panic. He could smell it, as pungent and acrid as body odor. Finally he spoke into the mike. "Whattya mean—with my heart?"

"First, I want to ask you both a question."

"Anything," Lucas said quickly.

"Just a few moments, will you accept some of these things I'm telling you are true?"

Lucas looked over at Sophie and saw her nodding. Lucas felt his stomach hitch painfully. He flashed on the image of his vomit boiling on the pavement of the Stuckey's parking lot like spit on a griddle. The icy fear closed around his heart. He could barely speak the words, "What difference does it make whether I believe it or not?"

The answer came over a wave of popping static. "It makes a great deal of difference."

"Why?"

"Because the things we have gone through—they are just the beginning. It will get much worse. I am sure of it."

Lucas paused, then thumbed the switch. "How will it get worse?"

"You must tell me that you believe?"

"I haven't decided yet."

"You must believe."

Lucas felt his scalp prickle. It felt as though he had finally gone over the edge. Stark raving cross-eyed mad. He pressed the switch and said, "I believe you, old man."

After a burst of static: "I'm glad to hear that, Lucas."

"Now will you tell me just how the hell it could get any worse?"

But before the old man could answer, Lucas glanced down at the control panel and learned very quickly how it could get worse.

The fuel gauge needle was on *E*.

"Gotta be honest with ya," Baum said, motioning down at the corpse, "damn thing looks like your basic fire victim to me."

The body of the young black man was burned beyond recognition. His blackened clothes had fused to his flesh. His fingers and extremities were completely burned off. And his face had seared away from his skull, leaving only the death mask grimace of his teeth. Baum noted that one of the incisors had been capped in gold.

"Take a closer look, Dick."

"I'm looking closer—but what the hell am I supposed to be looking for?"

"Anomalies. . . ." Dr. Chester Gibbons peeled away the charred layer of clothing with his big wooden forceps. A rotund, double-chinned man with thick hound-dog jowls, the coroner wore a heavy-duty rubber apron and rubber gloves. He hovered excitedly over the brittle remains of Melville Benoit like a chef lording over a delicate soufflé. "See what I mean—!"

Dick Baum took a closer look. Beneath the outer layer of the scorched shirt was a capsule of fat that sheathed the belly of the corpse like a cocoon of aspic. The fat was the consistency of chicken dumplings, pink and gelatinous and greasy. "Still don't know what I'm supposed to be looking at—"

"Here," Gibbons said and probed the stomach of the corpse with the rubber tip of the forceps. The lumpy tissue gave slightly, revealing a lacing of blue veins and purple organs underneath. It reminded Baum of sausage casing. "See how the outer epidermis has blistered and bubbled but has pretty much stayed intact?"

"Yeah."

Gibbons pulled a corner of the belly away and clipped it open with a surgical clamp. "Underneath you got major deep dermal loss, subcutaneous veins seared away, and major damage to the epithelium . . ."

Baum looked at the parboiled viscera and swallowed hard. "Epithelium?"

"That's the tissue that covers the organs of the body."

"So . . ."

"So, it's kinda funny it would burn like that, ain't it!?"

"Funny?" Baum regarded Gibbons for a moment. The coroner was nodding anxiously. He looked like a man who had just landed a ten-pound cat fish.

The room was dead silent except for the hum of air vents and the buzz of fluorescent tubes overhead. The smallest of the three autopsy rooms at the Pennington County Morgue, the chamber was less than a hundred square feet and had only one stainless-steel autopsy table. Affectionately known as the Honeymoon Suite, it was filled with the constant drone of an air-conditioning system that sucked out noxious gases radiating from the subjects. But right now, the walls were starting to close in on Sheriff Baum a little bit. "Why don't you go ahead and cut to the chase, Doc," Baum said. "I gotta be home by Thanksgiving this year."

Gibbons pointed at the seared organs. "Think about it, Dick. Think about the goddamn burn pattern. . . ."

"Goddamnit, Chet—whattya getting at?!"

"The kid burned from the inside out."

There was a tense moment of silence as Baum thought about it. Somewhere in another part of the building, the muffled sound of a phone ringing began to echo down the corridors. Baum wiped his mouth with the back of his hand. "Inside out?"

"Looks like a wrongful death." The coroner licked his lips. "Wouldn't you say?"

" 'Be damned if I know," Baum muttered.

Gibbons tossed the forceps back into a stainless-steel caddy attached to the side of the gurney table. "But that ain't the weirdest part—"

Baum's stomach was churning now. "No kiddin'."

"Check this out, bubba—"

The coroner led the sheriff over to a metal scale hanging from the ceiling. In the carriage beneath it was a small object covered in cloth. Gibbons uncovered it. "Take a look at the boy's heart. Bisected it a couple minutes ago."

Baum looked down at the fist-sized muscle in the scale. It was the color of eggplant, apparently undamaged by the fire. Gibbons pulled a tiny metal probe from his pocket and separated the ventricles.

There was a pattern burned across the myocardia.

"Jesus—what the hell—?" Baum leaned closer and studied the brand. It was plainly visible, burned across the tender tissue of the heart.

The imprint of a hand.

Somewhere outside the room, a phone continued ringing.

"Think, think, think, think."

Lucas was gripping the steering wheel tightly, trying to

conserve fuel by coasting down the long grade outside the upcoming little hamlet known as Stouville. But it was pretty futile. They were running on fumes and they would soon be coughing to a stop if they didn't get some go-juice pronto.

Her brow beading with fear sweat, Sophie snatched the mike from its cradle. "Flaco—can you hear me?"

A moment later, the old man came back on the air. "This is Flaco, over."

Sophie pressed the call switch. "You've both been life-savers—believe me, we appreciate all that you've done for us—"

The voice returned. "We're in this thing together."

Swallowing air, Sophie pressed the switch and said, "I know this sounds crazy—but we need you guys to refuel us."

After a few errant pops of static the reply came. "You mean like this morning? While you're still moving? *Over*."

"That's exactly what I mean."

At that moment, Lucas snatched the mike from her hands and barked into it. "Stand by, you guys, stand by for a second." Lucas slammed the mike back into its cradle. "Sophie, listen to me. We gotta stop again."

"We can't." Her eyes were flooding with fear. Her lips were pressed tight and bloodless. "We can't stop."

"Gotta get some fuel. You know it as well as I do."

"They'll help refuel us in motion."

"It doesn't work."

"Lucas, we cannot stop moving right now. When are you going to realize it? We're fucked!"

Lucas took a deep breath, wiped his mouth. "We'll do it without coming to a complete stop. We'll get some more fuel and buy us a little more time."

Sophie let out a cold, humorless laugh. "More time for what?"

"Time to think."

"You can think all you want. Fact is, we're fucked and you and I both know it."

Lucas swallowed the urge to yell and gazed back through the windshield at the white lines rushing under the truck. They were approaching the outskirts of Stouville. One of a million blue-collar enclaves across the southern part of the state, Stouville grew up during the post-war bungalow boom. But now, after decades of recession and unemployment, the topography of the town was dominated by boarded-up strip malls, rusty Airstream parks, and decaying factories.

Gazing out the side window at the passing landscape, Lucas muttered under his breath, "Just a quick diversion to give us time to think."

Sophie fished in her pocket for her cigarettes. She had purchased a new pack back at the Round Knob Stuckey's and had gone through ten of them already. Sparking another, she took a long drag and said, "How are you gonna pump gas into us without stopping?"

Lucas turned to her and said, "You dump me out and circle the station. I'll grab enough gas in a can to fill it."

"Then what?"

"I'll chase you down and slam it in while you're creeping back toward the highway."

Almost choking on a puff of smoke, Sophie laughed again. Dry, empty laughter. "That's a good one, Lucas."

Lucas slammed his fist against the steering wheel. "I'm not gonna let this thing beat me—whatever it is."

"You can't do it, Lucas."

Lucas grabbed the CB mike and activated the radio. "Break one-three for Flaco and Angel. Come in."

Through the speaker, Angel's voice: "We're here, Luca'th."

Sophie took another drag. "Forget it, Lucas."

Lucas pressed the call button. "Gonna be backing down momentarily, boys. Up ahead about three mile markers there's a Dixie Boy. Gonna get some more go-juice."

Angel: "You sure that's a good idea?"

"Yes I'm sure that's a good idea."

Sophie bit her lip. "This is suicide, Lucas."

"If you guys are up to it," Lucas continued into the mike, "follow us down the ramp . . . and try to hang back a few car lengths . . . you know, in case anything happens."

Through the speaker: "Okay."

"Forget about it, Lucas." Sophie nervously puffed the cigarette.

"Over and out," Lucas said into the mike. Snapping it back into the cradle, he glanced over at Sophie's side mirror to make sure traffic was clear. "Just a quick diversion."

Lucas flipped on his blinker and prepared to turn off.

17

Against God

"Goddamnit, Delbert—you better start making some sense real quick or you're gonna find yourself back on crossing-guard duty!!"

Baum was standing in the basement of the Pennington County Morgue, talking on the extension outside Dr. Gibbons's office. Above him, an ancient fluorescent tube flickered and strobed. Less than a minute ago the call had come in from Delbert. The deputy had tracked down the sheriff at the morgue and was now dropping a bombshell that was burning in Baum's stomach like a dollop of Tabasco. "You hear me, Delbert?!"

"I'm tellin' you the truth, Sheriff." The voice on the other end was stretched taut as a high-tension wire. "Gonna have to trust me on this one."

Baum angrily spat a hoogie of tobacco juice into the drinking fountain beside him. "Witchcraft?! After all your goddamn correspondence courses, that's what you came up with?! Somebody's practicin' *witchcraft*?!!"

On the other end of the line there was silence.

"Answer me, boy!"

There was a soft muttering that Baum couldn't decipher.

"What was that? What did you say?"

". . . against God."

"Whattya mean—against God? What in Sam Hell did you find down there, Delbert?"

After an agonizing pause, the deputy's voice returned. "It was . . . against God . . . that's all I can say. What I saw in that cemetery—it was . . . against God."

"Can you be just a little bit more specific?"

"The deceased—his hand was—amputated. I got sick afterward, Sheriff. Satan's involved in this here case—I swear to Christ—this is Satanism, Sheriff."

"For Christ's sake, Delbert!" Baum's hand was sweaty as he gripped the receiver. With only one other deputy who was still home with the flu, this was the worst thing in the world that could have happened right now. It just didn't make any sense. Why would Delbert go off the deep end?

On second thought, it was par for the course. Things were happening all around the sheriff now that didn't make any sense whatsoever.

"Been thinking," Delbert's voice uttered over the line, sounding shellshocked. "Better get some backup—you know, the violent crime boys from Memphis—maybe Father O'Conner from down in Chattanooga, the one who—"

"A priest?!!" Baum picked a fleck of tobacco from his lip. "Jesus Christ, Delbert . . ."

"He can ride along with me—"

"No! You get your ass back to the courthouse. I'm gonna ride this pony from here on in."

"But, Sheriff, I don't think you know what you're dealing with here . . ."

Baum wasn't listening anymore. He was too busy staring up at the sputtering fluorescent tube, thinking about the marks on the burned corpse, recalling the skittish way the black truck driver had behaved in his office, wondering just what the hell was going on out there on the highway.

Cruising. Unseen behind the truck. The old woman repositioned her opera glasses to get the best possible angle on the action.

Angel was the first to see the sparks. They had appeared the moment Lucas had jumped from the moving cab, his cowboy boots churning against the pavement of the Dixie Boy parking lot. Tiny filaments of light were jumping from his heels.

"Luca'th! Wait!" Angel was leaning out the doorway of the bus as Flaco pulled into the parking lot only seconds behind the truck.

Lucas didn't respond. Lumbering toward the office of the truck stop, an empty thirty-gallon can clutched in his left hand, Lucas seemed hellbent on getting diesel into his rig before the sickness overcame him. And judging from the way he was lurching across the lot, the pain was coming fast and furious.

Flaco pulled the school bus next to the office and threw it in park. Angel hopped out. "Luca'th! Lemme do it!"

The door to the office sprang open and a wiry little attendant with wavy red hair sauntered out, rubbing his hands in a grease rag. "What's all the commotion?"

Thrusting the can in the man's face, Lucas said, "Gimme thirty gallons of diesel as fast as possible."

"Excuse me?"

"Do it quick and there's a big tip in it for you."

Lucas doubled over in pain. His expression tightened. His hands were beginning to tremble. But he kept fighting it.

Angel approached and tried to urge Lucas back to the truck. "C'mon, Luca'th, thith ain't gonna work!"

The attendant scratched his chin. "You gotta go to the bathroom, mister?"

"Fill the fucking can! NOW!!" Lucas hurled the can at the attendant. The attendant ducked and the can smashed against the office door, chipping glass and clattering to the ground.

"Son of a bitch!" The wiry little man backed away as if backing away from a rabid dog.

"Luca'th, c'mon!" Angel reached for the trucker's arm, but a voice suddenly rang out behind Angel that made the boy freeze in his tracks.

"Angel—the *hex*—do not touch him—!!" Uncle Flaco was

peering out of the bus's doorway, screaming at the boy, terrified the curse might spread.

The attendant was backing inside the office door. "Goddamn drug addicts! All of ya!"

Lucas snatched up the can and spun toward the nearest diesel pump. "I'll do the fucking thing myself . . ."

He lumbered toward the pump, gasping for air, holding his belly with his free hand as if it might spring a leak at any moment. Angel ran after him.

Lucas reached the pump and tore the nozzle from its slot. Another spasm of pain hit him and he doubled over again, cradling his gut and dropping the nozzle. A string of saliva looped off his mouth. It hit the pavement and sizzled like lard on a griddle. Lucas gathered up the nozzle and tried to insert it into the can but he was shivering convulsively.

Behind him, the attendant was lurking in the doorway with the telephone clutched in his hand. "Tired of you goddamn drug addicts! Gonna bust you sonsabitches once and for all!!"

Angel knelt down by the can and tried to help Lucas by guiding the nozzle into the hole. The nozzle was as hot as a branding iron. Angel burned his fingertips on the searing metal and jerked away.

Then the molten vomit came. Lucas retched all over the can. His stomach must have been fairly empty because only a spattering of steaming dark bile spewed out over the hot metal and pavement beside it. Lucas bellowed with pain. He sounded like an angry wolf caught in the teeth of a steel trap. His voice was mixed with the sputtering sound of something gurgling up from within him. Something deadly.

Straightening up, Lucas staggered backward, his boots shuffling against the grit of the pavement, raising sparks from the friction and the magic. More sparks issued forth from his fingertips in tiny spurts. Lucas howled involuntarily. A spot of oil on his shirt caught fire. Lucas madly patted out the flame. Filaments of sparks sputtered from his fingertips.

"Luca'th! Get back on the truck!" Angel gestured toward the circling semi.

Lucas made for the truck. Evidently, Sophie had been keeping close watch because the Mariah was roaring toward them, downshifting, hissing, and squealing.

Lucas dove for the foot rail. His hands caught the running bar along the door hinge and he latched on. Sophie floored it. The truck roared out of the lot, with Lucas holding on for dear life, a fountain of sparks coming from his metal boot toes as they brushed the pavement.

Thirty feet across the parking lot, catching his breath, Angel watched the truck roar away. Something caught his eye near the far fuel island next to the road. A small fire was burning where an errant spark had touched off a patch of oil.

"Uncle! Quick!" Angel called out to Flaco, who was waiting twenty feet away in the idling school bus. The old man put it in gear and floored it. The bus roared and lurched over to Angel. Flaco threw open the accordion door and Angel prepared to hop aboard.

Then Angel looked down and saw that his pant leg was on fire.

"Ángel!" The old man's voice was hoarse and weak, yet filled with alarm. "Look out!"

Angel bent down and madly patted out the flames licking up his leg.

In the shadows of the limousine, Vanessa had decided to help the game along. She touched a flame to a branch of dried locust leaf. It caught fire immediately, the delicate ribs and veins evaporating in the glow.

"*Mucho ojo!*" Angel spun around just in time to see the fingers of the flame creeping along the pavement. "*Jeeeee' thuz Chri' th!!!*"

The entire parking lot was veined in flames. The main artery followed Lucas's path. Other capillaries were spreading out from there, creeping toward the main fuel islands and the office. A low cloud of dark smoke was building and the fumes rose up and made Angel's nostrils sting and his eyes water.

Twenty feet away, the attendant dove from the doorway of

the office and sprinted for the neighboring trees. "Jesus Christ Almighty—whole damn place is gonna blow!"

Angel dove inside the bus and Flaco slammed the accelerator to the floor. The bus rumbled out of the lot, belching black clouds of exhaust. Catching his breath, Angel cried, "Hurry, Uncle . . . i'th . . . i'th gonna . . . GET OUTTA HERE!"

Angel turned and looked through the rear exit window.

Behind them, the gas station was engulfed in fire. Countless tributaries of white-hot light spread out from the main artery and zigzagged along the oily pavement toward the building. For a brief, horrible moment, Angel was reminded of a huge mutant hand with all its twisted fingers.

Then the explosion came.

The concussion rocked The Black Mariah like a tidal wave hitting a tugboat. The truck bucked. Sophie struggled with the wheel to hold it steady as the thunder exploded all around them. The wave of heat could be felt through their open windows even at this great distance.

"Holy shit!" Sophie was shifting her gaze from the windshield to the pyrotechnics in her side mirror. "The whole fucking gas station went up!"

Lucas could barely hear her. He was doubled over in his seat, holding his injured hands, palms up, in his lap. The pain was beyond anything he had ever experienced. Much worse than the last stop at the pawn shop, where it was limited to an overall, feverish discomfort. Now his whole body burned as if someone had served him acid. And worse, there was exceedingly intense pain focused in a series of severe third-degree burns on the end of each finger.

"The boy . . . the old man . . ." Lucas spoke in a choked, halting wheeze. "Are they—alright?"

Sophie scanned her mirror. "Right behind us . . . little scorched and startled . . . but alright."

Pain shrieked in Lucas's hands. An involuntary moan seeped from his roasted lungs and he doubled over again. The pain was making his forebrain throb. His temples were pounding out the rhythm to a Sousa march. He had never dreamed a pain could be this intense, never in a million years.

He looked down at his hands and gasped. Each fingertip had erupted into a bloody ooze, rimmed in charred skin, a pink glutinous bud in each center.

Lucas climbed out of his seat and crawled back into the coffin box. He found the first-aid kit under the bed and urged it out with his elbows. He found some ointment and applied it to each finger. Then he wrapped his hands in gauze.

Sophie's voice came through the doorway, strained and uncertain. "Lucas, what have we done?"

Lucas searched through a drawer for some gloves. "Just trying to survive."

"We're walking death."

"Funny thing . . . about curses," Lucas murmured, taking deep breaths and fishing through Sophie's T-shirt collection. "They tend to have that effect. . . ."

Lucas found a pair of leather driving gloves buried under Sophie's underwear. He carefully slipped his bandaged hands into the gloves. Then he dug back into the first-aid kit and found an unmarked pill bottle. It contained the codeine-Darvocet cocktails that most truckers lovingly refer to as Mariannes.

He had purchased the pills a year earlier, when Sophie had sprained her ankle unloading honeydews in Des Moines, Iowa. It had been a healthy strain, too—all purplish and swollen. In the aftermath, however, Sophie had refused the emergency room doctor's orders to rest. Lucas had pleaded with her to stay off it but the woman was adamant about getting back home to cash her check. So Lucas pulled a few strings with the local underground and got the bottle of Mariannes.

Lucas rooted out a couple of tablets and swallowed them dry. Then he reached up to a drawer beside the bed, fished around, and found a secret flask of Jackie D. He took a couple of healthy sips and put it back. In the rush of dizziness that followed, he got an idea. They had a duffel back somewhere just brimming with drugs. Accumulated over time, the bag was a virtual depository of discarded prescription drugs, illegal amphetamines, or whatever had popped their way over the many grueling miles. But where the hell was it? Where the hell had Lucas stuck it—?

He found it wedged behind the bed. He opened the bag and discovered a virtual drugstore. Dozens of plastic bottles of unused capsules, blister packs of contraband speed, cheap diet pills, and countless other goodies that psychotic truckers had pawned off on Lucas over the years. Lucas scooped up a vial of Ritalin to keep them going and a stray bottle of generic Demerol to kill the pain.

"Wait a minute!" Sophie's voice came through the doorway again, a notch sharper. "Our escorts are pulling off again."

Lucas tucked the drugs into his pocket. "Whattya mean?"

"They're taking this exit."

"Taking it where?"

"I dunno."

Lucas climbed back into the cab and settled into the jump seat. Sophie was gazing over at Lucas's side mirror. "Looks like they're heading for the Shell station."

Lucas checked his mirror. About five car lengths behind them, Flaco and Angel were tooling up the exit ramp toward a grouping of gas stations along the overpass. The school bus was farting a cloud of exhaust as it lumbered around a corner, ran the stop sign, and entered the Shell lot.

With both hands, Lucas carefully palmed the CB mike off its cradle and said, "Break one-three for Flaco. Come back, old friend. What's going on?"

Through the speaker, a rush of static crackled through the cab. A frail voice broke through for a few moments, but the words were indistinguishable.

Lucas gently pressed the call button. "Ten-nine on that, Flaco. Say again."

After more static: "—hand delivered—way—*Over*."

"Negative copy. Say again."

"I said, we are getting more fuel to be hand delivered on the highway. *Over*."

Lucas paused and took a deep breath. The heat in his chest

had subsided but his fingertips were still throbbing. "Ten-four, Flaco. We'll be ready."

Carefully replacing the mike, Lucas turned to Sophie and saw her chowing down on her lip, burning her gaze through the windshield.

"Try to calm down, partner."

Sophie brushed a strand of hair from her watering eyes. "Where does it end?"

"Sophie, listen—"

But Lucas's words were cut short when he heard the engine begin to fail.

18

Fever Dream

For Sophie, the worst part was the sound. It started with a whining in the crankcase beneath them. The engine sputtered. The exhaust stack spat and coughed loudly.

Then silence fell over the cab like a funeral shroud.

"Jesus! It's happening!" Sophie was glancing down at the fuel gauge to the left of the speedometer. The fuel-gauge needle was below E. The alternator needle was jumping wildly.

"Put it in neutral!" Lucas hollered.

Sophie glanced out her side mirror. On the distant horizon behind them, the Shell station was quickly receding out of sight. Below the station's sign, the rusty old school bus was parked next to a pump. But there were no people in sight. Sophie glanced back at the dash and struggled with the shift lever. "It won't go into neutral!"

"Lemme try." Lucas reached over and wrenched the lever backward. The gears disengaged, and the truck finally went into neutral and began to coast.

"We're losing electrical." Sophie's throat was raw, her voice had gone brittle and hoarse. She could feel the burning sensation starting in her stomach. "Steering's gone!"

"Hold it steady."

Sophie glanced through the windshield at the distant horizon before them. Her mind raced. The highway continued straight as an arrow, straight and level as far as the eye could see. Where the hell were the rolling hills of Georgia when you really needed them?! Damn Illinois cornfield roads were flat as glass.

Turning back to the CB radio, Sophie snatched up the mike. "Break one-three for Flaco! Angel! Anybody—come back!"

The speaker was silent as a block of stone. No voices, no reply. All at once, Sophie realized they had no power. They were in a dead coast.

The truck began to slow down.

"Jesus, Lucas—what the fuck are we gonna do?!!" Sophie's heart was racing now. The fever was building inside her, sending chills down the backs of her arms and legs.

"Stay calm, partner," Lucas uttered through clenched teeth. "Try to hold the wheel as steady as possible."

"I'm trying." Sophie struggled through her tears. Her eyes were burning. Saliva filled her mouth, announcing the arrival of fresh nausea. She glanced back at her side mirror. The Shell station was long out of sight. The highway was deserted and striped with the lengthening shadows of dusk.

She looked down at the speedometer. The needle was frozen at zero. Without power, the Mariah's control panel was as dead as a piece of driftwood.

"Hold it steady," Lucas called out.

Sophie held a vise grip on the wheel. She found herself rocking on the edge of her seat, urging the truck onward, as if her movements would keep the thing going.

The truck was crawling now.

The fever intensified. Sophie felt as if a million knives sterilized in white-hot fire were beginning to slice their way up her torso. Her ears began to pound. Waves of nausea crashed against the walls of her stomach. Her vision blurred. A hot, coppery taste filled her mouth as her bile threatened to rise up her gorge.

The truck crept slower and slower.

"Try to start it again—try to pop the clutch—try!" Next to her, Lucas could barely talk. His breath came out in pained gasps.

Sophie hunched over the dash and tried to turn the keys. "It's no use!"

Her nausea had turned to an icy hot fire in her belly and a seething pain behind her eyes. Her skin crawled. Her teeth burned. The soles of her feet felt like they were pressed against a fry griddle.

She turned to her partner. "Lucas—ohmygod!!"

He was in hell. Mouth open wide, lips drawn back, he was shrieking some soundless cry. Stringers of scalding drool looped out of his mouth. His body had gone stiff and palsied. His wounded hands clawed at the air. And Sophie could have sworn she saw spurts of electricity arching off his bandages.

"*Lu—cah—sss-sss-sssss!!*" Sophie couldn't form words anymore. Her lungs clogged with noxious heat and fear. Her vision blurred and her brain spun. There was no fighting it now. Pain was everywhere, in every pore, on every nerve ending, consuming her, singing some horrible aria in some elemental language that she was just beginning to absorb.

The truck was inching along now.

Through the agony she looked at Lucas. His gaping silent scream had widened. His stricken gaze had intensified. Sparks danced around his hands and face. Mucus bubbled from his ears and his nose. He was dying, he was cooking in his own juices, and the pain was so all-consuming, so savage, that he could not even scream.

In a moment of pure delirium, Sophie flashed on that infamous painting by Edvard Munch called *The Scream*. A solitary man, frozen in anguish, hands to his face, screaming in primal pain. It echoed with silent horror, rippling, swirling down the drain of her diminishing consciousness.

Then there was a sudden change.

Sophie felt the waves of heat subsiding and her vision coalescing back into focus. She struggled to sit up straight. She turned to Lucas. He was breathing shallow breaths, holding his bandaged hands curled against his breast.

The truck was moving again.

She gazed through the windshield. Evidently, at the last moment, they had topped a gentle rise. Now the truck was just beginning to descend a long downgrade that led into the Kaskaskia river valley outside St. Louis.

"Thank God." Her words were choked and half-whispered, as the truck began to coast down the hill.

And for the first time in her life, she really meant it.

"There they are!" Angel had pushed aside the blinds above the door. Now he leaned outside, his unruly hair tossing in the breeze, the can of diesel gripped firmly in his left hand. Flaco was driving. They had just rounded the curve and were heading down the hill.

Less than a mile ahead of them, the truck was coasting down the hill and into the valley.

"On which side is the tank?" Flaco had to strain his voice to be heard above the rattling cargo of the bus.

"Driver th'ide!" The wind was making Angel's eyes water. He wiped his face with his sleeve and took a deep breath. He knew from recent experience this wasn't going to be easy. But he also knew he had several things going for him. First, on a Kenworth the fuel tank was much more accessible than a car's. The K-Whopper tank rode along the lower panel, a huge cylinder with a cap pointing upward and a place to stand. Second, with Sophie behind the wheel of the receiving vehicle, as opposed to a twitchy gearhead named Melville, there would be much more control. Third, the truck was coasting along at a safe speed. "Pull up next to the tank," Angel hollered over the wind, "and hold the bu'th th'teady."

Flaco nodded and caught up with the truck within seconds. He pulled to within inches of the Mariah's tank and held the bus even. He glanced at his speedometer. They were going about thirty-five miles an hour. But before gazing back up at the road, something caught Flaco's eye that bothered him.

The needle was climbing.

Flaco grabbed the CB mike. "Hello, Sophie? Lucas? Come in."

Through the transistor radio speaker came the crackle of

empty static and garbled voices. No Sophie, no Lucas, no answer.

"Sophie! Come in!"

Angel hollered over his shoulder at the old man. "Uncle, forget it! They got no power! No radio!"

"Sweet Christ." Flaco tossed the mike aside and checked the speedometer. They had just passed forty miles an hour and were climbing. He gripped the wheel tightly and kept the bus even with the truck.

Angel made his move. He pushed the accordion door open with his foot and wrestled the can out onto the bus's exit steps. The gusting wind hugged his body and made his eyes sting.

He reached over and grabbed the Mariah's metal banister bar with his free hand. Then he took a giant step and landed his right foot on the Mariah. He steadied himself. Standing with one foot on the bus's steps and one foot on the truck's tank, he felt like a strange mutant surfer riding the cement waves of the highway.

The truck was picking up speed on the downgrade, beginning to rattle and pitch.

"Angel!" It was Sophie. She had stuck her head out the Mariah's window. Her cry pierced the wind and roar of the engines. "We're out of control! Do you hear me?!"

Angel glanced up and saw that Sophie's face was flushed and her eyes were gaping hotly. Angel nodded at her and yelled, "I know! Hold on!"

They hit a bump. Angel rode it like a champion, squeezing the can steady in the crook of his elbow. The school bus drifted. Angel scissored his legs and braced himself against the banister until Flaco pulled the bus back in line.

Holding the banister bar, Angel hopped onto the truck. Then he reached down and found the fuel spout. The broken nozzle from Stuckey's was still planted in it. The length of torn hose was flagging in the breeze. Angel uprooted it and tossed it into the back draft.

The truck was coasting out of control now, climbing past fifty miles an hour.

At that moment, Angel realized he only had one chance to

get fuel into the Mariah. The longer he waited, the more impossible it would become. Besides, Flaco would only be able to keep the school bus even with the truck for so long.

And the bus was Angel's only escape route.

But Angel refused to give up on his friends. In fact, the more dangerous the situation became, the more driven he was to help them. Sophie and Lucas had touched him in some unspoken way, touched his soul. In the short time he had known them, in the midst of this nightmare, they had become unconditional friends. Friends who looked beyond his misshapen face. The kind of friends he had never known. And now they were in mortal trouble, he was not going to let them down.

Angel slammed the spout into the Mariah's tank and refueled the truck.

Inside the bus, Flaco began to panic. They were approaching sixty-five miles an hour. Behind him, his belongings were beginning to skid off their shelves. Pans were clattering to the floor. The shrine was falling apart. Candles were rolling under seats. Photographs were fluttering to the floor. It was as if the bus were falling apart at the seams. In fact, Flaco was surprised to be maintaining such a speed without blowing up. The bus had never exceeded fifty before in its entire lifetime. Thank God Flaco had dropped in the new Diamond Rio engine a few years back. He had paid for the engine in chickens and it had taken every last bird to buy it. The junkyard owner had warned him about the Diamond Rio engine proving to be too much for the bus at high speeds. But Flaco never thought he would be testing its limits to this degree.

"Ángel! Get back inside!" Flaco hollered over the noise, but his frail voice was swallowed by the wind.

Flaco was becoming terrified on a deeper level. Perhaps this was not meant to be part of the prophecy. Perhaps he was putting his beloved nephew in harm's way for nothing. Perhaps it was Flaco who should be out there walking the precarious ledge in the wind.

Suddenly, Flaco wished more than anything else in the

world that he could trade places with his nephew. But there was no time to pause and reflect. He had to act quickly.

The truck was a runaway.

Through his windshield the old man watched the semi coast out of control. Barreling down the hill, a silent zephyr of steel and black molding, the Mariah was edging toward seventy miles an hour. Its wheels whined against the super-slab like sirens. The cab rattled and shivered convulsively, the fenders vibrated, and the trailer fishtailed wildly as Sophie struggled to hold it in line.

Flaco felt the bus hit its ceiling speed.

"Muchacho!" Flaco cried out.

At that moment, Flaco saw something quite unexpected. Across the gap between the vehicles, in the rush of wind, another figure had appeared behind Angel.

It was Lucas Hyde. He was climbing through the space between the cab and the trailer. His hands were bandaged, his head was wrapped in a bandanna, and his eyes were squinting into the wind. He had climbed out the passenger side and was making his way across the huge metal coupler toward Angel.

Another thought struck Flaco like an ice pick through his temple. What if the boy came too close? What if he came too close to the sickness and touched the—

Whhhhhissshhhhhhhhhh!

The truck rocketed past a billboard. Along the top edge, a flock of crows suddenly took flight. To Flaco they looked like a cancer spreading across the distant sunset.

"Nino! Muchacho!

"MUCHAAAAAACHO!!!"

Flaco's words were obliterated by the din. The school bus lagged farther back. Through the side window, Flaco saw his nephew get tossed backward on a gust of wind as the truck shimmied violently.

Angel was about to fall.

Then Flaco saw the worst possible thing happen.

Although it only took a moment to transpire, Flaco watched it unfold through the window like some horrible tableau in a fever dream from which he could never awaken.

In fact, he had no time to even cry out a warning to Angel. He had no time to stop the chain from closing. He only had time to flash on that faint, yellowed page of the New Testament . . .

. . . *in those days men will seek death and will not find it; they will long to die, and death will fly from them.*

"*Don't touch his hand!*" Flaco thought hysterically in his mind as he watched. "*Don't take it, Angel! Don't take his hand!*"

But the issue was already moot. The wind was about to claim his nephew. At the last moment, Lucas reached out for the boy and the boy took the trucker's hand. The two hands clasped tightly as Lucas pulled Angel aboard.

Falling back, drifting away from the speeding truck, Flaco knew he would never see his nephew again.

19
Falling

The keyhole. Of course, it would be so easy. Peering through the keyhole . . .

Pressing the edge of her wheels against the doorjamb, she paused and listened. Somebody was moving behind the massive oak door. Muffled noises were penetrating the walls. It sounded like somebody making dinner. The clink of porcelain. The slight splash of water in a basin. Cutting sounds. A metallic ring, a knife striking a chopping block. . . .

The only problem was, they were coming from her father's bedroom.

Ever since his wife had passed away earlier in the year, Maurice DeGeaux had fallen into deep despair, becoming a recluse behind the door of his bedroom. He would show his face only a couple of times per week, either to deliver a guest sermon at some ramshackle church somewhere or to perform some feat of healing. This left the servants to care for Vanessa, wash her, dress her, lift her in and out of her wheelchair. It also gave Vanessa plenty of time to worry. The doctors said her father was suffering from a severe case of melancholia and that it would run its course eventually. But

Vanessa was terrified it would drive the tall man to do something crazy . . .

She leaned over the armrest of the wheelchair and put her ear against the door. She could hear wet sounds. Dripping. Then, the clink of cutlery. The rattle of bowls.

The keyhole . . .

She finally broke down and looked.

At first, it was hard to see anything. The keyhole was miniscule and the late afternoon light was weak. She had to squint. But soon the hazy outlines of her father's figure came into focus.

He was butchering cats.

Vanessa felt chill bumps crawling up her good arm. Her mouth went dry. She was watching her father, a holy man, butchering strays on a pine bench in his bedroom. She counted them. Six tiny heads were lined up in a neat row, little pink tongues showing, eyes blank as buttons. Gore leaked over the table top and gathered in a bowl on the floor. Maurice was performing some silent rite over the carnage, dipping his fingers in the gruesome sacrament, mouthing some forbidden tongue.

Vanessa gasped.

It wasn't the repulsion of seeing her father performing such an obscenity. It wasn't the shame or the confusion or the rage. It wasn't even the tide of hate that was washing over her now. No, on the contrary, what frightened her most at that moment, what nearly took her breath away, was the unexpected music.

It was as if the dissonant, harsh noise in Vanessa's head had finally flowed into a beautiful liquid harmony. The strings took over, soaring, rising. Flutes added lovely counterpoint. And the deep rich bassoons burnished the melody.

Vanessa was transformed.

Before opening the door and welcoming her father into her heart, she watched the man conduct his secret black mass in the golden glow coming through half-drawn shades. It was sublime, like watching a silent ballet. Dressed in his practitioner's cowl, broad shoulders hunched, Maurice

*moved like a dancer. He lit the black candles with grace. He
burned the herbs with childlike wonder.*

*Then he made a gesture that would stay with Vanessa the
rest of her life.*

*Its roots were in Vanessa's early childhood. Maurice's an-
cestors were Belgian and were very devout Catholics.
Vanessa had been baptized and had attended mass until she
was nearly eight years old. Until Maurice had found other
gods. But all the powerful vestiges of Catholicism had stayed
with Vanessa well into her teens. These vestiges all rose
around her now like an otherworldly chorus as she watched
her father complete his rite.*

*It started with the blood. Maurice dipped the fingertips of
his right hand—his large, muscular, coarse right hand—into
the puddling gore. Then he thrust his hand at the floor, motioned back and forth, then brought it up and touched his
forehead. At first, it looked only vaguely familiar to Vanessa,
but after a few moments she recognized the gesture.*

He was genuflecting in reverse.

An inverted cross.

*Vanessa felt music trumpeting in her brain as she shoved
open her father's door and joined his new church . . .*

"Madam—?"

The chauffeur's voice. Coming through the partition.
Vanessa had been silent for some time now, thinking. The
chauffeur was probably getting worried. The old fool. Little
did he know Vanessa was about to make miracles.

"Madam—we need to talk."

Vanessa scratched at her keypad. *I S—T H A T—S O ???*

"About the truckers—"

Y E S ???

"I . . . I don't really know how to say this . . ."

J U S T—S A Y—I T—E R I C—

"What if we just let them go?" the chauffeur said. "They'll
surely die sooner or later. What if—"

N O !!!

"I'm just thinking of your health, Madam. This trip is taking its toll and—"

N O—N O—N O—N O N O N O N O N O!!!

There was a brief pause as the chauffeur stared at the screen. "I have a bad feeling about this one, Madam."

Vanessa shoved the keypad away from her. Then she spoke as loudly as she could. Her voice was nearly gone, but the anger forced the words out in a dry wheeze.

"Eric . . . please . . . keep your feelings to yourself."

Sophie was in the coffin box, getting some first aid. Lucas had decided to let Angel take the wheel for a while. Lucas badly needed time to recover from his last blast of pain. Settling back in the jump seat, he took deep breaths. He felt like his insides had been soured with an arc welder. His vision was still spotty. "Maybe I should take over till we cross the river."

"Don't worry, Luca'th—I'm fine."

Lucas thought for a moment. "Take Highway Fifty around the city and then pick up Seventy going west."

"Okay."

Lucas glanced over at Angel. The boy was holding the wheel like his life depended on it, eyes locked on the road ahead. Lucas managed a faint smile. "Never thought I'd be taking on such a young partner."

"I'll be nineteen next Feb'uary." Angel's reply was meant to be neither smug nor argumentative. It was simply a proud assertion of fact.

"You're right," Lucas said, acknowledging the mistake. "And you've got more balls than any nineteen-year-old I've ever met. Don't know where we'd be without you and your uncle . . ."

"Glad to help."

"What did we do to deserve you?"

Angel shot a glance over at Lucas. "You would do the thame for u'th."

Lucas told him that was true.

They drove in silence for quite some time. Lucas chewed some Tylenol and tried to ignore the pain and think of some way out of this nightmare. They crossed the Mississippi and circled around the suburbs of St. Louis. Now and again

Flaco's feeble voice would come over the CB and discuss stuff from *Revelations*, but none of it made any sense to Lucas.

At length, they found themselves weaving through moderately heavy traffic. But it only made Lucas feel all the more isolated. He knew if they didn't figure out something soon they were going to be toast.

Finally Lucas said, "How much go-juice did you say you got into us?"

"About twenty gallon'th."

"The needle hardly budged. Ain't gonna buy us much more than a hundred miles."

Angel nodded and kept driving.

Lucas said, "Think we oughtta cut your uncle loose."

Angel shook his head. "Uncle Flaco i'th fine."

"I'm worried about him following us."

"Why?"

"He's an old man. Goddamn school bus is a death trap. Don't want to see anybody else get hurt."

Angel gazed back at the road for a moment. "Uncle Flaco think I got infected by touchin' your hand. He wanna keep an eye on u'th. He wanna help."

A moment of rattling silence passed.

Lucas balled his wounded hands into fists and squeezed. The pain was bracing. It popped in his brain like a shot of smelling salts. "Gotta be a fucking way out of this mess— *gotta be*."

After another twenty minutes the traffic started to thin as they left the suburban sprawl. Lucas gazed at his watch. It was after nine. The Mariah's high beams were cutting a hundred-yard swath through the dark farmland ahead. They were heading west on Interstate 70 toward Kansas City and the white lines were ticking under them like a horrible clock.

Their time was quickly running out.

"Gotta talk to Sophie," Lucas muttered and turned to the boy. "Think you could mind the store for a while?"

Rusty nails were driving through Flaco's knuckles as he gripped the oversized steering wheel of his school bus. Each bump sent jolts of electricity up his arms. But he kept driving. He would not give up. No matter how bad his arthritis became, he would not abandon his nephew and his new friends in the truck.

The school bus hit another pothole and bucked violently. Pots rattled around the back. Bench seats rattled loosely on their moorings. The old man gasped and tried to ignore his throbbing knuckles.

Flaco was not unaccustomed to driving with pain. Back in the days when he worked for the school district, he used to get up before dawn on creaking knees. He used to drive with the worst chest colds imaginable. He used to drive through the nastiest weather. One time he even drove his entire route with a hundred-and-two-degree fever, hiding his illness from the kids by vomiting into his thermos after every other stop. But none of it seemed to compare with what his amigos were going through at the present moment.

Taking a deep breath, Flaco ignored the pain and tried to think of a solution. He was convinced that his friends had stumbled into the Devil's trap, just as he was convinced it was his fate to fight alongside them. But how does a person fight a curse? How do you battle something so *tan como un hechizo*—so insubstantial? Flaco knew nothing of witchcraft. He knew nothing of spells and charms and hexes. He was a man of the Lord. All he knew was that the Devil was an evil magician—

The bus hit another bump. Pain shot up Flaco's wrists, and his belongings continued rattling around in back.

Flaco found himself remembering *Peter,* verse ten.

Be watchful, your adversary the Devil prowls around like a roaring lion, seeking someone to devour . . . resist him—

"*Un momenta,*" Flaco uttered under his breath. A new feeling was rising in his gut, unfocused, yet urgent and powerful. It was as if he had been trying to remember something which was on the tip of his tongue—the title of a song or a person's name—and it had suddenly begun to form in his mind. Perhaps there was a way to beat the curse. Perhaps there was a way to—

Something caught his attention in the side mirror. In the

darkness behind the bus, several car lengths back, a pair of headlights hovered. Dimly glowing, too small and close together for a late-model car, they were the color of urine; and for some reason they sent a shudder through Flaco.

"*Un momenta.* . . ." Flaco tried to get his bearings but could not get those yellow headlamps out of his head. They were like bothersome insects, stingers poised, buzzing around the back of his neck.

In fact, they were so incessant that for several minutes Flaco did not even notice the other lights approaching from behind.

Lucas pushed the accordion door open and found Sophie sitting on the edge of the bunk. Her eyes were raw from crying. She had removed her T-shirt and had draped a sheet over her shoulder. A glimpse of her left breast was visible and she covered it quickly as Lucas entered.

"You alright?" It was strange for Lucas to be sharing the coffin box with his co-driver while they were still moving.

"Guess so." Sophie was squeezing a dab of ointment from a tube of first-aid cream into her palm and applying it to a series of burns along her upper arm and shoulder.

Lucas sat down next to her. "How bad is it?"

"Feels like my skin was sand-blasted."

"Let me see." Lucas carefully removed his gloves, tossed them aside, and held Sophie's arm in his bandaged hands. Sure enough, her left arm was dusted with reddish blisters. It looked as if it had been passed through a microwave oven.

Sophie took a deep breath. "Not too pretty, is it."

"Does it hurt bad?"

Sophie managed a dry chuckle. "Compared to what?"

Lucas nodded and let go of her arm.

Gazing up at him, Sophie's eyes had gone hard and sharp. She was not ready to throw in the towel just yet. "You believe in witchcraft yet?"

"Very funny."

"We're in deep shit, Lucas."

Lucas rolled his eyes. "Another understatement."

"Got any ideas?"

Lucas studied her expression. It was an odd mixture of panic and concentration. After thinking about it for a moment, he said, "Keep moving."

"But then what?" Sophie angled her head toward the cab. "Can't keep moving forever—right?"

A jolt of pain shot up Lucas's arms. His fingers felt like steak tartare. "You got a better idea?"

Sophie took another deep breath. "I've been thinking—you know—"

"Yeah?"

"Thinking about our options."

"Options?"

"What do we know about this thing—this fucking curse or sickness or whatever you call it?"

Lucas grimaced at the fire worming through his fingers. "Well, let's see—we caught it from a dead man's hand. Now, we gotta keep moving or we're dead meat. What else do you want to know?"

Sophie glared at him. "Seriously—"

"I dunno, you tell me—what do we know about it?"

"It starts out gradually."

"What do you mean?"

"You didn't get sick immediately. It happened a few hours after you touched the hand."

"So what?"

"So I'm thinking it might be a progressive kind of thing."

Lucas studied her for a moment. It was dawning on him just where she was heading with all this. "Wait a minute—you're saying, if it's progressive—"

Sophie nodded. "—then maybe it may run its course."

Lucas thought about it for a moment. "Then what are you saying? All we gotta do is—?"

"Keep moving till it runs its course."

Beneath them, the wheels rumbled over some bad road. Lucas fought the pain. As plans go, it was thin. It was mighty thin. Just to keep moving without trying anything else seemed pretty ludicrous. But was it any more ludicrous than Lucas sitting here, shaking like a puppy, scared shitless of stopping? He glanced over at the doorway to the cab and felt the vibration of the engine, the joints squeaking, the fuel burning away with each passing mile marker. "Options. . . ."

"I remember one time years ago—" Sophie's gaze had wandered slightly, as if some fervent memory was bubbling up from her subconscious. "My dad took me rock climbing in Yosemite. Made a big deal out of it, too. Got up before dawn. Brought along all the gear, the nylon ropes, high-tech hardware. You know Harry."

Lucas nodded. "The weekend warrior."

"Exactly." Sophie nodded emphatically. "Dad was really into it and of course he thought his little tomboy daughter would be the perfect climbing partner. Anyway, we found a good slab of rock rising out of the forest and Dad strapped me into this knotted cradle of rope. Then he started leading me up the surface, over the crags. You know, real macho stuff."

She paused and rubbed her eyes. Lucas watched her. "What happened?"

"Halfway up, maybe a couple hundred feet, something went wrong," she said. "My rope got tangled. I tried to untangle it and I started to fall. Dad went berserk. But he just made matters worse, pulling and tugging and screaming at me. Eventually, I fell about fifty feet and landed in a tree. Broke my arm and punctured a lung. But you know what I remember most about it?"

"What's that?"

"The feeling of slipping backward," Sophie said, her eyes hot with the memory. "At first, I panicked. My heart was in my throat, my whole body was encased in ice. I was fighting it, slipping backward faster and faster. But then, there came a point where I just surrendered. If I was gonna die, I was gonna die. I just kind of gave in. And I think that was the worst feeling of all. Totally out of control. Just giving up."

Lucas got the message. "I hear ya."

Sophie turned to Lucas and burned her gaze into his eyes. "Lucas, I'm scared shitless."

Returning her gaze, Lucas said, "Join the club." Then a wave of feeling washed over Lucas and he added, "We're gonna beat this thing, Sophie . . ."

Sophie looked away. A single tear had tracked down her cheek and she quickly wiped it away. Suddenly, a hitch of pain made her wince. "Fuck!"

"What is it?"

"Goddamn arm."

"Here, lemme give you a hand." Lucas reached out for her arm but Sophie pulled back and stared at him with an odd look in her eyes. Lucas met her gaze. "What's wrong?"

"Last thing I want from you is another fucking hand." Sophie smiled wryly through her tears.

Lucas grinned. "Always the smart ass."

He took a closer look at her arm. He took the tube of cream and applied more ointment. His touch was tender and cautious. He reached into his pocket and pulled out a Darvocet caplet. "Here—take this."

"What is it?"

"Something to take the edge off."

"I don't want it."

"Take it."

"No."

Lucas held it by her lips. "C'mon, open."

Sophie rolled her eyes and took the pill. Lucas handed her the flask and she took a gulp of Jack. Grimacing, she shook her head and said, "That oughtta finish me off."

"You're gonna live."

"Lemme see your fingers," Sophie said and helped Lucas unwrap his hands. Upon seeing his wounds she gasped. They were swollen now, verging on being infected. "Jesus, you gotta get some antibiotics or something."

"I'll survive." Lucas was starting to feel dizzy, flushed. He could smell the spicy aroma of her hair, the powdery scent of her pale skin. There was something hot stirring in his loins, and it was embarrassing the hell out of him. He was in the middle of a crisis, for God's sake, and this was his motherfucking partner!

"Think there's a bottle of alcohol in the kit." Sophie leaned down and reached under the bed. As she searched through the first-aid kit, the sheet bowed away from her torso for a moment and revealed the curve of her back, the pale crescent of her breast.

"It's okay, forget it, I'm fine, just fine." Lucas was mortified. The urge to hold her was so strong he felt woozy.

Sophie sat back up with a damp swab in her hand. "Promise I'll be gentle."

"Go ahead." Lucas held up his hands and closed his eyes tightly, not because he was frightened of the pain or because he couldn't stand to watch. On the contrary, it was because he could not take his eyes off his partner.

"Ouch!"

The first touch of the swab startled Lucas more than anything else. He jerked back and opened his eyes. The sheet had fallen away from Sophie, revealing her breasts. Sophie quickly replaced the sheet.

Sophie dropped the swab and cupped Lucas's big weathered hands in hers. "Did I hurt you?"

"It's okay, I'm fine," he said softly.

There was an awkward silence. Looking up into his eyes, Sophie seemed to be wavering over some deep-rooted conflict. She chewed her lip for a moment. Then she reached up and touched his face. Her hand felt tender and reassuring on his cheek.

"I'm fine, really. . . ." Lucas reached up and put his hand on hers. Their gazes met and lingered there for a moment.

Lucas felt the urges tearing him apart inside—the longing to hold her, to comfort her, to wrap his arms around her, to reveal his true feelings. It was excruciating. His mind was spinning. Tears were stinging his eyes. Gooseflesh broke out along his arms and shoulders. He tried to express it in words but the powerful feelings were suddenly poisoned by the bittersweet sting of reality.

For reasons he could not understand, he would not allow himself to pursue it any further.

Lucas pushed himself away and said, "Better start thinking about getting some food in our bellies."

"Ángel! Come in!"

Flaco's voice pierced the noisy silence of the cab. Hurriedly reaching over to the CB controls, Angel turned the volume down. He did not want to disturb his two wounded friends in back. Gently lifting the mike from its cradle, he said, "Angel here, Uncle Flaco. Over."

The old man's voice came crackling through the speaker, taut with tension and perhaps even a measure of resolve. "Big trouble on the way, Nephew. Big trouble."

"Wha' the matter?" Angel said into the mike.

But before the answer could reach him, the entire cab lit up with an intense light. It was coming from behind them. It bounced off the side mirrors and momentarily blinded Angel.

Then came the amplified voice of a man who had a major bone to pick with The Black Mariah.

20

Rain
from Heaven

"ATTENTION WESTBOUND EIGHTEEN-WHEELER LI-CENSE NUMBER HYX-7557! PULL OFF IMMEDIATELY! THIS IS THE PENNINGTON COUNTY SHERIFF'S DE-PARTMENT, MISSOURI STATE POLICE, AND FBI! PLEASE PULL OFF, IMMEDIATELY!"

About a hundred yards behind the Kenworth, charging forth in a spectacular clamor of noise and glaring lights, Baum was leading the pack. He rode in the fast lane, his speedometer climbing past seventy. His cruiser was lit up like an insane party.

"REPEAT! PULL OFF IMMEDIATELY! WE HAVE A WARRANT FOR THE ARREST OF REGINALD LUCAS HYDE AND SOPHIA COHEN!"

Baum was barking into his PA system, beads of sweat filming his forehead. He was stewing in a mixture of rage and excitement. In one afternoon he had seen a fatal blaze take a colored boy's life, had seen his deputy lose his marbles, and had seen a gruesome stigmata burned into the dead boy's corpse. Then, early this evening, word started coming over the wires about some bad-ass *banditos* in a big black truck hitting pawn shops and blowing up gas stations across

Missouri. For a simple little backwoods sheriff like Baum, this was turning into a red-letter day.

"PULL OFF NOW BEFORE ANYBODY ELSE GETS HURT!"

Behind him rode the Feds, Hawkins and Massamore, in their unmarked '91 Pontiac Grand Prix. Dressed in identical wool suits, razor-cut hairstyles, and grim dispositions, they seemed like buffoons to Baum. Company men. Baum had no use for them. But it was still a good idea for them to accompany the sheriff; it lent an air of gravity to the situation that the sheriff wanted to take advantage of.

Ernie Parrish was bringing up the rear. A twenty-five-year veteran of the Missouri State Police, Ernie was an old drinking buddy from way back. He and Baum would usually get together on Easter weekends and go quail hunting down around Poplar Bluff, bringing along plenty of Wild Turkey and small bills for midnight poker marathons. When Ernie had heard that Baum was after some trucker high-ballin' across the Show-Me State, Ernie immediately called up the Feds and put together a posse. But even though the whole rhubarb was taking place in Ernie's jurisdiction, Ernie knew he was merely along for the ride.

This was Dick Baum's show.

"ACKNOWLEDGE AND PULL OFF! YOU HAVE ONE MINUTE!!" Inside the cruiser, Sheriff Baum continued hollering into the public-address. He could hear his amplified voice reverberating outside, clanging above the wind and roar of the engines.

He was approaching the semi. Most of the other traffic around them had either dropped back, pulled over to the shoulder, or exited the highway. Only a battered old school bus hovered between him and the truck. Baum glanced at his speedometer. He was going a little over sixty-five, gaining quickly. The school bus was losing speed, weaving, threatening to fall apart. It was obvious the bus driver was pushing it to stay up with the truck. Why? Why the hell would this friggin' bus be risking oblivion to stay behind the truck? Baum wanted answers so bad he could taste them.

Baum rushed past the school bus on a cloud of carbon monoxide and fury.

Approaching the rear of the speeding truck, Baum swept his searchlight across the back of its trailer. The words SACRAMENTO ALLIED LEASING were printed across the dusty loading door. Beneath it, mammoth wheels were churning wildly, sending chinks of dirt and gravel up into the bright lights.

Baum swallowed air. The semi was speeding up. Squeezing the PA mike in his moist palm, Baum spat his words, *"GODDAMNIT! PULL OVER OR WE TAKE YOU DOWN RIGHT NOW!!"*

Sudden static crackled through the cruiser. Baum reached down and adjusted the squelch on his scanner. Lucas Hyde's voice was trying to seep through the interference. "Breaking—Sheriff—back—*fffffht—fht-fht—*"

Baum fiddled with the knobs on the CB. The voice returned. "Break—break for Sheriff Baum!" Lucas's voice sounded high and brittle on the speaker. "Put your ears on, Sheriff—you got Lucas Hyde here. Come back."

Trading microphones, Baum barked into the CB handset. "Hyde, this here's Sheriff Baum. Don't make it worse than it already is—pull the fuck on over."

"Can't do it, Sheriff."

"Why the hell not?"

A momentary burst of static, then the reply. "Can't stop."

"Son," Baum began, squeezing the CB a little harder than necessary, "I've been in the law enforcement business in one capacity or another for over thirty years and I'm telling you I've never run across a person who had more of a reason to pull over!"

Breathing hard, Baum lifted up on the call switch and listened.

The trucker's reply came on a crackling cough of static. "Listen to me, Sheriff—if you make us stop right now, there's gonna be more deaths. I guarantee it."

"Bullshit!"

More static, then Lucas's anguished voice. "We haven't done anything."

Baum snapped the button down and barked into the mike. "Stunts on the highway, gas stations blowin' up, shit stolen from cemeteries—I'm gonna give you one last chance to pull over."

Through the speaker, the trucker said, "Sheriff, I told you we didn't purposely start those fires. I know you don't believe me, but we didn't!"

The sheriff screamed into the mike, "Whatever you yahoos have gotten into—it's over! You hear what I'm sayin'?! IT'S OVER!! YOU READ ME?!!"

"I fucking told you," Lucas's voice came back over the air, "this stuff isn't our fault!"

"Goddamn black grease-ball! I'm gonna take you out personally!'"

"You fat redneck! Can't you understand what I'm telling you?!"

Baum lost control. Veins pulsed at his temples, his color darkened. He crushed the button in his grip. "Don't you sass me, Nigger!! I'LL DROP YOU LIKE A BAD HABIT!!"

A sudden burst of static cut through the dark interior of the cruiser. It was Special Agent Massamore, his rich, modulated voice oozing from the speaker. "Sheriff Baum, perhaps we should step in and—"

Baum cut the Fed off. "Put a cork in it, G-man! This is my tag!" Then Baum growled into the mike at the trucker. "I'm gonna give you ten seconds to pull off, Nigger. Then it's Hail Mary time!"

Through the speaker: "You dumb, racist, backwoods, cracker motherfucker, you're gonna be killing three people!"

"Ten . . ."

"Sheriff, I'm not gonna stop—"

"Nine . . ."

"You copy what I'm saying—?"

"Eight . . . seven . . . six . . ."

"Fuck you!"

"Five, four, three, two, one—bingo!" Baum shot a glance in his rearview and saw the headlights of the Feds' car hovering one length behind him. He pressed the button and said,

"Hawkins! Massamore! Take over! I want to break this fucking pony right now!"

A moment later, Special Agent Hawkins's voice returned through the speaker. "Appreciate it if you could move aside and give us some room to work, Sheriff."

Baum dropped back and let them pass.

The first shot zinged past the cab just as Lucas was stepping over Angel.

"What the hell was that?" Sophie was perched on the edge of the shotgun seat. Gripping the steering wheel with her left hand, holding the accelerator down with the edge of her foot, she was keeping the truck on course while the boy traded places with Lucas.

Lucas quickly climbed into the driver's seat and took the wheel. He slammed the clutch in, shifted, and stomped on the pedal. The truck groaned away from the cacophony of sirens and light behind them.

"Gunshot," Lucas said absently. He was all too familiar with the dry popping noise of a high-powered rifle. He remembered it coming over the rooftops of the projects again and again during the Watts riots. It wasn't the clichéd cherry-bomb sound of Aaron Spelling TV-movies and bad cop shows. Instead, it was a bright subsonic crack that always raised gooseflesh along Lucas's arms.

"They're shooting at us." Sophie announced it not so much with alarm as doomed resignation.

"Stay away from the windows, lean inside!" Lucas had the accelerator pedal pinned to the floor. The truck was climbing past ninety-five. Beneath them, the DAF power plant raged. The cab shivered and vibrated. Twenty tons' worth of torque surged through the transmission.

It felt as though they were riding a blast furnace.

The next shot took the right Goodyear. Lucas felt it go like a heel breaking off his shoe. The impact goosed the rear end and made the truck weave violently. Lucas strained against the g-force and held the beast steady. Another shot chipped the back corner of the trailer and ricochetted past the cab.

"Jesus Christ." Sophie had her hands over her ears.

Lucas scanned the dark horizon ahead of them. In the throw of his headlights he could barely make out the silhouette of an ancient overpass a mile away, approaching fast. A pair of side ramps coursed off the highway on either side of the overpass. And for a feverish moment, Lucas contemplated tearing down one of those ramps, killing his lights, and escaping into the darkness of the farm fields. But his editorial voice deep down inside him put the kibosh on that idea real quick. . . .

Sure, that would be a great idea, just zip down one of those exit ramps and lose the cops on a side road . . . but you should also be prepared to die in a fiery crash when the g-force tips the top-heavy Mariah over into the gravel and slams the truck into the barricade like an overripe insect against a windshield . . .

Sophie was looking into her side mirror when another bullet strafed the side of the truck, shattering her mirror and taking a chunk off the hood. Rearing backward, Sophie screamed. "Son of a fucking bitch! Unmarked sedan breathing down our necks!!"

"You alright?" Lucas glanced over at his partner. Sophie was shaking convulsively, shielding her face with trembling fingers. Only inches away, a spider web of cracks had spread across her window from the ricochet impact.

"You're bleeding!" From the doorway of the coffin box, Angel pointed at Sophie's collarbone. A half-inch shard had pierced her T-shirt just below the neck. Blood oozed along her collar. "Hang on!" Angel hollered over the wind and the whine. "I'll get a bandage!"

Another bullet connected with the truck. This time it was underneath the tractor, the right rear tire. The explosion rocked the cab. The truck weaved madly. Lucas wrestled with the wheel, struggled to hold the rig steady. A rivulet of sweat tracked down the bridge of his nose and dropped onto the wheel. He quickly wiped his face with the back of his sleeve. "Not gonna be able to withstand many more of those," he hollered over the din.

The engine was complaining noisily. With two tires gone, the drag was a thousand times heavier. They were losing speed, fishtailing, bucking wildly. It felt like they were traveling over a sea of loose bricks.

"Looks like they got a piece of the engine!" Sophie was pointing through the windshield at the vapor billowing up from the grille. In the darkness it looked like a veil being pulled over the scene before them.

"Must have pierced the radiator!" Lucas slammed the shift lever down a gear and coaxed the rig onward against the drag of the wounded tires. The truck was faltering. Its gear groaned like a dying pachyderm.

Angel returned from the back and tended Sophie's wound with a HandiWipe and a bandage. Gazing over his shoulder, Angel said, " 'There any way to unhook the trailer?"

"Good idea, but impossible," Lucas said.

"I could climb out there and uncouple it," Angel offered.

Sophie glared back at the boy. "No way, José!"

"You've seen too many movies, kid," Lucas said and fought with the vibrating steering wheel.

"But I could—"

At that moment, another barrage of bullets lashed the truck. It sounded like the Fourth of July, like someone had lit a brick of firecrackers just outside their windows. Sparks rose all around them. Chinks of metal and fiberglass erupted through the darkness.

More tires went. Two in back, another one under the cab. The truck lurched. Then it began to skid. Lucas wrenched the wheel against the skid, held it steady, and put the pedal to the floor.

The truck was weaving out of control.

"Lucas, we gotta get off the highway!" Sophie's voice was as shrill as an alley cat's.

"Can't do it!"

"We're gonna jackknife!"

"Not if I can help it," Lucas hissed and threw the shift lever forward. The steering wheel had a mind of its own now. It convulsed in his hands, raising shivers of pain up through his arms. But he held tight. Unfortunately, the truck was losing speed in fits and jerks.

"We got company!" Angel pointed past Lucas at his side mirror.

Lucas gazed into the mirror and caught the lights of the Pontiac Grand Prix in his face. But what he couldn't see was the FBI agent on the Pontiac's passenger side attempting to end the entire situation very quickly.

"Get me just a tad wider, John," Special Agent Stephen Hawkins said to his partner. "It'll cut the angle down and maximize the kill zone."

"Affirmative." Special Agent Massamore pulled the vehicle across the fast lane to the edge of the far shoulder. They were going just over seventy miles per hour now, cutting through the dusty draft behind the runaway semi. Although their present rate of speed was well under the prescribed safety threshold for rural pursuit scenarios, Massamore was still a trifle concerned about being so close to the truck. With a half a dozen tires blown and a subject unwilling to surrender, the rig was unpredictable. At any moment, it might weave into them.

"Good," Hawkins said, raising the scope to his right eye and preparing to fire. "I've got an outstanding line now. Stand by for a quarterback sneak."

The sharpshooter took a breath and held it. Through the greenish hue of the night-vision scope he could see the subject swimming into focus behind the cross hairs. Early forties, black, male, stocky build, the truck driver was fighting to keep his wounded rig on course. One quick shot to the head would close the scenario.

Hawkins fired. At the same moment, the truck lurched and swerved violently out of range. The bullet caught the left quarter panel of the cab and ricochetted impotently off the metal and into the night.

"Darn it!" Hawkins was irritated. He didn't like to miss. He didn't like to let his teammates down. A mediocre trainee at the academy, Hawkins had nonetheless been tops in his class on the firing range. And after six years of field service, he had developed a reputation for being one of the best shots in the Midwest Bureau. "One-shot Hawkins," they called him.

"That's okay, Steve," Massamore said, encouraging his partner. "You'll score on the next play."

"Thanks, John," Hawkins said, while cocking another bullet into the firing chamber. He was using a Winchester bolt-action Model X with .25 caliber factory loads and a Dooley Extra-bright night scope. It was an outstanding weapon. And there was no reason it wouldn't work on the second try.

Hawkins lined up the shot again. He took a breath, held it, and prepared to fire. But before he could squeeze the trigger, a pair of headlights loomed behind him, throwing his concentration completely off.

Then came the impact.

"Chingado!!" Flaco was not prepared for the violent reaction that followed. He had pinned the bus's foot-feed to the floor and had rammed the FBI agents' car with everything he had. The impact carried him over the steering wheel and slammed him into the bus's windshield. His forehead collided with the glass. Stars burst across his field of vision. Hairline cracks spread across the windshield. And all his worldly possessions came tumbling off their shelves and across the floor. Cups and dishes and cans and saucers struck him from behind, collided with the dash, and shattered against the windshield.

Flaco slammed back into his seat and grasped the steering wheel. The school bus was skidding across the gravel shoulder. "Sweet Christ!"

He pulled back onto the road and held the bus steady. In front of him, the Pontiac skidded into the other direction, tires screeching and searchlight arcing wildly across the sky. Then it pulled back into its lane. The rear end of the Pontiac was a crumpled mess.

Flaco squeezed the CB mike with his crooked right hand. "Ángel! Can you hear me?!"

Static crackled through the speaker.

"Mr. Hyde?!"

Static.

"Sophie?!"

Nothing.

"Sweet Christ, Luisa, Lord in the Heavens," Flaco prayed frantically under his breath to the memory of his late wife. This was his moment of truth. He was about to slam into the Pontiac again and anything could happen.

From the sky above, a sudden burst of light enveloped Flaco. It was angelic light, pure and silver and omnipotent. It filled the interior of the bus like holy water and made everything turn luminous.

Flaco's heart began to race. The light from above was throwing giant shadows across the front of the bus, across the FBI car and the truck in front of it. The shadows danced, swam, slid back and forth across the dark highway. Flaco recognized these shadows. For most of his life he had dreamt of these shapeless, formless shapes. These were the shadows of his visions.

In that single instant of revelation Flaco realized what he had to do.

"Mr. Hyde—!" Flaco hollered into the mike.

Through the static: "—*fffffffffht-fht-ft*—Flaco?"

"Mr. Hyde, can you hear me?!"

"Get out of here, Flaco! Get out n—*sssshhhh-fffh-fht*—"

Static drowned the voice. Flaco pressed the call switch and said, "My friends! Ángel! You must do as the Bible says! Do you hear me?!"

The roar from above mingled with the din of interference and the rumble of the bus's engine. Flaco hollered into the mike, his voice breaking, deteriorating. "Do as the Bible says—resist the power—be firm in your faith—whatever that faith is—!!"

Flaco gazed through the veil of light ahead of him and saw the big Kenworth truck escaping into the night, wobbling on ragged tires and plumes of vapor, moving farther and farther away. The ringing in Flaco's ears worsened. But layering over the sound was a chorus of noise from above. It was weighing down on him like a thick rain. The light intensified.

Something struck his leg. He looked down and saw that a

candle from his shrine had rolled clear across the length of the bus. It was burning.

He glanced over his shoulder and saw the miracle.

The shrine was lit up. Dozens of the tiny candles had spontaneously ignited and now were glowing softly within the body of the altar. Some of them had fallen and were rolling around the floor of the bus. Others had ignited bits of old newspapers and corners of the ratty upholstery.

Flaco gripped the steering wheel with one hand and held his free hand palm-up to the heavens. "Luisa! My sweet love, help me!"

Another searchlight struck Flaco from behind. It was Sheriff Baum. Flaco glanced into the side mirror just in time to see the sheriff's windshield, distorted by the wreath of blinding light.

Now Flaco was immersed in brightness. From the FBI agents in front of him, the sheriff behind him, and God above him. And the ethereal symphony rose to such a thunderous level that Flaco could no longer hear the engines, the wind, or even his own thoughts. There was only the penetrating sound.

Flaco's time had finally come . . .

With his last ounces of energy, he leaned out his window, craned his neck upward, and looked into the sky. In the nimbus of light he saw the blur of rotor blades, the glint of glass off a fuselage, a dark insectoid tail. It was an angel in the shape of a police helicopter, its klieg light aimed down at Flaco's puny world. . . .

Then the seventh angel blew his trumpet, and there were loud voices in heaven, saying, "The kingdom of the world has become the kingdom of our Lord and of His Christ, and He shall reign for ever and ever . . ."

The rays of light that fell upon the hood of the school bus began to transform. Like beautiful ghostly spider webs, they began spinning, coalescing, forming the outline of a plump Mexican matron. She wore a lovely white bridal gown, bonnet, and train. Her merry face, dimples, and soft brown eyes gazed upon Flaco and smiled warmly.

"Do not be afraid," Luisa thought at him, *gossamer tendrils of light pouring from her lips.*

"Is it time?" Flaco asked.

"Sí, mi amor."

"May I have the honor of this dance?"

Luisa nodded and brilliant magnesium light cascaded from her eyes and mouth. "It would be my honor."

Flaco felt something flutter up his leg. He looked down and saw that one of the errant candles had caught his trousers on fire. The yellow flame curled up his leg and embraced him. The warmth was sublime.

Once and for all, Flaco knew his destiny . . .

He pressed the accelerator pedal to the floor and shot toward the Pontiac, but before he could make contact, a storm of bullets rained down upon him and delivered him from this world forever.

"UUUUUNNNNNNNNNNNNNCCLE!!!!"

Angel was leaning across Sophie's lap, hanging out the passenger window of the truck, watching the whole thing happen like it was all a bad dream. His body quaked and convulsed with shock. Sophie grabbed him for fear he would fall out. But Angel seemed oblivious to any dangers right now. "No, no, no, no, no, no, no, no, no, no."

Sophie pulled him back in and hugged him tightly. Tears poured from the boy's eyes and saturated Sophie's shirt. His wiry little body trembled like a wounded bird in her arms.

"He knew he wa'th gonna die!" Angel cried. "He knew!"

Sophie held him tight and softly stroked his hair.

"Jesus Christ!" Lucas was watching the conflagration unfold behind them in his side mirror. The police helicopter had appeared out of nowhere. Hovering overhead, it had carpeted the school bus with a full clip of M-16 fire. The bullets took the bus apart. Bursting at the seams, its windshield imploding in on itself, the bus had hiccupped into the air and had begun to roll.

As Lucas watched, the bus tumbled into the Pontiac. In a hideous chain reaction that unraveled with an unreal quality of dreams, the Pontiac skidded out of control and rolled across the median a hundred yards behind the Mariah. Landing in the center ditch, the Pontiac slid upside-down across the dirt like an unpended prehistoric beetle, its wheels scuttling uselessly in the air.

Then the bus crashed into it.

The two vehicles exploded on contact. The initial concussion was a brilliant white burst that rose up into the night sky and nearly roasted the helicopter. The shock waves reached the truck and jarred the cab like a battering ram.

"Oh, my God!" Sophie was instinctively shielding Angel's eyes, gazing through the window at the flames lighting up the heavens.

Lucas couldn't tear his gaze from the mirror. Behind them, the helicopter had emerged from the flames and groaned upward like a twisted version of the great phoenix. The inferno had threatened to gobble up the helicopter, but at the last minute it narrowly escaped destruction by pulling into a vertical climb. It sputtered in midair for a moment. Then it banked away from the scene and soft-landed in a nearby cornfield.

Lucas wrenched his gaze back to the road ahead.

"Madam! The truck is getting away!"

The limousine was hovering a quarter of a mile behind the chaos. Eric had discreetly dropped back to watch from a distance. The flashing light from the police vehicles was strobing through the windshield, painting the chauffeur's terrified face in bursts of silver.

A moment later, the limo passed the burning vehicles.

In the back seats, beneath the dome light, Vanessa began the ceremony. She used the spring-loaded arm to open the tin box. Inside, she found the beaker. The beaker was nearly a hundred years old, made of jellied glass with a nickel cap. A lovely pentagram figure was etched into its side. Her father had first used it to store lamb's blood for his rites. It rattled with the movement of the limousine. The liquid inside jiggled.

She opened the beaker and breathed in the odors of the oily brew. It smelled like sweet copper. In terms of ingredients it was relatively simple. Ninety percent was animal blood. The thickening agent was grave dirt—a substance the Cajuns called "goofer dust." The final ingredient was so costly and esoteric that Vanessa had to send Eric all the way to Honduras to obtain a single tincture. The mountain people called it adder's essence. In truth it was the strongest poison known to man. In small amounts it made for powerful magic.

It was Vanessa's holy water.

She worked quickly. As the limousine rattled over potholes in a furious attempt to keep up, Vanessa brought the beaker down to her armrest. She dipped her palsied index finger into the liquid. She closed her eyes. She made the sign of the inverted cross as best she could in her condition. Then she lightly touched her fingertip to each eyelid. The damp spots stung sharply where the poison clung to her skin. But the magic was delicious.

"Bringer of pain . . . Bringer of visions . . ." She whispered with her last ragged reserves of breath. "Let the being . . . man or animal . . . see the vision . . . be touched by it . . . be destroyed by it . . ."

She imagined the shape.

It took a few moments for the object to materialize in her mind. She relied on memories, fragments of things she had seen along the road over the years, in the corners of photographs and pictures from books.

Soon the shape began to form.

Lucas blinked.

At first there was nothing. Then there was something, rising up from the scarred pavement a hundred yards away, undulating in The Black Mariah's headlights like a fume from the very concrete itself.

A roadblock.

Smack dab in the middle of the westbound lanes, it had just appeared out of nowhere and exploded in the headlights. An enormous rampart of giant timbers. Festooned with red flags. Screaming death and destruction. No warning. No signs. Just the end of the line.

"LUCA'TH! LOOK OUT!!" Angel was pointing straight ahead, mouth gaping, eyes hot with urgency.

"I SEE IT!!"

Lucas didn't have time to think. He didn't even have time to aim his evasion. He only had time to wrench the steering wheel to the left as far as it would go and close his eyes. The truck fell into a skid and hit the roadblock going about sixty.

It was like passing through air.

There was nothing at all.

Lucas screamed. Not in anger or defeat or anything meditative like that, but more as an expression of pure primal awe. All of a sudden Lucas had become Primitive Man. He had discovered fire and had singed his fingers. The world had abruptly turned on its head. Cows were flying. The sky was green. It was raining toasters.

Then the confusion turned to white-hot panic as Lucas felt the feeling he had always prayed he would never feel. The g-force sucking him out of his seat. The churning of the wheels. The crunching sound.

The Black Mariah was jackknifing.

It felt like being on one of those teacup rides at the county fair. The seats swam beneath them. The steering wheel propellered wildly and all the momentum belly-flopped to the right as the cab curled around the coupler. The chassis bellowed the death wails of an enormous animal. Lucas was tossed out of his seat. Sophie and Angel were thrown against the passenger side like bearings in a pinball machine. Luckily, no one was crushed. Each of them landed against the hard vinyl panel of the door and there was enough metal around them to prevent the cab from collapsing.

Then came the aftershock.

The trailer's momentum ripped the back off the cab and the cab rolled. In a shower of dust and sparks the world turned upside down. Roof became floor. Wall became liquid rapids, spinning, spinning, a molten blur, arms flailing, limbs colliding, tumbling to the roof in a heap.

Pain sliced up Lucas's back and legs, rushed up through his lungs, sang in his ears. A blast of hot noxious air was filling the cab. The sound of screeching tires rose outside the wreckage.

Lucas madly scrambled to his feet and shook the chaos from his head. He scanned the darkness and peered through the ragged hole in the back of the coffin box. His heart was about to explode. Behind him, Sophie was crawling, shrieking, clamoring to get out. Lucas turned, grabbed her, grabbed the boy, and dragged them toward the opening.

Outside the cab, the sound of screeching tires rose to an unbearable level. Lucas reached the opening just in time to see the pandemonium.

Sheriff Baum swerved to avoid the overturned trailer. The cruiser hit the median ditch going about seventy. It fell into a violent roll, throwing Baum clear like a broken rag doll and pinwheeling fifty yards or more though the cornfield before crashing to a halt right-side-up.

Ernie Parrish wasn't so lucky. He tried to stop in time and skidded directly into the trailer. There was a sick baritone concussion of shattering glass and metal as Ernie's black-and-white collapsed like a paper bag, killing the patrolman instantly, sending torrents of shattered glass and metal shards whirling through the air.

Lucas wrenched Sophie and the boy out of the wreckage. Agony exploded inside him. Blasts of heat erupted in his belly. Searing daggers sliced through his chest, his arms, his legs, his mind. His vision swam. Orange sparks whirled like airborne cinders before him.

Lucas fell to his knees.

Through the pain he heard another vehicle weaving out of control behind him. It came skidding across the oily debris, its brakes locked, its tires screeching. Careening through the wreckage, it slammed sideways into the flaming trailer. It was an antique car. A limousine.

It was the last thing Lucas saw clearly.

21

Transformation

For Angel, the next few seconds unraveled in dream-lapse slow motion. He knew their only chance of survival rested upon his bony little shoulders.

He locked arms with Lucas and Sophie and wrenched them across the carpet of broken glass. The sheriff's cruiser was buried in cornstalks and smoke fifty yards away. Its bubble lights still strobed impotently. A trail of flames spewed off its tail like an arrow pointing at it.

It was their ticket out of there.

"The cop car! We'll take the cop car!! C'mon!!" Angel huffed and puffed frantically. It was like pulling along a pair of pregnant cows. Sophie was racked with spasms, eyes wincing, drool flagging from her mouth. She was trying to say something, but the convulsions were hacking off her words. Lucas was worse. He was dead weight. His legs were wet cement. Vomit and bile roiled off his lips.

Angel could smell something burning. He realized with sudden dread that it was coming from inside his friends.

"C'mon!! Another few feet!!!" Angel pulled them into the corn. The razor leaves and spiky tassels tore at their arms and legs. The smoke engulfed them. They swam toward the

cruiser, their clumsy steps chewing through the moist earth.
The cruiser was thirty feet away, still idling dumbly.

Angel stepped in something wet.

Before he had a chance to look down, a hand shot out of
the darkness and clutched at his ankle. Angel yelped and tore
himself free. There was a loud popping sound behind him
like a cherry bomb exploding. Corn silk erupted next to Sophie's head. The bullet barely missed her left ear.

"*QUICK!!*" Angel shoved them toward the cruiser and
looked back over his shoulder in time to see Sheriff Baum
crawling after them.

The sheriff was baptized in blood. His scalp was soaked in
sticky crimson. His shoulder had been torn open and the
milky gleam of clavicle poked through his ragged shirt. His
legs were useless, ravaged by multiple fractures. His eyes
glistened with shock and rage.

"Bah—baaahhhsss—!!" The sheriff couldn't get the words
out. Again he raised the .38 and fired, but the bullet just
strafed the soil in front of him. A paroxysm of pain stiffened
his body and he collapsed.

The sheriff's glassy gaze stayed riveted to Angel for endless moments, until Angel couldn't tell if the man had died
or was still watching.

Another piercing sound exploded in the darkness. Angel
spun toward the car. It was Lucas. He was on his knees,
shrieking like a newborn baby, clawing at the driver's-side
door handle. His face was contorted worse than ever. Tears
streamed down his cheeks and his body heaved with violent
twinges of agony. Sparks were spurting from his nostrils. Sophie was on the other side of the car, crawling on her hands
and knees toward the door. Sophie's breath was visible in
tiny plumes of smoke.

Angel's friends were burning like fuses.

Angel dove toward the car.

In real time, the next few moments encompassed no more
than ten seconds; but for Angel it seemed an eternity. The
pain was beginning to throb inside his own belly, the curse
incubating inside him. But he ignored it. He ignored everything but the driver's-side door of the cruiser. Only later

would he realize that it was quite a lucky break that all the doors of the cruiser were unlocked, because at this point every second counted.

Angel threw open the driver's-side door and shoved Lucas inside. The big man sprawled across the front seat and clawed at the steering wheel. Angel jumped in the back. Sophie was halfway inside the other door when Angel grabbed her by the shirt and pulled her in.

Lucas slammed his foot down on the accelerator and the cruiser blasted off. In a spray of corn silk and earth, the car fishtailed toward the highway. Angel scrambled to shut the doors, which were flapping wildly.

A moment later they made it back to the road.

Tires screeching . . . hitting the pavement and spinning off into the dark distance . . . fleeing . . . rats fleeing a sinking ship . . .

And the odors . . .

The odors of spilled diesel mingling with the coppery bouquet of blood . . . swirling inside her . . . the currents of liquid pain and hatred. . . .

She was drowning in her own hatred.

The accident had thrown Vanessa off the edge of her safety seat and onto the floor. Her brittle legs had folded up beneath her, the kindling of her bones snapping within her. She was face down. Her hair was sopping the spills. The tang of blood clogged her nose. She could not move but she could still hear. She could hear the sound of the sheriff's cruiser receding into the distance.

How ironic it was that it should end this way. Eric, the idiot lummox chauffeur, following too closely. The vision causing the accident. The chain reaction sucking the limousine into the broken glass and fire. And the final indignation . . .

Dying on the floor of the rear compartment, face pressed to the sodden carpet, drowning in the mire like a mongrel . . . like a bitch dog . . . crawling . . . crawling through the offal . . . through the excrement . . . through the stench . . .

The stench of wet hay and manure . . . the horrible memory flooding back . . .

The genesis of her pain . . .

Running . . .
Down by the mill house. Up Tassiter Hill. Across the bean
fields and out behind the DeGeaux farm. The dairy barn sat
in a clearing behind the main house.

Vanessa led Thomas through the doorway and into the
darkness. They found a private place behind an empty horse
stall in the corner. Vanessa's heart was racing. This was
turning out to be the most exciting night of her thirteen-year-
old life. She had already kissed a Negro boy once. Now, she
and Thomas were going to reveal all their secrets to each
other.

They lowered themselves into the hay. Thomas told her
she was beautiful. Vanessa told Thomas he was the most
handsome boy she had ever seen. They kissed again. Their
lips lingered, tasting, probing. Thomas began to gently urge
Vanessa's dress over her shoulders . . .

A sudden sound.

Thomas froze. Vanessa's mouth went as dry as sawdust.
Across the barn, near the double doors, the sound of a twig
snapping echoed through shadows. Footsteps. Thomas
turned and searched along the wall for a way out. Vanessa
began to panic. Soon a figure appeared at the mouth of the
horse stall and gazed down at them.

In the moonlight, Maurice DeGeaux looked to be about
ten feet tall. Decked out in his preacher's coat, high-button
collar, and hat, he radiated authority. His voice was a
glacial breeze in the darkness. "Lament like a virgin girded
with sackcloth," he said with his eyes burning into the pair
below him. "She is unclean now."

Behind Vanessa came the sound of splintering wood.
Thomas had pushed open a rotting plank and was shimmying
through the gap. Within moments he had escaped.

"THOMAS!!"

Vanessa made a move toward the opening but felt a huge
hand on her ankle. It gripped her like a vice and pulled her
back in the shadows.

"It's the blood that makes atonement!" Maurice was rolling up his sleeves.

"Please, Daddy—!!" Vanessa tried to pull herself away from his grasp but the man's hand was like a leg iron.

"You have sinned, Vanessa!"

"Pleeeeeeeease—!!"

"Take your medicine, child."

Vanessa screamed then, but it had no effect on the righteous avenger Maurice. The tall man flipped Vanessa over onto her tummy and held her there. Vanessa ate a mouthful of moldy hay. Tears rolled down her cheeks. She tried to see what was going on but the tears and horror and shame were clouding her vision.

Then came the first spank.

Maurice was widely recognized as one of the strongest men in the Mobile Bay area. Before his wife had passed away, he had participated in strong-men contests at the Baldwin County Fair every year. He could lift an entire buggy and change the wheel at the same time. He could drive a nail through a timber with his bare hand. Through the years, Maurice had slapped Vanessa only once before—when she was ten—and it had raised a welt that had permanently scarred her little bottom. But this was different. There was insanity behind these blows.

Vanessa shrieked at the pain. It felt like her rear end had been strafed with buckshot. She turned and glimpsed her father's face, luminous in the moonlight. The righteous fury positively glowed in his dark eyes. But the worst part was his hand. His muscular right hand. Fingers webbed together, cupped, rigid as metal, tendons pulsing in his wrist, the hand had become a deadly weapon.

Maurice spanked her again. Vanessa shrieked again and choked on her sobs. The pain was gargantuan. It exploded up through her body as if she were being struck with a cattle prod. Surely he would stop soon.

Vanessa prayed he would stop soon.

The third spank made her ears ring and her body vibrate sickly. She tried to scream. This time her breath was gone. She could only lie trembling, mouth gaping like a fish, legs

*going numb, staring through the jagged opening in the wall
through which Thomas had escaped only seconds earlier.*

*The fourth, fifth, and sixth blows did most of the damage.
Later, the doctors would explain in hushed tones behind the
curtains of the DeGeaux house what had happened. The repeated impact of her father's hand had collapsed a delicate
bone around the base of Vanessa's spine. This led to a sever-
ing of the cauda equina nerve—resulting in gradual spinal
stenosis, severe sciatica, and eventual paralysis.*

*But in the darkness of the barn that night, in the heat of
Maurice's thrashing, it didn't matter anymore. By the time
that massive right hand had delivered its seventh blow,
Vanessa couldn't feel a thing. Her body had gone completely
numb. All she could do was silently weep and continue gazing out through the splintered breach in the wall.*

*In the distance, she could see Thomas silhouetted against
the moon. He was running for the tree line on the western
horizon. Running as fast as he could. Running for his life.
Moving like a frightened deer. Skittering over deadfalls,
weaving through trees, moving silently. Moving.*

Abandoning Vanessa.

Damn him to hell.

The hand came down again. . . .

The coughing ripped her out of the memory.

Writhing on the floor of the limousine, Vanessa was
dying. Her lungs were filling with fluid. Her heart was about
to explode. Agony seized her good arm and the right side of
her face. It felt as though a rusty band saw was carving her
shoulder off at the collarbone. It was a rippling pain. Radiating through her insides and drawing darkness over her eyes
like a shroud.

She coughed and blood came out.

With all her effort, she tried to look beyond the floor of
the limousine. In the collision's violent aftershock, the limo
doors had sprung open. Over the edge of the front foot rail
she could just barely see a pale liver-spotted arm, its hand
curled up and frozen in death, lying halfway out the front
door.

Evidently the collision had finished the chauffeur.

Pathetic old fool.

Vanessa managed to turn her head just enough so that her face pivoted toward the back seat. She saw the desecrated crucifix. It had landed on the floor near her chin. The Christ figure's little black eyes were gawking up at her.

Vanessa closed her eyes and began to pray. She prayed to her dark gods. She prayed that they would transform her hatred into a black tide that would roll across this wretched highway of fools. She prayed that they would bring the fire.

A change slithered over her with the inevitability of a snake. Her body began to vibrate. It was as if someone were drawing a giant bow across her frozen bones and tendons. The vibrations rose and grew and swelled within her like dissonant harmonies.

She opened her eyes. She saw that the bucket of fingers had spilled with the impact of the collision. Now the shrivelled white digits lay around her like filings aligned around a magnet.

They were all pointing at her.

The last thing she noticed was the antique beaker of unholy liquid. It had also overturned in the accident. But unlike the other containers, it had remained perched precariously on the end of her armrest. Now the poison brew dripped languidly like molasses onto the floor next to her. Vanessa watched it and thought about bringing visions to the mongrels of the world.

The prayer.

Bringer of pain . . . Bringer of visions . . . Let the beings . . . Man or animal . . . see the visions . . . be touched by the visions . . . be destroyed by the visions . . . for the visions are pain . . .

For I am the visions . . .

Vanessa used her last ounces of life to position her face under the beaker so that the last drops of poison could kiss her trembling lips.

Earl Coonts was among the first on the scene. A seventeen-year veteran of the Columbia Emergency Medical Service, Earl rode shotgun as his partner, Barry Straythairn, guided the E-Unit through the wreckage and skidded to a stop on the litter-strewn shoulder.

Both paramedics hopped out.

The place looked like Beirut after a tornado. Diesel poured from a jagged breach in the tractor's gas tank. A patrol car was wrapped around the base of the trailer. An old antique limousine was canted off the edge of the shoulder and a trail of tiny fires burned along the pavement beside it and well into the adjacent cornfield.

The fires looked like footsteps.

Earl hustled with his trauma box over to the body of Ernie Parrish, which lay charred and bloody a few feet from the trailer. Barry went over to check the cab.

Kneeling down by the body, Earl snapped open the lifepack and prepared to get some vitals. A stocky little man with thick glasses and thinning hair the color of old brass, Earl wore the standard white duty togs of a paramedic. A neat, little, red bow tie was tucked under his chin behind his stethoscope. Some of the other EMTs had fun ribbing Earl about his fastidiousness, some even called him fruity, but Earl didn't care. He believed in running a neat ship.

He put his fingertips on Ernie's throat. There was no pulse. Cold as ice. Earl began prepping the defibrillator when a sudden noise startled his attention back over his shoulder.

There was movement over by the antique limousine.

The rear door of the limo burst open. The hinges tore away and the crumpled door fell to the ground like a dry leaf. A figure emerged. Wiry and bow-legged, moving with insectlike sureness, the figure headed for the driver's-side door.

"Hey!" Earl stood up and faced the figure. "You okay?!"

The figure paused, turned around, and faced the paramedic.

Earl felt his scalp tingle. "Ma'am? You alright?"

The old woman was covered with blood. But something was wrong. She was standing as though a steel rod was running up her spine. Her legs were like twisted spirals of bloody flesh. Gun-metal gray hair fountained around her skull. Her eyes were luminous, with pupils like tiny fireflies.

When she smiled, her teeth showed black as cinders.

"Coontsy—!!"

The voice came from the old woman, but it was all wrong. Gravelly, masculine, burnished with lust, it sounded vaguely familiar to Earl. Worse than that, it was a nickname that Earl hadn't heard since grade school.

"Little Coontsy . . ." The hag was moving toward him on her insect legs.

Earl Coonts dirtied his pants. The shit crept out of him on a spasm of fear and he could feel its warm and tacky protein fill his boxer shorts under his uniform. He tried to focus on what he was seeing, tried to understand it, tried to categorize it. But all he could manage was a rabbit stare and an impotent flapping of his jaw as the devil woman's face contorted into a familiar visage.

The face of a sadistic gym teacher who had raped little Earl back in the sixth grade.

"Gonna suck my dick like a good little bitch?" The old woman's mechanical voice washed over Earl as she approached. Like a pull-string doll, the voice was a perfect reproduction of Earl's childhood assailant. Earl fell to his ass and began to cry. It was the grief and shame of a little boy. It tore Earl's tentative sanity up by the roots.

A moment later, Earl collapsed on the ground and buried his face in the broken glass.

It was lovely . . . the sparkling shards . . . the points of blood glistening in the sodium light . . . the quivering form beneath her . . .

Vanessa stood there for quite some time, gazing down at the trembling paramedic. The festering spirit inside her now had blossomed like a black butterfly, shivering out of its cocoon and filling her sack of skin with heat and energy and miraculous new talents . . . talents to absorb pain . . . to transform fear into visions . . .

She turned and strode back to the limousine.

It felt as if she were commanding a ghost ship, the force

inside her pulling the puppet strings of her ruined legs and arms and fingers. She was weightless now. Powerful as lightning. Infinitely more deadly.

It felt sublime.

She reached the limousine. The driver's-side door was blocked by the cooling corpse of the chauffeur. She cradled the chauffeur's head and tried to wriggle the blond giant free. His broad shoulders were wedged tight within the twisted metal. Vanessa pulled harder and Eric's head suddenly ripped free of its stalk like a pumpkin being harvested. Blood spumed lazily from Eric's dead cartilage and ragged jugular. But it served as a good lubricant because Vanessa was then able to shove the remains aside and climb behind the wheel.

She prepared to drive. Of course, during her mortal life Vanessa had never operated a car, but the talent was in her now and among its other skills, it was an excellent driver.

She put the battered car in gear and set out to finish what she had started.

PART III

The Maelstrom

"And they shall go forth and look on the dead bodies of the men who have rebelled against me; for their worm shall not die, their fire shall not be quenched, and they shall be an abhorrence to all flesh."

—Isaiah 66.24

22

Shrieker

"Look for the—!"

"Lucas, we gotta—!"

"—first-aid kit!!"

"Where?!"

"Look—"

"Lucas, goddamnit—!!"

"—under the seats!!" The words hissed out of Lucas, his throat raw and scorched from the sickness. His mind was spinning with painkillers and fear. His entire body was buzzing with agony. Although the fact that they were speeding along at a fast clip certainly helped, the deep tissue damage would not go away.

Gazing around the interior, Lucas quickly took a mental inventory of his new surroundings. The car was a factory-model Ford Taurus customized with extra horsepower, searchlights, and a heavy-duty rack of radio gear. Though the body had sustained major damage in the accident, the reinforced chassis and interior were practically unscathed. Lucas attributed it to good ol' American manufacturing and a lot of dumb luck. There was also a 12-gauge pump shotgun bracketed to a mount on the dash. In the darkness, all the lights gave the car a real carnival atmosphere. Plus, it smelled of Sheriff Baum, his old pomade and stale coffee.

To make matters worse, Lucas had lost his beloved Black Mariah. All his childhood dreams, all the shit work, studying for his Class-A license, driving the company Freightliners, working weekends, saving up enough to buy the basic power plant, all the meticulous spec work, all the years of being an owner operator, nearly five million miles logged in his black beauty—it was all down the motherfucking tubes in one fell swoop. The shock and grief and tears were welling up inside him. But he didn't have time to weep.

At the moment, there were more pressing issues.

Lucas found the switch for the cruiser's bubble lights and turned them off. Searing pain suddenly flowed through his body. "See if the rear seat pulls down," he uttered hoarsely at the darkness in back, "maybe find something in the trunk."

"We gotta get to a doctor, Lucas!" Behind him, Sophie was sobbing dryly, tearing at the back seats. Next to her, Angel was curled into a fetal position against the window, moaning and taking deep breaths. His face was a twisted mask of anguish and grief for his uncle. Sophie finally located the flip-down seat and revealed the greasy contents of the trunk behind it. She found a small, plastic first-aid kit. She dug out a couple of tubes of balm, tossed one over to Angel, and climbed back into the front seat to help Lucas.

"Do yourself first!" Lucas hissed, cocking his head at her. "Get something on those arms!"

Sophie went to work. She sklirched a gob of cream into her palm and coated her own arms and face and neck. Then she quickly applied some to Lucas, to his blistered cheeks, to his neck and chin and lips. There was a blossom of soot shooting out of his nostrils. Sophie wiped it away.

Lucas choked back the urge to scream. At first, the cream stung like a million fire ants burrowing into his skin, then it began to turn everything down to a low simmer. He dug in his pocket with his free hand, rooted out a couple Demerol and a benny, popped the capsules into his mouth, and grimaced. They tasted like shoe polish.

Lucas took a deep breath and kept his hands riveted to the wheel.

The biggest challenge now was to stay alert. If they were going to survive, Lucas knew they had to stay alert. But over the course of the last few hours he had lost track of how many drugs he had taken. Was it four caplets of painkiller and two doses of Benzedrine? Or was it six caplets of Demerol and four tabs of bennies? For that matter, what kind of weird interactive effect was he creating by swallowing these cocktails? A sudden surge of dread passed through his gut. Maybe he should have allowed the pain itself to keep him alert.

"Jesus God, Lucas . . ." Hoarse, choked, and horrified, Sophie's voice sounded like it was coming from a mile away.

"Take it easy, girl." Lucas tried to concentrate on his driving. It was bizarre being in a four-wheeler. It had been years since he had even sat in a car.

"Lucas, those cops—they—"

"Calm down, Sophie."

"Jesus Christ, we're in some deep shit . . ." Sophie glanced over her shoulder and saw the boy huddled in the back. He seemed okay. Physically fine.

They drove another few moments until Sophie turned to Lucas and said, "Gimme a damage report."

"Car's fine."

"I mean you."

"Never been better," Lucas lied.

"Talk to me, Lucas."

"I'm okay."

Sophie wiped the pain-tears from her eyes. "How much gas do we have?"

Lucas looked down at the dash and saw that the cruiser had a full gas tank. Thank you, Sheriff Baum, wherever you are. Chalk up one for the good guys. "Tank's full."

"You okay to drive?"

"Yeah."

"You think we ought to get off the main road?"

Lucas thought about it for a minute. She had a point. That chopper might be making another sweep of the area. They had a better chance of evading the authorities at least for a while if they stuck to the farm roads. "Yeah, you're right. Why don't you see if the sheriff kept any maps in his glove box."

Sophie rooted through the glove box. She found a few half-empty boxes of cigars, an old greasy car manual, a couple of tins of Copenhagen smokeless, a blank ticket book, and a flashlight.

"No maps," she said.

"Shit."

"Wait a minute." Sophie pointed out the window. "Here comes a sign."

Lucas saw the green placard looming in the throw of the headlights. It was a mileage sign. It named a couple of small Missouri towns—Concordia, Oddessa, Grain Valley. The bottom line said HIGHWAY 15—TWO AND A HALF MILES.

Highway 15 . . .

Another lucky break. A couple of years ago, Lucas and Sophie had been on a coast-to-coast for Metric Incorporated, hauling a half ton of circuit panels. Destination was Trenton, New Jersey. Midway through the trip, Lucas had tried a shortcut around Kansas City. Sophie had been skeptical but Lucas had assured her it would shave an hour off the trip. Especially since they were scheduled to pass through KC at rush hour. Unfortunately, the best-laid plans of Lucas Hyde often went awry. The shortcut had forced them to trundle across seventy-five miles of deserted farm road that snaked endlessly through oceans of crops. No truck stops, no coffee pots, no turnoffs, no street lights . . . in fact, there weren't even any roadside reflectors. It was so narrow and winding, the truck had nearly jackknifed a dozen times.

At the moment it was exactly what they were looking for.

Lucas snapped his fingers. "Highway Fifteen will keep us underground for a while."

Sophie wrinkled her brow. "Jesus Christ, we're in Kansas already."

Lucas thought about it another moment. "No, Toto . . . I don't think we're in Kansas anymore."

Sophie was hurting too much to smile.

A minute later, they took the exit ramp and found themselves tooling down a lonely blacktop. Five minutes after that, they crossed the Kansas border. The landscape changed immediately. The patchwork of hills vanished into a sea of beige. Corn, winter wheat, sorghum, barley. It was all a vast plain of dirty beige undulating in the night breezes. Through the jagged broken glass of the driver's-side window, Lucas could smell the thick perfume of damp earth and manure.

Sophie broke the silence. "Lucas, what the fuck are we gonna do?"

Lucas shivered. He couldn't give her an answer. The sickness had faded to a low rumble deep in his gut, but he could still feel it inside him. It was festering there like a low-grade infection. Looking in his rearview, Lucas scanned the darkness behind the cruiser. The road was dead still. No cops. No vehicles. Not even any locals coming home from the graveyard shift. Lucas half expected to see the helicopter loom up over them at any minute. The chopper could finish them off in the blink of an eye. One spray of high-velocity slugs from the sky and poof! Game over.

"Wish I could say I had a plan," Lucas finally said. "Fact is, I don't know what the fuck we're gonna do."

Then they drove in pained silence for quite a few miles. Thinking.

Police helicopters had always reminded Lucas of East L.A. They represented the paramilitary oppression that occurred on a daily basis in the 'hood. Truckers called them "eyes in the sky." Homeboys called them bogies. Folks in Inglewood and Torrance simply called them sadistic motherfuckers. Lucas remembered how they had crept into his nightmares during the L.A. riots back in the summer of '91.

He had been home in Santa Monica working on his motorcycle when the shit had hit the fan. The news had come drifting across the garage in crackling sound bites from his portable TV. The infamous case against four L.A. policemen who had been caught beating a black motorist on America's Most Candid Home Video had ended in an innocent verdict! A motherfucking innocent verdict!! Lucas remembered throwing his crescent wrench through the window of the garage.

An hour later, Lucas had set out for Simi Valley, where the trial had taken place. When he got there, he found a huge, multiethnic crowd of protesters gathered outside the Simi Courthouse. They were waving placards, angrily disapproving of the absurd verdict. Lucas had joined in, yelling until he was hoarse. Somehow it had made him feel better: At least somebody was voicing their outrage.

But on the way home later that night, tooling down the San Diego Freeway, Lucas had seen the tiny dots of orange spreading across the horizon. It was the beginning of the apocalyptic riots, spreading out over South Central L.A., across Torrance and Compton and Inglewood. And Lucas had begun to feel a weird, exhilarating, contrary mix of emotions. It was almost as if his own personal anger at the thinly veiled but deeply ingrained racism of this country had exploded into a million tiny fires across the horizon of his childhood home. His anger had found its perfect metaphor. His wrath had become solid. His childhood was devouring itself.

Then he had seen the helicopters. Dozens of them had risen out of the east like horrible glowing Valkyries, descending on South Central with their deadly ballet of searchlights. In that one terrifying moment of recognition, Lucas had realized that true killing power would always be with The Man. His brothers might rage and burn brightly for a moment, but the fucking Man with his faithful army of storm troopers would always control the serious firepower. Riding home that night on his secondhand Harley, face in the wind, he could not help but weep. In fact, he cried all the way home, his tears destined to dry forgotten on his cheek in the endless draft of motion.

In some weird way, Lucas had been moving ceaselessly ever since.

"Emporia, Kansas?"

Sophie's voice broke the silence. They were passing another sign. Threading her trembling hands through her hair, wiping her mouth, she said, "Had an uncle that lived in Emporia."

"Does he know anything about voodoo curses?" Lucas kept his gaze on the road.

"He died when I was twelve."

"Sorry to hear that."

Sophie nodded. She was feeling woozy from the drugs and lingering terror. She reached into her pocket for a cigarette and a stitch of pain pierced her spine. It felt like someone was branding her pelvis with a white-hot poker. The sudden twinge took her breath away. She fell backward a moment, sucking air and trying to figure out what was wrong. She must have injured her back during the accident. Must have wrenched it all to hell.

"Sophie—?" Lucas had noticed her twinge.

"I'm fine." Sophie stiffened against the seat and waited for the pain to pass.

Lucas looked at her for a moment, then he dug a couple of caplets out of his pocket. He handed the drugs to her. "Here—take another Darvon—maybe half a Benzedrine."

Sophie looked at the capsules for a moment. She didn't want to mask any more of her pain with narcotics. It was like being on a life raft with a shark swimming beneath it. She knew her wounds were still there. No matter how languid and warm and orange her mind became, she knew she was going to wake up to the pain sooner or later. Finally, she shook her head and stuffed the capsules into her jeans. Then she glanced over her shoulder and said, "What about you? You okay, kiddo?"

Behind them, Angel put his elbows across the seat-back and nodded. Tears were drying in his eyes. Although he didn't seem to be hurting as much as Lucas or Sophie—mercifully, his sickness seemed to still be in the early stages—he seemed racked by grief and shock.

Sophie pulled her Marlboros out of her pocket and dug around for a smoke. Most of the remaining cigarettes had been crushed or broken in the crash, but she found one last survivor and lit it up. Her hands were shaking badly. "Cop car like this is none too discreet."

"Tell me about it," Lucas grunted.

"We gotta get help, Lucas. Gotta get out of this fucking car before they find us."

Lucas laughed bitterly. "Who the fuck is gonna help us? Think about it, girl—who the fuck is gonna help?"

"We gotta do something."

"Who the fuck would even believe us?"

"Who do we know in Kansas City?"

Lucas shook his head.

"How 'bout Lawrence? Maybe there's somebody crazy enough at the university."

"Whattya mean?"

She puffed her cigarette. "You know—some kind of crazed professor of folklore or student of the occult or religion or philosophy or something, I dunno—somebody who wouldn't laugh at this fucking insanity we're going through. . . ."

"And what are they gonna do for us?!"

Sophie took another deep drag. "I dunno—help us with some kind of fucking counterspell."

"Gimme a break."

"We gotta do something!" Sophie's voice was rising, becoming shrill. "Goddamn sickness isn't going away!"

"We're moving—right now that's enough for me."

"Great!! Just great!!" Sophie shouted at him. "What happens when we run dry! What happens then, Lucas?!!"

"We get a motherfucking sun tan!!"

"QUIT IT!!" The voice came from the back, and it was like a sudden cold dash of water on the argument. Angel leaned forward against the seats. The dashboard lights revealed his wet eyes. "We gotta th'tick together . . . fightin' don't help nobody!"

There was an agonizing moment of silence. Sophie and Lucas exchanged a glance. Then Sophie turned back to the boy and brushed a strand of hair from his eyes. "You're right . . . when you're right, you're right."

Angel went back to the shadows of the rear seat. His voice was barely a whisper. "Uncle Flaco th'aid we gotta have faith . . . gotta be firm in our faith."

Sophie thought about it for a moment. She didn't even realize she was uttering the words under her breath, "—firm in our faith."

She glanced down at the dash, her gaze playing across the radio, the shotgun mount, the CB, the glove box. Then she noticed the phone. Mounted underneath the radio and tucked out of sight, it was a small cellular job.

A tiny green LED blinked at its base.

". . . faith . . ."

She picked up the cellular receiver and punched in a number.

"What are you doing?" Lucas was watching her.

"Calling a friend."

A moment later, after several clicks and beeps, a woman's voice said, "Directory assistance—what city please?"

"Berkeley—Milo Klein, please."

It was so obvious, Sophie had no idea why she hadn't thought of it earlier. He was the only person in the world who would believe this macabre predicament that she and her friends were in. Born in Prague, educated in Israel and New York, Milo was a fountain of esoteric knowledge. He was the one who had first introduced Sophie to Jewish mysticism and all the fascinating lore in the Kabbala. The ancient Judaic spiritual systems. The unseen forces in the cosmos. And never before had it seemed more relevant to Sophie.

The operator asked Sophie to spell the name. Sophie spelled it. Then the operator gave her a recorded announcement of the number. Sophie listened to it once and then dialed.

It took five rings. The voice that answered was hoarse and groggy, maybe even a little shaken. "Hello?"

"Milo, it's Sophie. Sophie Cohen."

After a stunned silence the voice said, "Don't tell me you're in some kind of trouble."

Sophie felt a chill creep over the back of her neck. "You win the Kewpie doll, Milo—I'm in deep shit. How did you know?"

"People don't call at this hour with tension in their voice to get a recipe for blintzes."

"Touché."

There was a long pause. "Is it weird?"

"What do you mean?"

"I mean—is it weird?"

"Define *weird*."

The voice replied, "Weird, you know—strange, unusual, unexplained."

Sophie couldn't avoid smiling wearily. "Yeah, Milo . . . you could say that."

Sophie listened to the dead hiss of satellite air. After a pained sigh, the voice of the rabbi returned, "I knew this was going to happen."

Sophie swallowed hard. "What do you mean, you knew?"

The answer was instantaneous. "You always seemed like the girl most likely to get herself mixed up with something weird."

Sophie stared at the highway for a moment, then found herself shaking her head and smiling. "Same old Milo."

"And you're the same old Sophie Cohen."

Sophie agreed and then proceeded to tell the rabbi everything.

23

Skeleton Keys

Don Bischoff sat on the rear gate of his Chevy S-10 and waited for a car to come down Route 15. He had blown his right rear Goodyear a half-hour ago and since then, not one good Samaritan had passed his way. Not one. Not even the sheriff's cruiser that had roared past him a few minutes ago would stop.

He glanced at his watch again for the tenth time and felt his stomach tighten. It was already past Cindy's bedtime and now it looked like Don was going to miss his daughter's birthday party for the second year in a row.

"Why did I give my only spare to Burton?" he asked himself rhetorically. "Why?" Don had loaned his brother-in-law the tire just last week and was now kicking himself for it.

He fished in his pocket for another smoke. A stocky young man with broad shoulders and a generous face, Don didn't much look like a banker. In his flannel shirt, Royals cap, jeans, and work boots, he resembled a farmer's son more than anything else. But that was okay with Don. In the wake of the endless recession and countless farm foreclosures, managing a bank had dropped several notches on the popularity scale around these parts.

The wind picked up for a moment and carried fertilizer smells from the neighboring fields. Don found himself shivering despite the mild temperature. Maybe his cold was coming back. Just then he heard a car off in the distance, approaching from the west. "Maybe this is the one," he muttered, "the last kind soul in Coffey County."

Don lit up another cigarette and thought about little Cindy. This birthday was so important to her. She was entering the land of fifth grade, boys, makeup, and baby-sitting. Don wanted so badly to share the moment with her. Cindy was his only daughter, his little princess. It just killed him to disappoint her.

Of course, the child was all the more precious to Don because of the near-fatal drowning two summers ago. Cindy Bischoff had gotten her ankle caught on a log at the bottom of Biminy's Pond. Thank God, Don had been right there to fish her out. Other than swallowing a couple of gallons of stagnant water and wounding her pride a little bit, the child had gotten out unscathed. But the trauma still haunted Don. To this day, at least one night per month, he would wake up in a cold sweat, screaming his way out of the mossy depths of that pond.

Headlights were approaching. Don hopped off the gate, tossed his cigarette to the gravel, and ground it out with his toe. He walked over to the edge of the shoulder and got ready to flag the car down.

Funny, the oncoming lights looked a little screwy to Don. They were less than a mile away now, two pinpoints of yellow, close together, almost like tractor lights. But the closer they got, the harder it was for Don to tell how fast they were going. At first, the vehicle seemed to be speeding toward him at an unbelievable rate. Then his eyes started playing tricks on him.

About a half a mile away the oncoming car seemed to be crawling.

Don started feeling funny inside. Nervous. The tiny hairs on the back of his neck bristled. His stomach seized up and his chest felt heavy as if a sudden wave of dread were rising inside him.

The headlights approached.

"Wait a min—" He heard something over the noise of the oncoming car. Above the rattle of cylinders and whine of its tires. A thin, warbling gurgle. Vaguely familiar. The car loomed closer and Don smelled the marshy stink, the slimy texture of the air, the cold, murky depths, and the watery cry of his daughter.

"Cindy—?"

The antique limousine passed in dream motion, with the molasses pace of a photo developing. Don staggered. His mind was spinning now. Dizziness was threatening to take him down to the gravel. But before he fell, his gaze landed on the driver's-side window of the charred limo. His daughter was there, haloed by the green glow of swamp water.

The bloated little corpse was staring out at him.

"No—God—please—" Don tore his cap from his head and grabbed a handful of hair. He was staring into the face of his nightmare.

As the antique passed, the Cindy-thing stuck out a puffy purple tongue at her father.

The sound of Don's scream was swallowed up by the clamor of the Rolls Royce as it roared away in pursuit of bigger game.

"So you think you've stumbled into this thing?"

"You could say that—yeah."

"And it's like you can't stop—like you've been cursed to never stop moving?"

"I know it sounds ludicrous."

"Did I say that?"

"No, you didn't, but—"

"Did I once use the word *ludicrous*?"

"No, but—"

"Did I once say your situation was anything remotely like ludicrous?"

Sophie managed a thin smile. She had switched the cellular phone over to intercom so that Lucas and Angel could also hear the rabbi's rapid-fire voice. And now the sound of it was making her long for those carefree days back at the coffeehouses of Baker Street. But the temporary pleasure could not penetrate the film of terror and pain that clung to her at the moment. She snubbed out her cigarette and let her smile fade. "Well, it sounds ludicrous to me, and I'm the one with the sauteed stomach."

Milo's voice returned. "Who cares how it sounds. You saw some horrible things, people have died—let's work from there."

Sophie swallowed air. "What do you make of this, Milo?"

"Might be honest-to-goodness diabolism."

"Diabolism?"

"It's a silly, fachacta term for black magic. Tell you the truth, nobody really knows what to call it anymore. Lots of religions around these days involve magic—santeria, Ifa, voodoo, wiccanism. It's mostly decent people trying to help and heal each other. But the diabolists—they're a whole other can of toxic waste."

Sophie took a quick drag. Lucas was next to her, listening intently, his wounded hands cupped around the steering wheel. It was so moonless outside that only the glow of the dash and the blinking LED display illuminated their owlish faces. "Assuming you're right—" Sophie said into the speaker phone "—and it's this diabolism or whatever you call it, then how do we deal with it?"

There was a brief pause before the rabbi's voice returned. "Interesting question."

Sophie chewed her lip. "Gee, thanks, I thought it up all by myself."

"Your biggest problem is the struggle itself," the voice said. "It's in your heads now. The seed is planted."

Lucas spoke up. "What are you saying, exactly? We're imagining all this shit?"

"Put it this way, diabolists can't do bupkiss without the human mind. Early on, you might have stepped where you shouldn't have stepped, might have stuck your tootsies where they didn't belong, but now your heads are doing the work."

Lucas shook his head. "Gimme a break, man! You're telling me these blisters are all in my mind?!"

"No, Lucas, listen—I'm not saying it's psychosomatic. I'm saying the brain is like a pipeline for spells and dark magic and nasty stuff like that."

"What do you mean—pipeline?" Sophie asked.

"The brain is the conduit. The medium. Somehow all the negative magic—especially with antagonistic spells like this—it all incubates in the mind. It grows there."

"What's the answer, Milo?"

After another stretch of silence, the voice said, "You gotta fight on the only battlefield that matters."

"The brain."

"Give the lady a stuffed poodle!"

Lucas thought about it for a moment. "I'm sorry, Rabbi, I mean no disrespect . . . but this ain't exactly a Bar Mitzvah, know what I mean? Where do you get all this stuff?"

"I'm a rabbi, not Pat Boone."

"But where did you learn this kinda stuff?"

The voice on the speaker became measured. "Lucas, a lot of people don't realize Judaism is filled with layers of mysticism. Jewish folklore is chock-full of ghosts and demons. It's in the Kabbala, the ancient books. In rabbinical literature you see references to sorcery all over the place—"

Lucas tried to interrupt. "I didn't mean to—"

"Did you know that the Seal of Solomon is very commonly used in witchcraft?"

"The Seal of Solomon?"

"Yeah, the Star of David. In witchcraft it's used to repel evil spirits and ward off misfortune."

Lucas shook his head. "Wish I had one right now . . ."

"Look at what happened in fourteenth-century Europe," the rabbi continued. He was on a roll now. "During the Black Death, Jews were accused of spreading the plague in order to kill Christians. Hundreds of thousands of Jews were massacred. In fact, because the Jews kept their ghettoes so clean, they were accused of being witches and burned at the stake. Yes, Mr. Hyde, Judaism and witchcraft share an unexpected number of intersections. . . ."

"The thing to remember," the voice went on, "is that the mind and the cosmos are linked. It's in the Kabbala, it's in the ancient books, and today quantum physics is bearing it out—the soul and the physical worlds are one."

Sophie stared at the blinking LED. "You're saying we should fight this thing in our minds—"

"Exactly."

"What, by praying?"

The voice came back through the speaker. "King David said, 'Open mine eyes that I might behold wondrous things from my Torah.'"

Sophie took a final drag off her cigarette and tossed it through her window. "Milo, I gotta be honest—it's been a while since I've read my Torah. Plus, we gotta mixed bag of cultures here, know what I mean? It's Heinz's Fifty-Seven Varieties."

"Doesn't matter," the voice replied. "There's a monolithic religion out there. Kabbala says it's our duty to remove the illusion of darkness. Simple as that. You're on the right team, boopie. You're the good guys."

Lucas was restless. "With all due respect, Rabbi—there's gotta be something else we can do. Something tangible. Spit to the east—throw salt over our shoulders—something. . . ."

After a moment of hiss, the voice said, "There are so many different spells and charms and countercharms, it would make your head spin."

"Gimme an example."

"Oh . . . I don't know . . . there's the witch's ladder, for instance. To curse somebody you make a string of knots and hide it. Unless the poor *schmendrik* can find it and untie the knots, he will slowly die."

Lucas swallowed hard. "That's charming. What about the hand? What did you call it—the Hand of Glory?"

The hiss returned, then the voice: "Supposedly, the Hand of Glory is made from the right hand of a murderer severed during an eclipse of the moon, then it's dried and preserved. It's used in many different spells . . . supposedly . . . but listen, I don't really think it can—"

Lucas interrupted. "What are the counterspells like? What

are the universal elements in fighting these things? How do people usually deal with these goddamn things?"

Another beat of silence. "I don't really—"

"C'mon, Rabbi Klein, please—how do people usually fight this kinda stuff?"

After an awkward pause, the voice returned sounding very uneasy. "In the end, I am only a rabbi. I'm not some kind of mad sorcerer. But I will tell you this—it usually involves some kind of sacrifice."

Lucas looked at Sophie. "Sacrifice."

"Yes, that's right. Some kind of sacrifice."

There was another stretch of silence. Sophie threaded her fingers through her hair and looked over at the fuel gauge. They had a half tank left. "Milo, I'm sorry to say we're fresh out of virgins to sacrifice."

"Go on your guts, people," the voice instructed. "That's the only real way to really fight it. . . ."

Sophie stared at the blinking LED light. "Go on our guts, huh?"

"Yeah."

Swallowing thickly, Sophie said, "What does your gut tell *you*?"

No answer. Only the thin hiss of the dead air.

"Milo . . . ?"

After another moment, the voice said, "Where are you guys right now?"

Lucas said, "On our way to Wichita, Kansas."

"I could be on the red-eye by 6 A.M."

Sophie shook her head. "Forget it, Milo. You'd never find us."

Suddenly the voice said, "Sophie Cohen, you were always the wild one."

Sophie smiled sadly. "You taught me everything I know."

"Sophie, how can I help?"

Sophie stared at the phone. "Milo, we're gonna have to call you back."

"I'm telling you, the red-eye leaves Oakland Metro in less than five hours."

"We need time to talk this over."

"I can be there by morning."

"No, we gotta work this out among ourselves."

"Sophie, don't hang up—I want to help."

"You already have, Milo."

"Call me back—you know, when you figure this thing out."

Sophie promised she would call him back. They said goodbye and Sophie disconnected the line. She put the receiver back and rubbed her eyes. Her voice was barely a whisper. "This is fucking nuts . . ."

Lucas was scanning the darkness ahead, thinking. "He's right about one thing, Sophie—"

Sophie stared through the windshield at the rushing white lines. "Yeah? What's that?"

"We gotta go with our guts on this one."

She turned to Lucas. It was obvious he had an idea. "What's on your mind, Lucas?"

Licking his lips, Lucas said in a low, fervid tone, "Something that'll buy us a lot more time."

Sophie looked at him. "I'm all ears."

Lucas nodded at the darkness ahead of them. "Bet you a hundred bucks I can find a back road into Wichita."

"So?"

"Take us straight through Park City."

"So what?" Sophie's forebrain was throbbing. Milo's bizarre call had only served to tighten the screws. "Why would we drive directly into a populated area?"

"You remember the time we took the Bird's Eye load down to Tulsa?"

"Yeah. Flip-flop was a nightmare."

"You remember why?"

"Because of your brilliant idea to take the Pony Express Highway through—"

Lucas pointed a bandaged finger at her. "That's right! Motherfucking two-lane took us around the north end of Wichita—remember?"

"We were waiting for hours—" Sophie realized what he was getting at and froze. The realization made her skin crawl. He just couldn't be serious. *He just couldn't be.*

"—because of the goddamn trains," Lucas finished her thought for her. "Huge switching yard is located down there near Park City, operates the whole region."

Sophie studied his feverish gaze in the green light. "You're fucking nuts, Lucas, if you think we're gonna jump one of those trains."

"Time it right, we could hop the back of an Amtrak commuter train."

"Those things go a hundred miles an hour."

"Not through the yard."

"Lucas, they'll stop at every podunk town from here to Vegas."

"Then we'll jump a freight."

"What?!"

"We'll hop out of the car while it's still moving and jump aboard a freight car."

"What are we, hobos now?!"

Lucas punched the edge of the steering wheel with his wounded fist. "Goddamnit, Sophie—there's gotta be a way! It's the only thing that makes any sense! There's gotta be a motherfuckin' way to do this—!!"

"—we can do it." Again the meek voice came from the back seat. Angel had muttered something under Lucas's tirade but neither Sophie nor Lucas had heard it clearly.

Sophie turned to the shadows behind her. "What was that, Amigo?"

"I know a way."

"A way for what?"

Angel leaned forward and crossed his arms over the back of the seats. A stripe of green luminescence fell across his misshapen features. "A way we can hop a train."

24

Idiot Child

She drove in silence. Brittle bones creaking. Translucent skin stretched taut. The steering wheel was clutched amidst her crooked fingers, which were tingling, wired to the magic. Inside her flesh, the talent streamed through her like liquid hate. Stirring up poisonous memories. Mingling sensations . . .

Dry flowers rotting . . . a flock of blue geese spanning the sky above her father's plantation house . . . ink blots spreading across the dusky heavens. . . .

The spring equinox.

That evening, nearly seventy years ago, Vanessa had rolled her wheelchair out to the edge of the veranda to get a better look at the birds. "Why do they return to the north every year?" she had asked her father.

"Idiot child," he said. He was standing nearby in the shadows. In those days, it seemed he was always lurking on the periphery like a ghost. Brooding. Haunted by grief. "Don't you know those birds have the need?"

"The need?"

"It's inside them."

* * *

It was inside her now. The need. The talent. Forcing a fault line through the wrinkles of her face until something like a toothy smile appeared.

As black as a well bottom.

25

Bat Out
of Hell

Since the day they had met, Sophie had kept something from Lucas. It had to do with a secret phobia that had plagued Sophie since she was a little girl. Unlike all those classic fears catalogued in the diagnostic manuals, this one was rather unique to Sophie. And considering the way she made her living, it was also highly ironic.

It had originated years ago, during a traumatic event on the highway between Paradise Valley and Fresno.

Her family had been vacationing at the Grand Canyon. It had been one of those package tours that had included six days of white-water rafting, camping, and a naturalist's guided tour through the canyon. It was fun, but by the end of the week Sophie and her parents were exhausted. The trip home turned out to be a monster. Harry Cohen owned one of those little Dodge Darts with no air conditioning. The heat had caused tempers to flare and bare arms to stick to the vinyl seats. Sophie had gotten so desperately car sick that they were forced to stop for three separate puke breaks along the way.

By the time they had crossed the California border into

Death Valley, the Cohens weren't even speaking to each other.

The blood had come out of nowhere.

Sophie had seen it first, gazing feverishly out the front windshield. It had started in the center of the road . . . a tiny point of red . . . then a strand . . . then a thin trail . . . then a thick spoor of guts snaking wildly toward . . .

Carnage! The remains of a bighorn sheep had been scattered in half a dozen pieces across the center line. The Dart had been going too fast for Harry to avoid it. He had no choice but to plow through the mess. The tires had hydroplaned on all the blood and entrails. Evelyn Cohen had made a retching noise and the Dart nearly swerved out of control, but Harry cursed at it and pulled it back in line.

A minute later, things had returned to normal. Harry and Evelyn resumed their bickering and the incident seemed virtually forgotten. Forgotten by everyone except Sophie.

In the heat of the impact, a spattering of blood had splashed the side window in back. Sophie had seen it happen and could not take her eyes off that blood. Drying in the wind, making tiny tracks across the glass, the blood had refused to go away. Sophie had stared at it for hours. All the way back to San Francisco. It had hardened to a thick scarlet web. An eternal reminder of the random violence on the slab.

For many reasons, that spattering of blood stayed with Sophie the rest of her life. In her dreams. In her momentary flashes of panic on an icy road. In her paranoid ruminations. That blood seemed to be a scarlet letter stamped across her life. The stain of the sacrificial lamb upon her machine.

Sometimes she thought she was crazy to think back to that little tendril of blood. She figured it was typical middle-class neuroticism. Guilt. Guilt for choosing the machine over humanitarian endeavors endorsed by her parents. Guilt for choosing the open road over the mortgage. Guilt for choosing freedom over commitment. Guilt for living her life the way she wanted. Goddamned guilt. Sophie was so tired of guilt she could scream.

Lately, though, the memory of that blood had been resonating differently for Sophie. About a year ago, she started having increasingly potent dreams about it again. Dreams that lingered in her mind for days. At first, she figured it was merely due to the stress. Her bills had been piling up lately and the Mariah's business had been slow. Over the past months Lucas had become edgier. And Sophie just couldn't get the feeling out of her mind that Lucas had put up an implacable wall between them. But the more she was haunted by the memory of that blood, the more she realized it had gained a new significance in her mind.

Now that the curse had found them, the blood image road along with her over every mile. Around every turn. The horrible possibility buzzing faintly in her subconscious.

The realization that the blood might not always belong to some desert bighorn sheep.

Soon it might be her own.

The closest road that intersected Wichita's system of train tracks was Old 79 outside of Newton, Kansas. It took Lucas a little over fifteen minutes to find the ancient highway. Much to his amazement, he remembered every bump, every dip, every weather-scarred mile of the lonely two-lane. Old 79 wound along the lip of Rainkiller Lake and the surrounding communities of Towanda, Whitewater, and Furley. At this time of night, it was as deserted as a cemetery.

"Angel, you're gonna get yourself killed." Sophie was chewing her lip again, gazing over her shoulder at the boy.

"I know what I'm doing, Th'ophie."

"Do you?"

"Ye'th, ma'am." There was a strange color in the boy's voice. A mixture of resolve and anger.

Lucas glanced over at the kid. Angel was gripping the seat tightly, the dashboard lights making his expression look like something out of a forties horror film.

In a delirious moment of dissociation, Lucas flashed back to the late shows he used to watch as a boy. He remembered Rondo Hatton, the handsome character actor who'd been stricken with a fatal disease called acromegaly, a disease that severely distorts the facial features. Forced into playing evil freaks and heavies in B-movies like *The Brute Man*, Hatton had tried to make the best of his condition before dying of the illness in the late forties. As a kid, Lucas had always suspected old Rondo was really a good guy underneath all the low-key lighting and quivering strings. In fact, Lucas had grown up rooting for the bad guys—not due to any deep-rooted antisocial urge, but merely because movies demonized the outsider. The circus freak, the foreigner, the lunatic, the ethnic. These were the people Lucas identified with. And it took him a lifetime of wading through bullshit to discover that these were often the types of people who made the biggest difference, who did the greatest things, who changed the world.

Lucas pondered Angel's anxious gaze for another brief moment and then said, "You ever point a gun at a man before, kid?"

"No."

"Ain't like the TV shows."

"I know."

"Hardest thing you'll ever do. Almost harder to point at somebody than to get one pointed at you. You know why?"

"No, thir."

"Because that motherfucker you're pointing at just may be the one who's gonna force you to pull the trigger."

Angel thought about it for a moment and said, "I'm ready, Luca'th."

Sophie just shook her head and murmured, "God help us . . ."

Lucas checked his watch. It was almost three in the morning. Glancing back up through the windshield, he surveyed the road ahead. Old 79 had definitely seen better days. Cutting a serpentine swath through the farm fields, hewn from weather-beaten asphalt and streaked with ancient skid marks, the road looked otherworldly in the rush of their headlights. Almost like the surface of some uncharted planet. Along each side was a gravel shoulder fringed with weeds and carcasses of old tires. Flashes of broken glass sparkled every now and then. It was the perfect road on which to keep a very low profile.

The trouble was, Lucas had no idea if they could make it

to the train tracks before running out of gas. The fuel was nearly half gone. Lucas figured it would keep them healthy for only another hour or so.

The boy's plan was simple enough. Since Angel was in the early stages of the sickness, he could bail out of the cruiser somewhere outside the train yard and sneak into the switching area on foot. Holding an engineer at gunpoint, he would then commandeer one of the commuter trains and rendezvous with Lucas and Sophie at the nearest highway crossing. It wasn't exactly foolproof but Lucas was willing to bet this feisty little Latino had the balls to do it.

"How close are we?" Sophie's voice sounded as if it had been passed through a meat grinder.

Lucas glanced at the horizon. "Guess we're about twenty miles outside of Wichita."

"Got enough fuel to get there?"

"Yeah, absolutely."

Sophie chewed her bottom lip. "And you think this is the best plan?"

Lucas glanced at her. "I know what you're thinking—"

"Lucas, I just want to—"

"Listen to me . . . I know we're just buying little bits and pieces of time, but the train can give us enough time to get our heads on straight."

She didn't say anything. Lucas glanced at her again and pondered her tense features. She was chowing down on her fingernails now. It was a miracle she had any cuticles left. Her face was knotted with stress, her gaze focused like a beam of sunlight through a magnifying glass on the darkness ahead. Her hair had gone even further askew, the auburn rattails spiking off her crown like one of the Little Rascals on heroin. Her ear was bloody and missing half its earrings. Her sleeveless T-shirt was soaked under the arms. She was a mess, but somehow Lucas got an unexpected shot in the arm by just looking at her.

In so many ways, Sophie was the only family Lucas had left. Both his parents were in the ground. His sisters had completely lost touch with him. And it was next to impossible to maintain any kind of normal friendship while humping

overland every waking and nonwaking hour. Sophie was all
he had left. She was his best friend, his sister, his partner, his
. . . *lover*? Is that what he wanted to say? His *woman*? Why
did that very idea taste so sour? In a way, they were already
married. For Christ's sake, what was it about Sophie that
scared him? Right now he would do anything for her . . .

A wave of chills passed over Lucas. In his mind, he came
to the inevitable question: Would he lay down his life for Sophie? It was a frightening query to pose. Given their present
circumstances, in fact, it was especially frightening. The
worst part was the fact that Lucas did not, in his heart of
hearts, know the answer.

"We'll come up with something," he added awkwardly.

Sophie shot him a glance. "I'm trying real hard to believe
you, homeboy."

"Look at it this way, we've only got—"

Lucas stopped abruptly. The words seemed to hang like
icicles in the noisy darkness of the cruiser.

Something in the rearview mirror had caught his attention.
A pair of headlights. They had materialized on the horizon
behind them and were gaining quickly. Lucas looked at his
speedometer. He was going sixty-eight miles an hour. The
posted speed limit was double-nickels. This guy behind them
was coming up like a bat out of hell. Must be going at least
ninety.

"What is it?" Sophie was looking over her shoulder.

"Headlights behind us."

"Shit—what if—?"

"Just stay calm. It's probably some gearhead out for a late-
night joy ride."

"But when they see the police car—"

Lucas finished her sentence. "—they'll slow the fuck
down."

In the rearview the headlights were approaching. Gooseflesh rashed over Lucas's arms. His scalp prickled. The
lights were a dim yellow. The color of bug lights. Close together. Definitely too close for a late-model car.

"Wait a minute . . ." Sophie was looking over her shoulder, muttering. "That's no gearhead."

"Whattya mean?"

"Looks like a tractor or Model T or something."

"Model T?" Lucas quickly glanced over his shoulder and looked out the back.

The cruiser's rear window had been shattered in the collision. The center gaped open like a maw of jagged, icy teeth. Through the breach Lucas saw the headlights approaching. They were about a quarter mile away now, steadily closing the gap. As they loomed, the body around them became visible. The sweep of the fenders. The lines of the bonnet.

"I'll be a motherfucker . . ." Recognition flooded Lucas with ice water.

"What?! What is it?!!" Sophie was panicking.

"Fucking limousine."

Lucas realized he had been noticing the vintage Rolls, off and on, for the past twenty-four hours now without thinking too much of it. He wasn't exactly certain when, but he thought he had first seen it on the highway outside Round Knob. He was pretty sure he had noticed it parked in front of the pawnbrokers' shop. He was almost positive that he had seen it getting tangled in the pile-up after The Black Mariah had jackknifed. But he had never really given it much thought. Now it was dawning on him that this motherfucker had been following them.

Sophie's face was illuminated by the oncoming headlights. "A limousine?"

"Yeah . . . and you know how I *hate* limousines." Lucas sped up a bit. Past seventy. Past seventy-five. The antique continued to gain. It was as relentless as the Santa Ana winds.

Sophie turned to him. "You recognize it?"

"Sort of."

"What do you mean, sort of?"

"I saw it a couple times. I think it might be following us." Lucas looked up at the mirror and a surge of panic seized his throat.

The antique car was changing.

* * *

Through the hole in the rear window, Angel watched the limousine approach.

It pulled up to within twenty yards and hovered back there, its headlamps reflecting off the rush of pavement like a pair of moons on black rapids. Angel sensed the limousine was sniffing them. Hovering and sniffing. At this distance, the driver was barely visible. Angel could only make out a pale face behind the windshield.

Then the limousine edged closer and all of a sudden something broke through its roof.

Angel stopped breathing.

It was the shape of Angel's fear.

Back when he was only six years old, while his alcoholic mother was drying out at a local clinic, Angel had become a ward of the state. His father had skipped town a year earlier. Uncle Flaco was away in Mexico, so the child welfare people saw no other alternative than to send Angel to a foster home in Memphis. The McCallister house had been less than perfect. Three adopted kids living bare-bones cheap in a run-down farm house is tough enough. In the farm-crises 1980s it was next to impossible. Mary and Ben McCallister were both honest people who were forced to spend way too much time away in the fields, working the crops, struggling to make ends meet. Angel was left alone too often.

One particularly blustery night, Angel found himself locked in his bedroom, all by his lonesome. A storm had been brewing outside and the heat lightning strobed in through the windows at violent intervals. Angel had been drifting in and out of sleep all night, thumb planted in his misshapen mouth, blanket clutched at his neck. At around 3:00 A.M. he had awoken to the sound of thunder. He cried and cried and cried but nobody came.

At last he had crawled from his bed and fumbled through the dark toward the door. He tried to get out but the door was locked. Turning back toward his bed, he tripped over something. Lightning burst through the room. A tiny voice jangled out at him. In the flash of light, a figure suddenly sprang from the shadows. Little Angel screamed bloody murder and fell against the locked door and shrieked and sobbed and chewed his blanket. He had never been frightened this badly. It was a searing terror that cut through his little six-year-old body and changed him forever and ever.

A jack-in-the-box.

He had inadvertently grazed a metal jack-in-the-box with his shin and had sprung the little man. Synchronized with the lightning, its garish clown face had lunged up at him. The tiny mechanical laughter bleated at him. The tinkling music-box noise filled the room. And the face. The ghost-white face. The big yellow eyes. The red grin.

It had been a *jack-in-the-box*.

Thirteen years later, this same jack-in-the-box had just managed to burst up through the roof of the limousine. In a spray of metal shavings, grit, and particles of light, it sprang from a battered trapdoor in the roof. The clown face materialized like a photo developing.

Angel found his voice.

The scream awakened the others.

"What?!!" Sophie snapped her gaze around to the back.

Angel kept screaming and pointing dumbly through the broken glass portal in back. Through the jagged opening, the enormous toy was lurching toward him, its giant jack head craning in the wind, eyes like yellow embers, bloody grin spreading. Impossible moisture flagged from its lips and sprayed into the wind, as if the wooden thing was drooling. Angel got the distinct impression that it was about to gobble him up.

"It ain't real—it ain't—*IT AIN'T PO'TH' IBLE!!!*" Angel's tears began to flow. Fear constricted his throat. His testicles sucked up inside him as he cowered down on the floor. He was ten years old again. He was ten years old and was dying of fright.

"Angel—!" Sophie was screaming at him as if she couldn't understand his terror. "What is it?!! What's wrong?!!"

"I'th—i'th comin'—!!" Angel tried to tell her. The toy monster was getting closer, its mechanical laughter crowing over the wind and noise. It sounded like a cat being skinned inside a long metal tunnel.

"Angel—?!!"

"—the jack—*I'TH THE JACK!!*"

"I don't understand what you're saying!" Sophie's tense face was luminous in the yellow glow.

Through his wave of horror Angel realized that Sophie couldn't see anything. She couldn't see the jack at all. She couldn't see the monster. She had no idea what Angel was talking about.

The monster was meant for him and him alone.

Alone.

Angel turned around and saw the mammoth face orbiting closer, an asteroid, impossibly huge, looming in the portal of jagged glass, its red grin parting, hungry, hungry, hungry rows of rotting, moist, maggot-ridden fangs . . .

Angel buried his face in his hands and waited for the jaws to close around him.

Sophie saw the boy collapsing to the floor. Head in hands. Eyes locked. Was he praying? Was he having a breakdown? Had the grief and fear finally gotten to him?

"Angel—?!" She reached down and nudged him gently. His body vibrated with fear. "Angel—what is—?!!"

Sophie heard the sound.

The droplet.

She spun toward the windshield and saw the first drop. It had pinged against the cracked glass and had made a tiny spattering no bigger than a quarter. The wind flattened it into tendrils. Another one spotted the glass beneath it. A big fat drop. Wind splattering, spreading, rippling . . .

"What is that—muddy rain—?" Sophie turned to Lucas and saw something wrong in his eyes. Head cocked, gaze angled, Lucas looked like a dog listening to a whistle. "Lucas— what's the matter?!!"

Lucas gripped the wheel tightly and stared at the silent CB radio. "Fuck you!" He was yelling at ghosts, his eyes a million miles away, his lips trembling. "Fuck all of you!"

"Lucas?! What's going on?!"

The rain was picking up.

Sophie turned back to the windshield and felt her heart leap into her mouth.

The rain was deep scarlet. Rising to a steady drizzle, it spattered the glass and rolled sideways in wind-blown rivulets. It was coming from the darkness above. From the shadows below. From the rush of dark pavement beneath their wheels. Splashing up and cleansing the dirty fenders.

Rich arterial blood.

Sophie brought her hands to her mouth. "Jesus Christ—!!"

The crimson storm raged. A torrent of blood lashed the front of the cruiser. Deep-red serum washed across the hood and blew in freshets over the vents. The vacuum sucked some of the blood in through the broken side windows. Sophie could feel the mist on her cheek. It was rich and coppery smelling.

She recognized the smell from a lonely desert road long ago.

Sheep's blood.

Sophie clawed at her face, wiping the hallucination from her flesh as if scrubbing away acid. There was nothing there. But it didn't matter. She could feel it. She could smell it. She could sense it penetrating her pores.

She began to tremble. She began to lose control of her body. She had never shaken this badly in her life. It was convulsive. It rocked her against the seats in heaving spasms and forced a tremolo mewling from her throat.

"NOOO!!"

The blood was coming down like cats and dogs.

It rolled over the hood and tommy-gunned against the roof. It washed across the cracked windows. Soupy and opaque, it sprayed up from the churning tires. It began to form delicate, wind-tossed patterns of gore across the glass. Lacelike webbings of blood-streaked messages.

Sophie gasped. The cruiser was being blotted in bloody Rorschachs of her deepest fears.

Suddenly Sophie bawled like an infant. The cruiser was beginning to hydroplane on the sheets of blood. The rear was fishtailing. Sophie instinctively grabbed at the steering wheel and tried to pull it back in line.

Lucas shoved her away.

His eyes were glowing with terror. It was clear that Lucas was fighting his own private war.

"Lucas, boy, you hear me . . . ?"

It was a new voice.

Up to this point, there had been only ghostly fragments of voices coming through the dead CB speaker. Voices from Lucas's past. The shrill yammer of Miguel Torres, a local Hispanic tough who had beaten Lucas many times as a child. The gravelly baritone of Sergeant "Bull" Simmons, an old racist cop who had frequented a bar near Lucas's apartment. Even partially formed words of unidentified bullies from Lucas's reform-school days. They had all spurted through the dead speaker like angry threats spoken but unheard, like reverberations, like the ripple of after-echoes fading in an empty room.

Bits and pieces from Lucas's nightmares.

But this new voice was something else altogether.

"You hear me, boy . . . ?"

Charles Hyde's speaking voice had always possessed a distinctive timbre. In fact, even though he had merely been the owner of a small grocery store, he had always possessed the pipes to be a narrator for network TV or one of those late-night DJs on WKQX. Rich and modulated, Charles's voice had also carried a certain sadness. A quality that made Charles a highly respected deacon at the local Baptist church. He would deliver special messages at Christmas time. He would make announcements every Sunday. And occasionally, with a little prodding, he would sing the solo part of "That Ole Rugged Cross" with the choir.

It was this voice—the voice of his late father—that Lucas heard sizzling through the powerless CB.

"Lucas, I told y'all to come straight home after you dropped those eggs off at the Vincents' place . . . now you be draggin' in here at all hours, waking up your mama and God knows who else . . . come here, boy . . . y'all are smarter than that . . . I know 'cause I raised you right!"

Lucas felt long-forgotten emotions tearing at him, a lump

growing in his throat, tears stinging his eyes. He tore his
gaze away from the speaker and looked into the rearview.
The car was less than two hundred yards away now, headlights blazing, body gleaming in the moonlight.

It was a perfect replica, although Lucas knew it was impossible.

The hearse behind them was an ebony-black Dynaglide
version of a stretch Cadillac. Low-slung and oversized, it had
all the right options. Landau rear panels, opera windows, and
angular back. In the darkness rimmed in the glare of the
headlights, it looked like a glistening wild panther.

Lucas swallowed a mouthful of horror and muttered at the
radio, "You're not—not my dad! You're nothing! You're nobody!!"

*"Son, y'all remember what I told you . . . be a brave little
man now . . . gotta take good care of your mama and sisters.
Understand what I'm saying? 'Cause you the man of the
house now. You a good young man and I know you gonna do
good. Gonna make me proud. Gonna be a brave man. . . ."*

The words bleated through the tinny speaker, metallic and
weak. They were Charles Hyde's last words to his only son.
The sound of them opened up Lucas's chest and tore his
heart out by its roots.

*"You a good young man and I know you gonna do good.
Gonna make me proud. Gonna be a brave man. . . ."*

Lucas wailed.

It was a scream poisoned by rage. Sharp enough to slice
the air like a straight razor.

Next to him, Sophie jumped at the sound. Her eyes were
ablaze with fear. Her voice sounded as it if were a million
miles away. "Lucas, it's not real—it's not—!!"

All at once, Lucas shook the grief from his head and
stomped the accelerator. The cruiser lurched forward. In the
glare of the rearview mirror, he saw the hearse staying glued
to his tail. Glowing yellow, jaundiced, and poisoned.

Lucas slammed his wounded palms against the steering
wheel again and again. "It's a trick—it's a fucking trick—!!"

Through the CB another voice gusted.

It came in spurts.

"FFffhhhhhttt—friend's a gooooohhhh—good nigger—ssssssshhhpp-shp-shp—good   nigger's   a   dead—deeeeeaahhh—ffht—dead nigger!!"

Lucas smashed his fist through the CB. The radio's face plate shattered, its underbelly snapping off at the base. Pain shrieked up Lucas's arm but he barely felt it. His rage was feeding him now.

Behind them the hearse seemed to absorb his rage and pain like a sponge. It rumbled closer. It flirted with the rear of the cruiser.

"Take the wheel!" Lucas hissed at Sophie through gritted teeth.

"What are you gonna do?!" Sophie yelled over the clamor as she gripped the edge of the steering wheel and held the cruiser steady.

Lucas ripped the shotgun free of its brackets. He checked the breech. It was loaded to the gills, at least a half a dozen shells tucked inside. Evidently, Sheriff Baum had taken the initiative before he had embarked.

The voice of hate was everywhere now, spurting through the air vents, through the heater, through the cracks in the doors, rising, cacophonous, and violent.

Lucas cocked the shotgun, turned around, and hollered, "GET DOWN, ANGEL!"

Then Lucas fired over Angel's head into the darkness behind them. The explosion flashed like a photo bulb. The concussion ripped through the remaining shards of jagged rear window and into the wind outside.

The voice stopped.

The loud report from the gun was still ringing in Lucas's ears when he dropped the shotgun at his feet, took the wheel, and muscled the car back under control. "I think I got the motherfuckers," he uttered stupidly, his heart racing. "I think I actually got—"

A wave of light suddenly washed over the cruiser and curled around the left side. The hearse had swung out into the oncoming lane and was passing the cruiser. Lucas saw it coming in his side mirror. He saw the gaping hole in its grille, ripped open by the buckshot. He saw the flickering headlamp. He saw the silhouette of a figure behind the wheel.

It was wearing mirrored sunglasses.

"No—Jesus—no—!!"

The hearse roared past the cruiser and pulled back into the lane in front of them. Lucas recognized the rear of the hearse from that horrible day. The day they took his father away. It was tilted at a sweeping angle. Framed in dusty chrome. Oval taillights. A window embedded in its top third.

Through the window, Lucas could see his father's coffin.

"This—" Lucas swallowed hard. "—can't—"

The top of the coffin sprang open.

"—this can't be—"

The corpse of Charles Hyde sat up and waved. His face was the color of spackling putty. His teeth were cinders and his eyes were gone.

"—*happening*—!!!"

At that moment the hearse's taillights flamed on.

Sophie's scream was like a bracing slap in the face. Lucas acted on instinct. He crashed his boot down on the brake pedal and swerved. G-forces slammed Sophie and Angel against the far doors.

At the last moment, Lucas clipped the rear corner of the hearse and careened toward the shoulder.

The car hit the gravel going a hair under seventy. They were lifted momentarily out of their seats as the cruiser bounded over the shoulder and into the neighboring cornfield. The wheels bit into the turf. Detritus sprayed everywhere as the car bulldozed through the crops. The steering wheel convulsed in Lucas's hands, bringing new explosions of pain. The rear of the cruiser bucked wildly.

Behind them the yellow lights entered the corn.

"Goddamn you to fucking hell—!!" Lucas screamed over the chaos.

He concentrated on the darkness ahead of them. A wall of green loomed in their headlights. The cruiser was mowing down stalks like a combine gone mad. Lucas had lost all sense of direction. The only thing he could do was keep on coursing along in a straight line and hope they didn't meet anything in their path.

"I'th following uth!!" Angel was bouncing around the rear seat, trying to keep tabs on the light behind them.

Lucas saw it in his side mirror. A whirling dervish of yellow light was moving through the corn behind them. It made a rustling sound like a wildfire out of control.

"God—damn—you!"

"Lucas—!!" Sophie was holding on to the dash like a life raft.

They were swimming blind. Their headlights were swallowed by the endless green in front of them. The shocks pistoned furiously as they cobbled over the corrugated earth. Lucas spun the car into another direction. Dirt exploded all around them, washed up across the hood, blew into the car.

Behind them the yellow light was gaining. Lucas could sense it like a shark charging its prey. It was going to catch up and eat them alive. Sledgehammer fear slammed in his chest. He struggled with the wheel. His lungs were heaving painfully. His flesh was crawling. He pinned the pedal to the floor but the car dug deeper into the mud.

Angel was screaming. "The jack—i'th gonna hit us—!!"

The yellow light exploded behind them.

"—look out!!"

The first impact was more of a sensation in the back of Lucas's mind than a real experience, though violent nonetheless. It seemed to rock the entire car down to its very core, nearly spinning it into a cloud of earth and corn silk and making a sound that was indescribable. A low, wet, organic after-thud that sent seismic vibrations through the frame and the seats.

Angel was the first to see the bugs. They came pouring into the car from the darkness behind the back seat. Countless species of beetles, roaches, ants, and aphids, they carpeted the darkness. Shiny, undulating, glistening, they sounded like the crackle of a roaring fire rising around Angel's ears, covering him, burrowing into his skin with an infinite number of needling feet.

Angel screamed.

Lucas snapped his head around in time to see the wave coming over the seats. It was a cloud of buzzing bony blackness, tiny whirring mandibles flowing over him. Sophie shrieked. Lucas turned away and cried out, "They're not real, goddamnit. *The motherfuckers are not real!*"

Lucas pinned the pedal and swerved. The car spun away from the hearse and cut through a virgin section of corn.

"NOT REAL!!"

The bugs swirled around Lucas, engulfing his head, buzzing turbulently. Soon they were turning into smoke. Then they were turning into vapor.

Then they simply ceased to exist.

It happened with such violent abruptness that Lucas felt the air pressure around him hiccup with an audible pop. He concentrated on the wall of corn. The rush of stalks. The endless green sea. He could feel Sophie's anguished gaze beside him, her eyes frozen with the hot terror of someone caught in a dream. In back, Angel was still frantically clawing at the invisible bugs.

Then came the next impact. The hearse kissed the cruiser again and the cruiser spasmed with the muffled after-echo of metal on metal, then fishtailed wildly in the dirt.

A cloud of locusts erupted from the back. It filled the interior with a thick fog of humming, churning menace. Sparkling in the yellow back-light were cicadas, dragonflies, moths, mantises, even clusters of huge ancient insects long extinct. Seeping up from every corner and cranny, choking the dimness, they pulsated angrily.

Lucas opened his mouth to cry out and inhaled a clog of wasps. It was like breathing in a gob of needles. He gasped for air, heaved, and spat. The car went out of control again, shimmying across the shoulder, tearing through the gravel, and scraping the guardrail. Sparks erupted all around them, the metal on metal coaxing another howl from Lucas.

Again the insects streamed around Lucas like a hideous wreath of smoke. Their incessant buzzing grew to such a shrieking volume that Lucas began to howl inarticulate cries of rage and fear and hate just to hear his own voice, until—

On a lightning crack of static electricity, the horde of insects vanished.

Lucas gasped for breath. Brain swirling, he madly scanned the void of corn for a way out. The cruiser was beginning to falter. The engine was racing and clattering. Dizziness was cloaking Lucas's brain, threatening to make him pass out. Beside him, Sophie was gasping for air.

In back, Angel was bouncing around violently. He began to say something but vomited instead. His stomach was fairly empty so nothing other than thin stringers of saliva and bile came out.

"Kid!" Lucas screamed at Angel. "Are you al—"

The words froze in Lucas's throat.

They were in someone's backyard. The car had emerged from the cornfield without warning and had entered a farmer's residential lot. Thirty yards ahead of them was a two-story farmhouse, white picket fence, and garage.

Lucas turned sharply.

The cruiser plowed through a swing set. The metal poles snapped out of the ground like matchsticks, shattering the cruiser's right front headlight and bouncing off its roof. Lucas turned sharply again and the car went into a spin.

For a moment everything was up for grabs. The g-force slammed Angel and Sophie against the far wall and the car swam out of control. Vision blurred. Motion melted. The vapor lights of the backyard and the yellow glare of the predator streaked into one horrible halo. And in that insane instant of horror, Lucas flashed back to that awful fucking racist fable of Little Black Sambo where the tigers circled around and around and around until they all turned into butter . . .

Lucas finally grasped the steering wheel for dear life and pulled the car out of the spin.

The lights in the farmhouse began to blink on as the inhabitants were jostled awake by the noise. The spill from the porch light illuminated the driveway on the opposite side of the yard. Lucas threaded the cruiser between a tool shed and a rusty well, then pointed it in the general direction of the driveway and put the pedal to the floor.

They reached the driveway in a heartbeat, bit into the gravel, and clamored toward the access road fifty yards away. Behind them the yellow lights followed.

The access road was an asphalt snake. Heavily traveled. Worn by the weather. Minefields of potholes. Barely wide enough for two-way traffic. It took Lucas five seconds to reach it. He screeched around the base of the driveway and floored it. The cruiser angrily rattled down the asphalt.

A moment later, Lucas forced himself to look over his shoulder.

Through the jagged maw of the rear window the yellow lights were still looming. Through the narcotics, Lucas felt his heart palpitate painfully. His mouth was dry as stone. He felt as if his soul had been ripped from inside him by the teeth of a rabid animal. He couldn't get the image of his father's dead face out of his fevered brain. The pain was unendurable. And for the first time all night, the concept of surrender began to creep into his frenzied thoughts like a leak in the hull of a ship . . .

Lucas froze.

A new pair of lights had materialized in front of him.

"FUUUUUHHHHHKK!!!!"

There was a semi coming at them.

Less than a mile away, the truck had just rounded a curve and had its running lights fired up like a Christmas tree, its air horn bellowing. There definitely wasn't enough room for both to pass. If Lucas didn't do something immediately they would collide and that would be all she wrote.

Lucas jammed the steering wheel to the right.

The cruiser went into a skid across the shoulder and nearly swiped a row of birch trees. The rear end raised a thunderhead of dust and gravel. Lucas snapped the wheel back and the g-force tossed Sophie against Lucas, Angel against the far door.

The truck whooshed past them.

The impact that followed cracked open the darkness of the night with a sonic boom, metal on metal fury, and Lucas felt it on the back of his neck. The truck had collided head on with the hearse.

The explosion sent out a shock wave that goosed the cruiser and sucked the air right out of the night. Lucas managed to glimpse the afterimage in the retina of his rearview. It looked like an insane mating ritual. The semi had consumed the ancient limousine, humping over it in a spasm of bucking metal.

Lucas wrenched the wheel back to the left. The cruiser fishtailed through the dirt and gravel and nearly spun to a halt. But an instant later they snagged the edge of the road and Lucas put the hammer down. The engine roared and complained, and the cruiser groaned, kicking and screaming, back onto the access road and into the distance.

Toward the highway.

The cab was a blast furnace inside. Flames crept up the sides of the tractor and the windows from the wreckage underneath. Smoke seeped in through the vents. Another couple of seconds and the whole damn thing was going to blow. Unfortunately, Shawn Snowden wasn't moving too quickly. The burly, tattooed truck driver had cracked his skull in the collision and was now swimming in and out of a severe concussion.

He pulled himself up into a sitting position next to his door. His T-shirt, imprinted with HONK IF YOU'RE HORNY, was saturated with blood. It was running down his neck from his sticky, matted hair. He wasn't sure how bad his injuries were. As a matter of fact, at this moment, he wasn't even sure if he could remember his own name.

Shawn pushed his door open.

He was greeted by the searing heat of flames and the thick aroma of spilled diesel. Somewhere in the depths of his injured forebrain he sensed a warning. *Get outta there,* it cried, *get outta there now before the whole goddamn places goes up.* But Shawn was a decent man and was worried about the car underneath his rig. It was a long shot, but Shawn had heard stories of miraculous freak accidents where people had been cut out of crumpled wrecks like this and had lived to tell the story.

Struggling down his ladder, Shawn climbed to the ground.

With his last surge of energy he knelt down and looked under the truck. Low-lying flames sizzled along the puddled pavement and thick black fluids leaked here and there. Shawn blinked. His mind swam for a moment and he struggled to stay conscious. This was wrong, this was goddamn wrong. He must be imagining this, hallucinating or something.

The crumpled carcass of the antique limousine was gone.

"Everybody okay?" Sophie was taking deep breaths and gathering her bearings. She glanced around the car. She saw Angel huddling in the corner of the back seat. Lucas was driving silently. His eyes had changed. He looked wounded somehow. He also looked as if he had made his mind up about something.

It took them several minutes just to recover enough to speak. Sophie finally said, "You guys—okay?"

"Yes," Lucas muttered, breathing steadily. He was beginning to worry Sophie.

"I'm okay, Th'ophie." The boy was swallowing back his panic.

They drove for another moment in silence. Sophie glanced in the side mirror. The wreckage was a couple miles away now, a tiny dot of flame receding into the ocean of blackness behind them. "You could drive six months straight on these little back roads and never see a truck."

Lucas nodded. "Lucky for us that poor son of a bitch came along."

Sophie shook her head. Her mouth was tingling with the sharp taste of fear. "What the fuck are we dealing with here, Lucas?!"

He didn't answer.

Sophie just kept on shaking her head. She realized that none of them were mentioning the worst part. None of them were outwardly acknowledging it. But each of them knew deep down inside, the worst part of the whole confrontation had just taken place a few seconds ago. Whoever—*whatever*—was inside that limousine was most certainly linked to the curse; but in the confusion after the limo had collided with the truck—in those brief moments following the limo's destruction—the cruiser had nearly come to a stop.

And in that instant of panic, they each felt the sickness.

Still inside them.

A mileage sign loomed in the wash of their broken headlights. It said PARK CITY 5 MI. That was a good thing, too, because the cruiser's engine was starting to rattle ominously. It was only a matter of time before it either ran out of gas or simply gave up the ghost altogether.

Sophie took one last look in the mirror. "Whatever it was, it's gone now."

"Yeah," Lucas muttered softly, and Sophie could tell there was more he wanted to say but he was not letting on about it.

He simply kept on driving.

26

Odor of
Burning Metal

The engineer's name was Barney Hollis and he loved to read the funny papers. *Blondie, Dick Tracy, Peanuts, Dennis the Menace*, and especially *Beetle Bailey. Beetle Bailey* reminded Barney of his stint in the Fifth Army during the Second World War, all those beautiful Sicilian sunsets and those gorgeous olive-skinned women. Barney turned the page and shifted in his seat. His ass itched something fierce. Damn hemorrhoids. Curse of the railroad man—hemorrhoids and bad coffee and waiting in these blasted lonely switchyards.

"Situation normal," Barney mumbled to himself, turning the page to *Rex Stuart, MD.* "All fouled up."

Barney had been waiting for the signalman's call for over fifteen minutes now. It was a moderately busy night in the Park City hump yard and there were a number of freight jobs in line ahead of Barney. But for Christ's sake, did he always have to wait like this? Just once, Barney would love to see a nightly jaunt run on time. He checked his watch. It was going on three. At this rate he wouldn't get started until three-thirty, maybe even four. Darn it, he was getting too old for this aggravation.

It's all those young tadpoles up at the yard office, he

thought to himself and polished off the last gulp of tepid coffee from his thermos.

A gangly, fair-skinned man with thinning gray hair and weathered features, Barney wore greasy overalls and sat cross-legged on his chair like a big old stork all folded up. He was several years past retirement age but the railroad had let him stay on part-time. One or two trips a week on the old Dodge City commuter line was just enough to keep Barney active and out of trouble at home.

Barney had first learned about trains during the war. As a deskbound depot clerk, he had seen more action in the bordellos of Messina than on the battlefields of Sicily. But every few weeks he had visited one of the switching yards to requisition new supplies and learn about minutiae like automatic couplers, electric relays, trip stops, and interlocking signal systems. By the time he had shipped home, he was ready for a career as a railroad man.

During the early years, Barney worked as a signal repairman for the Northern Pacific and Burlington lines. He cut his teeth on the big freight trains out of Washington and Oregon, learning the business from the greasy foundation up. He got married, had three kids, and settled into a simple life. But his dream had always been to command a big deluxe passenger line like The Chief or The California Zephyr, shuttling thousands of travelers in style and comfort across the great wide-open spaces. It seemed the perfect way to spend a life.

In 1971, Barney got his big chance. Out of the new government rail subsidies, many of the old regional routes were taken over by Amtrak, and Barney was put in charge of the new Dodge City–Newton shuttle service.

Of course, as an engineer, Barney never dreamed he'd get stuck on the same route, week in and week out, for the rest of his life. But the weeks turned into months, which turned into years, which turned into decades. And the hundred-and-fifty-mile jaunt between Wichita and Dodge City became part of Barney, like a well-worn rutted road down the middle of his life. He came to know every gradient, every turn, every signal, every junction, every last frigging bump like—

Barney looked up from his paper.

An odd sound had clamored across the yard outside his window. Though muffled and indistinct, it sounded like someone digging around in the gravel behind the train. Barney couldn't tell how far away the source of the sound was, but after nearly fifty years at this game, his ears were tuned to any suspicious sounds from inside or outside his engine.

He went over to the window, threw it open, and leaned out. In the darkness in front of the engine he could see his coaches extending back into the shadows of the yard. At only six cars, Barney's cut was one of the smallest in the region, but then again, Park City was no Grand Central Station. Barney sniffed the air. It smelled of oil and cinders and dust.

He gazed around the yard. The switching area spread out in all directions, a cat's cradle of concentric tracks humming with the whetstone sounds of metal on metal. Signal lights and vapor lamps dotted the darkness. Great plumes of smoke came from the distant roof of the crest tower. Partially automated, the yard worked on gravity. All trains entered the area at the top of the bordering hill, and then were allowed to coast into the center tracks for maintenance.

"Pervis?" Barney called over the baritone of his train's idling turbine. The sound of footsteps was churning through the gravel, coming down the adjacent track. Barney thought it might be his motorman. "Pervis? That you?!"

There was no answer.

"What in hellfire is going on—?!" Barney turned back to his thermos and paper and stuffed the items into his lunch bucket. He had a sick feeling in the pit of his stomach all of a sudden. Usually, during an especially long delay, when somebody came out of the yard office it meant only one thing—bad news. It was either some kind of technical malfunction with the switching equipment or some problem down the line somewhere.

Barney reached over to the intercom and pressed the switch. "Granger—you back there?" Granger Tollifson was Barney's conductor. A pleasant little man in his late fifties, Granger had been on the Newton run since Jimmy Carter was in office. But right now he was no where to be found. "Granger? You anywhere near your station?!"

Still no answer.

All of a sudden the door to the engine burst open.

"What the—?" Barney saw a young boy standing in the doorway, holding a pump-action shotgun, breathing hard and shaking like a leaf. The kid had hair like a girl's and a face like an oblong gourd. From the way he was waving the gun he looked like he meant business.

Barney's feeble old heart began to race. In all of his twenty-two years as an engineer, he had never been a victim of a crime or seen a major accident. For that matter, Barney had never seen anything out of the ordinary.

Now it looked like his luck was about to change.

"Get your hand' where I can see 'em!" Angel felt like his body was crawling with scorpions. The fever was so bad he was starting to hallucinate. But he was trying to stay calm and avoid using sibilants. He wanted the engineer to understand every word the first time. "Get 'em up!"

The old man raised his greasy hands.

Angel gestured at the control panel with the tip of his shotgun. "Git thi'th train moving!"

"Think it over, son," the old man said. "Gonna get yourself in a mess of trouble."

"I th'aid—get thi'th crate movin'!!"

"What did you do with Granger?"

"What?!"

The old man motioned through the window. "My conductor—he'll be checking in any second now. Fella's armed and pretty nasty."

It was a lie. Angel knew it, and the old man knew he knew it. Before breaking into the engine, Angel had forced the conductor into a tool shed out behind the train. Now it was just the engineer and Angel and time was running out for both of them. Stepping closer, playing the gun barrel closer to the old man's face, Angel said, "You got about two th'econds to get thi'th train moving! YOU HEAR ME?"

"I can't!" The old man was gawking at the barrel. He looked scared now. Scared and confused. "Switches ain't cleared yet!"

Angel shoved the barrel closer. "Not gonna tell ya again! GET THI'TH TRAIN MOVING!!"

"Son, it won't do no good!"

Angel cocked the gun. It made a loud clanging sound that stiffened the old man. "Get it moving or I shoot!"

"Son, I'm tellin' ya—"

"NOWWWW!!" Angel pressed the barrel against the old man's head.

The engineer turned and hobbled over to the control panel. He disengaged the brake handle and grabbed the stick. The turbine came awake beneath them. "Can't go east, son! There's a stack of cars in the way!"

"That'th okay—" Pain erupted in Angel's stomach. He staggered for a moment, struggling to hold the shotgun aloft. His stomach heaved and he retched air. His throat felt like a blowtorch was blasting through. "—want to go weh'th! Under-thand? Weh'th!!"

The old man was vexed. "Say again, son. I can't understand what you're saying."

Angel pointed in the direction of the coaches. "Want to go wwwwwehhh'th."

"West?" The old man was trembling now. After seeing Angel puke, there was no telling what was running through the old codger's mind.

"YE'TH, DAMN IT!! WWWE'TH!!"

"Can't do it, son!"

"GO!! NOW!!" Angel was burning up. It felt like his eyeballs were going to pop out of his skull.

The old man leaned out the window for a moment. "Utility car's blocking the way!"

"RAM IT!!"

The old man licked his lips nervously. He grasped the stick. His eyes were filling with panic. "Ain't gonna happen, son."

Angel fell to his knees. The heat was coursing through his lungs now, through his arteries, his marrow. His vision blurred. The shotgun wavered for a moment. "—rrrraaaahh-hhh—"

The old man looked down at the boy and contemplated

grabbing the gun away. But something stopped him. It wasn't the risk of discharging the shotgun. It wasn't even the prospect of getting hurt in the struggle. It had more to do with the pain in the young kid's misshapen face.

Angel looked up at the old man and uttered through gritted teeth, pronouncing the sibilant as best he could, "—pleea'zzz—"

The old man looked at the boy and said, "Gonna have to go 'round the block."

Angel nodded.

The old man turned back to the stick and started the train in the direction of the west gate.

"How do we know it's him?" Sophie pressed her nose against the window of the cruiser. "Last thing we want to do is pull alongside the wrong train." She had taken another half a Darvocet and the painkiller was starting to kick in. But the dull throb of fever and terror continued festering within her. The passing landscape looked surreal to her, like a deep-purple munchkin land with scarecrows and silos and barns rushing by in the wee-hour moonlight.

"Look for the blinking light," Lucas murmured under the rattle of the cruiser's engine. He was writhing in pain, keeping his eyes peeled for any sign of a friendly train in his rearview.

"Suppose Angel gets busted," Sophie speculated. Her skull felt too tight. Her brain was filled with noise.

"He'll make it. Kid's tough as nails."

"Suppose he gets sick."

"Stop it, Sophie."

"Suppose—"

"Stop!" Lucas shook his head. "Help me find a place to pull along the track."

They were speeding down a rural access road between Mount Hope and Colwich. For miles, the road ran parallel to the train tracks. They knew the little Amtrak train ran this hundred-mile stretch every morning. Lucas had learned about it during his ill-fated Bird's Eye run.

With a little luck, the train would be fully fueled and able to continue westward past Dodge City into Colorado.

"There's a crossing!" Lucas nodded at an upcoming intersection.

Lucas slowed down and turned off the two-lane. He passed over the tracks and got a good look at the lay of the land around the rails. There was a sizable shoulder of gravel along either side, whiskered with weeds, big enough for a cop car to negotiate.

"Lucas, look out—!!"

Lucas was making a U-turn back toward the tracks when the lights of a pickup loomed behind him. He nearly turned directly into its path. The truck clamored by in a cloud of dust and exhaust, leaning on its horn. Lucas swerved back on the road and held the car steady, then completed his U-turn.

"Wait a minute." Sophie was craning her neck to see down the distant reaches of the railroad track. "Train coming."

"Lights blinking?"

"Yeah."

Lucas pulled back over the tracks and turned sharply. The cruiser shambled over the lips of asphalt and dug into the gravel. The tires spun in place for a moment and Sophie felt her head fill with pain, her throat constrict. Then the car lurched forward down the shoulder, its tires rimming the edge of the wooden apron, lifting clouds of gravel dust against the indigo sky.

They climbed to thirty-five miles per hour, then forty. The cruiser was vibrating furiously, threatening to rattle apart at the seams.

Sophie looked over her shoulder. Through the gaping maw of the rear window, the blinking lights were swelling. The train was a hundred yards away. It looked to be going about thirty miles an hour. Its front strobe light was slicing the darkness like a fiery scythe.

"C'mon, Sophie! Climb over!" Lucas was looking in his side mirror.

"Wait a minute!" Sophie's head was spinning. The drugs and the fear were creating a poisonous brew within her. "Hold on a second!"

"Hurry!" Lucas watched his mirror as the train loomed.

Sophie's brain seized up like a jammed clockwork. A vision flashed through her back-brain. Body flailing, bones shattering, teeth hitting the rail and smashing through her skull. Then the eruption within her, washing it all away. The end. The image tore through her mind in one frozen instant.

"Lucas—!!" Sophie was searching for the right words. "Maybe we oughtta—"

"Sophie, goddamnit—hurry!!" The metal beast bore down on them. The ground vibrated. A rumbling, clacking noise rose all around them.

"Lucas, listen—it's not gonna—"

"SOPHIE—GODDAMNIT!"

She looked into his steady, penetrating gaze. His eyes said everything. He was no longer scared. No longer vexed. He seemed to have found a kind of lunatic calm in the eye of the storm around them. She quickly inhaled all his courage, as if taking a gulp of oxygen. The feeling was bracing. "Fuck it!" she yelped and climbed over him.

"SOPHIE—GO NOW!!"

Sophie felt big hands on her ass, urging her out the window. She climbed out into the wind. The noise was excruciating. She tasted cinder dust in her mouth. Her head was buzzing with adrenalin. Leaning back inside for an instant, she touched Lucas's sweaty cheek and hollered over the wind and noise, "Just be careful!"

Then she climbed over him and struggled out the window.

"Hold it th'teady!!" The kid was in the doorway of the engine, leaning out over the rail. With his free hand, he held his shotgun poised on Barney.

Barney stood at the control panel next to the door, gripping the caliper stick in his sweaty palm. He was holding the train at a modest thirty-five miles an hour, keeping his eyes open for any unusual signals or obstructions along the track ahead of them. He was still pretty tense. Less than ten minutes ago, he had rammed his way out of the switchyard, completely ignoring the frantic voices crackling over the radio from the tower. Now he was rolling toward Dodge City with a gun at his neck and a group of God-only-knows-what climbing aboard.

Strangely enough, the old man was no longer scared. There was an electricity in the air. He could sense it like the hot odor of burning metal. And the smell of it thrilled him. Finally, he was going to see some excitement on this old tired line. At last, he was going to be part of something big. Heck, most of his cronies were either dead or in nursing homes. If only the old Burlington Northern boys could see him now. . . .

Outside the doorway, the police cruiser hovered next to the train. The car's engine was rattling like a banshee. Gouts of black smoke were spewing from under its hood. Barney figured it was going to blow real soon.

Then the woman came through the doorway.

The kid helped her into the engine. Breathing hard, eyes wet, and face flushed, Sophie tried to say something but couldn't get the words out. She just crawled across the floor and sat against the far corner of the cab, catching her breath.

Barney turned to the woman and nodded.

Sophie still couldn't speak. To Barney, she looked to be in her middle thirties. Boyish haircut, no makeup, clothes drenched in sweat and grime, she looked like she was sick. But there was a quickness in her eyes. She reminded Barney of his own daughter and he wondered just what it was these folks had done. Barney knew they must be fugitives—that much he could figure out on his own—but what the hell had they done to be on such a desperate run from the law?

The black man came next. Evidently, he had jammed something into the steering wheel and had wedged the floor mat against the foot feed to give him enough time to climb out. He lurched through the doorway of the train and crabbed across the floor to safety. Behind him, the cruiser floated away from the train, careened through the weeds and bush, and disappeared in a cloud of dust and smoke.

An instant later, the crash rang out over the clatter of the train.

Barney's pulse quickened. He thought about all those true-life crime shows on TV that his wife liked to look at. Stories of kidnappings and insurance scams and jewel heists. Boy, howdy—if they could just get a load of these folks! "'Evenin',"" Barney finally said to the black man. "Welcome aboard."

Lucas glanced around the interior of the engine like a frightened circus animal getting the lay of its cage. His eyes burned with urgency. His body was also soaked with sweat and blood and moisture. He also looked sick to Barney, if not more so. In fact, this guy looked as though he had been passed through a deep fryer. His skin looked raw and blistered.

The kid rushed over to his friends. They spent a few minutes getting their bearings, checking themselves for any fresh wounds. The kid whispered a few things in their ears about Barney, pointing up at the engineer, explaining how harmless he was, how he wasn't going to get in their way.

Finally, Lucas came over to the engineer and spoke between anxious breaths. "Just keep her at a reasonable speed—nothing out of the ordinary—and try to conserve fuel. Above all, keep her going."

"Mind if I ask a question?"

"Ask."

"What are you folks running from?"

Lucas wiped his mouth with the back of his hand and caught his breath. He looked like he was running a temperature. "It's complicated—"" Then he smiled a pained, weary kind of smile.

"What is it?" asked the old man.

"Nothing," Lucas said. "Just something I remember a dead man saying over the CB radio. Dude's name was Melville. He also thought things were pretty damn complicated."

27

Black Fire

They huddled in the belly of the engine for nearly thirty minutes, gathering their wits, keeping an eye on the old man. Through the greasy front windshield they watched the train's xenon arc light sweep across the changing landscape. They saw the darkness of western Kansas bulge and buckle as they made their way into the rolling grasslands of Colorado. They saw the great buttes rising into the sky. They saw the vast reservoirs passing by, one by one—Nee Shah, Muddy Creek, Seven Lakes—their surfaces reflecting inky clouds like black mirrors. All the while, Lucas was plotting his next move.

For the first time since the whole nightmare began, Lucas knew exactly what he had to do. He picked up the shotgun, stepped over to the controls, and stood next to the engineer. "Lemme ask you a simple question."

Barney raised an eyebrow and listened.

"Can I trust you?" Lucas asked.

"Depends."

"Depends on what?"

"Depends on what you're trusting me to do."

Lucas rubbed his mouth. "Can I trust you to keep the train on course while we regroup in the back?"

Barney turned and regarded Lucas. "Yessir, I believe you can trust me to do that."

Lucas studied the grizzled old engineer for another moment and thought it over. There was something oddly childlike about the old man. A strange softness in Barney's eyes. It made Lucas think of his Uncle Will. Will had been a stable hand down at a horse ranch in Houston for over fifty years. On many occasions, while visiting the old codger, Lucas had marvelled at Will's affection for the horses. Up until the day he died, Uncle Will's eyes had literally sparkled every time he brushed one of his beloved thoroughbreds. Somehow Lucas knew it was the same with Barney and his train. The old engineer had a certain wonder in his manner that couldn't be banished by age.

Lucas decided he trusted the old man.

"Okay, here's the deal," Lucas said. "I want you to keep us moving along at a steady pace."

"Yessir."

"Do not stop under any circumstances. Understand?"

"Yep."

Lucas motioned at the distance ahead of them. "Any chance of us running into any cops or rail authorities for the next hundred miles or so?"

Across the cab, Sophie and Angel listened intently. They both appeared to have recovered from the pain and heat and nausea, but neither looked particularly frisky. Sophie appeared especially haggard. Her eyes shone with equal measures of fever and terror.

After a moment of looking through the windshield, Barney replied, "Shouldn't be anything out of the ordinary along the route tonight. Don't think the dispatcher who noticed us skedaddling outta the yard even gives a shinola. If we're gonna have trouble, it's gonna be around a depot."

"How often do we pass through depots?"

The old man shot another sideways glance at Lucas. "Not too often if you know how to bypass 'em."

Lucas nodded. Although he didn't have much of a choice, he was satisfied that the old man was trustworthy. The fact was crucial to Lucas's plan. The train must be kept on course at all costs. No matter what goes down on board. In order to emphasize the point, Lucas grasped the old man's arm and said, "Promise me you won't try to be a hero and call in the Mounties."

Barney shot a glance at Sophie and the boy. "Ain't nobody gonna call any Mounties."

Lucas pointed at the control panel. "You have a way to alert us in back—in case anything happens?"

The old man thought for a moment. "Yessir, I can flash the cabin lights."

"Where's the radio?"

Barney pointed at a small panel to his left.

Lucas lifted the butt of the gun and slammed it down hard on the tiny panel. The radio crunched beneath the impact. Shards of plastic and cheap metal skittered across the panel. The elderly engineer gazed down at the mess and softly said, "Message received."

Lucas turned to Angel and handed the boy the shotgun. "Angel, you got the first shift in the caboose. You see anything coming, you shoot first and ask questions later."

Angel nodded. But Sophie stepped forward and raised her trembling hands. "Wait a minute—wait a minute, Lucas— what's the Duke Wayne stuff?"

"Whattya mean?"

"What are you up to? What's the plan?"

After a moment's hesitation, Lucas said, "Let's talk about it in back."

To get to the dining coach, Lucas and Sophie squeezed through the emergency exit of the engine and stepped over the massive iron couplers outside. The night wind was cool and sharp on their faces. The train shimmied precariously beneath them. Lucas shook the dizziness from his head and urged Sophie through the next portal.

The dining car was dimly lit. Twenty-seven feet long and filled with the smells of stale grease and old cigarettes, it was a relic of the Fabulous Fifties. It still had its original booths and tables. The lighting fixtures were ancient. Scuff marks from decades of weary travelers tattooed the narrow floor. Inside a small lavatory in back, Sophie and Lucas took turns relieving their aching bladders. A minute later, they were sitting side-by-side on the edge of an empty steam table.

"Whattya got in your head, Lucas?" Sophie asked while lighting another Marlboro. Her hands would not stop shaking. She had found a cigarette machine in the lavatory and was now going through the fresh pack like it was going out of style.

Lucas studied her. "You oughtta eat something, Sophie."

"I'll just puke it up."

"Shouldn't go so long on an empty stomach." Lucas scanned the car. He slid off the steam table, went over to the bar, and found a small mini-fridge. Nothing much inside, just scattered breakfast items such as juices, donuts, pre-made microwavable eggs, and the like. But it was enough to fill the emptiness.

"Gotta eat—" Lucas gobbled a donut and took a swig from a half-gallon carton of milk. The cool liquid had no taste but at least it was coating his raw stomach. He found a plastic bottle of orange juice, fiddled with its foil top, and handed it to Sophie.

"I hate orange juice." Sophie took a couple of sips of juice, grimaced, and then handed it back. Taking another drag off the cigarette, hands trembling, she said, "Just tell me what you're thinking. I know you've got something in that scheming little brain of yours."

Lucas put the milk down and rubbed his ravaged fingers over his scalp. His nerve endings were raw. He felt a slimy wetness between his fingers and saw that the powdered sugar had mixed with blood. "All I've got in my head is pain."

"We're all hurting."

"I'm talking about other kinds of pain."

Sophie looked into his eyes and shuddered. "Other kinds of pain?"

Lucas nodded. He couldn't find the words to paint the feeling growing inside him since the onslaught of the dark-green limousine. It was a cancer. It was a black fire raging through him. But in some horrible twisted way it was good. It was like a magnetic surge aligning every fiber of his being, pointing him in one direction. It was liberating.

Sophie took another quick drag and said, "What other kinds of pain?"

Lucas looked into her eyes. "That thing on the road—"

"The limousine?"

"Yeah, the limousine—"

"What about it?"

"The motherfucker inside that limousine—"

"They were trying to stop us." Sophie was shivering again, wired, drawing in anguished drags of smoke.

"That's right," Lucas said to her. "They were trying to stop us—whoever—whatever was inside that limo—it was trying to stop us. That's correct—"

"You think they were responsible for the curse?"

Lucas didn't answer at first. He wandered over to the window. His legs had finally grown accustomed to the gentle shimmy of the train; but he still felt every little vibration. Every bump, every shock, every slight shifting of weight traveled up his legs and made his testicles contract. He no longer had control of the vehicle in which he was riding. At any moment he could grind to a halt and go down in flames and there wasn't a damn thing he could do about it.

Looking out the window at the dark landscape rushing by, Lucas thought about his plan. He wondered how close he really was to death. Rubbing his mouth, he turned back to his partner and said, "Yeah, I think they're responsible."

Sophie's eyes were filling with tears. "They're gone now, Lucas. They're gone and we're still fucked—"

"Wait a minute. Hold on. There was something else—you know, when the limo was bearing down on us—"

"You heard stuff coming through the CB speaker."

"Yeah, I heard some stuff . . ." Lucas measured his words carefully. He still didn't know exactly what Sophie had heard or seen back there on Highway 79. "I heard some stuff coming outta that CB that nobody could have known about. Stuff from my childhood. Stuff from back home in L.A.

Stuff that went right to my motherfucking central nervous system—know what I mean? Ugly painful stuff that won't go away . . ."

"What are you saying?"

"I'm saying I don't think any of us ever had any idea what we were dealing with—"

"What do you think we were dealing with?"

"I don't know."

"What do you think it was?"

"I don't—"

"C'mon, Lucas—do you think it had anything to do with what Uncle Flaco was talking about? Was it the Beast?"

Lucas shook his head. "No, no, no—listen—it doesn't matter anymore anyway 'cause the thing is gone. All I'm saying is, it hit pretty hard."

"Lucas, what's your plan?"

Lucas started to answer but stopped himself and studied the wiry little woman for a moment. For as long as he had known her, he had prided himself on the naked honesty upon which they based their relationship. They kept nothing from each other. Nothing. It just seemed to fit their friendship. It seemed the best way to keep the business rolling smoothly. But now, for the first time since he had met Sophie Cohen, he had decided to tell her a great big lie.

"My plan," he replied, "is to stay on board this train until the fucking curse wears off."

Sophie snubbed out her Marlboro on the stainless steel counter next to her. Panic was rising in her face, as deep and scarlet as a sunburn. "That's your plan?!"

"That's my plan."

"You're shitting me."

"No, ma'am."

"Lucas—we're dead meat on this train. If nothing else, we're gonna run out of fuel before the curse wears off—if it ever does . . ."

Lucas looked at her. "These diesel-electric jobs carry tons of fuel."

"They'll stop us sooner or later, Lucas."

Lucas listened to the wheels rumbling and clacking beneath them. Sophie was right. At their present rate of speed they were due to reach Pueblo, Colorado, by dawn. But there were so many variables. At this very moment, regardless of what the old engineer said, Amtrak was probably alerting every depot from here to Vegas. Trip stops were being set, signals changed, tracks redirected. And even though old Barney Hollis had become their ally, it seemed only a matter of time before they were stopped. Which was exactly why Lucas had to act quickly. An element of surprise was critical to his plan.

All Lucas could think of saying at that moment was, "I told you we're gonna beat this motherfucker."

Sophie was shivering uncontrollably now. "I think we should give ourselves up. Get close to a hospital."

Lucas shook his head. "No way."

"Lucas, maybe they can stabilize the sickness—"

"No fucking way. We'll be cooked before they get us through the emergency room doors. Besides, if you remember, we're also running from the law. You think they're gonna give us priority medical care?"

There was a stretch of silence. The muffled vibrations rumbled beneath them. Lucas felt another wave of nausea and fever wash through him. The food was lying in his stomach like a wad of metal cable. Finally, he turned to Sophie and said, "Girl, you just gotta have faith. Gotta remember what your pal Milo said about—"

Lucas stopped suddenly because he noticed that Sophie had lowered her head and didn't seem to be listening anymore.

"Sophie—"

She looked up at him. She was crying.

"Sophie—?"

Tears tracked down her cheeks, a shiver of recognition passing through her. It took a moment before she was able to speak again. "I always believed—you know, I never—I never had much faith—"

Lucas felt a familiar ache in his chest. A dull bittersweet

ache. And the pain was unbearable, not from the sickness but from his need to comfort Sophie. He went back over and sat next to her and said, "Take it easy, girl. . . ."

Then, for lack of anything better to say, he added, "It's all gonna be over soon."

Angel Figueroa was sitting on a pine mail-trunk in the back of the caboose, eyes stinging with tears, shotgun poised between his bony knees. He'd been gazing through the tiny barred window in the rear, thinking about his Uncle Flaco and how the old man used to love the magic hour.

The magic hour was the moment in any given morning where the world turned mystical. Just before the horizon begins to color. Before the birds begin to sing. Before the stars fade. The sky would be at its deepest purple. The shadows would be pickled in aspic. The air would seem so still that the slightest sound might shatter it like delicate crystal.

On many different occasions Uncle Flaco would share this part of the day with Angel. There were early-morning fishing trips, frog-gigging expeditions along the creek behind the old man's property and other times when Flaco would take the boy on long predawn hikes over the surrounding farmland. The Tennessee highlands, with their forests of yellow pine that nearly glowed in the dark, were especially well-suited for these walks. And while hiking, the old man and Angel would talk about everything under the sun. They would talk about the folklore of Flaco's boyhood, Mexican myths, Mayan legends—everything mystical and wondrous. For Angel, each and every single one of those mornings was indelibly etched in his memory.

It was at the peak of this part of the morning that Angel looked up from his lap and saw the object on the tracks behind him.

At first, it looked like a black smudge in the darkness about a quarter-mile back. Angel thought it might be the shadow of a cactus or desert scrub brush. But upon further scrutiny, he realized it was moving. It was clattering along in the moonlight, raising sparks and dust as it came.

Angel rubbed his eyes.

It looked like a twisted piece of metal singing along the rails, moving at a pretty good clip, too. Forty, maybe fifty miles an hour. A plume of black smoke trailed behind it and bits and chinks of metal and broken glass sparked from its side every few yards. For a moment, Angel thought it might be some strange railroad contraption, a single-man car or a repair vehicle.

But all at once, the boy's bemusement turned to panic as he realized what it was. A tide of dread rose in his gut. It felt like someone was pumping ice water into him.

He should have known something like this was going to happen. After the events of the past few hours, he should have known. But unfortunately, there was still a small kernel of hope inside Angel that it was all a huge cosmic mistake. He was a good person. His uncle was good. Lucas and Sophie were good people. None of them deserved this. It was all a mistake. God's mistake.

No such luck.

Angel pushed himself off the trunk. He carried the shotgun over to the side window. He leaned his head outside for a better look. A gust of wind whipped his hair. The breeze smelled cool and clean with a hint of pine. It made his eyes water. Angel blinked a couple of times and concentrated on the flat, crumpled monstrosity approaching from the darkness behind the train.

"No way. . . ." Angel's whispered words were swallowed by the wind.

The limousine was only a couple of hundred yards away and gaining. It cobbled down the center of the track like a wrinkled steel crab, vibrating over the crossties. It seemed to be moving on some hideous internal reserve.

Angel pulled back into the caboose, his heart beating out a mariachi tune in his chest. His scalp tightened around his head. His skin prickled. But he fought the terror and forced himself to think clearly for Lucas and for Sophie and even for Uncle Flaco.

Angel cocked the shotgun.

A wave of chills crawled up his arms. He had never fired a gun before in his life. For years, Uncle Flaco had kept an old squirrel gun mounted on the wall of his bus and Angel had occasionally taken it down for cowboys-and-Indians. But nobody could remember ever shooting it. The firing pin had been missing for decades and the hammer had been frozen with rust.

But now he was prepared to fire the bulky police weapon in his hands, because now the cowboys and Indians were real.

Outside, in the pale dimness, the Rolls Royce was gaining. It was maybe a hundred yards away now. At this distance, Angel could barely make out the shattered windshield and the silhouette of someone—something—inside. The roof had peeled back like a flap of gray flesh. The sides were curled like an old sardine can.

The headlamps still glowed dimly.

"Guess I'm really acting like a helpless female."

Sophie had finally broken the silence. They had been sitting side by side on the empty table for nearly five minutes without saying anything. Sophie had gotten her crying under control. But now fear was hardening her gaze. She wiped away her tears and added, "Feels like the time I was driving on the ice in Utah and I didn't know where the goddamn turnoff ramp was."

Lucas reached over and wiped the moisture from her cheek. "I yelled at you till I was hoarse."

Another moment passed. Sophie clasped her hand around his and looked deep into his soul. "Bastard."

Lucas swallowed hard. It was getting a little too quiet in the rattling diner car. A little too close. He found himself edging away from the woman. Not a lot. Just a few inches.

"You're doing it again." Sophie squeezed his hand, tight enough to draw pain.

Lucas pulled his hand away. "What do you mean?"

"You're pulling away from me!" Sophie shoved him. Lucas bumped the carton of milk and it tipped over, spilling white liquid across the adjacent booth. Sophie continued angrily, "All this shit going down and you're still scared to get close!?!"

Lucas was stunned. "What?!"

"Fuck you! After all that's happened you still can't even touch me?!"

"Sophie, stop it. . . ."

"No, I'm tired of this shit. You and I both know we dig each other but we keep it platonic, right? Business, right? No touchy-feely on the superslab. But now we're fucking dying together and you can't touch me?!" The tears were coming again, hitching painfully in her chest, but this time they seemed to fuel her anger. She was jumping off the edge without a parachute. "What is it, Lucas? What the fuck is this brick wall between us?!"

"Sophie, cut it out . . ."

Sophie pounded her fist against the steam table. "You didn't have any problem touching a fucking dead hand! Getting us all fucking infected! Did you?!!"

"Cut it out!"

"What the fuck are you afraid of?! Afraid to get too close to your obnoxious Jew-bitch partner?! What is it?!! What are you so fucking afraid of—?!!"

"Cut it out!!" Lucas grabbed her and shook her. "Cut this shit out right now!!"

Tears tracked down Sophie's face but she was too filled with anger to fold up yet. She just stared cold and hard into his eyes. "I think that's it, isn't it!? Because I'm a Jew-girl! That's it! I'm a Jew and that just ain't down with the brothers in the 'hood! Right?! Guess ol' Lucas is as fucked up as the white racist fuckers that he hates sooooo—"

"SHUT UP!!" Lucas threw her across the coach. Sophie hit the floor and slammed her back against the legs of the opposite booth. An involuntary cry burst from her lungs. She folded up for a moment, cringing at the pain and stunned.

Lucas froze. His ears buzzed with rage and adrenalin. His heart slammed in his chest. But the worst part, the absolutely worst part, was the realization. It pierced his brain like a poisonous stinger.

Sophie was right after all. All the bullshit rationalizations for not getting involved were just that—bullshit. He was afraid. He was afraid of loving a white girl. After all his years of righteous anger he was turning out to be the very embodiment of all that he hated.

It made him realize all the more that his plan was the right thing to do.

"Jesus, I'm sorry—" He rushed over to her and knelt. Cradling her head, he spoke softly. "I'm sorry, Sophie. I'm so sorry—I didn't mean to hurt you. Are you alright? Girl—are you okay?"

Sophie looked up at him. Her eyes were wet, dilated, unfocused. "I'm okay—just a little—dizzy."

Lucas caressed her cheek, stroked her hair. "Please forgive me."

Sophie managed a smile. "I think I hit a chord."

Lucas nodded. "You could say that. You could also say that you're absolutely fucking right."

Sophie tried to keep her faltering gaze on him. "Gonna have to work on this problem."

"We will."

"Lucas," Sophie licked her lips, her speech slurring, "I feel kinda weird all of a sudden. Can't see straight. Mouth is really dry."

Lucas brushed the tears from her cheeks. "You remember that marathon apple run we went on back in March? Coming back on the flip?"

Sophie spoke slowly. "We were both wired on dexies . . ."

"That's right."

"You wanted me to take something to counteract the speedballs."

Again Lucas nodded. "It's Dalmane. Had some left in the stash. I put a couple in the orange juice."

For a moment, Sophie's eyes widened with terror. She tried to grab his shirt but her hands were too clumsy. Her words were coming with some effort now. "Lucas . . . what are you gonna . . . Lucas . . . ?"

"Just sleep," Lucas said. "When you wake up it'll all be over—I promise."

"Lucas . . . what . . . are you . . . ?" Her slurred speech was deteriorating into thick mumbling.

Lucas tenderly brushed her hair off her damp forehead. He knew she hadn't drunk enough of the orange juice to go completely under, but the trace of barbiturates would still keep her out of commission long enough for him to execute his plan. "Just sleep," he said softly.

Then he got up and started toward the caboose.

28

Angel Behind
the Glass

With horrible wonder he watched it coming.

Behind the train. On the tracks. The limousine was falling apart at the seams. The first thing to go was the left front wheel. It snapped off and bounded into the neighboring grassland. The car dragged itself another fifty feet and then snapped its front axle. The rear bucked into the air and the limousine crumbled apart.

"Jee'thuzzz!" Angel put his hand to his mouth. He sucked in shallow breaths and tried to fight the deadly panic that was washing over him, threatening to paralyze him.

It was clear that something equally awful and powerful was powering the limousine. As if electric current were sending it along the gravel. A hideous magnetic field. For a feverish instant, Angel flashed on an image buried in his subconsciousness. Something from long ago that had deeply disturbed him, seeped into his dreams, festered in his memory undetected for seventeen years. Now it trumpeted in his brain like a hellish little nickelodeon.

It was the image of a winged beetle that had escaped the clutches of some sadistic kindergartener, a straight pin driven through its shell. The insect was running on pure pain. A whirling dervish, spinning around the surface of a school desk, unstoppable in its throes like a tiny toy overloading.

Unstoppable.

Angel looked back out the window and watched the ancient car collapse. Its front bumper buckled under a crosstie and the entire limo windmilled into the air. With a great muffled explosion, it landed upside-down in the weeds. A storm cloud of dust coalesced around it.

Angel felt a nervous laugh bubble up within him. "Fuck you! Bath'tard!! Fuck you!!"

Speeding away, Angel kept his eyes glued to the wreckage receding into the distance behind him. There was movement in the mangled heart of the limousine. Something was forcing its way up through the flaps of crumpled steel.

Angel's smile evaporated.

Out in the dim light, a figure emerged from the torn metal and crawled out of the ruined car like a hermit crab. At first, it looked like an animal. Crooked limbs and leathery flesh tangled in rags, it moved with an odd turtlelike gait. But soon it revealed its full form in the silver moonlight reflecting off the ravaged bonnet of the limo.

The old lady.

The beetle impaled on a pin.

Wild gray hair flowing, electric eyes scanning the distance, she hobbled back up to the rails and started after the train. Loose flesh jiggling, brittle bones creaking furiously, she looked like a mad rag doll. The brace on her withered left leg was a shiny blur. The axis of her deformed hips pistoned steadily. She was an ancient machine.

Inside the caboose, Angel swallowed acid. He turned and frantically searched the interior for a way to quickly alert the others. Bare light bulbs encased in tiny metal cages swayed overhead. A huge ceiling fan harmonized with the muffled rumble below. In the center of the caboose, stray boxes rose to the tiny windowed cubicle that served as the watchtower. Cannibalized from a freighter many decades ago, the little car was used mostly for storage.

Gooseflesh rolled across the back of Angel's neck and

scalp. He rubbed the sweat from his eyes and rushed back to the side window.

In the predawn glow, Vanessa was approaching. She was less than fifty yards away now, sprinting toward the train, loose flesh shivering with each stride, crooked arms and legs wobbling violently like a bent and ruined tractor. At this distance, it was impossible to tell whether she was grimacing or grinning. But something was flaking and spurting off her limbs as she approached. Either blood or tissue or fragments of bones or shreds of clothing or all of the above.

Angel didn't stick around to see which it was.

He turned and made for the door.

By the time Lucas reached the doorway to the last passenger coach, he had planned out his entire course of action down to the last second. He was moving at a fast clip, muscles straining just like the old football days.

The old kamikaze slant play.

The narrow aisle made for tricky maneuvering. Every few seconds, Lucas would bang a knee into an armrest or scrape his shin across a footrest. But he kept churning toward the caboose, grinding and churning and muscling his way toward the goal line.

As he approached, he found the boy on the other side of the rear door.

"Luca'th!!" Through the glass, the kid's voice was muffled and filled with panic. He was on the coupling area between the caboose and the coach. Less than three feet wide and coated with grease, the coupler was treacherous to cross, something advisable only for railroad personnel. But from the terrified look on the boy's face, barely visible in the faint dawn, safe footing was not exactly a priority.

"Luh-luh—Luca'th!" Angel stammered as he shoved open the coach door and fell inside.

"Easy, kid." Lucas reached the boy and grabbed hold of his arm. The boy was holding the shotgun, shaking like an October maple leaf. Lucas gripped his shoulder tight for a second. "Slow down!"

"Th'omebody's comin'!"

"What?"

Angel gasped for air. Swallowed. "Th'omebody's comin'! Luca'th—they're comin' down the track!!"

Lucas shook him gently. "Calm down, Angel. You're seeing things, okay—you're just—"

"No, no, no, no—Luca'th—!!"

"Kid, listen," Lucas tried to speak gently, as if corralling a frightened animal. He didn't want the kid freaking out and fucking up his plan. "I'm here to relieve you. You're tired. Need some sleep."

Angel tried to catch his breath, his gaze burning with panic. "But they're comin' right now!"

"Who's coming?"

"The old lady."

"The who?"

"The old lady! From the limo'thine!"

It took a moment for it to register in Lucas's mind. "Kid, the limo is wasted. You saw it happen with your own eyes."

Angel swallowed air. "It'th her, Luca'th!"

"Calm down, Angel."

For a brief frenzied moment, Lucas pondered the anxious face of the boy. His tangled hair fell across horror-stricken eyes. His malformed lips trembled. It wasn't like him to get hysterical. It wasn't like him at all. Lucas felt a ringing in his own ears. A chilling of his bones. Maybe the thing from the limousine—whatever she was—maybe she was back. Maybe it was true. The more the merrier. The more the merrier for what Lucas had in mind.

Lucas glanced through the exit door and into the dimness of the caboose. Shadows played across the caboose's interior, caged lights swaying. "Lemme have the gun."

The boy handed Lucas the shotgun. "What are ya gonna do?"

"Gonna relieve you."

The boy froze. "You can't go in there alone!"

"I'll be okay."

"You can't go in there!!"

Lucas shoved the boy aside and opened the exit. The wind

slapped his face, the odor of metal on metal sharp in his nostrils.

The boy grabbed Lucas by the belt and pulled him back in. "Luca'th, pleeeeeeeaze!"

Lucas turned and threw Angel across the coach. The boy struck a bench and slid down between the seats. Lucas said, "Sorry, kid—I gotta do this thing myself."

Then, before turning back to the wind and noise, Lucas nodded at the boy. "Kid, it's like your uncle said—gotta be firm in your faith."

Lucas turned and stepped out onto the coupler. The greasy metal undulated beneath him. The rush of the track roared below the coupler. The wheels sounded like knives being sharpened. He slammed the exit door shut and smashed the butt of the gun across the hand lever, breaking it off and jamming the door.

Inside the coach, Angel rushed back to the door. He tried it, found it jammed, and started yelling. His voice was drowned by the noise outside the train. But it was fairly obvious he was clamoring for Lucas to come back.

Lucas turned and staggered across the coupler.

The door to the caboose was still open. Lucas paused inside it. He turned and stared back at the rear of the coach, all the diesel fury and energy sucking him forward. He pondered the panicky face of Angel behind the glass. The kid was pounding his fists against the window, screaming, begging, pleading. God bless him.

Lucas cocked the shotgun.

A surge of emotion rose in Lucas's heart. His eyes burned with tears. He fought the urge to scream, to wail at the heavens. He was on the verge of falling apart. God in heaven, he hoped that he was doing the right thing. The tears were streaming down his face now, vanishing in the wind. The pain was enormous. It threatened to pull him down and suffocate him. But the rage kept him going. The rage and the fear and the love for his comrades on the train.

He aimed at the uncoupling lever and fired.

The recoil kicked him back against the doorjamb and he nearly fell. The shell expanded on impact with the greasy

iron and tore a six-inch chink from the lever. But the seal
held. Although ancient and rotting with age, the uncoupling
lever was welded to the chassis of the train and was built to
withstand decades of vibrations Lucas screamed into the
wind and fired again. This time the lever tripped and the
hoses popped apart with a loud snap and hiss.

The caboose broke free.

Several things happened simultaneously. All the lights and
power inside the caboose went out. The sound of rumbling
sickened to a low whine and the caboose seemed to grow
pregnant with weight. Lucas watched the rest of the train
pulling away. It didn't happen as quickly as he thought. The
rear window, framing a cameo of a screaming boy, seemed
to hover endlessly, inches away, drowned by the rush of
movement. Then the gap began to widen.

Lucas turned and climbed into the impotent car.

In the darkness a word echoed in his mind. *Sacrifice*.
From the moment the rabbi had said it over the cellular, the
word had lingered in Lucas's fevered mind. Counterspells involved some sort of *sacrifice*. Animal, virgin, whatever.
Lucas was no virgin but he was a perfect candidate for sacrifice. For his friends on the train. For Sophie. For his family.
For himself. He had been running his whole life. It was time
to ante up.

He edged his way through the dark car. It was still moving
along at a pretty good clip but was slowing incrementally
with every passing second. The pale light of dawn was beginning to peek in the overhead cupola. Thin strips of light
were peeking through the slats in the walls. The car smelled
of soggy cardboard and tar. The wheels continued to rattle.
Lucas estimated it would take less than ten minutes to come
to a complete stop.

Then he would see if his magic worked.

He heard a sound. Outside the rear door. Just underneath
the knifing sound of the rails. For a moment, it sounded like
the canter of a horse. The snort of its breath was accompanied by the clapping of hooves. Then it faded away again
under the noise of the rails.

Lucas checked the shotgun. It was a reflexive thing to do.

Wishful thinking. At this point, the 12-gauge was pretty useless. Whatever was about to happen was beyond guns. Besides, he realized as he opened the breech and looked inside, the damn thing was as empty as a Baptist coffer.

He tossed the shotgun in the corner and pulled an empty crate out into the center of the caboose. Then he sat down and waited for the pain to come.

"Th'ophie!!"

Angel was frantic. He had found Sophie on the floor of the dining car in a pool of her own vomit. Now she was like a limp rag in his hands, drunk with dizziness. Angel shook her. He slapped her cheeks and begged her to snap out of it. She seemed to be recovering from a bad cocktail.

"Th'ophie—c'mon! We gotta help Luca'th!!"

Sophie pointed at the puddle of bile. "He—tried to—put me to sleep—but I got it out of my system. Stuck a finger down my throat . . . then I found a spare Benzedrine capsule in my pocket that I took for—"

"Th'ophie! Li'then to me—!!"

Her voice was still syrupy. "Better trucking through chemicals. . . ."

"Th'ophie—Luca'th cut the caboo'th off the train!!"

Sophie's eyes sharpened, the life shocking back into them. "He what!?!"

"He cut the caboo'th off! He'th gone!"

"Jesus—" She started to rise but the dizziness shoved her against the wall. Her knees threatened to collapse. She felt the nausea rise in her throat. "Help me, Angel!"

Angel got her up and moving.

They started toward the back of the train when all at once Sophie stopped moving. A warning had sounded in her swimming brain. Through the years, she had developed a kind of sixth sense about time. It stemmed from constantly fighting a schedule. Constantly battling the clock. At every stop, every weigh station, every overnight, Sophie would just intuitively know how long they should allow themselves before getting back on the road. Now her built-in alarm was screaming. She knew they had only a few minutes to do anything about Lucas's situation. Grabbing Angel by the shirt, she said, "Wait a minute—wait—you said he cut himself loose?"

Angel quickly nodded.

"Then there's only one thing we can do." Sophie began dragging him in the opposite direction. Toward the front of the train.

Toward the engine.

29

Welcome
to Hell

Lucas had expected the fever to come but now something entirely different was happening.

It reminded him of the time he was unloading sides of beef and had inadvertently locked himself inside a reefer truck. In retrospect, it had been no big deal; within seconds, the foreman had noticed it and had gotten him out. But the few panicky moments after bumping the door with his ass and hearing it latch shut would occupy a special place in Lucas's nightmares for the rest of his life. The sudden panic. Fed by the chilled air. Gripped around his heart like icy fingers.

Now that same dread was seeping into him as he coasted along in the powerless caboose.

The tingling started in his hands, as if he'd been pricked with needles of Novocaine. The sensation sharpened. His joints tightened like ratchet bolts. His extremities throbbed. He looked up and scanned the dimness of the cabin. The slatted walls were frosting over. Pale light was filtering through the cracks. In the delicate rays, he could see his own breath.

He stood up and kicked the crate out from under him. He tried to inhale a deep breath but the cold was seizing his throat. He hacked and coughed. A delicate spray of blood

317

spattered his chest. His knees felt as if metal cables were tightening around them. His spine was frozen. The weathered floorboards seemed to crunch beneath his boots as he began to move around the cabin, trying to warm himself against the killing chill.

The caboose continued to slow.

Lucas began to pray.

He had never been a religious man. His childhood on the mean streets of L.A. had soured him on the whole idea of worship. He just couldn't understand why The Big Dude Upstairs would subject good people to this kind of shit. With apologies to his Baptist mother, Lucas couldn't care less about God because God never seemed to give a shit about him. Even amidst the bizarre events of the last twenty-four hours—with Flaco's ranting and raving about the apocalypse and Milo's rap about the hidden world—it hadn't really occurred to Lucas that he could draw strength from his faith. But now a powerful current was cycling through him. Liquid and immutable, it sprang from deep within his soul. It was his essence. The source of his spirit. The nameless place inside him where he was most human.

His own brand of magic.

I'm ready for you motherfucker because I'm ready to die for my family and my people and my friends and my miserable fucking life because I've been running too long—

There was a ripping sound outside the caboose.

Lucas snapped his eyes open.

The rear door was rattling wildly. Something was assaulting the rusty hatch from the outside. Through the tiny barred window, Lucas could barely make out a shadowy shape clawing at the metal. The door shivered, hinges straining. Then came the first impact. Loud as a battering ram. The door buckled inward like a tin one in a cartoon, nearly ripping off its hinges. Another impact popped the bolts from the frame. But the heavy safety latch held firm. The next assault rattled the entire chassis.

Angry sounds erupted outside like a million high-pitched dog whistles. Violent chills vibrated through Lucas. Teeth on edge, joints freezing, Lucas staggered back into the corner and covered his ears. The sounds were unbearable. Cutting and metallic and relentless. A million banshees. The windows in the cupola cracked in unison.

By now, the caboose had slowed to a gentle twenty-five miles an hour.

Lucas prayed frantically, *if you want a sacrificial lamb, motherfucker, well here I am and I'm ready to die because I'm finished running—*

As if fueled by the prayer, the horrible thing outside began debauching the caboose. Crawling obscenely up the back wall and across the roof, rocking violently, searching for an orifice to invade. An opening. A way inside. Tiny rips in the ceiling formed and spread. Beams of light shaved through the cracks and seeped into the caboose. The air grew so gelid it was nearly crystalline.

. . . her gaze falling on the black man . . . a memory deep inside her stirring . . . the memory of another young man . . . the same defiant eyes, strong chin, broad shoulders . . .

. . . *Thomas* . . .

. . . the word was poison on her lips . . . poison odors from the past . . . the dew on the grass . . . the clutter of fallen magnolia blossoms . . . and the smell of his perspiration . . . sweet and rich like peach brandy . . .

. . . fueling her magic. . . .

"WWWWWWWHHHHY!?" A lunatic voice hissed behind him. Lucas managed to turn around just in time to see the impossible intruder fill the doorway behind him.

She resembled an old woman.

Lucas tried to get away from her.

He didn't get very far. Tripping over his own feet, he stumbled to the floor. He crawled for a few feet, then gazed over his shoulder.

In the doorway, she was howling, vapor spewing from her gaping divot of a mouth. She was blocking out the light with her shivering form. Draped in a gore-stained pinafore and flounce, she looked like a bloody rag doll fashioned from broken sticks. Bones rattled loosely inside her.

Through all the terror, Lucas could only think of escape: *Get away from her. Crawl. Slither. Roll. Whatever it takes, just get the fuck away from her!*

He tried to struggle to his feet.

The old woman lunged out at him, grabbing at his ankle and knocking him back to the floor. Pain shot up Lucas's leg, cutting off his thoughts. Spindly talon fingers clamped onto his ankle. It was like being caught in a power tool. Behind him, the monster crouched simianlike, eyes aglow, lips drawn back over rotting turtle teeth. Her right hand had turned black. Shrivelled and charred with decay, it was now the shrunken hand of her late father. The Hand of Glory. Glowing with an inner antilight. The root of all the cruelty and pain and anguish and evil.

All at once, Lucas realized who this was. The wicked old grandaunt. The hag. Vanessa DeGeaux. The bitch who had started all this misery in the first place. With her magic. With her father's hand.

The wrinkled thing shrieked at him. *"You shall not forsake me again, Thomas . . ."*

"Fuck you!!" Lucas fired back, trying to tear himself away. The old woman gripped his ankle tighter. Squeezing like a metal vise grip down to the bone. Igniting nerve centers with a blowtorch of pain.

"Retribution, sayeth the Lord!"

Then she struck.

The bracing slap sent a jolt up through Lucas that took his breath away.

Sensations flooded his mind . . . the stench of old urine . . . the peal of church bells . . . the yellow stains of sickness splashed like graffiti across hospital sheets. Lucas tried to scream but no sound would come. He looked back down at his legs. They were rashing with psoriasis, tightening. His knees were buckling painfully, his feet cramping, his toes curling inward and hardening.

"RETRIBUTION!!"

Her hand came down again.

Pain exploded. Crystals of agony spread quickly through him like sand in the cogs of an engine. His legs seized up with rheumatism, bulged hideously at the joints. Varicose veins spidered up his drying flesh. His toenails blackened and curled and shrivelled. His eyes were burning with tears. He was nearly paralyzed now, as stiff as a block of stone . . . the sensations assaulting his brain . . . the smell of viscous bed sores seeping through gingham . . .

The caboose slowed.

Vanessa struck him a third time.

Lucas became inert. Frozen with arthritis, he could only move his face and eyes enough to see the rest of his body transformed beneath him. Hands twisted into palsied remnants of his former self, legs crooked and impotent, feet toed inward in Christlike prostration, he was completely immobilized on the moldering floor.

Vanessa was laughing. It sounded like bones rattling in a metal box.

The caboose was creeping along now, less than fifteen miles an hour.

Lucas closed his eyes and thought: *You bitch, I'm ready to sacrifice myself for the people I love, so go ahead and give me your best shot and kill me kill me kill me kill me KILL ME NOW!!! . . .*

The next blow took his vision away.

The impact drove his face against the floor. Fireworks erupted in his brain. A surge of inky blackness washed over him, stealing his breath, drowning his senses. The air turned syrupy. The light dwindled and Lucas felt himself sinking into pitch black.

Then the light was gone.

Then there was nothing.

Lucas awoke to darkness.

How long had he been out? A minute? An hour? An instant? Was he still moving? He was like a broken gyroscope. No sense of direction. No sense of up or down. Only the cold darkness, the charnel smells, and the dead weight of his body. He tried to move. His legs were encased in blocks of ice, his arms were made of lead. He felt a presence somewhere close by, in the shadows, but he could not remember its identity.

Only the danger.

Something stirred behind him.

He struggled to see. His eyes were stinging and watery. His pupils were still adjusting. Above him, a pale beam of light shone down and shellacked his flesh with silver. It wasn't daylight. It wasn't artificial. It was the *moon*. A big fat harvest moon, coming through a jagged, gaping hole in the wall. Coming from some other time and place.

Lucas gazed around the room.

He was in a barn. The slatted walls rose to an A-frame ceiling. Cobwebs choked the crossbeams overhead. Needles of moonlight pierced the motes. A patina of dust and age clung to the wood, and the ammonia smell of decay hung thick in the air. Here and there, buried in shadows, were remnants of old wagon wheels, horse tack, and blacksmith tools. The corner where Lucas lay was carpeted with moldy hay.

Again, the stirring sound behind him. Like old wood creaking. Beneath the sound was a faint, mucus-clogged breathing. Craning his neck, Lucas glanced over his shoulder at the shadows behind him.

The slender hand shot out of the dark.

Before Lucas could even react, the hand wrapped around his neck.

"Thomasssss!!" Crooked nails dug into the flesh of Lucas's collarbone. It was like being wrapped in cold, iron stocks. Fueled by the falsetto voice, higher and shriller than before, Vanessa had changed. *"You betrayed me!!"*

Lucas swallowed razors. The old woman's face had emerged from the shadows, striped in the moonlight. Her complexion had gone white as curdled milk. Her hair had thickened and darkened, framing her sharp gleaming eyes. Even her clothing had changed, transforming into a bright print dress.

A garish parody of her youth.

"NO!!" Lucas wrenched himself away, turned, and clawed through the dirt toward the ragged breach a few feet away. Beyond the breach lay a vast dark void. Lucas struggled to-

ward it, swimming away from the insane nightmare . . .
swimming through the currents of her lunatic charges . . .

Coward!

COWARD!!

Lucas struggled through the opening, stoney legs dragging
behind him. Jagged splinters ripped at his shirt, rusty nails
dug into his flesh, but the smells of freedom drove him onward, into the magic landscape. Outside, the night was coalescing into a tunnel. Like a telescope turning backward.
Darkness hurtling into the distance. A new landscape opening up. A deserted grassy field. Bathed in shadows. Silhou-
ettes of the trees beyond it. Southern pines. The smell of it
shocked Lucas out of his paralysis. Climbing to his feet, he
shook the needles of pain from his legs.

Then he ran into the impossible new world.

The night was cool on his face. His shoes were gone. The
blistered soles of his feet stung against the rough grass. But
he was moving. Goddamnit, he was moving through this
nightmare and he was alive and he was free.

Behind him a banshee howled. *"THOMAS!!!"*

As he ran, the howling swirled through his brain, stirring
up chaotic voices. *She's not real—she can't be real—can't
be. She thinks I'm Thomas—Thomas who?! Who the fuck is
Thomas?! Can't be—I'm answering for some motherfucker—who's—not real—not—me!!*

Lucas sprinted into the forest.

The cool darkness swallowed him. His brain churned,
mixing fear with confusion. On either side, the line of imaginary trees glistened like shiny velveteen cutouts in a story-
book. The lights of distant fires dotted the darkness ahead.
The smells of swampland and black earth rose around him,
fueling the fear, adding to the sense that something horrible
and important was happening behind him.

"THOMMMMMMAAASSSSS!!"

Lucas stopped in a dark clearing. Catching his breath, he
listened to the mournful cries in the darkness behind him.
The temperature was plummeting. A straight-razor cold.
Much sharper than before. He turned and saw the barn,
through the trees, twenty yards away, rising out of the shad-

ows, the gaping hole in its back wall. Inside the hole, the old woman lay prostrate in the filth, her face contorted with pain, her palsied hands reaching for the moonlight.

Behind her, something was materializing in the shadows.

At first, Lucas thought it was merely a column of smoke, as if the hay was smoldering. But when the smoke moved, Lucas realized it was an apparition. A tall man. Raising his smoke arms. Gesturing to some nameless god. Rearing back like a cobra coiled to strike.

Then it struck.

Vanessa's scream shook the earth.

In the forest Lucas trembled. Flesh crawling, brain seized with terror, he stood there watching the old woman get spanked by a ghost. Every fiber of his being wanted to turn and haul ass deeper into the dream woods. Escape the old woman and this man made of smoke. But something was stopping him. Something in the recesses of his mind, buried under the avalanche of fear. An ember of recognition. The man made of smoke was the key. Like the black hand. Like the old woman's hate. Like the curse.

He was the source.

The apparition struck the woman again. Her scream rose and filled the night air like a clarion. It made Lucas's scalp crawl. It wasn't exactly the volume, or the way it sliced through the air, or the way it severed the stillness of the forest. It was the *tone*. The mournful, agonizing tone. It reached down into Lucas and ripped his central nervous system up by the roots. It was the deepest grief he had ever heard.

He had to make it stop.

He took a few tentative steps back through the trees and out toward the barn.

Halfway there, he saw the change. In the shadows behind Vanessa, the Devil was transforming. Arms thickening. Fluid, inky tendrils lengthening, taking on a new shape and color like a horrible chameleon. Painted in neon chiaroscuro. A uniform. Navy-blue epaulets. A newspaper tucked under one arm. Eyes like faint silver coins.

Mirrored sunglasses.

"Hey kid!" The voice wobbled like old sheet metal. *"Easy on the jalopy!"*

Lucas froze about twenty feet from the barn, testicles crawling up inside him. His body wouldn't work anymore. The grass had become tar paper. His feet were stuck. His fists clenched and unclenched rhythmically. His heart, a child's heart, raced. Icicles clogged his throat and threatened to suffocate him. He found the word *sorry* floating up through his subconscious but he refused to say it.

"Your daddy's a good nigger," the man made of smoke hissed, and continued striking the old woman. With every spank, the monster's silver eyes pulsed magnesium bright. Obscene. Iridescent. Below the monster, Vanessa wept, her wrinkled visage creased with fury and pain.

The smoke man continued bellowing and striking. *"Only good nigger's a dead nigger and since your daddy's deader than a ten-penny nail, he's pretty goddamn good."*

Tears welled in Lucas's eyes. Grief sizzled in his chest. The voice had summoned back all the pain of his daddy's funeral. Paralyzing pain. Pain that had kept Lucas silent. Pain that had kept him in his place. Pain that had kept him running throughout his entire adult life.

Now the running was over.

"Stop it," Lucas said, his voice coming from a great distance.

The man with the silver eyes just tossed his head back and bellowed and continued beating the woman.

Lucas walked the remaining length of grass toward the barn. As he approached, the apparition seemed to grow. Bloating with rancid energy, opening its mouth, it laughed with black razor teeth and serpent tongue wiggling.

Welcome to Hell.

Lucas stood his ground, the rotten wind on his face, the black chill radiating off the smoke man. Thin tendrils of smoke curled out of the barn and smelled of the grave. They swirled around Lucas and sent a wave of dread through him that was colder than hate.

Lucas gazed up at the Devil and found his voice again. "I SAID, STOP IT!!!"

Lucas heard a sound from below.

He gazed down and saw the old woman. She was staring up at him, her face drained, her eyes shiny with tears, her lips trembling delicately. Her rage was replaced by a look of awe. She seemed completely and utterly surprised by Lucas's presence.

"Thomas . . . you came back . . ."

Knees trembling, Lucas gazed down at the woman. He couldn't speak. He couldn't move. His body was threatening to collapse, but he kept his gaze locked onto her. Something about her wounded voice . . .

"You came back . . ."

Lucas felt a sudden tremor. An abrupt shift, as if the very air pressure around them had been sucked violently away. The shadows froze like the glitch of a ragged video transmission. In this frozen tableau, something struck Lucas like a sudden jolt of electricity.

Looking down at the old woman's milky eyes, Lucas realized what it was. It was pity. Instead of hate, Lucas felt pity for this grotesque old ruined thing. Then it dawned on Lucas, all the terror, all the smoke, all the visions, all of it had emanated from this pathetic old woman.

She was the source.

Lucas looked up.

The man made of smoke was gone. The barn was gone. Only a canopy of shadows lingered, slowly closing in like a giant black iris. Tightening. Until only the old woman remained, framed in the center of the dark spiral, her gaze penetrating Lucas. Waiting. Waiting for an answer.

"You came back. . . ."

Then Lucas noticed something else in the old woman's face. Something that sliced through his soul. A glimpse into another woman's destiny. Another angry white woman. Alone. Unrequited. Wounded, not by the power of the dark magic, but by Lucas himself. By Lucas's own fears and superstitions.

It was Sophie.

It was as plain as the ravaged terrain of the old woman's face. Twenty years in the future, alone in her bitter memories, Sophie would become an old maid, abandoned by the black man she had always loved. It reached into Lucas and wrenched open his heart. There was only one thing left to do.

"That's right," Lucas said softly. There were tears tracking down his cheeks. "I came back."

Then he reached out.

. . . starting in her fingertips . . . flooding up her arms . . . filling her veins . . . an opposing force shocking through her . . . an opposing magnetic force . . . galvanizing . . .

. . . awakening a part of her that had lain dormant for over half a century . . .

. . . a hidden source within her . . .

. . . tenderness . . .

At the precise moment Lucas gently took Vanessa's hand, the magic suddenly blew apart at the seams.

The concussion nearly knocked Lucas over. Shreds of smoke and odors and textures tore past Lucas's face, whistled past his ears. The hallucination was collapsing in on itself, a house of cards, tumbling apart, imploding. Shadows opened up, exposing old wounds underneath. Smoke swirling away on a gust charged with voices, disembodied chants, whispering . . .

"*. . . YOU CAME BACK . . .*"

Then the first flames erupted from the old woman's mouth and whirled through the darkness, searing the air, sucking all the black smoke and magic into its vortex. The discharge threw Lucas backward. He tripped over his own feet, landed hard on the dirty floorboards, and gasped for air.

The smells of axle grease and diesel rose around him. Above him, the pale light of dawn was slicing through the broken glass of the cupola. A few feet away, the exit door revealed a glimpse of early morning Colorado countryside. Lucas realized he was back on board the caboose. Somehow the entire vision—*the entire confrontation*—had only encompassed a few moments . . .

More importantly, the caboose was just now coming to a complete stop.

Vanessa combusted. A crown of fire blossomed from her head as she rose on spindly legs. Shivering. Cocooned in brilliance. She raised her crooked arms to the heavens and opened her mouth. A torrent of flame poured out, licking the ceiling, snaking across the rotten wood. Daylight filled the car. Twisted fingers rising, luminous eyes shocked open in ecstasy, she was bathing in fire. Her eyes hemorrhaged yellow like two ancient headlamps. Her clothing blackened. Her mouth gaped and let out a death shriek.

It was as if the air had been electrocuted.

Lucas shielded his face. Flames curled through the caboose. Horrible and beautiful in equal measures, clashing in pure violent brightness, devouring the dark. Lucas tried to watch, tried to keep his gaze on her figure in the nimbus of fire, but the conflagration was drowning everything. Lucas could feel the heat on his eyeballs. His breath cooking in his lungs. His burns awakening and exploding in his belly. He struggled to his feet, joints screaming, tendons singing with pain. It felt as though his body had been parboiled. But he was still able to move. Just barely.

A few feet away, Vanessa had become pure flame.

The caboose was about to fall apart. It sounded like a hurricane. Lucas realized he had better act fast if he was going to get out. Both doors were blazing. The floor was collapsing. Lucas saw a single patch of wall across from him that wasn't burning. He took a breath and exercised his only remaining option.

He put his head down and ran the old kamikaze slant play.

30

End Dance

Amtrak Number 507 was three hundred yards away when the caboose erupted into flames.

"Jeeezu'th!! Look!!" Angel was leaning out the window of the engine, gazing back down the length of the train, his face in the wind. He could see the caboose in the distance ahead of them—which was now beyond the rear cars, since the train was going backward.

"I see it!" Sophie was behind him, craning her neck to get a better look. Only a few minutes earlier she had talked Barney into stopping and reversing the train. Of course, the moment the train had ground to a halt, Sophie had expected to eat fire. But it had miraculously not happened. For some reason, it seemed both she and Angel were cured.

"We're gonna hit it!" Angel yelled.

"Slow down, Barney!" Sophie hollered over the engine, tears of panic clouding her vision.

Ahead of them, a body burst through the crumbling skin of the caboose. It was aflame. It fell to the embankment below and rolled several feet.

"Holy Bejesus!" Barney exclaimed as he gazed into his

mirror, navigating the train toward the caboose. "Who the hell is that?!"

Sophie strained to identify it. "Wait a minute—!!"

Angel leaned out farther. "Who i'th it?!"

Sophie grinned. "That's Lucas!"

"Luca'th?!!" Angel called into the wind.

"Thank God . . ." Sophie whispered. She could see him in the distance, rolling across a ditch. He was partially in flames but he seemed to be patting the flames out. He seemed to be okay.

"Sweet Christ, who the hell is that?!" Barney was referring to the caboose.

"Faster, Barney!" Sophie's smile evaporated.

"Whattya mean?!"

"Faster!"

"You're telling me to—?!"

"Do it!"

Barney goosed the engine. The train climbed to thirty miles per hour, then thirty-five, then forty. The caboose was looming, a hundred yards away now. Something had appeared on its roof. Something dressed in flames.

"What is that?!"

"Can't you make it go any faster?"

"Yes, ma'am!" Barney poured it on. They were fifty yards away now. Thirty. Twenty-five. Twenty. Barney's sphincter muscles tightened as he yelped, "But what in the Sam Hell is that thing?!"

Sophie braced herself. "Fucking dead meat."

Another set of eyes would have surely missed it. Another observer would have only taken in the whole of the burning caboose, the blossoming flames curling up the sides, the thick columns of smoke rising into the morning sky, the ribbons of fire flagging out the windows. But in the brief instant before the collision, a moment no longer than a single frenzied heartbeat, Lucas witnessed something within the heart of the inferno that would stay indelibly burned into the back of his brain for the rest of his life.

It had come up through the roof, emerging through the

broken portals of the watchtower like a rat escaping a sinking ship. Wrapped in flames, arms and legs dressed in white-hot incandescence, it managed to climb to its feet. Then it did something that made Lucas's breath freeze in his throat.

A spindly leg sweeping forward. Body turning gently. Elbow raised.

It was dancing.

Sheathed in flames, shrivelling like a dry bag of dead branches, Vanessa was dancing. Dancing some old waltz with an invisible partner, a partner whom she never really knew.

Then the rear of the train arrived.

The caboose exploded.

The impact shook the ground and Lucas put his face in the dirt and felt the concussion threaten to tear the top of his skull open. Bits and pieces of flaming debris rained down upon the apron along the track and the surrounding trees. The heat washed over the ground, singeing Lucas's hair, oxidizing plants, and scorching the earth.

Lucas gazed back up, dizzy, head throbbing from his plunge through the wall of the caboose. Squinting into the haze, he saw the train coursing away from a smoking heap on either side of the tracks that used to be a caboose.

He struggled to his feet.

He felt strange. Buoyant. It was as if he could feel his body for the first time in over two days. He looked down at the belly of his workshirt. It was covered in ash. He looked at his hands and felt the itch of his wounds healing beneath the soiled bandages. He felt very strange. There was a soft buzzing in his ears. Tinnitus. A gentle dizziness floating around his head. Then, all at once, he realized what was so strange.

He wasn't moving.

The hiss of air brakes filled the air. About a hundred yards away the train had slowed to a stop. The door to the engine sprang open and figures emerged. Angel came first, then Barney Hollis.

Lucas staggered toward the train, his heart beating, brain

swimming with dizziness. He was looking for one person in particular.

She was the last to emerge. She hopped to the gravel and then started toward Lucas. She didn't walk. She didn't jog. She didn't even run. She sprinted. She sprinted toward him as fast as she could.

A moment later they collided and wrapped their arms around each other. It was their first embrace ever. Oddly enough, their bodies fit each other perfectly. Like a glove.

"Jesus, Lucas—why—?" Sophie was trembling, uttering softly into his ear. "Why did you—?"

"Don't say it."

"Always gotta be the hero."

"That's right." Lucas held her tightly, savoring the scent of her hair, memorizing the curve of her back. "I never was too smart."

She looked up into his eyes. "We're standing still, Lucas— and we're not burning up."

"Imagine that. . . ."

Sophie closed her eyes and began to cry.

Lucas started to say something else but stopped when he saw Angel and Barney hovering nearby, keeping a respectable distance. Barney was nervously gazing up and down the track as if expecting another train to come along soon and break up the party. Angel's face was filled with questions. Lucas wanted to tell the boy everything. But there would be plenty of time for that. At the moment, there was something else on Lucas's mind.

"I want to say something—" Lucas began awkwardly.

"Yeah?"

"I want to say—I mean, you were right about me—I mean, I really do—"

Sophie studied his gaze. "What are you trying to say, Lucas? You trying to say you love me or something?"

Lucas looked into her eyes for a moment. He was still woozy with pain, reeling from the burns and the visions. But at that moment he found himself grinning. "Something like that."

Sophie touched his cheek. "The feeling's mutual."

Lucas kissed her forehead.

"C'mon," Sophie said and took his hand. "Let's get outta here."

But Lucas couldn't stand anymore and collapsed to the ground at her feet.

The ground felt cool and sweet on his face.

EPILOGUE

Time
Standing Still

"That afternoon many in the town hurried to the river to swim, for it was one of the hottest days of the year. And it was reported by many witnesses that a black hand the size of a tree trunk had risen up out of the water, made a fist, and cried out, 'What's mine is missing!'"

—Howard Schwartz
Lilith's Cave

Seven o'clock in the morning. Outside the window there were voices drifting through the air. Two voices. One high and shrill. The other tinted with a lisp.

Lucas closed his eyes and stretched. He didn't want to get up just yet, didn't want to leave the warmth. Not yet. He pulled the ratty patchwork to his neck and settled closer to her warmth.

She was still sound asleep next to him. She smelled of pine needles and lemons. She had been out in the grove until well past sundown last night, pulling weeds and moving stone borders around. The grove was her baby. She had grand schemes of someday selling lemon products in the station's gift shop. Lemon juice, lemon candy, lemon ice cream, lemon jelly, lemon pepper, lemon wine. He loved the idea.

He loved lemons.

She moaned softly. The voices were piercing her sleep as well and now she was fighting the need to get up and pee and get dressed and face life. Eyes welded shut, she turned and snuggled next to him.

Amazing. How their bodies fit each other so perfectly. How her shapely ass cuddled into the crook of his thigh and

belly. How her shoulder nestled under his arm. Legs inter-
twined. Toes whispering against each other. He could feel
the heat rising from her back. His big hands began playing
down her body. She wore a thin sleeveless T-shirt. Still
slightly damp. He found her breasts and lingered there, savoring their soft warmth.

She stirred. She murmured groggily, then gently took his
hands and lowered them between her legs.

"Good mornin', li'l schoolgirl . . ." he whispered, his erection announcing itself on a surge of electricity rushing up his
spine. Evidently, she had forgotten to wear her panties to bed
last night and now she was on fire down there.

"Make love to me," Sophie said and pulled him into her.

He obliged.

The little brass bed squeaked a rhythmic tattoo through the
stillness of the back room that sounded quite a bit like the
drum track to Lucas's favorite tune. A remake of "Everyday
People" by Arrested Development. Everyday people. That's
what Lucas and Sophie were now. Everyday people. Everyday love. Every day they made time stand still in the little
back room of the Amoco Oasis.

This morning the voices would not go away.

"Oh, for Christ's sake," Lucas mumbled as he gently disengaged himself and rolled off her sweaty form.

"Sounds like the lost boys club."

"Yeah."

"You want to go take care of it or should I?"

Lucas was already pulling on his pants. "I'll do it." Then
he leaned down and planted a kiss on her nose. They were
closing in on their second anniversary as husband and wife
and still lusted after each other every waking minute. "You
keep the motor running."

He walked out and strode down the hallway toward the
front office. The Oasis was really nothing more than a glori-
fied gas station on the edge of the high desert outside Ger-
lach, Nevada. Angel lived in a trailer out back and was in
charge of the two-car service center. In addition to two is-

lands of unleaded and diesel, the place also had a small office and retail space in front. Sophie had big plans for the space but right now money was tight. They had spent most of their savings on court costs and attorneys after giving themselves up to the Colorado police nearly four years ago. Of course, nobody had believed their curse story. Forensic psychiatrists had been called in. Plea bargaining had forced them to drop the supernatural talk.

It was all a moot point now. With the passing of time they had stopped believing it themselves. Now all they needed was each other.

Lucas reached the front office, pushed the screen door open, and walked out into the sun.

Angel was over by the pop machine, trying to fix a little plastic scooter. Next to him, a little boy in engineer pants was throwing a tantrum, jumping up and down, squealing, tiny fists clenched. Evidently, Angel wasn't fixing the scooter quickly enough.

"Go now!" the three-year-old bleated. "Want wheel go now!"

Lucas barked at them as he approached. "Seven o'clock in the morning, guys—people still trying to sleep!"

"Th'orry, Luca'th—Flaco had a minor crackup." Angel wiped a bead of perspiration from his forehead. He was dressed in mechanic's coveralls with a tiny patch on the breast that said ANGEL. He pulled a small screwdriver from his pocket and continued tweaking the scooter's rear wheel.

The little boy darted toward Lucas. "Daddy—want wheel go now!"

"Whoa there, Kemosabe!" Lucas scooped the toddler into his arms. Head full of curly dark locks, skin the color of cappuccino, little Flaco had Sophie's soulful brown eyes and Lucas's generous mouth.

"Daddy—make wheel go now!" The little boy kicked in Lucas's arms.

Lucas kissed the boy's forehead. "Take it easy, little man."

"Wheel go now!"

Lucas gently put the boy back down, held him by the shoulders, and spoke softly but firmly. "You cool your pits, Flaco . . . your scooter's gonna be ready when it's ready. . . ."

Then Lucas glanced up at Angel. "Besides, nobody likes a dude who can't stop moving for a measly five minutes."

Angel grinned. The little boy ran back to the scooter and continued waiting restlessly.

Lucas shook his head and started toward the office. Halfway up the sidewalk he noticed that Sophie was waiting for him inside the screen door, sipping her coffee. She was dressed in her robe and Lucas just couldn't help but grin at her. She had never looked so content.

Content to stay in one place.

Lucas walked the remaining length of sidewalk feeling precisely the same way himself.